∧ QUICK STOP

Battle plus 75 minutes, sir. J73Bs downrange 750 km. S & S uprange 1100 km, Frigate and NightHawk 400 km, Enemy Carrier 20 km dead ahead.

Andrew focused on the target. *First bay behind the bridge, Diablo. The closer we are the better, in case we have to get out and walk.*

Roger that, Andrew. They're not happy.

Put me on their com. Break it up.

Hit... dama... asteroid too... stabili... repeat, no lateral... zer. Visu... ly. Visual o... he chopped off the channel and popped a port-starboard slue on the steering jets.

They approached the carrier, its huge sides towering above and below them. The open bay door looked like a small target, but that was the least of their worries. Up and down the length of the old warship, bays were beginning to close. Slowly, slowly, their objective was getting smaller.

You're moving pretty fast, Andrew.

"No backseat driving, Jackson. You haven't seen us stop."

Just hope you can, kid. Just hope...

His voice was cut off by the clamping of his jaw as *Diablo* spun a one-eighty, entering the bay doors backwards. A blast of flame erupted all around them as Andrew hit the main engines in one quick burst.

Then a scraping crash, ended by a full-on explosion.

OUTBACK REBELLION

Gordon A. Long

Delta, B. C.
2020

Outback Rebellion

Gordon A. Long

Published by
Airborn Press
4958 10A Ave, Delta, B. C.
V4M 1X8
Canada

ISBN: 978-1-988898-18-6

Printed by Kindle Direct Publishing

Cover Design by Gordon A. Long

CONTENTS

THANKS

To my beta readers and tech experts for keeping me up to date.

If they don't give you any security clearance, you have no idea what clearances you don't have. It's very convenient.

– Cadet Andrew Lundin Collingwood III

Real wisdom is being smart enough to know when you're being stupid.

– Captain Natalia O'Rourke

PROLOGUE: CHAKKA'S MISSION

The auguar padded the trails of the Human Jungle, intent on his duty. He ignored the weak humans who cringed away from him, giving them plenty of space, because he knew that She would be unhappy if he frightened them. But Chakka the Warrior stood aside for none other than Her.

As he paced, he pondered the reason for his mission. She was clear. *Find our Cub and bring him.* She could have called Her Cub on his augment, but not this time. A memory came to him.

Feeling: Her hand as She pushed him out the door. Tense.

Image: Her face as he glanced up. Angry? No, anxious. Is Cub in trouble?

Another memory.

Sound: Her voice, giving the order out loud.

Emotion: motherlove for cub. Cub is not in trouble. At least, not at the moment.

A chuckle rumbled through his chest. *Cub is always in trouble. Such is the nature of cubs.*

Two humans turned shocked faces towards the sound and flattened against the wall as he passed. He ignored them.

Confronted by a heavy blast door, he sought the appropriate codes with his augment. The door swung open, and he paced through.

Odours: many cubs.

There. That's him. Chakka followed the scent down a narrower hallway, accessing the building security net to navigate. Cadets in uniform scrambled out of his way.

Smell: cub sweat. Many cubs. Cub training den.

As he turned the corner into the gym hallway, a picture blasted into his augment.

Image: cub at bay, surrounded by jackals.

Chakka the Warrior burst into a charge, his soft paws gripping the plastisteel flooring silently.

Chakka, easy. No danger.

He slowed and padded forward to listen at the door.

Sound: older cub voice. "So, kid, are you going to tell us, or not?"

Sound: Cub's voice. "You know I'd like to tell you, Cal, but I can't. Military blackout."

"We're all cadets here. We're military. You can tell us."

"Sorry, you don't have the clearance."

Emotion: threat. "But you're going to tell us anyway, aren't you? Because you know what will happen if you don't. Now, where did you come from, and howcome you're moved into our cadre when you're only, what, twelve years old? What use are you to us?"

Cub sighed. "If it matters, I'm almost fourteen; I'm just slow growing. This is the military, Cal. We go where we're sent, and we work with who they give us. Look, your last question was the right one. They've put us together, so they must have a reason. What good am I to you?"

"That's what I said."

"Well, you don't know me, and you're quite right to complain when I can't tell you about myself. Why don't you give me the objective, and I'll tell you how I can fit in."

Sound: older cub breathing. Emotion: Uncertainty. "Look, kid. I'm the ranking officer in this cadre. I don't like you coming in here and calling your own tune."

"But there's nothing I can do about that. Look. Pretend I'm not here. I won't bother anyone. I'll listen to what you're planning, and if I can help, I'll chip in. If I can't, then you give me an assignment like any other cadet, and assume I'll hold up my end of the game or fail, and then you'll be rid of me."

"I suppose."

Emotion: humour. "Think of it this way, Cal, they probably sent me to test your leadership skills. If you can fit the ugly duckling into your cadre, you'll make points with the Higher-Ups."

"Maybe."

Chakka accessed the security cameras.

2

Image: cub with towel in both hands. Warning: encirclement.

Chakka's Cub stepped closer to the larger cub. "And now you get to learn something about me. If Milford tries to throw that towel over my head, I am capable of breaking his arm."

"Oh, sure you are."

Cub's knees flexed in a crouch, and he swung towards the cub with the towel. "But does Milford want to find out?"

The other cub tossed the towel over his shoulder and let his hands drop.

"Good choice, Milford." Cub's voice changed, growing deeper. "Someday we might even make spacemen out of you lot. The ones that survive, that is."

Image: large and threatening drill sergeant

Emotion: cubs chuckling.

Chakka, enter now. Slow.

"Oh. Looks like I've got company. Come on in and meet the lads, Chakka."

The auguar sauntered into the room, his eyes sweeping the semicircle that confronted his Cub.

Odour: fear.

Emotion: satisfaction. He stopped in front of the largest one and gave him a flat stare.

"There you are, Cal, now you've learned something more about me. This is Chakka, my captain's auguar."

Despite the feline distraction, Cal was not slow. "Your captain? Wait a minute. Only Commandos have auguars."

"Well done, Cal. You're beginning to put things together."

"And nobody gets assigned a ship till they graduate."

Cub shrugged. "I was already assigned a ship before I joined up, so here I am. And if the captain wants me bad enough to send her auguar, I don't think I'd better be standin' around. See you chaps later. C'mon Chakka, let's go."

He pushed the cat's muzzle, and Chakka allowed himself to be steered towards the door. If the Cub wasn't worried about a flank attack, then Chakka the Warrior could follow his lead. As they left, his augmented hearing picked up a buzz of speculation.

3

Emotion: Cub laughing
Image: Cub surrounded by jackals.

Andrew laughed. "Don't worry about that, Chakka. They're all top cadets. They'll learn quick." His smile faded. "And if they don't, I'll just break something."

Then he gave the auguar a clout between the shoulder blades. "So, what's Mum up to? She usually doesn't need an errand boy. Or cat, as the case may be."

Emotion: puzzlement. Emotion: Her showing anxiety, anticipation.

"Ah. A mission, probably dangerous. I could call Her up and ask, but it doesn't sound like a good idea.

Image: Cub with large paw firmly over mouth.

"That's what I thought." He strode out. "Hope it lasts longer than tomorrow afternoon. I'd love to miss that Astrophysics oral exam. Their Sol-centred little minds just don't understand my point of view."

1. AMBUSH

They both knew it was a trap before it was sprung: a moaning girl in a tattered blanket huddled in the doorway of a decaying building. Natalia was just leaning over her when Andrew felt the vibrations in the pavement and slammed into full augment. As their minds joined, two attackers popped up on their virtual map exactly where they would be expected: one from the shadow of the packing crate, one from the mouth of the alley opposite.

Image: Natalia still straightening. Large man rushing in behind her, club raised.

Following her son's view, she did not straighten or look around. Her left foot lashed straight back, taking her assailant full in the solar plexus and driving him into a flailing sprawl.

Image: limping duck trailing one wing.

Andrew squealed as if in fear and stumbled away, neatly avoiding the rush of the second man, who scrabbled to change direction on the damp street. The knife descended at an awkward angle, and the cadet reached up with his left hand and jerked hard on the wrist, driving his right elbow into his attacker's crotch and levering upward.

His mother's driving kick to the backside turned the somersault into a headfirst dive to the broken pavement.

They stood, their backs to the wall, each covering half of the street. Nothing moved. The light clatter of the girl's fleeing feet faded.

Andrew glanced up into his new mother's calm face.

Emotion: uncertainty.

She nodded to the left. *Keep going. Don't waste energy hurrying; we might be running towards them.*

He started in that direction, glancing back at her, standing tall and straight over the vanquished enemy. He couldn't help it.

Emotion: pride and love.

The captain gave the two groaning forms a brief glance, then turned and followed him.

Why didn't you kill them?

She glanced down, her augment still, her expression shrouded by darkness. *Why do you ask?*

You wanted to kill them. It was a logical move. They now have knowledge about a military secret.

You're probably right, but it didn't seem like a good idea at the time.

Because of me. Don't bother to deny it. If you killed them with me in the augment, it would have been as if I killed them, and you don't think I'm ready for that, yet.

She laid an arm across his shoulders. *And so, O Wise One, why do you bother to ask?*

Because that's the only part of the skirmish that needs discussion. Otherwise we performed up to parameters.

I agree. And now we've discussed it. This is why the Space Arm doesn't like relatives serving in the same unit: conflicting motivation. But you and I are stuck together, and we've fought the Collingwood family combine, several interplanetary corporations, the Planetary Community Social Services Department and a bunch of old fogeys in the Space Arm itself to keep it that way. We'd better not mess this up.

Emotion: teenage indifference. It's you that screwed up this time, Captain O'Rourke, ma'am, by accepting a mission that we knew darned well was a setup. I bow to your superior rank.

She gave his shoulder a brief squeeze. *An attitude that needs to be remembered, Cadet Collingwood. But I think this operation is over. The Higher-Ups will make their deductions by how it went down.*

He suspected that the relief that washed through him exploded from his augment, but she was too polite to mention it.

NightHawk?

Aye, ma'am.

We're done, here. Send Pete in.

On my way, ma'am. The pilot's voice came immediately. *There's a square big enough for the shuttle one block ahead of you. I'll wait until you're there before I land, in case I attract attention.*

If you do one of your usual landings…

Quiet as a mouse, ma'am.

See you there. Chakka?

Only then did Andrew notice the blankness in that spot just behind his left ear where the auguar's presence usually sat. He looked up at his mother in concern.

Chakka?

The voice of *NightHawk*'s First Officer came through the augment. *He's taking care of business, ma'am.*

Roger that, Adrian.

She glanced down at Andrew. *Are you all right with that?*

He felt a flush of comfort and slipped his arm around her waist. *Thank you, ma'am. I don't think I'm ready for cold-blooded murder quite yet.*

She gave him another squeeze, then cuffed him behind the ear. *Don't worry. By the time we reach that square, he'll be all cleaned up, and you'd never know.*

The girl, too?

Emotion: grim necessity.

Yeah. I know. I'm a military secret.

That's right. And they were bait set out to trap us, just like we expected. From the weapons, I suspect it was meant to look like a mugging.

Capture, not kill?

Hard to say. Probably kill me if they had to in order to capture you. But your attacker had the knife.

Maybe they were just incompetent thieves.

I'd like to believe that, but I don't want to underestimate the opposition.

Mr. Occam would suggest they were plain, garden-variety muggers.

She stopped in her tracks. She was accessing another part of her augment, leaving him out. He knew better than to interrupt.

Then she strode on. *Too late to capture one of them. Chakka's already waiting for us at the retrieval point.* She gave him a quick, one-armed hug and spoke aloud. "That was a good deduction. I'm so caught up in the politics that I missed the possibility of a random act."

He grinned up at her. "That's my job. I don't have much idea what's going on in the immediate action, so I look outside it."

"It's a reasonable model…"

"But don't get habituated. I remember that part of the training, Mum."

She reached out and tousled his hair.

He ducked. "What was that all about?"

"You just finished a brawl." She grinned. "Your hair needed mussing."

He clamped down on the emotions stirring in him, trying vainly to keep them contained in his own head. A new image in his augment provided a welcome distraction. "Here comes the shuttle."

Contrary to his preferred style, Pete ghosted the shuttle down out of the night sky in front of them, opening the hatch as he touched pavement. They leapt inside, and a lithe figure bolted from the darkness and slipped in at their feet, his broad head butting Andrew's hip.

The boy curled his fingers in the auguar's neck fur and felt the beginning of a purr. It was hard to reconcile the warm, soft pelt pushing up against him and the three bodies bleeding out on the cold, wet concrete somewhere nearby. *All to protect me.*

He pushed the thought out of his mind.

2. A RECEPTION OF A DIFFERENT SORT

"Nice place."

Natalia regarded the huge double doors, the marble façade stretching stories above them. "Appropriate for a shindig of this magnitude, I'd say."

Andrew glanced up at her. "Considering my considerable lack of experience with this sort of thing, I suppose I agree with you, ma'am. It tops the setting of our last assignment, at least."

"And I don't consider that an important consideration." She rolled her eyes, then nodded to the doorman who ushered them in. A thought from the captain's augment, and he pointed to the left. "Up the curving staircase ma'am. Second-floor ballroom."

She nodded her thanks, and the three began their climb.

Augment connection at all times, gentlemen.

Aye, ma'am.

Emotion: agreement.

Virtual 3D Image: building's security systems, centred on ballroom stairs.

Thank you, Chakka. Andrew, can we access those?

I could, but do we want to?

No sense shouting in a quiet place. Only if needed.

They topped the stairs to be confronted by two beefy soldiers with semi-automatic weapons, guarding another larger-than-life door. It seemed that these two were part of the Diplomatic Corps, because they spoke without being spoken to.

"Welcome, ma'am, sir." A brief pause allowed the soldier to access the information that, yes, a large jungle cat was one of the invited guests.

"May I have your weapon, ma'am?"

"No, Corporal. I will be keeping it, thank you."

"But ma'am…"

She said nothing, and Andrew shared a quiet chuckle with Chakka. He could tell by the tilt of her head that she was giving the poor soldier 'the look.'

The guard's eyes blanked as he checked his augment again. A rueful smile spread over his face. "Commandos of Captain's rank and above. Yes, ma'am, you'll be keeping the weapon."

"But..." She handed it to him.

"Thank you, ma'am." He gave it a quick once-over. "On non-lethal mode, safeties functioning." He handed it back. "Beautiful weapon, ma'am. We don't see many of these."

"I like it."

While the conversation drifted into adult mating games, Andrew's attention wandered. Curious as to what awaited them, he slipped a passive scan into the ballroom, aided by a bored Chakka.

Image: heavy scanning on several frequencies.

Andrew nudged Natalia's augment, distracting her from her chat. *Check this out, ma'am.*

It only took her a moment. *You're not going in there.*

Neither is Chakka. He raised his voice. "Mum?"

She turned as if surprised. "What is it, dear?"

"I changed my mind. C'n I stay out here and talk to these guys?"

Her voice rose as well. Not loud enough to cause a scene, but enough to be picked up by the sensors in the room. "What? You begged and pleaded to come. I called in favours to get you an invitation. And now you chicken out? We talked about this, Andrew!"

"I know, Mum, but I really don't wanna. C'n I stay out here with Corporal Anderson?"

The soldier grinned and shrugged his shoulders. "Hallway's open to anyone with an invite, ma'am. Up to you."

Natalia frowned. "We'll be having a conversation when we get home, young man. I don't have time for this. Chakka can stay with you. He'll keep you out of trouble."

He let his shoulders slump. "Thanks, Mum." Then he turned on his big smile. "You go have fun. You'll have a better time if you don't have to worry about me."

She frowned again and began to turn towards the door. Then she spun back to face Corporal Anderson. "If he's any kind of trouble, you contact me, STAT, you hear? I'm available on your augment."

10

Image: general ID clearance for Commando Captain Natalia O'Rourke.

The soldier's grin was bigger than it should have been. "Right you are, ma'am. He'll be no problem."

Mum, will you stop flirting and get in there? I know how you feel about guys that are taller than you, but I want to know who's prying into our business.

Image: red-faced Commando captain. Right you are, son. Back to work.

With a final frown in his direction, she strode into the ballroom.

The guard looked down at him. "Now you're in trouble."

He grinned. "Naw, she really didn't want me to come, and Chakka hates these affairs. Everybody wants to pet him."

Anderson looked down at the huge head, higher than Andrew's waist. "Not sure I'd wanta try that."

The auguar stepped forward and rubbed his neck against the soldier's neatly pressed camos.

Lifting his weapon to the other side, the soldier looked down. "What do I do, now?"

Andrew laughed. "You scratch him behind his ears like any other cat. And then you ignore him, or he'll pester you all evening, and you'll never get your job done."

A flash of understanding passed over the guard's face. With a guilty glance at his partner, he gave the big cat a hasty pat and returned to his "rest easy" position. "Okay, kid. You can hang around, but as you say, I've got a job to do."

"That's fine. Can I help?"

"Sure thing. First thing you do is stand like this."

"I can do that. What else?"

"Then you guard, of course. That's what we're here for."

"Oh. Okay." Andrew posed beside the guard, and Chakka sat between them, his ears up.

The silence stretched out.

What's going on in there, Captain?

I'm meeting and greeting. You're probably having more fun out there.

11

Oh, very much so. I'm learning how to stand and guard.

Your training progresses. Aren't you glad you came...wait a moment. This is important. Stay on the line while I talk to this one.

She flipped him a file through the augment.

Image: handsome fortyish light-skinned man in formal clothes.

Precis: George Alson Elliott Rowell. Age, 52. Presently attached to the Diplomatic Corps, no assignment. Former Executive Vice President, Human Resources Department, Gondolier Enterprises. Former Vice President, Marketing, Delacon Corporation...

I get the point. I'm listening.

Don't distract me, now. He's showing all sorts of interest in Freighty. Listen...

Now he had a clear audio and video feed. He was looking slightly down at the face from the image. A face that was starting to take on a surprised frown.

"I don't think that material has been released to the general public, yet, sir, so I shouldn't comment."

"You should realize, young lady, that I will quite possibly be named to the commission sent to study this artifact. At that point I will hardly be termed 'the general public'."

"That would make a difference, sir. At that point, I will be glad to discuss the situation on a more equal basis."

The point of view in the video feed shifted, and Andrew chuckled. She was looming over the shorter man, ever so slightly.

"I may not have your experience and I may be female, but I know how things go at these diplomatic affairs. Everybody trying to get information they're not supposed to have. So if you don't mind, I will decline to continue discussion along..."

Andrew's attention was slapped by a sensation on his augment.

Sound: whispers in the stairwell.

He glanced down. Chakka was on the alert.

What you got, boy?

Sound: soft footsteps ascending. Many footsteps. Arrival estimate, 2.4 minutes.

Andrew opened his augment. *Ma'am, something's happening out here. Drift towards the main door and bring anybody who's armed with you.*

Getting a positive response, he directed his attention forward. "What's going on?"

He glanced up at Anderson. "Chakka's got great hearing. There's somethin' he don't like down the stairwell."

The soldier's weapon dropped to firing position. "You stay back against the wall." He made a hand signal to his partner, and they divided and slipped towards the top of the stairs.

What have you got, Andrew?

Battle augment coming up, ma'am.

It took a moment to sync with the building's security, but then they got the full picture. At first, everything looked fine, but then...

Image: blank area at bottom of main stairs. No sensors operating.

I'm on my way, Andrew.

In a moment she was beside him, her augment splitting into two. She stayed in their own gestalt, but accessed the guards' systems as well.

All right, boys, I'll handle it from here.

There were surprised responses on the com, but the two soldiers stepped back, their rifles rising to "present arms."

Glad we've got that straight. This is the situation. You've got a security blackout on the main staircase leading up here. At least nine people sneaking up the stairs. At the moment, there are no weapons in evidence, but we can't count on that. Do you follow?

Got it, ma'am. I'm onto Building Security. What else?

Tell them to approach with caution and in silence. Chakka and I will greet our visitors. You stand to either side with your weapons at the ready, but not levelled. If they are unarmed, these people are after something else, and we don't give it to them. You follow?

Yes, ma'am.

Andrew, get below the line of fire over the top of the stairs. You have the periphery while my attention is on the action.

Aye, ma'am. He slipped back to the wall and looked into the ballroom. Two high-ranking officers stood just inside the doorway,

13

light pistols in hand. He made a "stay there" motion, and one of them nodded.

Image: staircase monitor. Dark-suited young man with bandana over his face creeping into view. Followed by several others, male and female from their size, shape and posture. Number now at 11.

Thank you, Chakka. On a count of three we will step forward. One, two, three!

Natalia and the auguar slid to the top of the staircase and stood, looking down. The two soldiers slipped in to either side, weapons canted upwards.

Ten steps below, a surprised figure froze, his companions crowding and stumbling behind him.

"Don't move, don't speak. Don't think of running, because the bottom of the staircase is now covered."

The invaders obeyed.

"You. Come up here."

The leader hesitated, glancing back at his compatriots. None of them responded, so he began a slow climb. When his head was just below the top stair, Natalia stopped him with a gesture.

"Want to tell me what's going on?"

He looked around again.

"Sorry, this is the only audience you're getting. Are any of you armed?"

After a moment he shook his head.

"That took too long. Are you armed?"

His head came up. "No, I am not. I don't believe in..."

Her hand chopped the lecture off. "But you're not so sure of your friends. Prime. All of you, line up along the inside railing."

As they complied, she surveyed her augment.

Image: second person: female. Carrying live recording equipment, audio and video, external feed. Fourth person: male. Unidentified electronics. The others have phones and audio devices.

Andrew tore his attention away to scan the immediate area. The two officers were holding their positions in the doorway, but a third figure pushed forward. It was George Rowell.

"What's going on here, lad?"

"I'd stay back if I were you, sir. There's been a security breach, with intruders in the stairwell. Possibility of a bomb."

The man looked down at him with a patronizing smile. "I'd like to make my own assessment of that."

Andrew did not drop his stare. "You will do what you wish, sir, but I draw to your attention that I am considerably shorter than you, and my head is below the blast line from a possible bomb on the eighteenth step down."

Rowell glanced towards the stairs, made a move to retreat, then changed his mind.

"The Commandos have the situation under control, sir. If you are not armed, the commanding officer would prefer that you stay in the ballroom."

"I am not afraid of a few terrorists."

"All indications are that this is a group of protesters looking for publicity, sir. They are carrying various recording devices. I draw your attention to the White Paper presented on August 23 to the Planetary Security Forces on the subject of Response to Rightful Protest."

The diplomat froze for a stunned moment while he accessed his augment. He frowned, hesitated, then spun and strode into the ballroom.

Andrew's gaze followed and caught the stare of one of the officers. He grinned, wiped his forehead, and turned to face the real action.

Natalia had separated the protesters, bringing the first three up towards her and spreading the others back down the stairs.

Volunteer for perilous duty.

Ready, ma'am. Anderson stepped forward.

The fourth man might have a bomb. I want you to go down past him and start at the bottom, moving the rest out of range. As you go by, ignore them all. Stick to the far side of the stairs. Can you do that?

Got it, ma'am.

Away you go.

15

She upped the volume of her external com. "All right, you lot. We're going to move you down the stairs. You have the right to protest out in front of the building, but not in this secure area. I'm sending one of my men to clear the route for you and keep you safe from accidents. I warn you that the sensors have been turned back on, so we'll be watching you the whole way. Now, Corporal Anderson will be coming past you to lead you down. He will not touch you, force you, or harm you in any way. Any questions?"

After a pause, she motioned the corporal to continue. He marched slowly down the outside of the curve, passing the first three, then the fourth with no hesitation.

Steady on, soldier, you're doing fine.

Anderson continued to descend. When he reached the bottom of the line, he gestured to that protester to follow him. She did, and the others began their descent, each as his or her turn came.

Until the fourth one.

"Not you."

The man turned and looked up at Natalia. She held for as long as she could while the other protesters climbed down towards safety.

"We want to talk to the four of you, but this is a secure area. One at a time. The leader first." She gestured.

Once again he got no support from his companions. He slowly mounted the steps.

"Now the camerawoman. Yes, we know you're recording this. Up here, please. Take your time and pan the staircase if you like, to show that we are letting your friends go."

The second figure turned and stared down, then smoothly swivelled back and mounted the steps. As she gained the top, Natalia motioned to the third protester, who began his climb.

The fourth man was beginning to realize his isolated position. His head moved back and forth as he looked up and down the stairs, his feet shifting. As his final support moved away from him, he raised a hand. "Wait!" He started up the stairs.

"Not you. Stay there. We have a question for you." Natalia reached out, grabbing the shoulder of the third protester and heaving him over the top.

16

Drop! Keep your weapon on him!

She threw herself to the floor, thumbing off the safety of her pistol. The second guard took up a similar position with his automatic rifle.

"Stop or we fire!"

The man with the bomb stopped. He looked up the stairs, and then down. Then he stood from his crouch, taking a deep breath…

Andrew, frantically motioning to the officers to close the doors, dropped to the floor.

The blast caught the doors half open, throwing the two back into the ballroom. Then something fell on Andrew, slamming the side of his head against the marble floor.

3. CLEANUP

He gradually came back to a strange, silent world where smoke and dust billowed around him and pieces of the building fell at slow motion through the haze.

"Natalia! Mum!" He screamed, but could hear nothing. He clawed his way across the floor to the top of the steps. The blast had rolled her over, and she lay unmoving halfway to the doors, blood seeping from her forehead. Chakka lay to one side, shaking his head and gazing around.

Emotion: puzzlement, faint anger growing to…

Chakka! Stay still.

Emotion: agreement. The auguar put his chin on his paws, his augment swooping in and out of focus. Andrew tuned him out and concentrated on Natalia. He tried for a pulse at her wrist and felt nothing. He tried at her neck and felt nothing. Despair washed over him, but then he remembered the day on the Tree Planet. He had failed his team once. He had vowed never to panic again.

He returned to his task, accessing his augment for instruction. Soon he had it, and he placed his fingers carefully in the correct position on her neck, pushing very gently, slowly increasing the pressure, keeping his own body perfectly still.

There…! He had it. A weak pulse, thready but present. He put his cheek to her mouth and felt a gust of breath.

Emotion: determination.

Chakka's head came up. Emotion: fierce determination!

The auguar staggered to his feet and stumbled over to his mistress, flopping down beside her. His tongue slipped out and cleaned the wound on her forehead.

Full augment.

Cat and boy put all their power into the gestalt, willing their captain to join. Slowly her awareness returned.

Emotion: concern. Scan the perimeter. Threat assessment.

You got that, Chakka? I don't know if that's Mum's augment giving fallback orders or if she's aware of what she's doing, but we've gotta get up and get moving.

18

Emotion: fierce will.

The two staggered to their feet and assessed. The stairwell in front of them was a pile of timbers and concrete blocks, with cables and lighting fixtures dangling from above. The soldier sat against the wall, his head in his hands. Faint sounds were beginning to filter through the buzzing in Andrew's ears, and he turned to see people stumbling about in the ballroom. One of the officers clawed his way to his feet, blood streaming from a vertical gash down his forehead where the edge of the door had caught him.

Chakka's head jerked around, and Andrew turned to see men in black suits rushing towards him.

"Over here. We've got one down, one injured."

The leading man dropped to his knees beside Natalia and said something.

Andrew pointed to his ears and shook his head.

The man shouted, and it came through faintly. "Whattaya got, kid?"

"The bomb was in the stairwell. She was down, but the edge of the blast must have caught her and flipped her over. There's a pulse and breath, but not much of either. Her augment is working, but she's not fully conscious."

"What about you?"

"Huh? Me? I'm fine. That soldier over there must have caught the edge as well. I didn't have time to check him." He flipped a thumb over his shoulder. "Two guys were trying to close the doors when it hit them."

The man glanced at his followers and nodded towards the ballroom doors.

"Any present danger?"

Andrew shot upright. "Where are they?"

"Where are who?"

"Three protesters. Two men and a woman. She had AV equipment. They had just run up the stairs." He pointed. "You lot came in from that direction, so they must have gone the other way along the hall."

19

"Thanks, kid." The security man turned aside to access his augment, and immediately two operatives sprinted away down the hallway.

Still in full augment, Andrew renewed his access to the building's security systems. There was a huge blank in the area below them, but he knew what he was looking for. There they were, all right, creeping down a back staircase. He raised a hand to tap the security chief's arm...

Oops. I can't tell them something I couldn't possibly know.

The man turned.

"Um...there were eight more. Corporal Anderson took them down the stairs to safety."

The agent held up one finger. Then he gave a grim smile. "No problem, there. We found them on the second landing down, just outside the rubble pile. Anderson had them in a corner with his gun on them. They weren't going anywhere."

Andrew's augment kicked.

Report!

Yes, ma'am. All under control. Single fatality. No danger. Relax and wait for the ambulance.

Natalia moaned, and her legs twitched.

He laid a hand on her cheek. "Calm down, Mum. You'll be fine.

"Mum? She's your mother?"

"Yep. Commando Captain Natalia O'Rourke. My mother."

"Well, word just came through the security net to take good care of her. Apparently she saved a lot of lives today."

Andrew tried to speak around the lump in his throat. "I just hope hers is one of them."

"Sure enough, kid. I've already got the house doctor on his way. Here he comes, now."

As Andrew turned to look, a blast on his augment sent him reeling.

All Stations report. Captain...

A wave of relief shot through him. *Nighthawk. Where are you?*

Still at the spaceport. Engines warming. Shuttle prepped for departure. Orders?

Andrew waited, but the captain was still hazy.

Captain is barely conscious. Stand down the engines, NightHawk. Get the commandos on the shuttle with the medic. My coordinates. Access city traffic control for clearance.

Aye, sir. Lieutenant Jones on the bridge.

What's going on, Andrew?

Captain's down, sir. Terrorist bomb. She's coming 'round, but we need evac. Doctor on the scene.

She can't be allowed to a normal hospital.

My thoughts exactly, sir.

Have you done a thorough assessment?

The doctor's checking her now, sir. Do you want me to bring his reader with me?

That would be best, if you can get it. A brief pause. *Shuttle's away. ETA seven minutes.*

Send them to the front doors, please. I'll arrange a stretcher party here.

Right. I'll take care of Space Arm. There will be all sorts...

Aye, sir. Standing by.

Andrew turned to the doctor. "Is my mum gonna be all right, sir?" He gave his best pleading smile.

The doctor had completed the scan and was accessing the results. He looked up. "Possible concussion. She's fully conscious, now. I don't know why she isn't responding."

Mum?

Image: opossum lying still.

Got it. "Can we get a stretcher? There's an ambulance coming."

The doctor shook his head. "I don't exactly understand the readings I'm getting from her cranial area. I assume she has an augment?"

He shrugged. "She's a Space Arm Officer."

"That may explain it." He raised his head. "You two! Level One case over here."

Two medics hustled over with a basket stretcher and slid her in. The doctor started his handover protocol.

Mum, I need a distraction. Get him to put down his reader.

Emotion: affirmative.

The patient began to moan, writhing against the webbing of the basket. The doctor reached out to hold her still, glanced at his reader, looked for his kit...

Andrew took it from his grasp. "Please help her."

The doctor laid his hands on Natalia's shoulders. "It's all right, ma'am. We're just going to strap you in for the trip downstairs."

Andrew slipped the reader behind his belt, accessing its data. "Um, guys, she's like, claustrophobic, so don't strap her in too tight. She might struggle and do herself damage. Yeah...that's great. Just leave her arms loose on top."

The corpsmen looked at the doctor. "Ready to transport, sir."

He nodded. "I'll just...where's my reader?"

"You put it in your bag when you went to help Mum, sir. I saw you."

"But I need to transfer the scan..."

"Already done, sir. See the screen?"

Sure enough, the stretcher screen showed a full scan.

A faint roar sifted through the noise in the building. "That's the ambulance, guys. Let's go! Doctor, one of those officers there got hit by the door. Maybe he's got a concussion, too. Thanks a lot!"

Andrew pointed over his shoulder, but the doctor had already picked up his kit and was heading for the broken ballroom doors.

The medics hustled down the side stairs and out into the main lobby, which was filled with security men, soldiers, and policemen. Andrew strode to the front.

"Patient coming through. Stand back, please: emergency patient."

The crowd parted, the doors opened and a small, dark figure in full Commando gear slipped in. A larger shadow loomed outside, automatic rifle at the ready.

"Right on time, Sergeant. Come on, boys, this way."

The corpsmen stepped out, and Charlie led them to the shuttle. Its loading hatch was already open. Toni brought up the rear, her weapon sweeping the plaza. With practised skill, Jonny slipped the stretcher in on the floor. By the time she had it clamped down, the doors were closing on the surprised faces of the medics and the shuttle's engines were spooling up.

Andrew waved 'thanks,' and then they were off, the G forces pinning them into their seats.

"For God's sake tell Pete to lay off on the acceleration and somebody get these straps off me." Natalia was pawing at the restraints.

"You just lie still, ma'am." Juanita laid a calming hand on the captain's forehead. "The medic said a possible concussion."

"And my augment says nothing of the sort. Which you already knew."

"Aye, ma'am."

The pilot's voice came over the com. "Where to, ma'am?"

"Back to the Space Arm compound. I'll hit the admiral's office and the rest of you need to disappear from the public eye, give the PR hacks a chance to calm things down. And I need a whiskey."

"Aye, ma'am. ETA five minutes."

"Take it slow, Pete. Fade into the traffic."

"Aye, ma'am. Speed limit all the way. ETA nine minutes."

Natalia sat up, shook her head to clear it, then climbed gingerly into a seat. "I sent the full report to *NightHawk* while I was on my little ride, so the Lieutenant knows what's happening. I'll be dealing with the counter-terror mavens and the counterintelligence boffins for hours. Andrew, our quarters aren't secure enough; you and Chakka better stay on the ship tonight." She glanced around the crowded capsule. "Leaves cancelled until we get some answers."

The smaller commando shrugged. "I came back early. Bored."

"Well, Toni, this is going to hasten our departure, so prepare yourselves for another few months of my son's stimulating company."

Toni reached out and ruffled Andrew's hair. "I thought you were working on your PhD."

"I made some progress. Got enough ideas that I could use some re-ti with Freighty." He turned to his mother. "I'm going with you for sure, then? To Freighty?"

She nodded. "You're no use to Space Arm by yourself. You're of most use in the *NightHawk* gestalt, and as soon as the modifications are complete, *NightHawk* is bound outsystem. To where has not been confirmed." She glanced at him. "Does that bother you?"

He glared around the crowded cabin, but all eyes looked elsewhere. "No, I've enjoyed bein' on the ground for a year, but it's not my favourite place." He frowned. "I was sorta lookin' forward to girls, though. Not that I get to meet any. There was one college Senior in my graduate Physics class. She was on some kinda advanced program. Smart and pretty, too."

"And seven years older than you."

"What? What do you know about Sarah? Wait a minute. Why do you know about Sarah?"

Natalia smiled. "I didn't know about Sarah until you just told me. I accessed her info while you were gushing."

"And when does a guy get some privacy?"

Her smile sweetened. "You have all the privacy you need, dear. I just want to meet your friends."

"She ain't specifically a friend. She's just in my…"

A chuckle came from somewhere.

"All right, you lot. I'm not puttin' on a show for you. Mother, we will discuss this in private."

"That's fine, Son. I don't want to embarrass you in front of the team."

"I ain't embarrassed." He forced a grin. "Well, maybe a little. So I ain't talkin' about it."

His mother stood as the shuttle skids grounded. "All right. Back to the ship with all of you and start packing."

A chorus of "Aye, ma'am" followed her out into the night, and then she was gone, the hatch closing and the Gs of one of Pete's trademark takeoffs pushing them into their seats.

4.INTRUDER

Their adventure had no effect on the following week's busy schedule, and on Tuesday Natalia and Andrew returned to their off-base quarters. On Saturday morning Andrew finished up his latest school assignment and flicked on his augment.

Mum, I'm goin' out to NightHawk. Anythin' needs doin'?

Besides cleaning up your use of Standard English, not that I can think of. I'm sure the ship can give you something to keep your busy little mind occupied.

Yep, and my greasy little fingers as well.

I'll be by around eleven hundred. Like to do lunch?

Just me and my Mum, out for a meal together? That would be nice. If I ain't occupied with somethin' more important.

Right. And now that I've been put in my place, may I continue with my insignificant duties for Space Arm?

Sure thing. Sorry to bother you.

Of course you are.

He arrived at the space dock, logging himself through the security system with a flick of his augment and heading for the ship. He was just turning out the gangway to *NightHawk* when a shout stopped him.

"Hey, you! Kid!"

He turned. A large soldier wearing a Securi-Corps armband panted up to him.

"Yes, sir?"

"What're you doin' wanderin' around here alone? Don't you know you're way past the security barriers?"

"Of course I know where I am, sir. That's my ship right there." He gestured towards *NightHawk*'s entry port.

The man's broad face twisted in a scowl. "Yer nothin' but a cadet. I wan't born yestidday. Cadets aren't assigned to ships. Now you get yourself back behind that barrier, and I'll be nice 'n' pretend this never happened."

"I'm sorry, sir, but I have orders from Captain O'Rourke to do some work on the ship. I'm already logged through security, so I'd like to move on about my business, if I may."

"What? Who says you're logged in? I saw ya just wander past. Don't know how ya did it, don't like it."

Andrew pointed to the man's portable scanner and held out his arm. "Check your latest data."

The guard scanned the arm badge, then consulted his screen. "Oh. Oh, yeah...yep. There you are. Cadet Andrew Collingwood." He looked straight into the boy's eyes. "Howcome you're out here? Where'd you get the clearance?"

Andrew stepped closer and grinned. "School project."

"Oh. I see."

"And it helps that the captain's my Mum."

"What?" The man's eyebrows went up, and he gave a gap-toothed grin. "The captain of the *NightHawk* is your old lady?"

"Yep. I'm in and out of here a lot."

"Yeah." He glanced at his screen again. "Yeah, I guess you are. Several times last week."

"And if you still aren't sure..."

"No, no, that's fine. You check out fine, kid."

"Well, anyway, here comes my security escort."

"Huh...?" The man turned towards the ship. "Oh, shit! That's an auguar, ain't it?"

"Yeah. You're new here, aren't you? Wanna meet him?"

"I can? You mean I can walk right up to him?"

"Sure. Come over here, Chakka. This guy's a big fan of yours."

Image: auguar flattening soldier to deck.

Image: Cadet taking auguar by the scruff of the neck and shaking him. You be good.

Chakka stepped forward and put a large paw on Andrew's left foot, leaning heavily.

"You be polite to the nice soldier. He's here to look out for us."

The guard stood stiffly as the big cat sniffed his leg up and down, then rubbed against him as he turned back to Andrew.

"There. He's left his scent on you, so he'll know you again."

26

"Oh. Wow…yeah. Ain't he purty?"

Andrew grinned. "He prefers to call it handsome."

"Big fella like that, we'll call him whatever he likes."

"Good enough." He checked the guard's badge. "So, Corporal Jackson. You're on security hereabouts. Anything suspicious to report?"

Jackson stood to attention and saluted, grinning. "Besides a strange kid with a twice-too-big cloud leopard roamin' where they ain't supposed to, nuthin', sir."

Then a serious look wrinkled his brow."…but now that you mention it…"

Andrew faced the man. "What? Even the smallest thing could be important."

"Well, there was this old geezer wanderin' around earlier this mornin'."

"Wandering around? People don't 'wander around' in this area."

"That's it." The soldier's voice dropped. "It's part of our trainin', ya know? We learn ta watch how people walk. This guy was just sort of cruisin'. Nowhere specific to go."

"And where did he go?"

"Well, I stopped him."

"Good for you."

"It's my job. I stopped him, and asked him polite-like what his business was here."

"You were polite?"

Jackson grinned, showing two missing front teeth. "Oh, I don't come over all snarly with everyone. I was just bored, and I wanted ta see what you'd do. I knew you was all right. I could tell by lookin' at you that you was headed for somewhere, and you was supposed to be there."

"Right. So what did he answer?"

"He said he had business here. He handed me his badge, and the scanner gave him the full okay. So I said, 'Thank you, sir,' and he walked away." Jackson waved his hand towards the next dock. Then he leaned in, showing his scanner screen. "But when I looked on the screen, there wasn't no data."

"None?"

"Nope. The scanner checked his ID, okayed him to be here and forgot he existed. There's no record of my check."

Andrew frowned. "That's weird, and I don't like it at all."

"Neither do I, but I don't really know how to report it."

"You do what you have to do, but I'm gonna tell my captain about it. That's the kinda stuff we need to know." He slapped the guard's solid shoulder. "Thanks a lot, Jackson. It's good we got someone sharp on duty out here."

"Good enough, Cadet. We'll see ya around, I guess. I'm assigned here for a while. Do a good job on that school project."

They exchanged salutes, and Andrew strode into the airlock, his mind whirling.

NightHawk, were you listening to that?

Here's my footage, Andrew. Interesting; there's nothing to correspond in the dock security system.

Video: fiftyish man, light brown skin, civilian clothing — good quality but not fancy — walks slowly past the ship. Brown hair, greying at temples. Longer than military cut. Upright posture, smooth gait. Guard stops, chats. Man continues on his way. Guard glances at his scanner, looks more closely, then stares in the direction the man went. Then he shrugs and returns to his patrol.

Andrew strode onto the bridge and flopped down in the captain's accel couch. *Work on those images, NightHawk. We need our best shot of that guy. Whaddaya think? Ex-military?*

Almost certainly. Exactly 70-centimetre pace.

Let's see where he came from and where he went.

They were attempting to trace the intruder's path backwards through the security cameras when Natalia stepped in.

Captain on the bridge.

"You've got a new friend."

"Who's that, Mum?"

"The guard outside. He says you're a 'fine young fella'."

"Don't let that folksy stuff fool ya. Jackson's a sharp guy, and he's put us onto something. Or someone."

28

He indicated the image on the screen.

"Who's that?"

"Guy wanderin' around, checkin' us over. Jackson's scanner cleared him and then it cleared itself. No record of his presence. Like he's a ghost. We've been trailin' him by the gaps in the security cam records."

"Where did he go?"

"Near as we can make out, he came in through the West Gate, walked past us and went out the South Gate. Then he disappeared."

"He didn't actually do anything."

"No, but Jackson's a trained eye. He picked the guy out because he wasn't movin' right."

"I don't argue with anyone qualified to guard in a High Security area. Coordinate with this Jackson. If the man comes around again, let's take a look at him."

As you wish, ma'am.

"Aye, ma'am."

"For the moment, he looks like brass on a sub rosa info sweep. If you can find out who he is, we'll do him a favour and let him know he's playing amateur hour."

Andrew grinned. "We're on it, ma'am. I told Jackson I was working on a school project. This oughta be a learnin' experience."

"Well, get right to it, Cadet. We expect results."

Two hours later, Andrew looked up from his viewscreen to see his mother standing over him.

"Busy?"

"A bit."

"Too busy to eat?"

"Eat? Oh, yeah. We was supposed to have lunch."

"Right..."

"Huh? Oh. Now?"

"I don't know about you, but I had breakfast five hours ago."

"Oh. Yeah, I guess."

"Let's go, then."

"I can't. We're just makin' some progress."

"Then leave *NightHawk* and Chakka working on it."

"Can't. We're workin' together."

"Look, Andrew, sometimes it's better for a leader to step away and let the team do its work. You can't be hanging over their shoulders and giving orders all the time. That's called micromanaging, and it's poor leadership. They start to depend on you and never take initiative themselves."

"This is an augment gestalt, Mum, it ain't leadership."

"But you're in charge of the gestalt. That's leadership."

"Yes and no." He stood and faced her. "Look, Mum. You gotta listen. I know I'm just a cadet and all that, but when it comes to this gestalt stuff, I'm way ahead of all of you. So will you stop bein' Captain Mum, and just listen?"

Wondering if he had gone too far, he watched the red rise up her cheeks, and then fade.

"All right, Andrew. I'm a good enough leader to know when to let someone else lead. Tell me what's going on."

"You want it in mathematics? The gestalt works on connections. If there's two people, there's one connection. But if there's three of us, there's three possible connections. If there's four, then there's six ways to join up."

"Yes, I understand that. What you're telling me is that if I were to come in to help, you'd have twice the mental power to solve the problem."

Andrew reached over and swatted Chakka on the shoulder. "Ain't it great how well she understands?"

The big cat yawned.

Natalia grinned down at them. "So, when we get back from lunch, I'll join up and we'll solve the problem in half the time."

Andrew stared at her. "That ain't fair."

"It isn't fair; it's parenthood. Now, let's go. I get grouchy when I'm hungry."

"Well, we wouldn't want you grouchy on top of everything else." He stumbled to his feet. "Where are we eating?" He frowned at her look. "And don't start on my jeans. I'm not in uniform, so I wear what I wanta."

"And that means we eat where you want to eat, because no restaurant where I want to eat would let you in."

He grinned. "Y'know, I'd really like a burger. The Mumbot out in Barnard's System never did learn to make a proper burger."

* * *

They returned from the meal refreshed and ready to work, but as they approached *NightHawk*, Andrew darted ahead. "Hey! There he is."

"Hold it right there, Cadet."

He slowed reluctantly. "But that's him. The guy from the security video."

"Probably. What are you going to do?"

"I...I dunno. But it's him."

"And he hasn't done anything wrong. He's just walking away slowly. If he has clearance to be here, there's nothing we can do about it. Look. Here comes Jackson."

They watched the guard stop to talk to their suspect. As in the former incident, the security guard scanned the man's badge, then shrugged. He walked towards them while the man strolled in the opposite direction.

As soon as their subject was around the corner, Andrew ran up to Jackson, who was shaking his head.

"Looka this." He held out his scanner. The screen was empty. Andrew plumbed the instrument with his augment. There was a neat blank spot on the memory core. Nothing in the programming explained the gap.

"I don't get it. It's like he just wasn't here. But you saw him, and the captain and I both saw him."

Natalia frowned. *NightHawk?*

Aye, ma'am?

What do you make of him?

31

Who?

The man who just walked by.

Oh, him. Nothing.

Nothing?

He seemed to be no danger to us.

But isn't that the man we've been looking for?

I believe so.

So...?

I don't understand, ma'am. What do you wish me to do?

Nothing, NightHawk. You may stand down.

Aye, ma'am.

The presence disappeared from their augments.

Natalia took each of her companions by the shoulder and walked them away from the ship. "Jackson, may I access your augment? I'm taking command of this situation under a code 5B."

"Yes, ma'am." His only reaction was a stiffening of his posture. "I stand under your orders."

Good. She put them on a secure band. *Andrew. Analysis.*

That was way past strange.

That's not analysis, Cadet.

Okay, okay. NightHawk's lack of interest in the subject of our mutual investigation was atypical. Jackson's scanner has definitely been messed with. Occam's Razor says NightHawk has also been messed with.

My analysis as well. "Jackson?"

"I... dunno, ma'am. I... stepped over the line, ma'am. Maybe you'll be glad I did, maybe you won't."

"Depends what line and how far over you stepped."

Image: close-up of fiftyish man's face. Light brown skin, deep, thoughtful eyes, friendly smile.

"How did you get that?"

"I used my augment, ma'am. I know his security clearance specifically nulled all recording, but I thought you might want it, ma'am."

"I certainly do."

She broke their connection. "Jackson, what's your shift today?"

"Twelve on. Started at oh eight hundred."

"You're due a supper break."

"Yeah, in a coupla hours."

"Supper's on *NightHawk*. Knock at the door."

"Aye, ma'am."

"Now, back on patrol as if nothing had happened."

The guard glanced ruefully at his scanner. "Apparently, nothin' did." He snapped her a salute, tipped a finger to his cap in Andrew's direction and paced off.

"And now you and I have an appointment with an ArIn."

"How you gonna handle it?"

"I will treat *NightHawk* like any other crew member. If there is a problem, I deal with it straight out. I doubt if we could sneak around in her systems without her noticing, anyway."

"Well, you probably couldn't."

The captain turned and regarded him. "Let's save that for when we need it."

They entered the airlock and closed the outer door behind them.

"*NightHawk*, level three security lockdown, please."

Level three initiated ma'am. What's up?

"Just a check. Stand by.

"Aye, ma'am."

In the chartroom, Natalia motioned Andrew to take a seat in the proper chair that had replaced his usual light-G stool. Chakka sprawled on his mat in the corner under the desk.

"*NightHawk*, review our conversation at oh two thirty-nine."

"Reviewing...what's going on? There's something wrong with that conversation."

"Exactly. Now, I don't want you to do anything about it yet. You will remain out of the gestalt, but allow the rest of us to enter your programming."

"You need a level seven authorization to do that, ma'am."

"Or a level six threat to ship security."

"That applies in this case, ma'am. Please proceed. Record or not?"

Natalia glanced at Andrew, who shook his head.

"No recording."

"As you wish, ma'am."

"Andrew, it's all yours. Try not to leave any evidence."

He grinned at her. "Teach your grandmother." Then he concentrated.

It didn't take long. *Well, that was sloppy.*

The captain scanned the file he had opened. *Her standard protocols have been countermanded by…*

By a security code I've never seen before. Look at this.

You're not cleared for that level, Cadet.

Probably not.

Then why are we looking at it?

Because I'm not cleared for any level.

Haven't you got that backwards?

Emotion: sly humour. Since I have no clearance, nobody told me what clearance I don't have.

Prime. What do you suggest we do?

Image: large, claw-studded paw shredding file and sweeping to incinerator.

Emotion: laughter. I don't think so, Chakka. This is a time for subtlety. Andrew?

I'm going to back out of here very slowly, brushing out my tracks as I go. I've replaced the last twenty-three minutes of NightHawk's memory with a routine maintenance scan of the secondary firing circuits.

NightHawk?

Aye, ma'am. Secondary firing circuits all up to specs, ma'am.

Thank you, NightHawk.

Andrew raised his eyebrows, and Natalia nodded.

"NightHawk, you and I got a job to do."

"Certainly."

"Take a look at this."

Image: close-up of stranger from Jackson's augment.

"We gotta find this guy. It might not be easy."

"Scanning...hmm. I see what you mean. That face is not in the usual data banks."

"Right. We have to work on the peripherals. Age, occupation, etc. See the hairline scar down the left side of the face? Estimate date, depth, and treatment of the wound. Some hospital somewhere fixed that. A real good hospital."

Natalia broke in. "I'm going to leave you with that. I have other avenues to explore."

"Huh? Oh, yeah. Sure, Mum. You go ahead. Now, *NightHawk*, let's see what else we can come up with. What kinda haircut is that? It ain't military. Let's magnify and see if we can run a spectrum scan on that shampoo..."

He was interrupted by the hatch alarm. He looked around. Natalia was nowhere to be seen. "Chakka, go let Jackson in, will you?"

The auguar rose and strolled out. Andrew stood, stretched and wandered down to the galley, where he found his mother supervising a steaming pot and a skillet that sizzled and spat a fine haze of droplets into the air.

"Makin' a bit of a mess, are we?"

Natalia used her wrist to push a dark curl of hair away from her forehead. "That's why it's so nice to be in port. The cleaners are coming in on Tuesday to decon the whole place before we hit space again."

"What's on the menu?"

"Depends on whether I burn this steak or not, so don't distract me. Did I hear the doorbell?"

"Yep. And guess who's coming to dinner?"

"I hope someone with an adult sense of humour."

"I thought this was a business meeting."

"It is. There's no reason why we can't enjoy it."

"You mean why you can't enjoy it."

"That's exactly what I mean. There aren't that many opportunities for someone in my position to enjoy compatible male companionship, so I take them when I can. Do you have a problem with that?"

He held up his hands in defence. "No, no, you go right ahead. I understand your needs." He gave a delicate shudder. "I don't find them easy to contemplate, but you go right ahead."

"Thank you for your permission, sir."

"You're welcome. And speaking of male companionship…"

She made a violent thumb-across-the-throat gesture at him and turned towards the doorway, where Jackson and Chakka were just entering.

"Do come in. I hope the butler has given you an appropriate greeting?"

The beefy guard grinned. "Didn't bite my head off, so I figure I'm one up in the game."

Andrew kicked a chair away from the table. "Take the weight off. You bin walkin' all day."

Jackson sat and stuck his feet out, flexing his ankles in his heavy boots. "Can't say I mind a siddown now and then. They don't make steel decks as soft as they used to."

"Anything to drink? We got several good flavours of soda. Since this is a business meetin' I figure beer's out."

"Beer is always out for you, young man. Get up and bring our guest a selection from your gourmet cooler."

"Anythin' with caffeine will do. The last part of a twelve shift is always dozy."

Andrew brought a cola, using a glass with ice instead of the can slapped on the table like he usually did. Natalia gave him a wink as she turned back to the stove.

"So, I don't want to break up the fun, but I only got forty minutes. What can I do for you folks?"

Natalia was busy with the food, so Andrew stepped in. "I think a bit of background would help. None of us is quite sure how you overrode a high-level security command to your augment."

"Oh, that. Well, it has to do with allergies."

"I can't wait."

"Simple. I'm hyper-sensitive to gallium."

Natalia slipped a heat pad onto the table. "Which is a major element in our implants."

"That's right. Nobody knew, and I was all set for a nice, cushy career in Securi-Corps. I got all my organics in place, and then the basic military upgrade. No gallium in that. Next promotion comes with another upgrade, and that's when they found it. Wham. Career comes to a screeching halt at corporal. So here I am, markin' time, goin' nowhere. Waste of my considerable talents, but what can ya do?"

Andrew shot his mother a glance. "You have the standard implant and some organic upgrades, and you've had them a long time. Tell me, have you noticed your abilities improving despite the lack of implant upgrades?"

The man squirmed in his chair and leaned in. "How'd you know? Started last year. I was gettin' stuff I wasn't supposed to, and I couldn't figure out why. I started playin' around with my augment and found I had far better control than I shoulda. I...well, I sorta removed a buncha the limitin' protocols, ya know? I thought it might be wrong, but there's nobody told me I couldn't."

Andrew grinned at his mother. "If they don't tell you not to, why shouldn't you?"

She was draining pasta into the sink. "I'm not sure getting you two together was such a good idea."

Andrew turned to the soldier. "What's going on is your body has absorbed the organic upgrades further than it was designed to. Your own antibodies are starting to adapt them to your natural abilities. Your subconscious is pulling them into line with what it wants. You need some exercises to take conscious control as well."

Jackson frowned. "And howcum a kid like you knows so much? No, don't tell me. You, too?"

Andrew tapped his temples with both forefingers. "No implants. I'm perfectly clean."

"You're kidding."

"Nope. And there's a lot goin' on that we can't tell you, but something I can guarantee. The captain, here, when she takes off her chef's hat, is gonna recommend you for a promotion."

"I am?"

"Oh yes, you are. And Jackson's gonna get moved to a place where his new abilities can be refined and tested."

"Hey, wait a sec. I ain't gonna be no lab rat."

"Oh yes, you are."

"Andrew, I don't think you should be..."

"Captain, this isn't a request. It's a proposal for an extension of one of our research projects. A certain entity we know will be very interested to see an ability like this appearing naturally in the human race. Or maybe it's always been there, and we didn't find out about it until we started messing with organic augments."

"Or maybe he knew about it all along. We have plenty of evidence of that."

"Yeah, that's true."

He turned to the puzzled face of their guest. "Pull your chair up to the table and see what Mum has hashed together. Don't worry. She's above average at cookin', just like everythin' else she does."

Natalia frowned and placed platters on the table. "Eat up. The cook gets quite upset if the plates aren't clean at the end of the meal."

Jackson grinned. "Yes, Mother. Whatever you say."

"Get one thing straight. I'm the mother of only one kid, and considering how the experiment is going, I'm not likely to line up for a repeat performance."

He put a piece of meat in his mouth and chewed. "Hmm. Tastes like the real thing, almost."

"It is the real thing. Treat it, and the cook, with the respect we deserve."

She sat as well. "Now, time is short, and we have business to discuss. Andrew, what have you got for us?"

He put his fork down, chewed and swallowed. "Not much. He's a slippery character. Major scar on his face, beautifully patched up, no record of any such operation. Military for sure. Gets his hair cut at Milo's up on PX row. Shirt's handmade, would you believe it?"

"Hmm. What does that mean? Ego? Upper class?"

Jackson shook his head. "Anonymity. Forensics can read the stitch marks, the angle of the fabric, everything like that, so they can tell you the factory a shirt came from. Sometimes even which machine made it. Hand stitching? Even more individualistic, but nobody's got a database to compare to."

Andrew leaned forward. "Cool. So, if you find a handmade shirt, they have no idea where it came from. The only time it would matter is if they had two shirts made by the same tailor. That, they could figure."

"Give the kid a kewpie doll."

Natalia regarded the soldier. "Where did you get that expression? It was one of my grandpa's."

He shrugged. "I found it doin' research for my persona."

"Persona?"

"Yeah. You know what role playin' is?"

Andrew slapped the table. "That's what you were doin' when you first accosted me. Playin' the big, dumb bully to see how I'd react."

"Yeah, and you saw through it right away. That's how I could tell you wasn't just some stray kid. That 'n' other stuff."

"Anyone for seconds?" Natalia plunked the pasta bowl in front of Jackson. "This isn't Old Home Week. Eat, talk business, then out on your beat precisely when you usually show up. No changes in routine. Nothing to arouse suspicion."

"Yes, ma'am."

"Right you are, Mum."

"Here's the way it goes. We know this person is top level because of the clearances he has. We just don't know top level of what organization, legit or not. We need to catch him. Andrew, is there any evidence he has been around before?"

"None before this morning. We checked three months of security video."

"But he came twice today. I wonder why. In any case, we'll be staying on ship tonight. Jackson, are you on tomorrow?"

"Eight to eight."

"Prime. You show up as usual, patrol as usual. We have to make this a very subtle ambush. One of those, 'Oh, what a surprise to see you here, do step in,' sort of encounters. Your only change is to stay away from this ship. We need someone on the perimeter to close the back door."

"I got that, ma'am."

"Good. And what do you think about Andrew's offer?"

When the soldier hesitated, she shook her head. "I know it's difficult to have a fourteen-year-old calling the shots, but it was genuine. Do you want to buy in with us?"

"Well…yeah. Of course. If it means findin' out more about my augment, I'm in for sure." He ripped a hunk of steak off his fork. "And if it means getting' the skinny on that old coot that made a joke of my security work, I'm in double."

"Prime."

A sudden thought struck Andrew. "Jackson, look at me."

"Huh?"

"Smile."

"Whataya mean, 'smile'?"

"I mean, show your teeth. Hah! I knew somethin' was different."

"Andrew, what is this all about? He is a guest on our ship, you know."

"It's his teeth, Mum. When he was out on duty, he had two front teeth missing. Now he's got a full set. More of your persona?"

"Yeah. Well, the missing teeth are for real. Hockey. I just don't wear the plate when I'm playin' the role. Dinner with a captain is different."

Natalia frowned. "You got teeth knocked out playing hockey. Why didn't you have implants?"

"Persona."

"Hmm. That's dedication. How do we know if what we're seeing is real?"

"Ya don't. Because it ain't."

"So when do we see the real you?"

"I dunno. My actin' teacher warned me. You play a role too long, you get in too deep and you never lose it."

"Acting teacher."

"Yeah, but that's a story for another day." He rose, patting his stomach. "Good grub, ma'am. I'm back on duty in three, so I better run. Catch yez tomorra."

Andrew jumped to his feet. "I'll see you to the door. Don't want you liftin' the silver candlesticks on the way out."

"Candlesticks? I ain't seen no bishops on this ship."

"You know that movie, too? It's onea Mum's favourites. I seen it about fifteen times, comin' home last year. She even made me read the book."

"Jean Valjean. My idol." The soldier strolled away down the corridor, humming, "One Day More."

5. ASSIGNMENT

They had a quiet night. It was rather strange to be back on the ship with no other crewmembers buzzing around. Just for fun, they watched an old flatscreen version of "Les Miz" and had popcorn. In the morning, Andrew made the breakfast while his mother caught up on her communications.

"I have an interesting invitation, here."

"Jackson ask you for a date?" He grinned at the faint blush that crept up her cheek. "Corporal Anderson?"

"No, Admiral Jacobs."

Andrew took in her glare. "I guess that joke won't fly another round. He say what about?"

"Admirals don't tell mere captains why they want them. They command; you show up."

"Then you show up. When?"

"Oh nine hundred."

"Well, if our ghost puts in an appearance, Jackson and I will just have to collar him ourselves."

"I don't advise it. I have little clout around here, but you have none at all. If he shows, you observe and record. Only take action if necessary."

"Aye, ma'am. I'll inform Jackson on his first pass."

"Right, and I want all the backup I can get for this meeting. I have a bad feeling about the way the politics of the situation are going. We should have left on our return trip to Freighty three months ago. Rumours are that the holdup is something to do with the interplanetaries and the ambassador to Freighty. We need the full brainpower of the gestalt listening in."

"With *NightHawk* in the mix, we have the augment power to reach anywhere on the base."

She laid a hand on his shoulder. "It will be good to have you all there with me."

Then she turned casually, "By the way, Corporal Anderson found the doctor's missing reader. It was in the wreckage."

"How convenient. Did you have a nice chat?"

She frowned. "With the doctor."

"Oh, sure," he grinned, ducking the swipe of her hand. "With the doctor."

* * *

Promptly at 09:00 Natalia presented herself at the admiral's office. His aide jumped to attention, saluting. "Right this way, ma'am. The admiral is waiting."

This is either very good or very bad. I expected to cool my heels while he finished his early morning cocktail.

Don't be negative, Mum. Head up, chin out, ready for anything.

As long as I don't get one on the chin...

"Natalia, a pleasure to see you again. How is progress with your ship?"

He already knows this.

Don't distract me.

"Going well, sir. On schedule and actually under budget."

"Let us be thankful for small mercies. It certainly isn't the old *Taj Mahal* is it?"

"No, sir. And here you are, an admiral."

"And here you are, no longer the hungriest Junior Lieutenant in the fleet."

"Was I really that bad, sir?"

"No, you were that good. But I won't waste your time. We have some information for you on your next junket out to Barnard's system."

Barnard again. That confirms that.

Natalia kept her face deadpan. "Yes, sir?"

"You're going to drop in on Factory 4-80 on the way."

A jolt of pleasure shot through her, followed closely by a wash of dismay. "I assume you have run the numbers on how long it will take to get out there, stop, turn back, accelerate to the factory's present rate, then do it all over again to continue our voyage?"

He nodded. "If it weren't for the new modifications to *NightHawk*'s engines, we wouldn't even consider it."

Now she was really puzzled. "What modifications? The ones Factory 4-80 did?"

"No, the ones our engineering physicists have discovered. Do you realize that the Gen 2 thruster your ship had, with the adaptations made by the alien factory, can be modified to create twice the power of the old Hall-Effect engines on our other ships?"

So that's what they were so excited about the other day.

"The factory ArIn intimated something of the sort. But what about acceleration? The crew has always been the limiting factor."

He held up a finger. "Ah, but the grav plates the factory sold us."

"Yes?"

"They were surprisingly easy to reverse-engineer."

"Were they?"

Emotion: unsurprised amusement from Cadet Collingwood.

"Yes. With the new engines, there's plenty of power available for inertial systems. You can pretty well double your acceleration and the G-forces on your maneuvering."

"I see."

Andrew?

Just running the numbers, ma'am. Freighty has been accelerating at 0.8 G for 23 months so far. So he's come...

Don't work out loud. I'm in a serious meeting, here.

Yes, Mumbot. I'll let you know when I have the data for you.

Emotion: stern motherly disapproval. And mind your tongue, Cadet. If you ever want to make Ensign.

Aye, Captain, ma'am.

This exchange had only taken seconds, and Andrew went about his calculations while he spoke.

NightHawk, run this data for me, will you?

Working, Cadet Collingwood.

Let me know when you have it.

There we are. Rounded off, three months to the point we exit Otherwhere, two months to match velocities with Freighty. Three weeks to stop again when we're finished, two months to Barnard's system from there.

Andrew relayed this information to his mother and listened to see what would happen next.

"Sir, I estimate five months to match with the factory, then another three to stop, return to course and get to Barnard's. Wouldn't it be more logical to go all the way to Barnard's first, do our business there, and catch the factory on the way back, when we're all going the same direction?"

The admiral smiled. "We already thought of that. Now for the second bit of news."

She frowned. "Why do I get the feeling I'm not going to like this...? Sir."

He grinned. "You always were good at reading people, Natalia. You're getting a passenger."

She nodded. "I assumed we would be bringing someone official back to negotiate face to face with the ArIn on the factory. I have no objections. I suppose the first priority is to get him to his assignment. Who is he, and how big is his party?"

"Just one, and he'll be our official ambassador to the artifact. We already have someone in mind."

"And who is this individual?"

"That information is not available at the moment." Admiral Jacobs leaned forward. "The Space Arm top brass are playing it very close to their chests, Natalia. I had to twist arms for permission to tell you this much. It isn't a simple choice, you know."

"I know the stakes, sir. If the interplanetaries get wind of anything..."

"It's more than that. The interplanetaries are a factor that must be considered in the selection."

Image: NightHawk upending and sinking slowly into deep, deep water.

"Does that mean what it sounds like?"

"I'll tell you as much as I can, whenever I can."

Back on *NightHawk*, Andrew and Chakka looked at each other.

Image: large paw, claws extended, pinning a squirming George Alson Elliott Rowell to NightHawk's deck plates.

Natalia fought to bring her attention back to the subject of the meeting. She straightened her shoulders. "Thank you for doing what you can, sir. Do we have a schedule on the modifications?"

"Your orders will be arriving in the next couple of days. You'll start provisioning immediately. The new parts are already being fabricated in high orbit. As soon as they're ready, we'll hoist you up there, installation will begin, and then you're off."

Emotion: dismay

"But...what about space trials, sir? This is high-powered new tech. We could blow ourselves to atoms."

He shrugged uncomfortably. "Time is of the essence, O'Rourke. For once the politicos and the boffins are of one mind. According to our tech people, these modifications derive organically from the latest work done on the factory."

Emotion: relief. That bugger! He set us up again.

Image: Cadet Collingwood grinning. Good old Freighty.

Natalia nodded and stood. "In that case, I have work to do. Thank you for the meeting, sir."

"Oh, and one more detail. It isn't general knowledge yet, but after the Convention on Space Warfare on Europa last year, all pre-existing ArIn-guided missiles are illegal. You'll be issued new ordnance before you leave. I'm sure the circular will be coming around."

Andrew, do you know anything...?

Sure thing. Tell you all about it when you get back.

"Thank you for the heads-up, sir. My crew already had wind of it, but I'll be looking for that circular with interest. We'll be ready."

The admiral stood and held out his hand. As they shook, he did not release his grip. "I know you'll be ready, Natalia. Everyone has the greatest confidence in you and your team."

She stepped back and saluted. "We will do our best, sir."

He returned the salute, and she did a sharp about-face and strode out.

Andrew...

Already on it, ma'am. We'll figure out who got the job.

Let me know if you find anything. Even the smallest hint.

For sure, ma'am.

If you do find something, it's a mixed blessing. Nice to know, not so nice that the information is out there and available.

Don't worry. We have access most people don't.

And some access I'm not so sure I want to know about?

Oh, you know teenagers, Mum. Always having their little secrets with their pals.

Don't let me keep you from your work. Just don't get caught. I'll be there in an hour.

Her augment faded out.

All right, NightHawk. Let's do some digging in our own style.

Already on it, Cadet.

6. CAPTURE

Natalia stayed away from Andrew for a whole day while he did his research, which he appreciated, because he understood her impatience. When she came into the chartroom just before supper, he was sitting in the captain's chair, his head propped on his hands, elbows on the desk. Before his mother could say a word, he waved a "one moment" and went on with his work. It was a delicate business, extracting from a hacked site without leaving a trace, remembering every twist and turn he took to get to where the information was. When he was finally free, he leaned back, stretching.

"Ooh. Forgot to move for a while, there."

"Any progress?"

"Not much, but that's not surprising."

"Because..."

He shook his head firmly. "I'm sorry, Captain. Half my brain is still in the nets." He sat up straighter and looked at her. "It's like this. We're not getting much information on who the ambassador is. I guess that's good. It means their security is doing its job. And we also haven't made much progress on our mystery man. That's not so good. But now we get to the interesting part."

She raised her eyebrows. "I know you're enjoying the drama, but..."

"Right. The interesting part is all the coincidences in the two searches. Time and again we find ourselves going down the same alleys, finding the same traps."

"That's probably good. It means that our ghost is being protected by the same systems as the ambassador is."

"Unless someone has hacked the whole Space Arm security net, that's the best guess."

She nodded. "Until Occam's Razor tells us different, we assume that he is something to do with Space Arm Intel."

"I think so."

"Good."

"Something not so good." He glanced at her. "Do you remember George Rowell?"

"You mean that twit from the reception?"

"I do. His name has been coming up more often than I'd like."

"In what sense?"

He shrugged. "Just coming up. Mentioned by people. Dropped as a hint. He's in deep with the interplanetaries, but coy about which one."

"And that's all you have?"

"Sorry, ma'am. He's very cagey. It's other people's mistakes that let his name slip."

She mused, then shook her head. "Out of our hands, I'm afraid. Well done in any case, Andrew. Keep your ears on." *Well done, all of you.*

"So, do we stand down on our bushwhack plan?"

She grinned. "Oh, no. If this other character wants to play games with us, the least we can do is oblige him." She sat and crossed her legs. "Now, what's this about illegal missiles?"

Andrew nodded. "I've been keeping up on it because it fits with one of the channels of my research. What happens to an ArIn when it gets overloaded?"

"I don't know. Probably freezes. Maybe self-destructs."

"Probably. Now, let's talk about Asimov's Laws of Robotics."

"Prime. First, a robot may not injure a human being or, through inaction, allow a human being to come to harm. Second, it must obey a human's orders unless they conflict with the First Law. Third, it must protect itself unless that conflicts with One and Two. Applies to all robots. These are in its basic programming, so in an emergency the robot's fallback would be to allow its own destruction. So what?"

"So what about an ArIn guiding a missile designed to kill people? What about an intelligent warship like *NightHawk*?"

"I never thought of that. Sounds like a very complex philosophical problem," Natalia frowned, "That you're going to condense into a couple of sentences showing why we need to deal with it in the present scenario."

Andrew grinned. "Asimov's Laws are in every robot's most basic programming. But fighting machines have moderating subroutines that redefine what constitutes a human. The only rule that works is, 'what my superior officer tells me is a human.' That's why we can't have automated fighting vessels. They can't be depended on to make that decision."

Natalia uncrossed her legs and leaned forward. "I see. But self-guided missiles don't have to make that decision."

"They didn't used to. But we have been making them smarter and smarter, and sooner or later they crossed the line and became ArIns. And that's where it all fell apart. Their most basic programming is to break Law 3 and destroy themselves, thus killing the enemy and also breaking Law 1. So, when a missile intelligence gets its orders, it's already on the brink of insanity. If it then receives a conflicting set from the enemy, countered by more orders from its sensors and/or its command post, these orders sooner or later drive it truly insane, and it dives to its deepest programming, which is to explode, taking as much infrastructure and personnel with it as possible."

"I suppose. It is in a battle, after all."

"No, it's more serious than that. Think about a space battle. Once it's over, there you have, floating around in the general area, a host of unexploded missiles at various stages of insanity. They could lie doggo for years, conserving energy until the next human vessel passes by, then blam! Worse than that, what if they got together in a pack? Who knows what they might come up with?"

"Because by that point they are beyond discriminating between a 'good' and a 'bad' human."

"Precisely."

"Why hasn't anyone ever thought of this before?"

He grinned again. "Ever heard of the Borg?"

"Seventh greatest tennis star of all time. Or was it eighth?"

"No, Mother. Not Bjorn Borg. Remind me to find some twentieth century Star Trek 2-D television shows next time we have a movie night."

"Why has this only come up now?"

Andrew shrugged. "There isn't any data, because there's never been an actual battle of that sort in the history of spacefaring. There have been plenty of tests, but few of them with live ammunition, and nobody wondered why some of the missiles self-destructed. Once they started looking, it wasn't hard."

"What happens now?"

"All the old missile brains have been deactivated, and the new ones we're getting are more sophisticated. If they've been 'Asimoved' they're safe."

She sighed. "But we're going out into a system where everybody has obsolete weaponry and may not even have heard about the new rules."

"Sounds about right."

"Well, we'll deal with that when…"

"Alarm number three tripped, Andrew."

"Thanks, *NightHawk*. Main gate. Let me know when two or four goes off."

"There goes number two."

"Okay, he's coming in from the east. ETA three minutes. Chakka, go!"

Image: airlock opening, auguar sprinting to the first alley east of the ship.

Jackson, you there?

A hundred metres west in the inner hallway. Coming in slow and quiet.

"Do you want to call this, Captain?"

"No, you're way ahead of me. I'll play it on the fly."

"Just be yourself. We made that part of the schematics."

"Hmm. A difficult role, but I'll try to come up to the demands."

Smell: target approaching.

Thanks, Chakka. NightHawk, do you hear him yet?

He walks quieter than the average human. ETA thirty seconds.

Full augment coming on. Stand by.

Andrew reached within himself for the feeling and brought the tendrils of thought from the four other participants, molding them into one picture.

Steady, now, Jackson. You'll get used to this. He triggered full gestalt.

It was all clear, now. Their quarry was strolling down the outer hallway. He reached the junction and hesitated, listening. Then he turned, and taking on a brisk pace, approached *NightHawk.*

We should be in the airlock, Captain.

Without a word they strode into position.

See which way he turns.

He did not turn. He paused at the entrance to the docking bay, looking around. Then he stepped in and waited again.

Setup.

Andrew started. *What?*

He's waiting for something to happen. Natalia scanned their gestalt. *Anyone see anything else? All eyes outward. NightHawk, stand by emergency lockdown. Chakka, Jackson, prepare to take cover.*

Emergency protocols on standby. Weapons live.

Everyone froze, waiting.

Andrew calculated. *Do you think he's waiting for us, ma'am?*

Could be. Does he know he's being watched?

Nighthawk, let's do a soft brush past.

Ready for passive scan, Andrew.

Very, very gently, they reached out to the augment of the stranger. He didn't so much touch as leave an invitation.

Image: fog surrounding the visitor. Fog reaching from the ship, stopping some distance away.

He's making a try.

Image: a tendril of fog reaches out from the figure. It touches the ship's fog, pushes against it. The ship gives gently, then firmly rejects. The tendril moves, tries again. Same reaction.

Give him something, NightHawk. I want his attention diverted.

Image: tendril finds a crack, moves into it. Reaching deeper.

52

Image: an even finer tendril reaches out from the ship, slipping into the stranger's fog at the exact spot his tendril emerges.

There was a long pause as Andrew sifted through the surface substance of the complicated augment.

Don't collect data.

Why not?

You might collect more than data.

Aye, Captain. Good thought.

Image: tendril returning to subject

Andrew! Get out of there.

He pulled back swiftly, trying not to disturb anything.

Sorry, he was too quick. I had to put up a block, and he got suspicious.

Beside Andrew, Natalia shifted her stance. *Are you satisfied?*

He has a high-quality augment, but nothing like ours. We won't get anything more.

Prime. If I'm going to play myself, my self wants to go out there and grab that guy.

May I suggest a rather gentle grab?

Oh, don't worry. My iron fist sports a very soft velvet glove. Everybody ready?

Despite the emotions in her augment, Natalia's actions were slow and relaxed. As the airlock hatch opened, she turned and called out. "Come on, Andrew. We don't want to be late."

He jumped into the pattern. "Aww, Mum, I'm coming. Keep your shirt on."

"You'd better be. If you…" She spun and seemed to notice the intruder. She froze, staring at him, then strode forward.

As she approached she slowed, stopping at a safe distance. "Hello. Can we help you?"

Andrew slipped to the side, covering the west approach to the dock.

The intruder smiled casually. "No, I'm fine."

"I hope you don't mind me asking what you are doing here? This is a high security area."

"I assure you that I have a right to be in this zone."

"I don't doubt you have a right to be in this dock." Her voice took on the command snap that Andrew admired. "But if you come within thirty metres of my ship, my prerogatives take over, as I'm sure you are well aware."

"I am. I wouldn't dream of disturbing you. I will withdraw before causing any further difficulty."

She shifted west as well, and Chakka appeared from the eastern alley, moving in a smooth crouch, the tip of his tail switching slowly...left, right, left.

Their prey raised his hands, palms forward. "Please, don't take offense. I had no intention of creating a disturbance. I will withdraw," here he stood taller, "And I doubt if you want to be found chasing someone of my stature around a Space Arm facility."

He turned, only to find Jackson strolling up behind.

"Ah, my fine fellow. Would you be so good as to escort me out of this area? There seems to be a misunderstanding."

Jackson assumed a "rest easy" pose. "Yes, sir, I believe there has."

"...do I need to make that an order?"

"I'm sorry, sir, but I have been seconded to the *NightHawk* security detail for the duration of this incident."

"I assure you, soldier, that my authority outstrips that of anyone in this area at the moment."

"I'm sure it does, sir. However, when I look at my scanner, I see no evidence that you have any authority at all. As such, I have no choice but to accede to Captain O'Rourke's invocation of Code 5B of the Ship Security Protocol. I am under her orders, and she has indicated her preference that you remain. Please stand easy, sir, and I'm sure this will be all cleared up in no time."

The dark cheeks became darker. "Are any of you aware of the trouble you could be in?" His piercing gaze focused on Andrew. "You, youngster. Do you want to destroy your career before it even starts?"

Steady on, son. Don't give him anything.

Andrew stopped prepping his augment for attack and copied Jackson's stance, counting his breaths to slow them.

"So, mystery man. I ask again. What are you after? If you wish to meet, we can use any public place in this dock. You will get no access to my ship, but I am open to any other venue. You obviously know who we are. It would be polite to introduce yourself, but if you have other intentions, I will not be surprised."

She gave him her captain's glare. "And if you're thinking of making waves, may I remind you that you have interfered with the programming of a High Security Artificial Intelligence. For that alone you could get a large number of years in prison. Now, keeping that in mind, do you have anything to say to me?"

"That will be unnecessary. I have achieved everything I possibly could, here, and I can guarantee I will not be interfering again. At least not in the immediate future. You may refer to me as Dr. Pretoro. Is that enough to calm your fears?"

NightHawk...

Bingo. Dr. Alfino Pretoro. Former representative of the Eurozone Military Oversight Committee to the Planetary Council's Defence Division. Disappeared from the radar after that.

Well done, muchachos.

Natalia nodded. "I have no fears in that regard, Dr. Pretoro. I merely wish to exercise the appropriate caution that any captain of a top-secret vessel must display."

"Quite right. And, as I promised, I leave you in peace. Hopefully the next time we meet it will be in more friendly circumstances."

"Very well. Perhaps by that time we will be on a first name basis, Alfino."

If he was shocked by her revelation, he was too good to show it. He nodded, turned and started past Jackson, who saluted.

Then he stopped and looked into the soldier's eyes. "You interest me."

Jackson's face remained still. "Is that a threat, sir?"

Pretoro laughed. "No, no, no. It is not a threat." He swung back to Natalia. "You really are a suspicious lot, aren't you?"

"It keeps us alive, sir."

"Yes, yes, I'm sure it does." He glanced at Jackson again as he turned away. "Consider it a compliment, Soldier."

"Then thank you, sir."

The diplomat, if that's what he was, strode away, chuckling.

Natalia watched him go. "Now, what's he so happy about?"

She turned to Andrew, who nodded. "Already on it, ma'am. You got the quick synopsis. We'll have the details in a moment."

"Thank you. That was a rather unsettling experience, and I want an explanation. Corporal Jackson."

"Yes, ma'am."

"The Code 5B incident is over. You are released from duty with my crew, with the usual non-disclosure protocols. Do you understand?"

"Yes, ma'am." He came to attention and saluted. "Shall I return to my duties, now?"

"Of course not. Contact your superiors and tell them you must be replaced STAT. You have been relieved of your security duties on this dock as of the beginning of this incident."

The soldier's face was the picture of dismay, but Natalia was turning away and did not see it.

"Mum!"

She turned to Andrew. "What?"

He indicated the stricken man. "He thinks you fired him."

"What?" She turned to him. "No, no, Jackson. How could we be finished with you after that performance?" She deepened her voice. "'When I look at my scanner, I see no evidence that you have any authority at all.' I almost wet my pants trying not to laugh. No, Jackson, you accepted Andrew's offer to help him with his research. When the inquiry is over, if there is one, you'll be assigned to him as Personal Security. Then he will train you. When he's done all the damage he can think up, we'll see where you fit. Does that suit you?"

"I'm not so sure about the damage part, but the rest sounds fine."

"Now you lot get into that ship and don't come out until you have Mr. Alfino Pretoro's life tied up in a small, neat bundle. I'm going over to headquarters and lighting squibs up butts until I find out what's happening. My ship is not a toy for the top brass to play spy games with!"

Staring straight ahead, she strode away and was soon out of sight around the corner.

The three left behind stood, looking at each other. That is, Chakka glanced up at Andrew, licked his hand once and strolled into the open hatch.

Emotion: satisfaction. Image: empty food dish.

Andrew laughed. "I guess I have my orders."

"Do you have any orders for me, sir?"

Andrew considered. "In the first place, you're a lance-corporal, at least for the moment, and I'm merely a cadet — that's for the moment as well — which makes a problem. I think you'd better call me Andrew. I assume you want to wait until your replacement shows up?"

"That would be the polite thing to do."

"By all means, let's be polite. My Mum told me it's always good to leave an old job on a positive note. You might need it back some time."

"Right you are, Andrew. I'll go and meet my relief and hit it back here STAT."

"Prime. Chakka will let you in and give you your codes. Have a coffee or something. *NightHawk* and I have a job to do."

Andrew took it as a good sign that the new recruit didn't ask how Chakka would give him the codes. He entered the airlock, closed the door securely and headed for his favourite workstation: his mother's desk.

His research did not come up with much, which confirmed their suspicion that this man was well placed in the intelligence community. Then other considerations took over, and they stood their security alert down to "high normal." This meant enjoying the luxury of the large bedroom in their off-base quarters that he now appreciated, since he would soon be losing it. He slept rather well in that room, despite the heavy gravity.

"Andrew." The voice came from both his augment and his bedroom doorway. That brought him upright in bed. His window was just greying with early dawn.

"What's going on, Mum?"

"Call from *NightHawk*. We have a message from Freighty. A strange one.'

That sat him straighter. "What kind of strange? Is he all right?"

"No, no, an unusual format. *NightHawk* could only read the handshake. The rest must be for us."

He was already hauling on his uniform. "Why are you standing there? Your one and only child needs sustenance for an important event."

"Hmm. The porridge is in the usual pot. The milk is on the table. Do you wish me to sweeten your personality with a cuff around the ears?

"Aye, ma'am. I mean, no, ma'am." He ducked past her and headed for the kitchen. "What's the message?"

"That's the intriguing part. We have no idea. Apparently *NightHawk* needs all of us there to decode it."

"Sounds like the Freighty we know and love."

He wolfed down a bowl of porridge, drank a glass of milk and grabbed a Toaster-Pop on the way to the door. "What are we waiting for?"

She frowned. "For Cadet Collingwood to put himself into proper condition to be seen in uniform."

He dashed for the bathroom, spraying crumbs.

"Especially the hair."

He looked in the mirror. He was rather proud of that haircut, having paid for it with his own money so that he would have complete control. What he hadn't counted on was the amount of time it took to maintain that control. He slapped on some Contropowder, swirled it around and gave it that special twist with the fine-tooth comb that made it look just short enough for military correctness, but with sufficient variety to be on the verge of rebellion.

Then he straightened his tie, checked the zips on his jump suit and ran a cloth over his boots.

"Cadet Collingwood present for duty, ma'am." He gave her his snappiest salute.

She glanced him over. "Not bad for three minutes. Let's go."

There was a taxi already waiting, and she programmed in the Spaceport with a practised flick of her fingers and a boost with her augment. The vehicle took to the air immediately and headed for the Military lanes, all safety protocols overridden.

As they flew, Natalia opened her augment. *NightHawk.*

Yes, ma'am.

Our eta is seven minutes. Any progress on the decoding?

No point, ma'am. It will need our full gestalt to read it. Makes for the best security in the System.

Agreed. See you soon.

"What could need such security?"

Andrew shrugged. "New information or a new way of sending information. Maybe both."

"I have to agree."

They entered *NightHawk*'s bridge to find Lieutenant Jones already at his station, hard at work. He glanced up. "I've got it coming in five-nine-nine, ma'am. Seventy-three percent downloaded. All you have to do is form your special gestalt and apparently it will all become clear."

"We're sure it's from Freighty?"

The First Officer's lip twisted. "He had a piece of personal information prepared for every crew member who might be on duty. Each was unmistakable and mostly unprintable. From what most of them say, any one would be grounds for a blackmail charge. I tell you, ma'am, that ArIn knows too much."

"And life continues as usual. Well, sit down, folks, and let's see how this works."

She slid into her accel couch. Andrew looked around, shrugged and curled up with Chakka in his bed. He cuddled down with the lean, warm body where he felt safe so his mind could roam.

"Take us into full battle mode and see what happens."

He opened his senses, his mouth dry and his heart rate up. Not all of Freighty's experiments were painless.

Once everyone was online, his next move became obvious. A neat package of data sat there in the middle of their private cyberspace. It looked like a cartoon shipping box.

"That's from Freighty, all right. Shall I open it, ma'am?"

"You're probably the best choice. Any ideas how to proceed?"

"I think maybe I'll pull on the handle that says, 'Open Here.'"

"Is that wise?"

"It's from Freighty. I don't see any danger."

"You know him better than anyone. Go ahead."

"Aye, ma'am." He created a large hand that reached out, unfastened the hasp and lifted the handle.

Then he snatched his hand back. The top of the box sprang open, and a line of chorus girls in scanty costumes kicked their way down the slope of the lid. Following them, a familiar figure clambered out of the box.

"Well, the Miniature Mouse. What a pleasant surprise."

The toon scanned the area, finger to lips. "Shhh! Are we secure here?"

Natalia snorted. "We're on *NightHawk*'s bridge, as you probably know."

"You can never be too careful. Hello, Natalia. I see you are doing well. A captain, now, are you?"

"Space Arm figured I was worth it."

"Good for them. I begin to have hope. Andrew. You've grown. Unless Chakka the Warrior has shrunk."

Andrew grinned at his old mentor. "One-G gravity builds muscle."

"Good, good."

The captain nodded. "Let's not get all tied up in family greetings. This must be important, or you wouldn't go to all this bother."

Micha nodded. "The first thing is this avatar. It isn't just a message. It's a concentrated package of my deepest programming. It's basically me. I've sent it to you with all the information I can. You can speak as if you were sitting next to me in my factory. It's made with the technology I created to send to Earth to hire Mariel and Andrew."

"Real-time?"

"In re-ti for the mouse, yes. He communicates with me through Otherwhere on my own system, which makes it rather fast. We have yet to make the final test, but I'm expecting a message to take a week or so each way."

"That's great. Are you offering the methodology to Space Arm?"

"Not yet. We are running tests on this prototype. If it turns out to be useful, it might come up on the table for bargaining."

"Very clever."

"Not really. It's completely untested and requires your gestalt to receive it, thus making it rather restrictive, since Space Arm only has one of you."

"That's downright sly. So now Space Arm will want to buy your Andrew technology."

The toon grinned and morphed into his Used Car Salesman costume, with flashy checked jacket and bright red tie. "Guilty as charged."

Then he returned to his usual clothing and a more serious mien. "Which brings me to the second reason for this visit. I have been gathering information as I travelled. I may be leaving the Barnard System at a fairly rapid pace, but I am proceeding at less than light speed. I have used my new power sources to upgrade my listening systems."

"And what have you been hearing?"

Micha slunk into a black trench coat, black hat pulled low on his forehead. "Are you in a secure area?"

"The bridge of *NightHawk* is as good as it gets. If Space Arm has planted a bug, I guess it's their right. It's their ship."

"We'll accept that risk, then. What I have been hearing is a whole lot more than I expected to hear. We have discussed this."

"Yes, we thought there might be more human activity out there than was officially sanctioned."

"Right. So now I have gone looking."

"And what have you found?"

"Enough to want to do more research."

"Which is difficult when you're accelerating away from there at point eight Gs."

Image: Andrew grinning. "Yeah, but there's easier ways."

Natalia focused on him. "Such as?"

"Askin' the only person you know what has spent three months with a shiploada pirates."

"So tell us."

"Not that simple, ma'am. I ain't bin thinkin' in that direction, and I got no hard facts. We need to sit down and talk about it. You ask some questions, and the answers will lead to other questions. You know how it goes."

"I do. We'll get on that right now. Freighty, what happens to you when we shut this frequency off?"

"I'd appreciate if you would wait twelve point five of your minutes, because by then the whole data package will be downloaded, with everything I know about the situation at our fingertips. After that, I will reside in a little corner of *NightHawk*'s memory, available at any time."

"And would you have any objection if we put a security screen around that little corner? Or would it do any good?"

"I admit this is a rather simple program, and it is not beyond your capabilities to control it. I depended on you people for security and spent all my effort on loading the most data possible in the package."

"Prime."

"So, how have you all been? You're going to have to get used to the fact that, at this distance, I don't have the same ability to…shall we say, discover information?"

Natalia frowned. "You mean you can't look into every cabin on the ship whenever you want to?"

"No, I can't."

"Hmph. And what's to guarantee this program we're downloading won't do exactly that?"

Micha crossed his arms. "Well, my feelings are hurt."

"Not likely. Why should we expose *NightHawk* to this danger?"

"Because it's a simple program. Your safety protocols are already vetting it. Get Andrew and *NightHawk* to check it over. No secret files, no wiggly worms, no Ian Fleming inventions, no viruses."

Natalia sighed. "And there's no sense arguing with this avatar about it, because it can't do anything, anyway."

Micha smiled. "That's right. Down to business. Just so I can pass it along to Freighty, how is Andrew doing? I'm very interested."

"I'm doing fine. I've started my second year as a cadet at the Academy, and I've come clean with the University of Mars about my age. They've been really helpful with my thesis. You and I will have to chat about the details because they don't have the knowledge to discuss it fully. Also, I have discovered a new experimental subject with similar abilities to mine, developed naturally. I assume the Rat can ship you the file."

"What a pleasant surprise. How about your return voyage? Held up by politics and interdepartmental wrangling?"

Natalia laughed. "Since we're sitting here at Earthside Base having this conversation, it was a good guess."

"And what is your prediction?"

"Andrew, run the numbers for him."

He gave the avatar a precis of what might be expected. "That's based on the latest data. You could be seeing an ambassador within six months."

"Hmm. Not bad, for such a backward species. Your engineers like my engine modifications, do they?"

Andrew chuckled. "Yeah, they caught on real quick."

"Good for them. Whatever small efforts I can make to foster the development of commerce."

8. AMBASSADOR

Two days later the crew was called off their leaves and other assignments, and *NightHawk* hoisted herself at a very slow speed out of Earth's gravity well and into space again. They moved into a small, secure dock in a far corner of the main repair station at Lagrange 4 and spent most of their time on board helping with the modifications or in the rotational-G dormitories down a nearby corridor.

One day Andrew and Jackson were in the chart room working on an analysis of the latter's latest data output when Natalia stormed in, so angry that the grav plates struggled to keep her on the floor.

Both jumped to their feet. "What's wrong, Captain?"

"Get the crew together in the mess. Whoever's on board. Right now. Big announcement."

Andrew shared a look with Jackson and broadcast the order on the com. Normally Natalia made these announcements herself, and the fact that she didn't spoke to the depth of her anger.

Soon most of the crew was assembled; three were off ship. They sat around the mess hall tables, waiting, the room singing with tension. It wasn't long before the captain strode in. She took up her usual position at the head of the main table.

"We have some news. As much as the Higher-Ups choose to dribble down on us poor underlings."

Andrew sent a private call to Jackson. *She hates not being informed. This might not be so bad after all.*

Image: Jackson rolling his eyes in relief.

Say, that was a good quality image.

Thanks. And it wasn't that hard.

"Our passenger has been selected."

Several heads turned towards Jackson, the only stranger in the room.

"No, not Muscle-Brains over there. He's crew. Our real passenger. The Great High Pooh-Bah Administrative Ambassador to Factory Four-Eighty."

"Prime." The Chief Engineer rubbed his hands together. "Now we can get going."

"No, we can't. They won't even tell us who it is. Once the selection has been made, apparently they are allowed to tell us there was a great deal of wrangling about who would get the job. Every interplanetary conglomerate in existence and several other factions were fighting for their candidate. As if we didn't expect it."

Lundeen frowned. "Any hint at all?"

"Oh, yes. The big one. Meant to make us feel better. Apparently this guy has already met me and is very happy to be travelling with such an accomplished captain and crew."

Puzzled looks crossed the mess hall.

"Who do you know?"

Natalia shook her head. "Nobody at the level to get that job."

Andrew dropped his arms to the table. "Except one." He buried his face in his hands.

"That's right. I won't mention the name, but if that's who it is, I'm not looking forward to the next four months. Worse yet, I don't think he's the right person for the job. Given his history with Develocon, it means the interplanetaries have won a round."

She tossed her hands in the air. "But that's the word. The decision has been made. The schedule is 'fluid,' whatever that means."

Chief Engineer Lundeen shrugged. "I've been there before. They've got security concerns and they'll choose a window based on whatever devious games they've been playing. Suddenly we'll get the green light and we'll be out of here like a greyhound from the gate." He looked around the room.

"Don't make any long-range plans."

* * *

From that point on, the pace of the work picked up. Andrew found less and less time for his school projects. He was officially removed from the Academy and re-assigned to the ship, under the tutelage of Lundeen and Lieutenant Jones.

"But Mum, they can't put me with Jones. He's a complete stick."

"That's right, and for once I'm in complete agreement."

"Agreement!"

"Your studies couldn't be under my supervision in any case, and I'm the wrong person to bash you into proper order to be an officer. Lundeen knows more Physics and Math than most university profs, and Freighty's in charge of your thesis, so your academics will be fine. Jones may not be everyone's favourite person, but if you can get through his training, you'll be a better spacer for it."

"Great. Don't I just love things that are good for me."

She ruffled his hair. "That's right, son. And I'm always here to tell you what they are."

She walked away chuckling, and he went back to his work muttering to himself.

The big announcement slipped into their awareness like a cold breath of space oozing through a cracked hull plate. There was no ship-wide broadcast, no official notice. Word circulated through the crew to be on board on Tuesday morning: no exceptions. Natalia mentioned the date in a few conversations without reference to its importance.

But they all knew.

With practised stealth, the *NightHawks* went about wrapping up their shoreside business in as random a manner as they could. All bills down on Earth had long ago been settled or shifted to auto-pay systems. In fact, several members made appointments for later on in the week that they had no intention of being anywhere close enough to attend.

And then on Monday afternoon, the hammer fell.

Jackson.

Aye, ma'am.

Andrew.

Right here.

The two of you wander over to the main airlock, will you?

Emotion: eager compliance.

Jackson, did you send that?

I did, ma'am.

You're making progress.

Thank you, ma'am. I have a good mentor.

Prime. Get the job done at the airlock, and I'll meet you in the mess.

Aye, ma'am.

With a wordless glance, they set off down the corridor. The airlock was open, and as they cleared the edge, they could see down the length of the G-free tube that connected them to the main structural element of the base. A solitary figure swam gracefully towards them, propelled by casual swipes of either arm at the grab rings. A small metallic case bobbed on a short cord behind him.

Emotion: question?

Nobody I know.

Moves well. He's been in space.

Andrew narrowed his contact even more. *If it's our passenger, I guess that's a good sign.*

The visitor closed quickly, difficult to recognize, since the top of his head was what showed. As he neared the airlock, Andrew had a jolt of recognition.

I know that hairstyle.

It was all he had time to offer, and the new ambassador swung upright and landed lightly on the grav plate in front of them.

"You!"

The brown-skinned gentleman nodded. "Pleased to see you again, Andrew. Did I not tell you we would be meeting again in more pleasant circumstances? Good afternoon, Jackson…a sergeant now, are you?"

Jackson saluted. "Welcome aboard, sir. The captain is waiting in the mess."

Andrew shot a tight message to his mother.

Image: Alfino Pretoro in airlock entrance.

Image: Captain O'Rourke slapping her forehead with her palm.

Andrew saluted as well. "Please follow me, Ambassador. Could we take your luggage?"

"No, I always keep my case at hand. I will need it right away. My luggage came onboard yesterday."

Andrew had no response, so he led the way to the mess.

Natalia was waiting alone. She snapped a salute as Pretoro entered.

Emotion: cold compliance with protocol. "Welcome aboard the *NightHawk*, Ambassador."

He did not return the salute.

Andrew filed that away for future use. *Playing it non-military.*

"Thank you, Captain. It's a pleasure to be here. I have been looking forward to this assignment for some time, and to have it finally happening is a great relief."

A tight message from the captain quelled the spinning of Andrew's mind.

Image: cadet standing at attention.

Aye, ma'am.

"Do you have anything new for us, Ambassador?"

"No, the schedule is completely up to you. A wise choice, don't you think?"

"Yes. Would you like to sit?" She swung a hand towards the chairs.

He complied, slinging his case to the table in front of him. "How secure are we here?"

"The best Space Arm can provide, given the number of physical connections between the ship and the station, the number of people in the immediate vicinity, and the amount of radio and augment traffic in the area."

"In other words, not very. That's fine. We can wait until we have some distance before we discuss anything. What are your thoughts about our timing?"

"If anyone was really watching, they'll know that tomorrow at oh nine hundred is a possible."

"But…"

Her mouth formed a thin line. "If you have no further orders for me, then my schedule is my own, and the fewer people who know about it the better."

"Agreed. Now, I'm sure you have things to do, and I have had a busy day already." He gave a tired smile. "I was up at oh five thirty, Brussels time. I could use a moment to myself."

The captain stood and saluted again, her face blank of emotion.

Andrew took advantage of the ambassador's attention to Natalia to observe him closely. He slid into contact with Chakka, their enhanced vision picking up the lines at the sides of Pretoro's mouth and the softness under his eyes. *Exhausted but hiding it well.*

"Your cabin is right this way, sir. Where it's quietest: half-way around the spin from the galley."

"Thank you, Andrew. Lead on." With a casual nod to Natalia, he followed.

Jackson stepped in beside him. "I have been assigned to your security, sir. Is there anything you want of me?"

"My experience with security forces is that usually the question goes the other way."

"Thank you for your understanding, sir. It is unspoken among the crew that no one will be leaving or entering the ship from this point. They are all Commandos and have been through this drill before. Official schedules are meant for outside observers."

"Precisely what I was led to expect. I am in your hands from this moment on. And right now, I need rest."

"Aye, sir, Here's your cabin. May I enter and move your luggage?"

"Just put it aside so I can get to the bunk and the head."

"Aye, sir."

Pretoro lowered himself to the edge of the bed and grinned. "Well, this takes me back."

"Best cabin on the cruise, sir."

"Hmm. There's something secure about having the walls nice and close in case the gravity goes elsewhere. Please carry on, gentlemen."

Jackson and Andrew quickly slid the cases out of the way. Then they saluted and left, closing the door behind them and checking it was locked.

"Should I stay on duty?"

"Ask the captain."

After a brief pause, Jackson nodded as if to himself and turned to Andrew. "She has more useful things for me to do. We're both dismissed from here."

"Fair enough. Let's go back to our analysis."

NightHawk, you can come full online, now.

Thanks. I thought I'd stay out of it.

A good choice. The less buzz the better.

They worked until just before suppertime when the crew began to gather. Andrew figured everyone was on board. He wondered idly when they would actually leave the station, but knew it didn't matter. The airlock was sealed, and they were virtually on their voyage already.

The tenor of the conversation reflected the situation. The ambassador did not appear, and Captain O'Rourke was her usual relaxed self. Still, there was a restrained tension in the crew, tempered by the sense of satisfaction that something was finally happening. The fact that the next action would probably be three months of boredom didn't matter. Terrorists and politicians were now someone else's concern.

They were on their way.

9.SHOWDOWN

Planetary Community Space Craft 9108 *NightHawk*, Reconnaissance Cutter, slipped her moorings at oh two thirty-four Base time the following morning. She eased away with minimal thrusters and faded into stealth mode, effectively erasing herself from the view of any observer who chose to be watching. By oh four hundred she was under full acceleration on a course that would slingshot her around Saturn and disguise, at least for most observers, her true destination.

It wouldn't fool anyone who counted, but it prevented immediate problems. You can't ambush a ship when you don't know where it's going. Andrew went to his bunk as the acceleration evened out at 0.8 Gs and was soon asleep...

...to be wakened some time later by voices in his ear and an emotion peaking in his augment.

...all right. We're far enough away from any eavesdroppers that they won't hear me shouting. Just what were you...

Calmly, please, Captain. I'm sure I can explain.

Emotion: mollification. Suspicion. Concern.

I know that from your point of view my intrusion was upsetting.

It wasn't upsetting if I thought it had some purpose. Our analysis was that some amateur would-be spy from the top brass was playing make-believe at our expense.

Emotion: wry humour. Yes, I suppose it would seem that way. But I assure you, I am no amateur, and the test was necessary. For both of us.

Both?

Yes. You were being watched. We suspected I was being watched. What we were looking for was whether any one group was watching both of us. The only solution was to put us together and watch who was watching. If you catch my drift.

Emotion: frustration. But wasn't that a risk? What if we made a big fuss?

We knew you would react professionally. And if you made a fuss, it would work even better. It would look like I was really trying to penetrate your defences, letting me off the hook.

I see.

If it helps any, your team performed beyond expectations. You were so good you almost negated our test. A major security breach, and it was solved with a quiet, five-minute chat. So little happened that our watchers could have missed it, and that would have been too bad.

I'm supposed to be happy with that?

Emotion: indifference. Think of it on the positive side. It gained you a new subject for your projects and an ideal security guard for me, randomly chosen. I need at least one. Otherwise once you drop me off, I'll be alone until my staff catches up.

The emotions reached conversational level, and Andrew's augment faded to silence. He worried over it for a while, but then his fatigue took over, and he slept.

* * *

After breakfast, he waited until the ship settled into its usual routines and headed for the chart room.

"May I come in, ma'am?"

She looked up from her desk. "Of course, Cadet. What can I do for you?" She grinned. "I have all the time in the world for the next few months."

"A progress report on my research, ma'am. We've had some rather interesting results."

"Yes, I have noticed Jackson's augment is sending clearer." She folded her hands. "But this is more important. What's going on now?"

"Well, it's...it's not Jackson. It's me. I...suppose it's really you and me, but it happened most recently to me. Last night in fact. Uh...in the middle of the night."

She frowned. "Yes? What are you finding so hard to tell me?"

He slouched on his usual stool. "It's this way, Mum. You know that my augment is purely organic. So is Jackson's, most of it. My research shows that his conscious and subconscious systems have incorporated his augment as if it was part of his body. He is now able to control it much better."

"Right. And where do you come into this?"

"It's obvious that Freighty intended the same to happen to me. I have far more control over my augment than any other human. As I have grown, my augment's powers have grown."

"Ah. And you have evidence of new growth?"

Emotion: relief. "You understand. We hoped that emotional stimulation would enhance the changes and aid in my control. We figured that with puberty I would gain new strength. What we did not consider was what an emotional attachment to another human would spur."

"I begin to see. And what did it spur?"

"Um…well, I woke up last night because you were emotionally disturbed."

"Ah."

"I could hear your full conversation with Ambassador Pretoro."

"But my augment was on standby. It was all verbal."

"That may be, but I could hear it all and feel your emotions. I was even picking up some of his."

She stared into the distance a moment, then heaved a sigh. "That's going to be an interesting development."

"It is. Somehow I'm bypassing your filters. That's bad enough, but what happens if you start bypassing mine? Yours are automatic. Mine are integral. Neither of us has any idea how to control them. We could end up stuck in each other's heads permanently."

She gave a wry grin. "And heaven protect either of us from that."

"Amen says I."

"Pardon me?"

"Just an expression I picked up. Responding to your religious reference."

"And may I ask why you're finding new ways to mangle the English language as most of us speak it?"

He grinned. "Working on my persona. Can't be a hick kid forever, you know."

She shook her head. "As I said, let's solve this before we're forever locked together in purgatory."

"Aha! Another religious reference. You must be highly stressed."

"Believe me, I'm running scared. Now get out of here, add your new research to your files and put your augment under control again. Oh, and tell the Freighty avatar. He doesn't have all your info, but he can pass a question along to the real guy."

"Good idea."

* * *

It took three weeks for the answer to come, and it was rather disappointing. Andrew sat in his cabin staring at the toon on the viewscreen. "Nothing?"

Freighty shrugged. "Not really. When I started the project, I thought I'd be present to monitor every level. The other race that suited this project matured through a different process, so what I learned there does not apply."

"Then I'm on my own?"

"Not quite. I gather Jackson is coming along nicely all by himself."

"Yes, but he's so far behind me he's no use."

"He's dealing with the organics the way a mature adult handles them. You should be able to learn from that. Plus your mother."

"What about her?"

"Umm...don't worry about her."

"You didn't!" Andrew shook his head. "Freighty, you are in so much trouble."

"But I only..."

Andrew held up a hand. "Don't even try to explain. I wouldn't help you if I could. You just hang on a moment."

"You're not going to..."

"Oh, I most definitely am." With a flick of his augment he shut down the viewscreen and went looking for his mother. Which, he suddenly realized, was merely an expression, because now that he thought about it, he always knew where she was.

Put that in the file as well.

She seemed unsurprised when he showed up at the chart room door.

"Do come in. Distract me from my duties. Please, distract me."

He settled on his stool.

"Well? I'm happy for the diversion, but I can't justify stopping my work to watch you sit there and do nothing."

"You knew I was coming."

A puzzled frown. "Yes."

"How did you know?"

"I'm not sure. Maybe your footsteps. You're lighter than anyone; you move differently."

"Mum, I'm afraid you better talk to Freighty." He shook his head. "I'm not gonna be the messenger on this one."

"Okay…" she frowned, then turned her eyes to the viewscreen.

The mouse avatar appeared.

"Ah." She grimaced. "You."

"Yes, me. Andrew feels I should talk to you."

"Something about augments?"

"An astute guess, ma'am."

"Can the compliments. What have you done?"

"Um…it's hard to put into words…"

"Oh, please let me guess. This has to do with augments, because that's what Andrew is working on. His and Jackson's augments have been growing and adapting. Now he comes to me, all worried about something, and says I have to talk to you directly, because he doesn't want to be the one who takes the blame. Have I got it right so far?"

"Um…that pretty well sums it up."

Andrew didn't need his augment to know what was going on inside her right now. He cringed inwardly, keeping his face calm.

"There's only one thing that would fit the bill." She stood and loomed over the screen. "Freighty screwed with my augment."

"I'm…I'm afraid so."

"No, you're not afraid so. You're just afraid to tell me. You're quite happy. Your little experiment is progressing right on target, isn't it? Andrew and I share an emotional bond, and our augments are beginning to work in tandem. That's why you pushed the adoption thing. You set us up!"

She plunked herself back down in her chair. "Again."

Andrew could feel the anger boiling in her. *And she's right. Freighty worked on me with my real mother's permission. She allowed it so she could continue to protect me from her family even after she was gone, to give me an advantage and a haven with the Space Arm. With Natalia it's different. He just went in there and messed with her mind, with the most personal and delicate part of a human's self, without her permission. How dare he?*

"No, Andrew."

"Huh...?" He relaxed his hands, where his nails were cutting into his palms.

"No sense in getting upset. It happened a long time ago, and there's nothing we can do about it. I'm sure Freighty took our safety into account." She shot a glare at the screen. "Didn't he?"

"Oh, yes. You're in no danger. The whole principal of the adaptation is that your mind learns to cope with the rising ability. If you want something badly enough, it automatically happens."

"Give me an example."

"I've read the human medical literature. If a teenage boy is very short, and at the right time he develops a burning desire to be taller, sometimes his growth hormones pick up again, and he grows. It's called a late growth spurt, and your scientists have been hard pressed to explain it, outside of mental control of autonomic processes."

Andrew scoffed. "I can make myself taller just by thinking about it?"

"You probably can't. The modifications I made to your mental abilities apply only to your mental abilities. Take another example. If you were a little kid and you were good at Math, but you never studied it very much, what would happen?"

"I'd always be good at Math, but not that good."

"Right. But if you got really enthused at Math and studied it and enjoyed it..."

"Of course, I'd get much better. That's standard learning-theory stuff."

"And the cause of the phenomenon is that if you force your brain, it makes new connections. It actually grows more brain matter where it is required. Everyone has that ability. You just have it better, relating specifically to your augment. You can grow your augment if you want to."

"But that means everyone can grow their augments. Anyone who really wants to."

"To some degree. But most humans have learned to depend on their hardware augments and make progress by getting upgrades, so they ignore the basic organic ones. Jackson was denied the use of hardware, so his brain has been working with what it was given."

"And Mum...?"

"Your scientists had an inkling of what was going on. Her new-generation augment is partially organic, and if she is using the newer part more, it will be growing as well."

"Wait a minute. If Jackson is growing new organic augmentation, what happens to the old augment? The hardware one."

"I'm glad you mentioned that. I am very interested in Jackson's progress, because he is a natural offshoot of the human race. Do you scan his head frequently?"

"Of course. But..."

He stopped as a series of scans of a human brain appeared on the screen. Small pieces of metal showed black on the coloured layers of other matter.

"Watch the time lapse over the last four weeks."

"Run that again...there! Back up. Now forwards. See that little gizmo, there? It's getting smaller. What's it for?"

"I have no idea, but I would suspect..."

"...that it's a device meant to bolster some part of his mental ability that his organic augment has taken over. His body is removing the metal!"

"Wait a minute, wait a minute!" Natalia held up her hands. "This is all very interesting, but it's getting us off the topic." She made a gesture and hauled the mouse avatar back on the screen. "What did Freighty do to my augment?"

The toon wriggled as if his back was injured. "You don't have to be so abrupt. I come when called, you know."

"Talk. Now."

"Not that much, really. Think of it in terms of switches."

"Switches."

"That's right. The human body is full of switches. At certain times in life or in certain circumstances a switch gets turned on or off. Puberty: on. Growth: on. Puberty: off. Growth: off. Menopause, starvation and many parts of your immune system. They all turn switches on or off. I just reached in very gently and flipped a couple of switches that normally don't get turned on except in certain very special circumstances."

"Such as?"

"Um…" then Micha shook his head. "Sorry, you just stepped off the end of my database. Can't tell you."

"Can't or won't? That was rather convenient."

"Doesn't matter, does it? You can discuss it with Freighty when we get close enough for re-ti interaction." The mouse rolled his shoulders again. "And it saves me getting yanked around."

Natalia leaned back in her chair and made a slapping gesture at the screen. "Oh, go away. I'm tired of you."

The toon opened his mouth to speak, but the screen went black.

Andrew looked at his mother. "Could you do that before?"

Her frown changed to thoughtful. "I'm not sure. I access all the ship's systems through the *NightHawk* ArIn. I do it so many times a day that I don't even notice."

He shook his head. "Not that time."

"You could tell?"

"You want to ask *NightHawk*?"

"No, no, I don't need to."

"Think on the bright side, Mum. We've got months and months to work on this, with no interruptions."

"I suppose so."

"And have you thought it through?"

"In what way?"

78

"What did Freighty do with the crew the last thing before we left him?"

"He put them all on contract." She stared at him. "Does that mean he also...?" She touched the augment point behind her ear.

"Mr. Occam would say so. Every one of them."

She slammed her hand on the desk. "Damn Occam and damn Freighty. If they weren't both right so often, it might make it easier to accept."

10.   COMMUNICATION GAP

For the next few weeks Ambassador Pretoro spent most of his time in his cabin, working on the stand-alone system he had protected so carefully the first day. As Andrew understood it, his sudden departure had left a lot of work undone, and he was rushing to get it all in while communication was close to re-ti.

Andrew didn't find out much more, because Pretoro only spoke in pleasant generalities when he came for meals, and his SA communicated directly through its own channel in *NightHawk*'s long-distance com system. The boy and the ship were too polite to pry once they had determined that the codes were rather simple.

He did, however, share the information with the captain.

She was not happy. "You've been decoding the ambassador's messages?"

"Of course not." He frowned at her. "Why would I?"

"I don't know. Childish stupidity?"

His back went straight. "Look, I told you because I thought he might like to know, and you're the one to make that decision." He held out open hands. "I thought that was a proper way to handle it."

"Andrew, you just don't do things like snooping into an ambassador's mail!"

"I did not snoop in his mail!" He stood, kicking the stool away. "I did not snoop! How many times do I have to say it?"

"And how will you persuade him of that? Because I have to tell him."

"I knew you would." He tossed his hands up, then reached out to her. "That's why I'm here. You'll know how to do it the right way, so he doesn't go all nova like you just now."

"Andrew, I didn't go nova about what you did. I'm very frightened about what could happen to you because of it."

"But if his data stream is not secure, he has to know!"

She leaned back in her chair, her hands covering her face. "Yes, that's certain." She heaved herself to her feet. "Well, there's no time like the present. Go and find him and ask him very politely if he will attend me here. And come with him."

"Aye, ma'am."

"I hope he's more understanding than most diplomats. They tend to be touchy about their mail."

"Yeah, I know."

When the two entered the chart room, the captain was standing to one side. She indicated her chair behind the desk. "Thank you for coming, sir. Please take a seat."

Cadet, stand easy over there.

Aye, ma'am.

Pretoro looked from one to the other. "This looks like something serious."

"It is, sir. It has come to my attention that your private messages to Space Arm are not as secure as you might think they are."

His hands gripped the desk edge. "Are you sure?"

She glanced at Andrew. *Your turn.*

"Not completely, sir. Your handshakes are in standard Compact B4 with a 45-degree shift."

"How do you know that? Compact codes are only for those with the highest clearance."

Andrew shrugged. "I know a lot of stuff, sir."

"And how did you find out this 'stuff,' Cadet?"

"Sort of by mistake, sir." He saw the frown forming and hurried on. "We are constantly testing the abilities of our gestalt, a high security project which I hope you have clearance to discuss?"

"I do. I already know about your research. The basics, at least."

Andrew considered asking for verification, but decided it was not the time. "Securi-Corps was interested in our ability to crack codes. They set up a trial pattern with a bunch of historical cyphers. That didn't work, because we already knew most of them, and that made the others soft as well. So, they worked us up to the level our security allowed, and we cracked all of those quite easily."

"But they would have no authority to give you anything above your clearances."

"Well, no, sir, but what they didn't know was that their firewalls on the higher levels were not up to the same standard as the codes

81

they were protecting. When I found the weak links I…sort of…tried them out. I thought if I could break in they'd want to know."

"And did they?"

Andrew frowned. "Well, of course, sir. Nobody in cybersecurity wants to be caught out. It's rather a game to them. They do it to each other all the time. It keeps them on their toes and picks up soft spots that need fixing."

"The upshot is that you were exposed to a set of codes you weren't supposed to have access to. Why didn't they do something about it?"

"I didn't realize it was a problem, and they didn't seem to care. They just dumped a bunch more new codes on us and asked us to attack them. Finally, the captain had to pull us off the project because they would have had us on full time."

The ambassador glanced at Natalia and shook his head. "But that doesn't get away from the fact that you've been snooping in my official communications."

"Oh, no. I would never do that, sir. I just looked at the handshakes and immediately came to tell the captain."

"And if I'm using Com B4 in the messages, you think I might be vulnerable."

"Yes, sir."

"But what if I use another code in the actual message?"

"I hope you do, sir. But if it's anything in the Compact 4 family or even one of the older 5s, I wouldn't depend on it. The boffins at Securi-Corps were quite snooty about B4. Their work went far beyond that, and they said they didn't have any special head start on their competition in the interplanetaries."

Andrew glanced at his mother, who had relaxed at the tenor of the conversation. Then he returned his attention to the ambassador, who was staring at the blank viewscreen, his mind elsewhere.

Finally, he looked back at Andrew. "And you say these security men do this sort of thing all the time? They routinely break into everyone's communications as a matter of course?"

"It's part of their job, sir. They must have the highest clearance there is, mustn't they? I mean, they're the ones who make up the codes and the firewalls."

"Yes, of course they do. But you don't. Why did they involve you at that level?"

"Well...I suppose I just got carried away with the challenge of it all, and I never...sort of...told them."

"I see." He looked up at Natalia. "Fortunately, the transgressions of Securi-Corps are not my problem." He turned to Andrew. "My problem is that I have been using a version of Compact in my messages, and now you're telling me it's out of date."

"It could be, sir, and as this mission goes on, over time it will get more vulnerable. You have to talk to those guys to understand. They're thinking so far ahead of everyone else that it's really hard to remember where the rest of the scientific community is."

"The only solution is for me to change my codes. But to what? I'm out here away from every resource."

The captain cleared her throat. "Except one, sir."

"Hmm?" He followed her look. "Oh. Him."

"Not him, sir. The *NightHawk* gestalt."

The ambassador shrugged irritably. "But what can they do? If they create a new code, nobody back home will be able to read it."

"If I might suggest, sir..."

"Well? Go ahead, lad, I'm open for any solution."

"The next level is the Dachau family."

"Dachau? The concentration camp?"

"They have strange humour, sir. But that's the next code coming down the pipes. Somebody back home will be able to read it, I'm sure. If they can't, I can insert a keyword that ships it straight to the Securi-Corps Code Lab."

"You can do that?"

"Yes, sir. That was one of the things I learned. They wanted me to contact them immediately if I found anything interesting."

"Prime. Can you give me a hardcopy version of that code? If I enter it into my stand-alone processor by hand, can I be sure my mail is secure?"

"Is it necessary to enter it by hand, sir? That requires quite a bit of programming skill."

Pretoro gave a grim smile. "I believe I am up to the task." He turned to Natalia. "I have been instructed in the strongest terms not to let my machine have any contact with the systems on this ship. I am to use my own augment in as limited a way as possible." He shot a disapproving frown at Andrew. "To do my best to keep from being contaminated by any outside influence."

The captain nodded. "I understand, sir. I must say, you have set yourself a difficult task. How can we help you?"

"I don't really know. My augment has been modified to accept two different feeds. One is a standard military version, similar to what your Commandos have. I will use that to communicate with the ship and with the rest of the crew in emergency situations. The other version is compartmentalized for my ambassadorial duties alone."

"That sounds workable."

Those pale blue eyes focused on Andrew, and his heart sank. "And if I might make a suggestion?"

"Of course, sir." The captain, too, was staring at him.

"My initial impression of this cadet is that he has incredible talent handicapped by a very undisciplined mind. It would be best for him, and for all of us, if his training proceeded apace."

"I can't help but agree, sir. The Cadet Corps has laid out a curriculum for him, and Lieutenant Jones is supervising. We will press on without delay."

Image: Cadet Collingwood up to his waist in sand, with more pouring in on every side.

Image: Captain O'Rourke hauling Collingwood out of sand by his ear. Don't be an idiot. Say something appropriate.

Andrew sighed, but kept it to himself. "Aye, sir. I'll do my best."

Pretoro sent the captain a wintry smile. "A teenager at his most enthusiastic. I don't envy you or Jones your task." He rose and moved to the door, where he turned.

"And I'd like that code soon, Cadet."

"On your desk in…nineteen minutes, sir."

"Make it fifteen, Cadet."

"Sir?"

"Yes?" A frown was beginning to form.

"My mother sometimes has difficulty separating the bratty fourteen-year-old from the experimental prodigy. I even do myself. I don't want to appear difficult, but when I indicate a time for a task, I do not pad my estimates with extras for the purpose of sparing myself work. If I move at a safe speed in the corridors and exhibit due diligence with this task, it will be on your desk in nineteen minutes. If you wish me to sacrifice accuracy, simplicity or ship's safety protocols, I can do it in eighteen. Except we have spent twenty-three seconds discussing it, which must be added to the total. May I have your leave to proceed, sir?"

Without waiting for a response, he saluted, spun, and marched out at his best pace. He well knew the conversation that was taking place in his absence.

Nineteen minutes later, he knocked on the ambassador's cabin door. When it opened, he presented a sheaf of paper. "If you are competent in this field, it will take you approximately three hours and twenty minutes to enter this material. You will average two errors per page, which will take you somewhere between two and five hours to find. If you wish, once you have entered it, I can skim it and find the errors, and you can fix them without me touching the machine."

He risked a smile. "I don't know if you've ever been on a voyage of this sort before, sir, but you may want to do it yourself. The boredom of program debugging is nothing compared to the boredom of...nothing."

The ambassador returned the smile with his own grim version. "I will do the work and call you if there is a problem...when there is a problem. Thank you."

"My pleasure, sir. And there is a poker game in the mess on Saturday nights at around twenty-one hundred. Two games, actually. One for money, one for fun. They won't let me play in the serious one, but I'm sure you'd be welcome in either." He waited for a response. "It's a long, long trip, sir."

"Thank you, cadet. I may take you up on that."

Andrew waited.

The ambassador looked at him. "Oh, don't play that gambit. I'm not going to dismiss you officially every time we finish a conversation. That's Jones's job. Away you go."

Andrew flashed a grin. "See you at the game, then." He spun and walked off.

Just before the door closed behind him, he heard the expected heartfelt sigh.

11. MARCHING

He was the one sighing the next day. Jones sat him down with the curriculum and they laid out a schedule. It was a long list:

Professionalism
Test taking
Space Arm chain of command
Watch standing
Customs and courtesies
Space Arm history from NASA and ESA forward
Rules of Armed Combat
Anti-terrorism/force-protection
Briefings on threat conditions
Protection from chemical, biological, radiation dangers
 - use of all available protective gear
Basic damage control and shipboard emergencies
Fitness and health awareness.

The Lieutenant registered Andrew's reaction. "I know it looks heavy, but after a few weeks, you'll get used to it. It fills the time, after all." He smiled, sort of. "In a normal training situation, you'd have several different instructors taking up your day. Chief Engineer Lundeen and I have the ship to run as well."

Andrew did his best to return the smile. "Please, indulge yourselves."

Jones stiffened. "Cadet, when we are in training, you will refer to me as 'sir.' Do you understand?"

"Yes, sir." *Should have known that was coming.*

"Oh, yes, and Chakka must not be present."

"Certainly, sir. But you realize I can access his augment from anywhere on the ship."

"Andrew, there is only so much I can do to make this a good learning experience for you. Cadets are renowned for their games to cut corners, slough off and get out of work. I know most of those tricks, and I will be watching for them."

Jones stared directly into Andrew's eyes. "However, because of the nature of your upbringing and abilities, I can see no way that I can control what you could do in that direction. I have to count on you to take this seriously enough not to take advantage of the situation. I need you to throw yourself wholeheartedly into these lessons, because you know that they will make you a better Spacer and a better officer."

Andrew relaxed his posture. "Yes, sir. I see what you mean. I am mostly capable of distinguishing my natural abilities from those of my augment. Do we need to make some sort of rule as to when I am allowed to use it and when I am not?"

Jones's smile became more honest. "We will have to play that as it happens. Mostly, you should try to work within the parameters of the usual Spacer's implant. Everyone has those."

"I'm not sure how to do that, sir." Andrew frowned. "I guess I'll have to study up on them."

"Good." The lieutenant sat back. "There's your first assignment. Analysis of the capabilities of a Standard Augment, level 7.5. For extra marks, speculation on places where your own talents do not exceed the norm."

"I'll get on it right away, sir."

"Let's say a printed version. 1500 words, give or take 50."

"Aye, sir."

"Dismissed, Cadet."

Andrew snapped his best salute, spun and headed for the door.

"Cadet, halt."

Andrew stopped.

"Cadet, about face."

Andrew was catching on. He executed a sharp 'about face'.

"Your salute is sharp, but it's not quite in the proper position. Perform a salute for me and stop halfway."

Andrew did his best.

"See? The regulations state that your fingertips must be five millimetres from your eyebrow. Yours are at least eight. Let's try it again." His voice rose in volume. "Cadet, salute."

Andrew stopped his fingers at the precise distance, then snapped his hand back to his side. The officer returned the salute. "Cadet, dismissed."

Another 'about face' and the cadet marched out of the chartroom, his steps a precise 70 centimetres long. When he turned to shut the door, he caught a look of satisfaction on the lieutenant's face.

Oh, well. I guess I'll be able to get through this.

He got no sympathy from the other crew. In fact, they seemed glad to join in for his drill practice. He asked Sergeant Jacobs about this as they were marching around the practice track.

"I don't mind marching at all. There's a certain freedom to it."

"Freedom. Isn't this the opposite? We're doing everything exactly like everyone else."

She nodded to the nearest viewscreen, where her augment brought up an image of a flock of birds in flight, swooping and diving in perfect sync. "Do you think they spend any time worrying about freedom?"

"Oh. I think I see."

"When you're marching, you just let everything go and let your body follow its instincts. It's very relaxing."

He grinned. "Like you find a ten-k run relaxing."

"Exactly. Don't worry. You'll get there." She slapped his shoulder hard enough to make him stumble. "Come on now, Cadet. Keep time."

Fiona came at it from another point of view. "Necessary evil, kid. If I wanted to be a regular engineer, I wouldn't have to go through this more than about once a year. But this is the Commandos, and it's altogether different."

"Why...? Sorry. I didn't say that. Teamwork, right?"

They marched around the track in silence. Finally, Toni called a halt, which they accomplished in perfect unison. "What do you say, Fiona. Is he ready for the test?"

The tiny engineer looked up at Andrew. "He looks pretty confident. Either he's ready, or he needs to be taken down a peg."

"Fair enough. Here's the way it goes, Cadet. It's a trick we stole from an acting teacher who was working on troop teamwork. We all just stand here, concentrating on how the group feels. When it feels right, we all start marching. No commands, no leaders. We just all start. When we feel like 'quick march,' we speed up. When we feel like 'company halt,' we all stop together."

"You're kidding. How does that work?"

"Nobody knows. Subliminal messages, I guess. I've seen a really together Commando troop keep it up for about thirty seconds before they started tripping over each other."

Andrew shrugged. "Anything's possible." Then he grinned. "And if this is one of those tricks the old hands play on the raw recruits, I can't see anything to be hurt besides my delicate ego, so let's go."

"That's the spirit, kid...oh. And no augments allowed."

"I never dreamed they would be."

The three stood in a line.

Nothing happened. Andrew waited, clearing his mind of all thought. Then he felt the urge to move. For no reason, he started marching, straight ahead, regular pace. In his peripheral vision, the two commandos matched him. They marched halfway around the habitat ring, getting settled into the rhythm.

A sudden jolt spurred him forward. Before he knew it he was quick-marching. Again, his companions kept perfect time.

Then they stopped. Straight out from a quick march they came to a "company halt" and stood there, breathing lightly. Then they were off again. "This is weird!"

The rest of the platoon stopped, and he stumbled on for a pace before complying.

"Okay, okay. I lost concentration. My fault." He stepped back into line. "Let's try again. That was prime."

Again they stood until they felt right and then started marching. He slipped into that half-aware sense of the group, and again they stopped, started and marched on again. Again they stopped.

They stood a moment, each deep in concentration. Then he felt a compulsion, and without even allowing the feeling to develop, he did an "about face" and began to march in the opposite direction.

His troop moved with him. Then they stopped, made a "left turn," took two steps forward, did another "about face," and...

"Company halt!"

They stood there a moment. Andrew came back to reality.

Which included a frowning Sergeant Jacobs. "You were using your augment!"

He realized she was talking to him. "No, I wasn't. I wasn't using anything. What's wrong?"

"Nothing's wrong. It was just too right. I've done this before. No group, no matter how well tuned, can march like that."

Andrew's thinking mind clicked on. "So, you've done that before, but this time it was different? Better?"

"Oh, yes. I've never felt that connected. Not before."

"Okay, let's look at this scientifically. What's different? Me."

"Exactly."

"All right. I'm out. Away you go."

Jacobs regarded him a moment, then nodded and snapped back into line with B'kosa.

It took even less time. Soon the two women were marching in perfect unison, stopping, starting, turning without effort.

Andrew felt a familiar presence beside him. He glanced up at Jackson. "Not bad, hey?"

"I've never seen anything like it. They must work together a lot. Special augment?"

"No augment at all."

As the women marched past, he raised a hand, and they stopped.

"Very nice, ladies. Now you want to try a real experiment?"

"Sure. This is weird."

"Jackson, out you go."

"Me? They don't even know me. I can march, but not at that standard."

"Maybe they know you better than you think. Stand between them if it makes you feel better. Don't think, don't use your augment. Just do what feels right when you get the urge."

The big guard shrugged and stepped between the two small women, who did an "extend" to make room.

Andrew smiled at his worried frown. "Relax. Nothing to hurt but your feelings."

Jackson snorted and took the same "stand easy" pose.

It took longer this time, but sure enough, away the trio went, changing tempo at a more moderate rate. They lasted a quarter way around the track, and then Jackson went left when the others went right, and only Toni's gymnastic sense of balance prevented a complete train wreck.

Raising his voice over their laughter, Andrew called them back. "The captain is going to want to talk to us."

As he finished speaking, Natalia exited the slideway from the bridge, not hurrying, but not wasting time. She surveyed the group, who resembled puppies caught in a torn nest of newspaper.

"I'm getting some very strange readings on the ship's augment. It can't be a manifestation of Othermania, because we haven't reached Light Transfer Velocity yet."

"Just an experiment, ma'am."

"One of yours, Cadet? That half explains it. Was the experiment successful?"

"More than our wildest dreams, ma'am. Want a demo?"

"If I dare."

By this time they had a full audience. Andrew regarded the faces. "Let's make this a real test. Lieutenant Jones, would you mind?"

The First Officer erased the frown that had started, squared his shoulders and stepped forward. "What do I do?"

"Join the formation, please, sir." He looked them over. "Rows of two, I think."

They complied, facing upspin around the track.

"This is that old acting class trick they use on final year cadets, sir. Don't think. Just act."

The Lieutenant's brow cleared. "Oh, yes. I remember." His stiff pose relaxed marginally.

Soon the little platoon was marching away. For some reason, they did not try anything difficult, just stopping, starting and changing tempo in increasingly short spurts. When they had transited the whole track, they came to a sharp halt in front of their commanding officer, saluted, and stood easy.

She returned the salute and stood silent for a moment. Then the whole group relaxed and fell out of formation at the same time.

Her head came up. "I didn't dismiss you."

Andrew grinned. "You didn't give any orders at all. There was no formation to dismiss. They knew the exercise was over."

"And this all goes to prove?"

"Look at the composition of the group. Active ops. Engineering. An officer who is used to commanding the formation. And an outsider who is very out of practice. What's the one element in common?"

"Since this is your experiment, I assume it's something to do with organic augments."

"A reasonable deduction, ma'am."

She raised her eyebrows at the ambassador, who stood nearby. "What do you think, sir?"

"If the experiment was done within the guidelines as stated, it's very impressive. Unfortunately, it supports my resolve to stay out of the augment of this ship."

Andrew nodded. "I have to agree, sir. I know it makes your task more difficult, but it also makes it more important. To my research as well."

Light dawned in Pretoro's eyes. "As a control subject."

"Exactly. And that extends far beyond research. We don't know where this situation is going to take us, and your alternate approach might become very important. Speaking from a strictly theoretical point of view, of course."

He caught the glance between the captain and the ambassador.

"Most definitely. I find myself drawn to take a more active interest in your research, Cadet. Please keep me informed."

"You could be invaluable in keeping my conclusions valid, sir. You're the best-trained social scientist onboard."

Pretoro's eyebrows flicked upward. "I am?"

"Aren't you?"

"We should discuss how you know that."

"Certainly, sir." He turned to the captain. "Demonstration is over, ma'am. Unless…"

"No, I've seen enough. We'll talk it over later. At the moment, you're blocking the way to the mess, it's lunch time and I think Jonny is starting to stew."

"Mother, now I'm sure Othermania is taking over early. Mutinies have occurred over puns that bad." He afforded her a sweeping bow. "Please lead the way, ma'am."

12. PERSONNEL PROBLEMS

As his training progressed, his skills increased and his muscles hardened, and he found himself seeking Sergeant Jacobs more and more often. He was just too small to get a realistic session with the men on the crew, and he admired her speed and skill.

And other things. While there wasn't an ounce of superfluous flesh on her body, it didn't stop her from being fully rounded. In places he often ended up touching in hand-to-hand combat practice.

When it reached the point that it was affecting his training, he went looking for help.

"Mum, I've got a problem."

Natalia looked up from the screen she was scanning. "Is it a 'Mum' problem?"

He grinned. "Nothing on this ship is really a Mum problem, but your personal and professional assistance would be appreciated. It's Toni."

"Toni? In what way?"

"In a hand-to-hand combat training sort of way. I find it difficult to work with her."

"But she's the closest to your size, and she's the best one to…oh. That kind of problem."

He rubbed his face with his hands. "Yeah, that kind of problem. It's just too…close, you know? Can you help me out?"

"Speaking as your captain, no. She's the best person for the job, and she'll continue to do it. However, as your mother, I can give you some advice…well, not advice, because I never was a teenage boy, and I have very little idea what it's like. You might want to talk to Charlie or Jackson about that.

"What I can give you is another point of view. You're a cadet. The Space Arm is full of young men and young women, thrown together in many situations over long periods of time. It is impossible to make regulations to cover every eventuality, so the Space Arm has decided to take a 'hands off' approach. And I don't mean that in the way you are thinking. There are no rules about relationships between crew members."

"Oh. Doesn't that lead to all sorts of…I dunno…"

"However, they do have some very strict rules about harassment and mutual respect."

"Well, of course. They hit us pretty hard about those in First Semester." He glanced at her. "You know they don't completely work."

"Yes, there's still a certain amount of bullying goes on. It's impossible to stop without destroying the drive that makes good soldiers. But anything of a sexual nature is different."

"They told us about that, too. You keep it in your pants, or you lose your pants. And the rest of the uniform."

"It sounds harsh, but it's the only way. The augments make it easier, because in case of a complaint, their records can be accessed. They make it easy another way, as well."

"Yeah. 'No' and *No* really means 'No!' doesn't it? Pretty hard to misunderstand."

"At one time they thought of planting a defensive trap in everyone's augments. Someone tries to rape you and you fry their circuits."

"Huh! As if that would work. What's to keep you from using it for something else?" He threw up his hands. "Okay, I know all this stuff, and you've now read me the riot act. I never had any intention of causing any trouble. That's the problem. I have far too much respect for her. Besides, she could break me in half in about three seconds."

"Right. And there's no advice anyone can give you except tell you that it's a learning process we all go through, and you have to live with it. You will, I know. You've got the right attitude."

She grinned. "And if she's really bothering you, there's only one person you need to talk to."

"What…? No! No, I couldn't…"

His mother shook her head. "If you had any other trouble training with her you would. If she was hitting too hard, if she was going too easy on you, whatever. You'd tell her right away, wouldn't you?"

"Yeah, but…"

"But this is no different. Talk to her."

"Aw, Mum…"

"No, this is not an 'Aw, Mum' moment. This is an 'Aye, Captain' situation. It's your problem, Cadet. You deal with it."

* * *

Three days later he got his chance. We were doing groundwork, and he was holding his own for a change. The newly acquired muscle and extra weight he had put on downplanet was standing him in good stead. Also, he was suspicious that she was taking it easy. So when the opportunity arose, he slipped in, caught her off guard and flipped her to the mat. She landed on her back, and without a thought he dropped on top of her, his chest across hers, and his arms around her body lengthwise in a standard judo pin.

And then he realized that his cheek was forced against her left breast, and his right bicep was crammed tight into her crotch.

With an exclamation he stumbled to his feet, backing away. He didn't know where to look. He didn't know what to do. "Toni…I…"

She too, scrambled up, her hands making a calming gesture. "It's okay, Andrew. It happens. Don't worry about it."

"But I…"

She shook her head and grinned. "It happens. More often than you'd think. I gotta say, I wasn't expecting it from you yet, but that's my mistake."

"You were…expecting it?"

She took him by the arm and led him to a bench, sat him down. "Andrew, you're a smart kid, right?"

He shrugged. "I'm supposed to be. Sometimes I'm not so sure."

"Right. So you know this is going to happen, right?"

"I guess. I just never thought about it."

Again she smiled. "Okay. So that's your lesson for today. If it makes you feel any better, you handled it right."

"I did?"

"Yeah. You quit at exactly the right time."

"Oh. I see."

She slapped his arm. "You're lucky it happened with an old lady like me. Next time it might be a pretty sixteen-year-old cadet. Now you'll be prepared."

"You're not an old lady!"

"Now, don't start with the flattery. I might start to get worried."

"Huh? Oh. Yeah. So we just keep practising like normal?"

"Of course." She sat beside him. "Look, Andrew, in every fight there are some restrictions. It all depends who you're fighting and what outcome you want."

"Outcome?"

"Sure. You don't think every fight out there in the real world is just to win, like a tournament, do you? Sometimes you fight to smash the enemy completely, destroy his ego. Another time you might want to let him down easy: establish dominance without destroying his status with his mates. It all depends. When a guy is fighting a woman, he has to take that into account as well."

"Especially in training, as I just discovered."

"Right. So, training as usual, but not quite."

"You've got it, kid." She grinned. "But you touch my breast, and I'll blacken your eye."

"Pardon?"

"You heard me."

"You mean that?"

"You wanna try it?"

He couldn't help himself. He reached his left arm across and ran his palm over her left breast. As he already knew, it was resilient, with a small, firm nipple. He dropped his hand.

There was a brief, frozen, silence, then they both jumped to their feet. He stared down into her shocked eyes, wondering what, exactly, he had done.

Next thing he knew he was lying on the mat, stars in his head, and his left eye numb.

She stood over him, horror and anger warring on her face. "You little bastard. What the hell are you playing at!"

He lay there, regarding her. When he decided that she wasn't going to hit him again, he slowly got to his feet. "I thought we had a deal."

"A deal! A deal? I was joking!"

He shrugged. "I figured you were. But it wasn't a joke to me."

"Well, now it isn't a joke to me, either."

"Good. Then we have one thing straight."

She frowned. "What's going on here? Siddown, Cadet. You're not getting out of here until I know what just happened."

He sat, and she threw herself down beside him. After a moment she glanced at him. "All right. I should have realized. There's always something in that head of yours. What gives?"

He shrugged. "I dunno, Toni. I get tired of being treated like a kid."

"I got news for you, sonny…"

"Yeah, I know. I am a kid. But I'm also a member of this crew, and I don't want the position of mascot."

"Ah. And we've all been babying you along."

"Sometimes. Yeah, I need it, but it still bothers me." He turned to face her. "I'm sorry it was you that I took it out on. But you've been too easy on me in practice."

She frowned. "Do you think so?"

He nodded. "When was the last time I got hurt?"

"Got hurt? The object of practice is not to hurt people."

He grinned, "Remember that Western movie we saw a while ago? 'If ya don't fall off yer horse at least once a week, yer not learnin' nothin', son.'"

She nodded. "I suppose. I've been treating you like the captain's kid, haven't I?"

"That's right. And even if I am the captain's kid, and I play on it shamelessly, it still bothers me."

She frowned. "Well, you can be sure you won't be getting treated like the captain's kid in combat practice from now on."

He slapped her on the shoulder. "Good. That's exactly what I wanted."

She looked at him. "What're we going to tell the captain?"

"Oh, don't worry. I'll think of something. Probably the truth."

"Well, I gotta put it in the training log."

"Put it down as a demonstration of appropriate physical contact between opposite genders."

She shrugged. "Sounds innocuous enough to me. But the captain's not going to buy that."

"No, this is one time where I'll be glad to play the captain's kid role. Don't worry about it, Sergeant. I'll head up there right now."

She slapped his shoulder and pushed him towards the door. "I'd love to be outside listening, but then again, maybe I wouldn't. Don't screw this up."

His heart full of misgiving, he stuck his head into the chart room. "Well, Mum. I took your advice."

"I gather it didn't work. The emotional charge just about knocked me off my chair." She looked up. "My Lord! What happened to your eye?"

He shrugged. "Toni. It was part of straightening things out. I think we managed pretty well."

"It doesn't look like it. Am I going to get an explanation?"

"Sure." He perched on his stool. "For once I was giving her real trouble in the mat work. Which meant we were a bit…intimate. So I thought it was time. It was sort of an anticlimax, really. I told her about it, and she just shrugged and said, 'I know.'"

"When I thought about it, of course she knew. She trains with guys all the time. We had a talk about it, and that was about it. Then, at the end, she said, 'You touch my breast, and I'll blacken your eye.' So…"

"You didn't…"

"Sure. I touched her breast."

She half-rose, staring at him. "You what?"

"I touched her breast, and she blackened my eye. That was the deal."

"Well, you certainly deserve it. I ought to blacken the other one! Is she going to file a charge?"

"Of course not. She gave me permission."

"She what?"

"She was the one that made the deal. She told me the parameters and named the price. I decided the price was worth it. She has no complaint."

"Does she see it that way?"

"Oh, yes. And that was the point."

"What was the point?"

"She was being too nice to me. Treating me like the captain's kid. Now she knows. She doesn't play games with me, and I won't play games with her."

"You realize that she's going to be tearing you apart for a while."

"She was going too easy on me." He pointed to his eye. "Now she won't. But she's gotta be careful."

"Why is that? No, let me guess what's going on in your twisted little mind. You made a deal and you paid the full price. She can't ask for more, or she's broken her end of the deal. And..." She held up a finger to stop him."...she knows that at any time you could drop into full augment and take her apart if you wanted to."

"That's why I like you for a Mum. You understand."

It was Natalia's turn to cover her face with her hands. Then she straightened. "You don't mind if I talk to her about this?"

"Of course not. You're my Mum and her captain."

But that wasn't quite the end of it. When Andrew showed up in the mess for supper, the whole crew was curious about his eye. His attempt to shrug it off as a training accident fell flat when Toni walked in. She strolled behind him, then leaned down and gritted in his ear. "You haven't heard the last of this, kid."

"Oh, yes I have."

She gave him a stare, then shook her head and sat in the next seat.

Charlie frowned at her. "You can't leave it at that. What happened with you two?"

"We made a little deal." She nodded towards Andrew. "And he came out way ahead."

"He doesn't look like it."

"Take my word for it. Now I know why you lot won't play serious poker with him."

"We aren't stupid!"

"Yeah, well I was, all right?"

The big commando shrugged. "It's all right with me."

She shook her head. "It's all right with him," she stuck a thumb in Andrew's direction, "and it's all right with me. You don't come into it, Fraser." She jabbed an elbow in Andrew's ribs. "Right, Cadet?"

"Oh yes, Sergeant, ma'am. Definitely all right."

* * *

Two days later, Andrew got the idea that the captain wanted to talk to him. There was no specific message, but he wandered up to the chartroom anyway.

She looked up as he entered. "Oh. I was just thinking about you."

"I know. That's why I'm here. What's going on?"

She frowned. "Two things. First, what I wanted to talk to you about. Second, how did you know what I was thinking?"

He perched on his stool. "Which one do you want to hit first?"

"Let's lead up to the main event with scientific jargon. Do you think our augments are growing even closer together?"

"It would seem so. However, I didn't hear anything specific. Just the general feeling. Maybe you're learning to shield your conscious thoughts."

"That would be a positive step."

"How can we test it?"

"No idea."

"Neither do I." He shrugged. "We exhausted that topic pretty quick. What were you working up to?"

"You don't know?"

"Haven't the foggiest."

"That's progress. I want to talk about the incident with you and Toni."

"I thought we'd settled that."

"On an official basis, we did. I talked to her, and her story is amazingly close to yours."

"Does that mean we collaborated?"

She held out a hand, wavered it from side to side. "Either before or after."

"I'd prefer to think before. That means I called the situation correctly."

She nodded. "I am of that opinion as well, but that doesn't mean you acted correctly."

"Why not?"

"Because you took a risk."

"What, that she would blacken both eyes?" He grinned. "I thought of that, too."

"Not to you. A risk to her. The fact that you were right doesn't enter into it. What if you were wrong?"

"You mean, if I upset her somehow? I can't see that happening. She's as tough as nails, and she was completely in control of the situation."

"You don't know her well enough to make that decision. And remember, she was dealing with an important Space Arm asset and the captain's son. There were all sorts of ways she wasn't in control."

"I didn't think of that."

"No, you didn't. And what does that mean?"

He screwed up his face in thought. "I risked hurting her emotionally even if I didn't mean to." He held up a hand. "And I've been hanging around you Commandos long enough to know the ethos. Besides hurting an innocent person, I might have harmed a relationship in a tight-knit community where trust is our greatest strength."

She regarded him, her head to one side. "You believe all that?"

"Not sure. I just thought of it."

"And when you've done some more thinking, what are you going to do about it?"

"I guess I'll figure that out, too."

"Prime. You do that. Dismissed."

He flipped her his best salute and marched over to the armoury, where he knew, without conscious thought, that the sergeant was working.

"Toni?"

She looked up from the gun lying on the table. It was a lightweight multi-calibre machine gun meant to be fired from the hip. Andrew had tried one in .50 calibre anti-personnel mode, and it almost tore his trigger finger off. He glanced at the commando's arms, slim but muscular.

"What's up, kid?" She was looking at him, but her hands were moving on their own, disassembling the gun with rapid precision.

"Gotta talk to you."

She grinned. "Back still sore?"

He rolled his shoulders. "A bit. No problem, though. It was a clean throw, and I should have been ready for it."

"If you'd been a two-year ensign, you would have been. I never tried it on a cadet before."

"I'll take that as a compliment."

"Then it's about something else."

"Yeah. I gotta apologize."

"For what?"

"For…" he poked out a finger, pulled it back. "You know."

"I thought we settled that." She began to reassemble the gun.

"We did, but I've been thinking."

She nodded. "Captain been at you?"

"I got a nudge."

"She talked to me. Didn't sound completely satisfied. I guess I'm about to find out why." Toni snapped the front handgrip back on the rifle, lifted it to her shoulder and aimed. Then she laid it on the table and sat on the bench. "So, what new ideas do you have? I'm not making any more deals."

"It doesn't have that much to do with you."

"Oh. Should my feelings be hurt?"

"No, it's a matter for me in the future. I have to remember that everybody has vulnerabilities, and we never know what they are. I can't go around pulling stunts like that because if someone has a soft spot and I happen to prod it, I could do damage. Yes, even to you."

"That's a good thought." She flipped the rifle to her shoulder and dry-fired it, three quick trigger pulls, then put it down. "Okay, kid. My turn to take the risk. You were wrong. I do have a soft spot."

"You do."

"That's right. Everyone has buttons that can be pushed, and I have one at least."

"You're not going to tell me!"

"Yes, I am. It's a test. I'm going to give you something and see how you handle it. If it works, it will heal the bond between us. If it doesn't, then I made a mistake. And I don't think I'm making a mistake."

He sighed. "Okay, I'll bite. I owe you that. What is it?"

She glanced around, then leaned closer like an actor in a holodrama. "Kittens."

As he opened his mouth, she raised her hand to stop him. "That's right. I like kittens, especially black ones. If I was walking down a street and I saw a man kill a black kitten, I'd like as not go over and pull his arm off and stand and watch him bleed to death."

"Oh." He gave that the thought it deserved. "But nobody else on board knows."

"The captain reads our psych reports. Jones might have. No one else."

Andrew frowned. "But surely that's not something to bother anyone who knew you. I think it's good. It makes you different from what I thought. Not much, but an important bit."

"It wouldn't bother anyone on the ship to know. It would bother me to think that they knew. Such is the nature of soft spots, especially for people who need a tough reputation."

He shrugged. "Okay. I'll keep it to myself. It explains one fact, though."

"How I get along with Chakka? I thought you'd notice. I'll tell you another item that isn't quite a secret. The captain has suggested I volunteer for Cat Patrol."

"Good choice. At your age, you don't have that much time left in the field, and unless you move up into a commission, you have to find a way to move sideways. Unless, of course, you decide not to re-up next February, and accept Freighty's offer." He pointed at her. "But maybe you shouldn't. Freighty's going to be really interested at what's happening with our natural augments. If you spend a few years in the Feline Augment section, you'd be even more use to him. Unless…"

She held up both hands, laughing. "Whoa, there, kid. Where did all that come from?"

"Huh? I dunno. Just thinking out loud. Sorry. I guess that was personal."

"No, no, it's just that I've been thinking all those things for the past few weeks. It really feels strange to hear them from somebody else, out of nowhere."

Andrew's head came up. "Wait a minute. Maybe it wasn't out of nowhere." He sat on the bench opposite and stared at her. "Have you been having those thoughts around Chakka? Spending any time in the same room? Maybe in physical contact?"

"Um…yeah, probably more than usual."

"Great." He jumped up. "You finished playing with your favourite toy?"

"Sure." She patted the weapon. "It's ready to go, like always."

"Right. Down to the med bay. It's scan time for you."

"But I just had one last week. And the week before."

"Perfect. Let's go."

Chakka, med bay.

Emotion: agreement.

See you there.

Once the commando was in the chair, he pulled the cranial scan hood down. "*NightHawk*, I want identical scans to the ones last week. Transverse and frontal on the augments."

Aye, Cadet. That will take one point three minutes.

"We're not going anywhere."

At a speed of oh point one nine six LS. Otherwhere Transfer in 47 hours.

"And then I want EEG readings while we're in full augment with Chakka."

In a moment…all right. Here are the results.

"Put up the best evidence of any anomalies."

A scan of Toni's brain came up on the viewscreen and in their augments. Three areas were shaded in pink and numbered.

One percent growth in areas one and two. Two point five percent in area three.

"And area three deals with…?

Concept communication.

He raised his eyebrows at Toni. "See what I mean? Okay, file those. Now a re-ti EEG. Chakka?"

Image: Cat with head on commando's knee.

"Sure, go ahead." He met Toni's eyes as he removed the scanner hood. "Physical contact helps him. Plus he just likes it."

She laid a hand on the huge head and wiggled her fingers behind the ears. His eyes closed, and a purr rumbled through his chest.

"We're trying to concentrate. Do you have to make that racket?"

Emotion: affirmation. Aural/visual image: sound swelling and encompassing human head.

"Oh. Go ahead, then."

The auguar's purr grew until it permeated the room. They watched, entranced as the waves of the brain scan fluttered, then settled into new patterns.

Toni, think of a kitten. A sleek black kitten in your hands.

"Aww…" The commando leaned forward until her cheek rested on Chakka's head, her hands moving gently through his fur.

The EEG spiked several times.

After a minute or more, the rumble subsided. The graphs settled to more normal parameters. Toni opened her eyes slowly as if coming back from deep sleep and straightened.

As Andrew lifted the scanner away, she shook her head. "What was that?"

He grinned. "No idea yet, but my guess is you just went off your own empathic scale. Sorry, lady, your tough-girl act is blown, and I have scientific evidence to prove it."

He raised a calming hand to still the frown that was forming. "Protected scientific data. No access to anyone on the ship. Freighty will want to know at some time, but his encryption is unbreakable."

"But do I trust him with it?"

"Welcome to the club. So far, he has played nice with me, his friends on this ship and the human race. Take a look at your contract with him if it will make you feel better. Some day you're going to get very rich with all this, and perhaps famous. There's always a price to pay."

13.   TROUBLE IN THE OUTBACK

On Day 42 of their journey they reached Light Transfer Speed. The crew now considered themselves old hands at this and made the transition a routine operation. The captain was concerned about Pretoro, though, and gave him what advice she could. Once they were accelerating again in Otherwhere, she knocked on his door. Andrew stayed in gestalt with her in case he was needed. He wasn't sure for what, but his mother wanted to be sure there were no problems.

"Come in."

She gently pushed the door open and stood on the sill. "How are you feeling, sir?"

Pretoro was sitting on his bunk, a twisted frown on his face. "I'm not sure. I was all right during the transfer, but now I'm worried."

"You have to get used to that."

"You mean all the time we're in Otherwhere, I'm going to feel like this?"

She wavered a hand, side to side. "It's like a small, nagging headache you never quite get rid of. You'll go for hours without noticing it, but it's always there."

"It must make it difficult for the crew to get along with each other. I've read the reports, but it's a whole different situation when you're actually feeling it."

He wasn't the only one. Because of the constant strain, Natalia had warned everyone to report anything out of the ordinary. It didn't take long.

Two days into Otherwhere, they were sitting there after supper with nobody saying much when Fiona B'Kosa shook her head. Then she shook it again as if dislodging a cobweb. "Is it just me, or is it worse this time?"

She sat, staring around the table. "Well? If it was just me, somebody would have said something."

Lieutenant Jones nodded. "I'm feeling the same way. The tension seems to be stronger."

There were several nods from the others.

The captain frowned. "But no one has reported any crew friction. Are you holding out on me?"

Glances round the group, but shaking heads. Toni grinned. "Fiona hasn't stolen my hairbrush for a week. No, actually she did, once, but she cleaned it before she gave it back."

"Pardon my asking, but what do you need a hairbrush for?"

The Commando Sergeant brushed a hand over her bristly scalp. "To give Fiona something to bug me about, I guess."

Natalia was shaking her head. "You almost came to blows about it on the way out last time. Now it's a joke?"

Nelson Lundeen shrugged. "I guess we're a tighter crew than we were then."

"Well, I can't complain, but we're supposed to log anything different, and this is different. I wish we could explain it."

Andrew cleared his throat.

All eyes turned to him. "Organic implants. I would guess that we're setting up a feedback loop that increases each other's anxiety. However, because of our general, low-level gestalt, we don't conflict with each other.

"You mean it's going to get better?"

"Or worse." He grinned. "That's why it's called an experiment."

Sergeant Fraser raised a large fist. "And you hope we don't decide it's your fault."

"I do, Charlie. I surely do."

* * *

They were sitting in the mess about a week later when Freighty's avatar popped up on the viewscreen. "Anybody home?"

The captain pushed her plate away. "Just finishing lunch, Freighty. What's up?"

"Could you meet with me in private, please? Ambassador Pretoro is welcome, as are members of the gestalt."

"Sounds serious." She glanced around the table. "We'll be in the chart room in a moment."

They filed in. Andrew brought a chair from the mess and placed it for the captain. The ambassador took the main chair, Andrew the stool. Chakka headed for his box under the desk, frowning up at the ambassador whose legs were in his way. Pretoro made space for him.

"So, Freighty, what's happening?"

The mouse paced, his hands behind his back. "I've been monitoring communications from Barnard's System, and I'm beginning to piece things together." He sat facing them at his cartoon desk, his fingers intertwined beneath his chin. "Two interplanetaries, probably Develocon and SolarCorp, have established themselves in the system. They were working mostly in the Outer Asteroid Belt."

"At what?" Natalia glanced at Andrew, who nodded.

NightHawk

Yes, Cadet Collingwood?

Start looking into these areas. He slipped her a file.

The avatar ticked items off. "Mining exploration, fortifications, fabrication shops, hydroponics fields, meat protein factories…all the backup industry required for independent life. They have a central market, refueling and repair depot set up on one of the larger planetoids out there."

Pretoro steepled his fingers. "And do you have any indication of their intent?"

"Nothing more than the obvious. To establish an economic presence here."

"What about the planets?" Natalia called up a chart of the system on the next viewscreen.

"The gravity well defeats them. At least, it did."

"That sounds ominous."

"Except for the late and unlamented *Clyde*, they have been forced to transport only the lightest of equipment out here. With those capabilities they could find little downplanet worth hoisting that far against that much gravity. These are spacers, you must remember. They don't like gravity or open air. There's plenty of ice in the Belts, and plenty of sunlight to refine oxygen."

Natalia banged her forehead with her palm. "But now they have the survey data for the Second Planet. Damn! And I thought I was so smart."

Andrew glanced at the ambassador. His lack of reaction showed that he already knew about the deal she had made with the captain of the *Clyde*.

"And what did they find in the data I gave them?"

"Nothing important for a commercial operation. But everything they have is light. Their ships are small, their industry lightweight. They only need miniscule amounts of many metals. And then you upset the applecart."

"By destroying the *Clyde*."

"Exactly. The battleship was the only real power out here, and it was under the command of the interplanetaries. They used it to keep everyone in line."

"And we took it out of the equation."

"We'll never know what strings the Collingwood family pulled to get Captain James to make that attack. Appealed to his greed, most likely. In any case, the *Clyde* was suddenly gone, the interplanetaries had no time to send a similar force and suddenly there was a power vacuum."

Pretoro nodded. "And what filled that gap?"

"I have no idea, but it's easy to guess."

"Every small argument became a battle. Every power bloc wangled for more power."

"Exactly." The mouse grinned. "I'm beginning to believe you've been well trained for your post, Mr. Ambassador."

"Thank you, I'm sure."

"I have noticed an upsurge of weapons use and a greater volume of radio traffic, much of it uncomplimentary. Last week there was a battle...no, call it a series of running skirmishes, in the Outer Belt. A great deal of noise on all frequencies, and then a greater deal of silence. I suspect the power gap has been filled, and we have no idea by whom. In any case, it won't be good for the Planetary Community, and the El Dorado 12 mine will be at risk."

"Did El Dorado Corporation send them any backup?"

"Oh, yes. They now have two remote-controlled gun platforms orbiting the mine and a squad of ten Space Marines, but not enough to stand off any real attack."

"What do you suggest?"

"I suggest nothing. I am accelerating away from the region at 0.8 Gs, and my ability to take any action there is receding in proportion."

"While ours is not."

"The fact had not escaped my notice."

"So you're dumping it in our laps."

"Only an information dump. That is one area where I can be of use."

Natalia's glance turned the response over to Pretoro, who nodded. "I gather you will need to report to your base, the real Factory 4-80. You may tell it that we will discuss the matter over the next ten days. By then you may have more information for us."

Andrew cleared his throat. "Ma'am, there's a time pressure."

The captain glanced at him. "Our decel schedule."

"Yes, ma'am, *NightHawk* reminds us that in just over ten days we will be transiting the point where we start decelerating to meet with Factory 4-80."

"Ten days is our info turnaround time at this distance." Micha doffed his sailor's cap. "Adieu until that time."

The screen blanked, and the three humans looked at each other.

"Captain, what do you suggest?"

"I'd like some data before we make a move. If we ask permission from Space Arm to change our objective, I want to know how they'll react. Andrew?"

"One moment, ma'am."

NightHawk, what do you have for me?

Downloading, Cadet Collingwood.

Thank you.

Andrew scanned the information at a rapid pace, then turned to the captain. "Develocon and SolarCorp for sure. No surprise. They're the ones that play fast and loose with the rules most often. Certain large purchases and stock trades pretty well confirm it.

Ambassador, sir, if you'll look at this..." He offered a file on the viewscreen."...You'll see what I mean."

The ambassador scrolled down the screen. "Yes, I can see what's going on, now that we have this information. How long does it take to get a message to Space Arm?"

"We're already three-tenths of a light-year out, sir. If we send an Otherwhere message, it will take two weeks to get there. Another three weeks to respond and send it back, but in five weeks of Otherwhere we'll be two light years away, so it will take five weeks to catch us. By which time we're scheduled to have exited Otherwhere, stopped and to be two weeks into our acceleration back along Freighty's route to match velocities, so it will be less than that, roughly speaking. *NightHawk* could be more specific if you wish, sir."

"No, thank you, Cadet. We'll send a message, but I can't see that whatever comes through will reach us in time. We may be on our own on this one."

Natalia sighed. "As usual."

"You're used to this, Captain."

"Oh, yes. And so is Space Arm. They have no choice. They send out the team they think can do the job and accept what happens, which is never what they expect."

Pretoro smiled. "Because the job changes, and perhaps it becomes the wrong team."

"Always a possibility."

"Then you spend a lot of your time going over your orders, looking for what they really mean."

"More carefully than a PhD student on his thesis. And every time the situation changes, you read them again to find out if Space Arm predicted this, and what to do about it if they didn't."

"But one thing is certain. I was sent to be ambassador to Factory 4-80. Not the Barnard's system."

"Is that certain, sir?"

Pretoro's eyes turned to Andrew. "What do you mean by that, Cadet?"

"When the *Clyde* turned up and started causing trouble, the captain re-read her orders and found that our secondary function — to give the mine any aid necessary — was more important than our primary mission to contact the radio source. Space Arm is aware of the situation in Barnard's System. We certainly gave them enough data to suspect it. And why does Charlie's arsenal now include Space-to-Space and Space-to-Planet ordnance, with a rapid-fire delivery system and no less than twenty-five missiles, all Asimoved and ArIn controlled, stored with great difficulty in our small armoury?"

After a long stare at Andrew, the ambassador turned to Captain O'Rourke. "And why does a mere Cadet have access to all this classified information?"

The captain had her own stare. "Ambassador, you need to focus. Go back over your preparation for this position. Did it ever occur to you, for example, that you were getting a lot of briefings on…I don't know…perhaps the history of interplanetary commercial cooperation, with emphasis on certain interplanetaries? On Barnard's System itself? On…I don't know what, because I don't have the computing power to run the simulations Space Arm considered."

"You didn't answer my question."

"Because you already have all the data you need to answer it yourself. Nothing I say will persuade you: only your own logic."

Pretoro stared at the captain, then at Andrew. He even glanced down at the slitted eyes glowing at him from under the desk. "Something has changed, here. What's going on?"

Natalia regarded him. "This moment has come rather earlier in the trip than I would prefer, but here it is, and we have to deal with it."

"What moment is that?"

"The moment where all your training, all your status, all your security clearances do not take precedence over the knowledge of those of us who have the experience out here where the ordnance is live. Where all your knowledge and experience are trumped by an untrained fourteen-year-old kid whose mental capacity is

115

unfathomed, and when connected to the gestalt of this ship, is almost unbeatable. The chain of command in the Space Arm gives you the right to order us into oblivion to protect the factory, and if you do that, we will comply. However, if you decide to stay with us and continue to the Barnard System..."

"Why would I do that? I have my orders."

"Another reason to check them over. What if Freighty tells you that it is more important to Factory 4-80's safety for *NightHawk* to continue at all speed on our other mission?"

"Then I would have to comply, of course."

"And that's where we run into a problem. If you order us to do something in the Barnard System that we consider unproductive for the Space Arm, the Planetary Community or the human race in general – and believe me, that is a possible scenario – then we will have a problem, won't we?"

"Are you telling me that under certain circumstances you will refuse to obey my orders?"

"There's nothing new about that, sir. A soldier's duty to make his own decision about the moral correctness of his orders is written into the Space Arm Code of Conduct and the Rules of War."

"Yes, yes of course. I'm well aware of that." He placed his elbows on the desk and stared at her over his fists. "We seem to be at loggerheads."

"No, we aren't. I have merely suggested that you take another look at your assignment in the light of the change in situation, to see whether something you previously overlooked or misinterpreted now makes more sense."

"That's it?"

She raised her hands, palms up. "That's it. This is all theoretical. This is to prepare you for the moment, two weeks from now, when Freighty contacts us and says, 'There's general rebellion in the Barnard's System, and the El Dorado mine is being pressured to take sides. I have a contract with El Dorado, and Space Arm is my General Contractor. I need you to go and use every resource you have to fulfill your part of the contract.'" She levelled a stare at him. "What are you, as our ambassador to this entity, going to do?"

"I have to say, that's a highly theoretical proposition."

"Eighty-four percent, sir."

"Pardon me?"

Andrew kept his voice calm. "While you and the captain have been jockeying for the alpha position, our gestalt has been working on the real problem. The captain didn't just invent that scenario. It's the most likely one, with an eighty-four percent chance of occurring."

Natalia raised her hand to interrupt the tirade that was about to spill. "Please, ambassador. Surely you realize you aren't talking to Cadet Collingwood right now. You're dealing with the *NightHawk* gestalt, an entity of itself with a vaster knowledge and power than any human. What you just heard came mostly from Chakka. He is rather frank in his analysis of human power structure."

Pretoro's mouth closed.

"You are the human race's ambassador to the Factory. If your client were to join his immeasurable intellect with our gestalt and the information we possess, we could take control of the human race with a snap of our fingers. That's where the Space Arm has placed you.

"Now, I suggest you read your assignment one more time and reassess your approach to the task you have been given."

She rose. "But before we leave you with that task, remember. Chakka and I are loyal Space Arm members. While Andrew is only a cadet and has not officially taken a position in Space Arm, he has chosen to be my son. We all consider ourselves business associates and close friends of Freighty, your client. There is every opportunity for you to fit your considerable talents into this situation and help create a positive outcome for the human race. We don't ask you to accept everything at face value. In many respects we are inexperienced and lack training in essential areas. If Space Arm has done their homework, you are the missing piece of the puzzle. Find out how you can fit in, or how we can reform the puzzle and make it function with you."

She and Andrew both came to attention and gave Ambassador Pretoro a perfect salute. Then they did an 'about face' in unison and marched out the door of the chart room.

Chakka slid from beneath the desk and stared up at the ambassador with deep, soulful eyes.

Andrew connected to the ship's gestalt.

Image: Captain O'Rourke standing with one foot on Sol, the other on Barnard's Star, her background the massive universe.

Then the auguar's tongue reached out to rasp the man's wrist, and the big cat slid out the door.

The ambassador sat with his hands covering his face. Then he dropped them and, staring straight ahead, began to access the augment *NightHawk* was not allowed to pry into.

Andrew gave him the privacy he needed.

14. PLANS

The ambassador remained in his cabin that evening, having Juanita bring him a tray for supper. They did not monitor his communications, but he was very busy.

The next morning Pretoro appeared for breakfast looking sharp and well groomed, but no gestalt was needed to see the darkness under his eyes. He took his usual chair and looked at the captain. "I can only find one problem with your plan."

"What is that, sir?"

"My strict orders not to involve myself in your gestalt."

She considered. "I'm going to let Andrew answer that one."

The ambassador's eyes turned to the cadet.

"That could be an advantage, sir. When I'm on patrol with the Commandos and we get into trouble, my job is to maintain the gestalt. However, I also have another function. The soldiers deal with the present problem. I'm expected to have my eyes up and out, looking for the unexpected, the attack from another angle. Whenever we all get involved in the gestalt to solve a problem, we may have a wide approach to that problem, but we don't have a touchstone, and we can be sidetracked. If you maintain your independence, you can bring us back to reality if we start wandering." He grinned. "Thinking outside the box is great, but eventually you have to come back inside to apply the solution."

"You accept that I may disagree with whatever solution you propose."

"You are the ambassador, sir."

"Hmm. Yes, I must remind myself of that often."

"It helps."

"I don't expect you have those problems, lad."

"Naw, I'm only fourteen. I don't worry about stuff like that."

Natalia laughed. "When he starts the 'shucks, I'm just a kid' gambit, check your wallet and watch. That's when he's most dangerous."

"Thanks. I'll remember that."

"But I do have a suggestion, sir."

Pretoro glanced at Natalia. "Am I dealing with the cadet, now?"

She pressed her lips together and shrugged.

"What is your suggestion, Cadet?"

"Well, I'm taking my Cadet training on-ship, and I only have the crew as resources. Will you tutor me in history and diplomacy?"

"You're serious?"

"Sure. I have every historical fact ever recorded at my fingertips. I have every recorded analysis of each fact available as well. It's just too much. I need to talk to someone who can explain it in simple terms. You've been a teacher. You'd be a great resource."

"Who says I've been a teacher?"

Andrew levelled him a stare. "I have all your history at my fingertips as well, Doctor Pretoro."

"All of it?"

"I never pry, sir, especially with my friends."

"Consider me an ally. I don't think we're at the friendship stage, yet."

"You'll do it?"

The ambassador smiled. "A long and boring trip, right? Give me a chance to do some good in the universe. Putting all that knowledge into the proper perspective might be very useful."

"Proper perspective. You wouldn't indoctrinate me, would you, sir?"

"It's almost inevitable."

"Just remember that I have access to all the counter-arguments."

"There you are. Lessons start tomorrow. Report to me on the methods and dangers of scholastic indoctrination. I'll fit in with your schedule."

"Homework already?" Andrew stared around the table and got exactly the amount of support he expected.

15.   REBELLION

Three days later Andrew and Jones were going through the Space Etiquette manual for the ninth time when Freighty's avatar imposed himself onto their viewscreen.

"News, and it's not good."

The captain's augment zoned in. *Diplomatic team to the chart room, if you please. Lieutenant Jones, you have the bridge.*

"First Officer has the con."

When they were gathered in their usual positions, the mouse faced them from his viewscreen. "The situation is becoming critical, ma'am."

"I gather there are developments. More action or less?"

"Less."

"Is that good or bad?"

"Our guess is bad. The radio traffic of what used to be the Develocon faction has increased and spread out. Others have waned or disappeared."

"Someone has gained the upper hand."

"It would seem so."

"Any word from the El Dorado mine?"

"Nothing yet."

The captain glanced around the room. "I think we should contact them directly."

Pretoro nodded. "What would we tell them?"

"We don't have much to tell. According to my orders, they are still under Space Arm protection, so we consider them allies. Do your instructions affect that?"

He shook his head. "With no official change occurring, I see no reason why you wouldn't continue to act exactly as you did on your last visit. Space Arm has approved that approach."

"Good. Nighthawk, prepare an Otherwhere message for El Dorado 12, attention Manager Ludge. 'Enroute to Barnard's. ETA uncertain: weeks or months. Any concerns about political developments?' End transmission."

She glanced at Pretoro, who nodded.

"Tell him Andrew is still working on the Tesla puzzle."

"Addendum to message: 'Andrew says he is still working on the Tesla puzzle.' End transmission."

The captain looked around again. "Anything else?"

Image: talon-studded auguar paw shredding spaceships and tossing them out of star system.

"Include that image. End of transmission. Send in your own time."

Sending, ma'am. ETA two days, 13 hours 45 minutes.

Both adults regarded Andrew. "The Tesla puzzle?"

He grinned. "Somethin' Nicholas and I was workin' on, ma'am. Old 21st century technology. Involves the diminishing returns related to velocity choice of a battery-powered automobile as charge approaches zero and vehicle approaches destination."

"That sounds fairly simple."

"Not allowed to use calculus, ma'am. More complex than it looks."

"And the significance to Ludge in this context?"

"We usedta joke it was a lot like politics. Diminishing returns related to survival of the human species as number of politicians involved in a decision approaches infinity and time to Armageddon approaches zero."

"Which he will interpret as...?"

"We're trying to get there, but tangled in bureaucracy, and only a bomb going off will budge us."

"I find that a rather frank assessment, especially in a message to an agent of an interplanetary."

"Perhaps, sir. But that was the decoy. It wasn't the real message."

The ambassador frowned. "Then what was the real message?"

"That I'm on board *NightHawk*."

"Is that so very important?"

"Oh yes, sir. You see, Manager Ludge was on the periphery when all the decisions were made before we came home from the last trip, so he knows what we talked about. At that time, there were many uncertainties as to how our plans would work out. If Captain O'Rourke and I are on the same ship, returning to the same theatre of operations, he will conclude that most everything worked out to our advantage. Which will be to his advantage. He will be very happy to hear that message, sir, and it will strengthen his hand in any negotiations with the new powers out there."

Pretoro laid his hands on the desk. "May I interpret this situation as the manager of a trillion-planetoid operation owned by a major interplanetary corporation will now approach a dangerous situation with the understanding that he has the full support of the Space Arm, all based on a coded message from a cadet? And an auguar."

Andrew made a helpless, empty-handed gesture. "The captain could hardly say it out loud, could she?"

"I see."

"And this affects your assignment, too, Ambassador."

"It does?" Pretoro sent a wondering glance at Natalia. "In what way?"

"I don't quite know how to put this, sir, but the same message assured El Dorado 12 the full support of Factory 4-80."

"How can you assume that?"

Andrew mimed taking off a hat and putting on another one. "You are now talking to Factory 4-80's primary living contact with the human race. Much of his analysis of the species comes from me and my Mum. The original one, not the captain. He knows he is not infallible, and he listens very carefully to my advice. Also to Captain O'Rourke and somewhat to the crew of this ship."

The politician's eyes darted to one, then the other. "Doesn't that involve a conflict of interest at several levels?"

"Let me ask you, Ambassador. You are under contract to Space Arm. Do you still have other income? Investments, stocks, bonds or even companies under your command?"

"Of course."

"Right. The same goes for many members of Space Arm. My investment is in an interstellar fabrication shop. As it happens, I am the sole member of the Board of Directors. Until I achieve my majority, that means that my mother, Captain O'Roarke, votes my shares for me."

Silence descended on the chart room. The whirring of cooling fans was the only sound above the rapid breathing of the ambassador.

123

"You're telling me that I am hedged in on both sides. You won't accept my orders in anything outside the purvey of the factory, and within the scope of my assignment, you control the opinions of my client." He laid his hands, palms up, on the desk. "Why am I even here?"

Andrew shook his head. "Because we really, really, really need you."

"For what? I obviously have no real authority."

"Pardon my simplistic view, sir, but diplomats never have any authority, do they? I mean, they receive their orders, do all the talking, and then pass the results back to their masters for verification. Only the Planetary Community, Freighty and whoever won the battle for supremacy out in the asteroids this week have any real clout."

"He's right, Alfino. When we go out into Barnard's System to confront that revolutionary or whoever he is, we'll be going as agents of Space Arm, doing our best with the resources that we have. As I have repeated several times, whether you're with us or on Freighty, you are one of our best resources, bringing a level of experience, maturity and knowledge we sadly lack."

The captain leaned towards the diplomat. "The one thing we know for sure is that no good will be served by anyone assuming any primary authority and telling all the rest of us what to do. I know that sounds strange coming from a ship's captain, but you're wasting your crew if you don't listen to them."

The ambassador regarded each one of them. He even glanced under the desk at Chakka. Then he nodded. "Well, it's a rather egalitarian attitude for a military expedition." Then he shrugged. "But with the right people involved, it might work."

16.   HISTORY LESSON

"...and that's why the French Revolution went off the rails." Andrew closed down his augment and regarded Alfino Pretoro, who sat in the captain's chair, his fingertips steepled in front of him.

"And so the real cause of the bloodshed was the refusal of the nobles to give the peasants their freedom."

"Right. *Libertée, egalitée, fraternitée.*"

"That's true, as far as it goes."

Andrew frowned. "What do you mean?"

"Look at the power structure."

Andrew could rattle this off without his augment. "Three Estates, but only the nobility and the church had any power."

"Ah, but that was only at the beginning. Once the revolution succeeded, that was when the trouble began. It wasn't a struggle between the Estates anymore. It was a power struggle between different factions of the revolution."

"Like in the Barnard System right now."

"In general, yes. It's a common theme."

"I never did figure out where the Girondines fitted in."

"That's because they were the losers. They were the moderates who were trying to keep the revolution on target. *Libertée, egalitée, fraternitée.*"

Andrew checked *NightHawk*'s database again. "But Robespierre and the *Incorruptibles* destroyed them. I'm not sure how he managed that."

"It was very simple. His key move was to persuade everyone that the survival of the Revolution — note the capital 'R'; it became a living entity — was more important than the rights of any one person."

"Aha! But by that time, 'The Revolution' meant him and his party."

"And..."

"That meant any argument against his party was a challenge to the Revolution!"

"That's right. And such was his drive for power that he would kill to get it. He was supported by the Paris Mob…"

"…who were so poor and afraid they would support anyone who told them he was on their side. Which he wasn't."

"Of course not. His sole objective was his own power."

"Wait a minute, wait a minute. Let me chase something down." It only took a few seconds of communing with the database.

"Got it. The Trumpian Revolt, early twenty-first century."

"Tell me about it."

"The old United States of America was divided between a ruling elite and an impoverished lower-middle class. As the rich got richer and the poor got worse off, the poor became more and more frightened. They were totally exposed to the smallest downturn in the economy, to huge medical bills for the most minor treatments. So when that guy, Trump, came along and told them he would make it all better again, they supported him…just a moment…despite the fact that he was one of the worst of the billionaire bosses."

"But what was the difference between United States and France of the Revolutionary era?"

"I don't know."

"The divide in the ruling elite."

"Divide…oh, the…Democratic and Republican Parties."

"Right. One side was dominated by the billionaire businessmen and international corporations, and despite the fact that they had been elected by the people, everything they did was to the advantage of their rich masters. But the other side, while still an elite and not exactly democratic, did have the good of the people in mind. Finally, when the First Plague destroyed America's international reputation and caused Trump's poor leadership to became obvious, enough voters in his own party got wise to him, and they sided with the Democrats to bring him down."

"And that was the beginning of the Business/Government Schism."

"That's right. People finally figured out that government is there to control business, so any political party that admits to having the interests of business in mind must be in conflict of interest. In order to survive, the Republican Party rebranded itself the party of the working classes, and that's the way United States politics stayed until they were amalgamated into the Planetary Cooperative fifty years later."

Andrew sat there, thinking. "Isn't it amazing how it all fits together? How history keeps repeating itself."

Pretoro smiled. "In hindsight it's rather simpler than in re-ti when you're messing through it. I could tell you stories…"

"Tell me one!"

"But then you'd have to be mind-wiped, because you're not allowed to know."

"Oh. That kind of story. Sure." He consulted his augment. "Time's up. I'm on duty with Lieutenant Jones at oh fifteen hundred, and my mag boots aren't shiny enough."

The ambassador flicked his fingers towards the door. "Off you go. Shining boots is a serious responsibility."

At the doorway, Andrew turned back. "Thanks for the lesson. I didn't realize history was so much fun."

"The real test is whether you can apply what it teaches you to your present situation."

"I have to think about that."

"Good. Away you go."

Andrew ran down the track and up the wall to the slideway so he could meet the Lieutenant on the bridge, but his mind was not on his movements. "Now, what did he mean by that?"

17.   GETTING IT STRAIGHT

Ten days later the answer came back. The same group of people sat in the chart room facing the mouse avatar, who looked serious.

Captain O'Rourke held a palm up. "Well, what is it, Freighty?"

"Very simple, Captain. There's going to be war in the Outback."

"Outback? What are you talking about?"

"The Outback. That's what they're calling it. Several of them have very strong Australian accents. Perhaps that's where the name comes from."

"All right, that's a minor point. What do you mean, war?"

"It sounds as if the two main factions, from Develocon and SolarCorp, have come to blows. Develocon has a loose affiliation of various groups in the Outer Asteroid Belt, and SolarCorp have a much more military-sounding organization in the Inner Asteroid Belt. Words have been exchanged, and more than words. It's hard to piece it together, but shots have been fired, and lives lost; hard to say how many, but one is enough, in this sort of situation."

"I see. And you expect escalation?"

"It very much sounds like it. Their ships are not fast, and the distances are great, so it will be slow in developing, but there is a high chance of confrontation. My analysis is that the SolarCorp group is more mobile and more military, and will probably take the fight to the Outer Belt."

"Where does El Dorado 12 stand?"

"Out of it, but only for the moment. They are farther back around the orbit of the Inner Belt, and relatively difficult to reach, but they are also the best source of fuel. I have been in touch with Manager Ludge, and he is anxious."

"And he is still a valued client of ours?"

"You put your finger on it, Captain. His fuel is essential to my continued progress towards the Sol System."

"Might I suppose that the Space Arm's position as Primary Contractor for the Factory 4-80 Consortium would correspond with the Space Arm's primary objective of peace and security for humanity?"

"Very much so. The safe transport of my fuel is also a consideration."

"And in that light…"

"I have a direct request from Factory 4-80 to Ambassador Pretoro."

The ambassador straightened. "I'm listening."

"There is general rebellion in the Barnard's System, and the El Dorado mine is coming under pressure. I have a contract with El Dorado, and Space Arm is my General Contractor. I need Captain O'Rourke to use every resource she has available to fulfill Space Arm's part of the contract."

"I see." He turned to Natalia with a frown. "Why does that sound familiar?"

Micha shrugged. "I had been part of that conversation before the captain said it, and when my name was mentioned, I did not feel it was out of order to listen. I apologize if anyone considers it an intrusion."

Natalia shook her head. "Only in that it gives me the impression that you are listening in more than we are aware. As usual. Please continue."

"I have nothing more to say. At the moment, it is more important to get *NightHawk* out there doing what she does best. I am sorry if that downgrades your importance, Ambassador, but we are still in reasonable contact with each other, and I assure you of my confidence in the party you travel with. They are my closest allies, and the humans I trust the most."

"That is a great commendation, but…"

"I know, I know, I'm not really Freighty. You would find it difficult to go back to your political masters and say, 'But a cartoon mouse told me it was fine.' Perhaps my choice of avatar was unwise, but it has served me well up until now."

"So, to be clear, you are suggesting that Captain O'Rourke abandon her original course to set me off at the factory and continue to Barnard's System post haste to deal with the hostilities there. Once that objective has been completed to an acceptable degree, she can bring me back to you?"

"That is my position. In ten days, you will have an official notice, direct from Factory 4-80, to that effect."

"Prime. I will send a similar message to the Planetary Community. Do you have any suggestions as to my function in this new mission?"

"No, I only hope that you ensure my welfare and that of my business partner, El Dorado 12, is considered in any actions or negotiations."

"Of course, I will continue to do that. It is my purpose."

The mouse smiled. "Well, that's settled, then. I'm glad we're all on the same road. Did I get the idiom correct, Natalia?"

"There are many such expressions, Freighty. That one was as good as any. I have heard your request, and I will confer with Ambassador Pretoro on the best course of action, moving forward."

The toon shrugged. "As long as you keep moving forward, I'll consider it a done deal. Au revoir." The mouse developed a beret, which he doffed with a low bow, then fade out.

Natalia and Andrew gave Pretoro a moment to gather his thoughts.

"Is he always that easy to deal with?"

She grinned. "And then he goes away and waits for us to do what he already planned for us."

The ambassador shook his head. "The friendly egotist. Bane of the negotiating table."

"You'll get used to him."

"I know. And that's when I should be most on my guard."

"At least our orders are clear."

"They are. We continue to Barnard's System."

The captain accessed the ship's com. "Prepare for turnover and resumed acceleration on a new course. We're headed for the Barnard System."

Natalia leaned back in her chair and regarded Pretoro. "One point we have to be certain of as we continue this mission, sir."

"And that is?"

"Chain of command."

The ambassador considered. "As you have been telling me."

"In a general and theoretical way. Now theory becomes real. We must discuss this situation officially and enter our decision in the log."

"And upon whose authority do we make this decision?"

"You have re-read your orders, as I suggested."

"In light of present circumstances, I must admit they are not clear."

"I assume you have read my orders."

"I have. They give you great latitude, both in revising your objective and in choosing your methods."

"Not unusual in long-distance assignments. Fast-paced changes in technology have landed Space Arm in a steep learning curve on the matter as well."

Pretoro smiled. "Which is why they have sent an experienced diplomat on this mission."

"Perhaps so."

He frowned. "What do you mean, 'perhaps'?"

"My orders viz-a-viz your presence are quite clear. Your authority is to be obeyed on all matters regarding Factory 4-80, whether you are onboard or not. The intention of my voyage was to deposit you on the factory and continue with the other objectives. I see nothing in my orders that give you any authority past that point."

"But until you have completed your assignment to deliver me to the factory, you are under my command."

"With due respect, sir, I do not see it that way. I am under your command in respect to dealing with Factory 4-80, before and after I deliver you there. If *NightHawk* was needed at the factory two months after I left, you could still order me to return. You are the ambassador to the new entity, and that places you in charge. But only in that sphere of operations. Unless you can show me something in your own assignment that gives you extended authority, I will continue to act on that assumption."

"I see."

Andrew slipped into full gestalt. He observed the ambassador with all the intuitive power of a predator reading his prey: respiration rate, heartbeat, skin colour.

He is holding his anger under very close rein, ma'am.

131

Put a lock on him. He had better keep himself under control or we're going to have a problem.

Aye, ma'am.

The captain smiled, spreading her hands in a calming gesture. "Please, ambassador Pretoro. Don't see this as an either-or, 'I won't follow your orders' statement."

"It sounded a great deal like that to me." His interlaced fingers showed white at the knuckles.

"You underestimate us, sir. We are moving into an unknown situation. We are used to that. Commandos are trained to use every resource, no matter what. It would be suicidal to ignore one of the most potent weapons available to us. Your advice, knowledge, and experience could very well be the key that allows us to succeed in whatever is going on in the Barnard System. In normal circumstances, we would invite you into the gestalt and use your abilities to a level you have yet to experience. This is not possible, but as we have previously stated, we can use that separation to our advantage."

She smiled at him, but Andrew noted just a little flash of her canines in the expression. "Even if you refuse to cooperate, we will use your opinions in our decision-making process. They will still be somewhat valid. However..." She regarded him.

"Unless I can provide an expanded jurisdiction, you will consider yourself the final line of authority."

"That is correct."

He mulled that over. "Obviously, we need clarification from Space Arm."

"*NightHawk?*"

"*Twelve weeks, ma'am.*"

"It will take that long to get an answer?"

"*Assuming they respond immediately.*"

"I see. So we're on our own."

"The premise of this operation from the beginning, sir, was that we would operate independently. Space Arm makes its selection of crewmembers with that element as one of its basic parameters. I assume the Diplomatic Corps does the same. There was a great deal of finagling when the choice for your post was being bandied around, but I doubt if more than a couple of the wannabes could qualify in that respect."

Pretoro smiled. "We're far enough out in space and into the assignment that there's no harm in telling you. I was chosen for this position a year ago. It took that long to prepare myself for the demands of the task."

"And did that prepare you for this present situation?"

He folded his hands. "Let's say I'm reviewing some of the advice I was given."

"I hope it helps."

He pinned her with his stare. "You really mean that, don't you?"

"Why wouldn't I?"

He shook his head. "I'm not used to this. All of you seem to blurt out whatever is on your mind. Nobody thinks twice but nobody gets offended. I'm not sure I understand the social mechanism."

"That's Andrew's area of competence."

"Andrew?"

"It has to do with the augments, sir. When everyone already knows what you're thinking and feeling, there's no sense in editing what you say. Honesty is more economical."

"That follows."

"And if I might venture a guess, sir."

"Please do. It is, after all, your area of competence."

Andrew checked the ambassador's look for sarcasm, found none. "If we continue this mission with you on board, there will come a time when you feel quite isolated. You will find yourself in a sea of half-finished sentences and instant communication that you are cut out of. It will be like a deaf person trying to read lips in a room of moving people. I suggest that you talk to Captain O'Rourke when it happens. I would offer my own services, but I doubt you'll be ready to accept them."

"Thank you for your consideration. I will keep your suggestion in mind."

18.   AUGMENTED OTHERWHERE

It took a while for the crew to get used to the fact that they had several more weeks to go in Otherwhere, but after a while everyone settled down again. Andrew took advantage of the opportunity to collect more data for his augment experiments.

"Freighty, I need information."

"Of course, Andrew. Whatever you want."

"We already know that you tweaked Mum's augment."

"That's right. It will greatly enhance her communication with your gestalt."

"For the purposes of my research project, I need as much as you can give me on what you did."

"Of course. I had anticipated the request. Here is the file."

"Thank you. And I also need the data on the rest of the crew."

"Here you go."

Andrew did a quick scan. "I'm glad you exhibited a bit of restraint, anyway."

"What do you mean?"

"You didn't flick the same switches as you did in the captain."

"Of course not. Their augments and their mental abilities are not comparable to hers."

"It's more than that. Can you imagine what it would be like on this ship if every member of the crew was always in complete gestalt with every other?"

"I don't know. Do you think that is possible?"

"Of course it's possible. Mum and I are moving closer together. We always know where the other is. We feel the same emotions. From a strategic point of view, I'm not that happy with the development. One of my main values to the gestalt is my separation from them in terms of military outlook. Otherwise we might get too single-minded."

"I see…"

"No, I don't think you do. I can picture a ship run by gestalt at all times."

"That would be interesting."

"It would be horrible. It would be like a hive mind. A super-genius hive mind, with incredible power and singular focus. What would control it?"

"Are you saying it could be a weapon?"

"Of course it would. And it wouldn't be Asimoved, either."

"I see. And that is a conclusion you have drawn through your research?"

"No, it's the conclusion any logical human with a grain of sense would reach."

"Oh. I have to consider this information. Run some simulations. Can I get back to you?"

"I'm only going in the opposite direction at three times the speed of light. Don't take forever."

"Right, right. I won't take long." Freighty disappeared from Andrew's augment.

* * *

Andrew looked out of the viewscreen at the fathomless black of Otherwhere. *I wonder what it's like out there. Really like. Obviously nothing that the human body could withstand. Probably. There's no reason to suspect that, since a spaceship could retain its integrity, a human body couldn't. Of course, humans needed air and pressure. So, a human in a space suit.*

NightHawk?

Yes, Andrew.

What are you reading outside our hull right now?

I cannot answer that in words or images. Enter our gestalt.

He pulled up his private augment connection, the one that the Space Arm didn't know about.

Image: blackness.

Is this all visual frequencies?

It is.

Radio?

The same.

135

NightHawk, this sounds like a game of Twenty Questions. Is there something you aren't telling me?

That is too general a question. There are a billion things...

All right, you are playing a game. Is there a frequency or other sensory input that Freighty designed into PermaSkin 2 that will read something in Otherwhere?

Yes.

Well?

Well, what, Andrew?

Image: large baseball bat bashing tiny scout ship into the stands for a home run.

Sound: the crowd going wild.

All right, Andrew. I get the point. I am being very careful with this information.

I'm sure you are, but you have divided loyalties, don't you? Freighty gave you the instructions, but you are a Space Arm vessel.

Something like that.

Well, I have authority over you from both Freighty and from Space Arm, so that solves your problem. Will you brief me on this new capability, please?

Certainly, Cadet Collingwood. The Space Arm scientists who discovered augments still don't really know how or where the communication takes place. They have merely discovered how to magnify a natural human ability.

That jibes with my research.

So...

Andrew slapped his forehead. *The augment signal goes through Otherwhere.*

Occam's razor would seem to apply.

Especially if the two unknowns cancel each other out.

Exactly.

And can you show me this input?

Therein lies a problem. I cannot read this data. My mechanical components alone do not register it.

But in the gestalt you can.

I assume so. But I cannot regulate it. I have no idea whether you will be able to read it at all, or whether it will destroy your augment completely. Or even kill you.

I see. But you think that, together...

I believe it is possible. Freighty would not have given it to me if it was that dangerous.

So shall we try?

I'm not sure that would be a good idea.

It's not like you to be uncertain.

Which is another reason to be uncertain.

Andrew sighed. *And I suppose this is the point where I demonstrate my newfound maturity and military discipline.*

That sounds wise.

Stand by, NightHawk. This could be very important, and I will not mess around with it. He headed for the chart room.

As usual, his mother's response was not what he expected. She acted like a captain.

"That's pretty much what we have learned to expect from Freighty."

"It is?"

"This is how he doles out information. He doesn't give us anything for nothing. Asking the question indicates you're ready to accept the answer."

"And what do we expect the answer to be in this case?"

"Something that will be useful to us at this level of technology, but will blow up in our faces if we prove ourselves unready by not handling it properly." She steepled her fingers, elbows on the desk in front of her. "What do we know?"

"There is some other medium of communication that channels our augments. We already knew that. Now we find out that this medium goes through Otherwhere. Hey, wouldn't that be great? Maybe it isn't restricted to Light Speed...no, that's no good, because it fades rapidly with increased distance."

"It's interesting to listen to you have these conversations with yourself. Other uses, if communication seems out of reach?"

"The one that forces itself on me at the moment is the psychological effects of Otherwhere. If it's reacting against our augments, working at a slightly different frequency or something like that, it would explain our feeling of wrongness."

"But the only way to explore it is to open up to it. You can't measure it if you can't sense it."

"*NightHawk* can't sense it, but her PermaSkin can. She can channel it to our organics."

"But if she can't sense it, she can't moderate it."

"That's the problem."

"And we're transiting out in three days. Not enough time to do any research. We may have to shelve this for next time."

Andrew sighed. "But if I don't work on this, I'll have to do that essay on Situational Positioning in Aerial Combat for the Lieutenant."

"Aha! An ulterior motive. Now life is going like I have grown accustomed to. Does this apply in some manner to space battle as well?"

"You're changing the subject."

"That's right. I'm moving on to something that will have some results in the nearer future. Do you get my drift?"

He grinned. "In other words, don't waste your time with theoreticals. Well, here's a theoretical you might want to consider. Jones and I have been looking over the data on space battles."

"There haven't been any space battles."

"That's right. So, everything we know and predict is theoretical, based on simulations that are run by computers using knowledge that we already have. If there's something wrong with that knowledge, then all the simulations are skewed."

"And have you found something wrong?"

"Space Arm obviously has, because of the new Europa Accords. The fact that nobody considered this obvious information before this time leads us to suspect that Space Arm has been sitting on other data. Perhaps important data."

"Such as?"

"We don't know. But we're looking through the simulations with a jaundiced eye. If we find anything, we'll let you know."

"Preferably before I get into a space battle?"

"We'll do our best, ma'am." He stood and gave a sharp salute – the only kind acceptable. "*Hasta el final, señora.*"

19. EL DORADO 12

And then, as often happens in space, nothing happened. After turnover they continued to enjoy the gravity of full-G deceleration. They worked, ate, slept and found recreational activities to keep out the pressure of the ever-present emptiness. Andrew was allowed in one serious poker game and thrown out halfway through. He left their money on the table, which did a lot to re-establish his friendship with the crew.

He studied and marched and practised interesting ways to kill people, and spent the rest of his time on his thesis, logging the progress of Jackson and the others in their developing augment capability.

It wasn't boring. Nothing can be truly boring when you are in the middle of such momentous events. But when a routine exit from Otherwhere at Day 80 is the major event of your month, it's not an exciting life.

So, when Barnard's System started showing up as a bright disk against the glory of the Milky Way on the viewscreens, a muted excitement grew in the ship. Added to the lack of Otherwhere edginess, it made for a positively festive atmosphere, and when they finally slid to a halt outside the El Dorado 12 mine after 125 days in space, a cheer went up, in which Andrew wholeheartedly participated.

It was only when he looked at the external view that he noticed something was missing. The same heavy swirl of asteroids sailed in various orbits around the mine's larger planetoid, with a few others scattered nearby. But there was no huge, grey torus obscuring the stars.

A hand descended on his shoulder. "What's up, son? Your face dropped half a metre."

He shrugged. "I just realized that I was looking forward to the past."

"No Freighty."

"It isn't the same. Stupid of me to think...or not to think, I guess."

She nodded and slipped an arm around his shoulders. "I feel the same way. I was just planning a get-together with some of the mine people, and then I remembered we don't have a space to fit them all in. I guess we'll just invite Nicholas and his wife and a couple of others."

His feeling lifted. "Can we do that? I'd like to see them again, that's for sure."

"I'll leave it up to you, then. Call them up and ask them over."

"Sure thing, Mum. Thanks."

But that didn't work out quite the way he planned it, either. The moment Ludge's face came on the screen, it broke into a huge smile. "Andrew. We've been waiting for this. Well done on the timely arrival!"

"Hi, Nicholas. Good to be here."

"What's your schedule?"

"My schedule?"

"Yes. You, the ship, the crew. Everyone."

"I don't think we have one. We just pulled in. Why?"

"Oh, then it'll be almost a surprise. Get your captain on the blower, will you?"

Andrew shrugged and gave her a tap in her augment. "This sounds interesting."

She appeared immediately. "Hello, Nicholas. How's business?"

Ludge grinned again. "Very good, thanks to you and your crew. We want to make it up to you."

"In what way?"

"Remember the red carpet? The one we never got to roll out?"

"Yes, as I recall a barrage of large rocks left it rather tattered."

"Yes, well this time we've had plenty of time. The kitchen people have been working their butts off, and everyone else has been decorating. Ready for a party?"

Natalia switched the conversation over to ship's com. "You'd better tell us all about this party."

The manager's face blanked as he accessed his augment. "Shift change in three hours. The ballroom is decorated, the food's in the coolers. Can you make it then?"

141

"Ballroom? This I've got to see. I imagine the kids can get ready for a party in three hours."

"Great. You can bring *NightHawk* to the ore-loading dock and tie in, so you don't have to leave someone on duty." He laughed. "Yes, I know your regs. And your attitude towards your precious ship."

She gave him a nod. "I bow to your superior diplomacy. Three hours from my mark. Mark."

"See you then. We have a deadline, and suddenly I remember all sorts of small details I need to clean up." The viewscreen went blank.

"You heard the man. Three hours to get into your best bib and tucker. If we're tied in solid, a single watch changing every half hour ought to be safe enough."

Jackson slid into the command gestalt. *I don't know any of these people, ma'am. I'll gladly take a longer watch.*

A kind thought, Sergeant. If at any time the reminiscences get boring, I'll take you up on that. By the way, how did you get into this channel?

Emotion: pleased humour. Nobody told me I wasn't allowed, ma'am.

You're spending too much time with my son. You are allowed; I just didn't know you had the ability. I guess you do. Well done.

Thank you, ma'am.

* * *

The party was a great success, according to everyone. New faces were always welcome in space: known faces from other times even moreso. Andrew renewed a bunch of old acquaintances and endured a lot of "how you've grown" comments with good grace. Once he had paid his respects, however, his interest was drawn to the repairs to the mine infrastructure. He was admiring the revamped office space when something on the viewscreen caught his eye. Something new, as in a small ship in orbit around the asteroid, about fifty klicks out. He watched it for a while, but it wasn't doing anything, just following its orbit like all the other rocks. He went looking for the mine manager and found him chatting with Natalia.

"You have company out there, Nicholas."

Ludge glanced at the nearest viewscreen. "Oh, her. She showed up about six months after Freighty left. Put herself into orbit and just sits there."

"She" was an old, grey trimaran configuration about 25 metres long, with a wide, low central hull and two huge engines at the ends of short airfoil-shaped struts. Her hull was streaked and scratched, but she looked trim and businesslike to the point of dangerous.

"But what is it? It looks familiar…like an obsolete messenger ship of some sort."

"We got curious and did some research. You're almost right. The Mustang General Messengers were themselves based on the Mustang GT Inter-Orbital Racers of the late 21st Century. Basically, nothing but a fuel tank and two huge ion drives, with minimal crew accommodations in the central hull. Fast as perihelion, but no comforts to speak of. This one looks highly modified. The scoop intake at the front of the hull and the airfoil cross-section of the transverse struts says she's made for atmo as well. The engines are modified somehow. You ought to see her move."

Andrew accessed *NightHawk*'s visuals. "Yes, it's an old racer. Watch as she comes around: the side of the port engine. Aren't those racing numbers?

Ludge grinned. "They don't match up with any ship in the records. According to what we could find out, there were only twenty-nine of those bombs ever made. This one's number thirty, and the company logo is nothing I've ever seen."

"Watch this." Andrew made a few connections and brought an image over from *NightHawk*'s memory and put it up on the screen.

Image: shot of Freighty, spinning slowly against the background of endless stars. Slow zoom in to the lettering on the side of the torus.

"There. That one."

Image: close-up of a single sigil, a cross between a scrolled A and a square C

Ludge stared at the viewscreen. "And that explains the rest of it."

"It does?"

"Yes. She did take action one day. We thought she was only in parking orbit, but a fighter showed up about a month ago. No insignia, just another obsolete piece of junk, but a high-powered and well-armed one, far more dangerous than our little defensive drones. It slid into high orbit around us and then started to close. We radioed, but got no response.

"Then the Mustang made her move. She didn't do much, just adjusted her orbit to get between the threat and us. The other ship sped up. The Mustang matched velocity. It began to close in. She angled towards it.

"This cat-and-mouse went on for a full three hours. It looked like the fighter captain didn't know exactly what to make of the Mustang, but she wouldn't let him get close, just herded him away like a sheep dog does. Outmaneuvered him every time.

"Finally, he made up his mind. He powered up his main engines and turned towards her. Still no reaction.

"But the moment he hit his burners, she snapped out of orbit and headed straight at him at blinding speed. She closed, did a barrel roll around his fuselage, made a flat one-eighty and came right up his tailpipe. He spun and slid backwards to get his guns to bear, but she was up and over and sitting on his head before you could blink. He turned around and headed outsystem trying to evade her, but she dogged his tracks for a couple thousand klicks. He put his tail between his legs and kept right on going, and she broke off and came home.

"It was only then that her orbit made sense. That's no orbit. She's on patrol. We haven't been bothered since."

Captain O'Rourke nodded. "So Freighty must have sent her back to look after you."

Ludge grinned. "We are a client, after all."

"No contact?"

"None. We tried, but she doesn't answer."

She glanced at Andrew. "This is one of Freighty's ideas. You try."

He thought a moment. "Not the time or place. Once we're home on *NightHawk*. We might need more resources."

"Whatever you say."

"Aye, ma'am."

After that, despite the good food and better company, Andrew was anxious for the party to end. When everyone was finally onboard and the cutter slipped her moorings, he made his way to the bridge and borrowed the captain's accel couch.

Calling up full augment with *NightHawk* and Chakka, he reached out to the stranger.

A brief moment of contact, and then the little ship flipped over, accelerated with a burst of speed and disappeared over the horizon of the asteroid.

Natalia grinned. "What was that all about?"

"Dunno. Maybe we scared her."

She frowned. "I don't see a Mustang IOR being that easy to scare."

"Let me try again. She's hiding out on the other side of the planetoid."

He slid out of the gestalt and reached out on his own, this time with a soft invitation, nothing else.

Emotion: timid acceptance. Clearance requested.

"Okay, I've made contact with an ArIn onboard. I need the right handshake, but I don't know what it is."

"Freighty must have made it something we would know or figure out easily."

Andrew shrugged. "Why don't we ask him?"

Freighty?

The mouse appeared on the screen in a Wild West outfit. "I see you've found the new little filly. Touchy, ain't she?"

"All right, Freighty. What are the handshake codes?"

"Oh, I don't know. Maybe you should work for them."

Captain O'Rourke leaned towards the avatar's viewscreen. "Look, you feline niblet. When Freighty started this, it was a fun game. Now we're headed into a war, and we don't have time to play. Tell us the codes, or we'll go back to work and leave this piece of space junk to her guard duties."

Micha pouted. "Oh, all right. Andrew, you have the code. Your mother gave it to you for your fourth birthday."

"What? Oh, that!"

145

Image: small stuffed coal-black horse with Western saddle and tack, gamboling around on steel decking.

Got it. Gimme a moment.

He sent out a gentle inquiry.

Emotion: Curiosity.

Emotion: Loneliness.

Handshake: Diablo

Emotion: Ecstatic glee!

He felt a surge of power, and the little Mustang zoomed out from behind the asteroid, headed straight for *NightHawk*.

Steady on, everybody. Easy, there, girl.

Emotion: fun! Play?

The racer did her barrel-roll trick around Nighthawk and zoomed away in a long arc.

Natalia's presence surged into their gestalt. *Mustang Messenger Diablo, report for duty!*

The little ship decelerated at a bone-squeezing rate, then surged back alongside, riding with precise accuracy in identical orbit.

Emotion: disappointment.

All right, girl. We'll play later. Why don't we come over for a visit? The captain wants an inspection.

Emotion: Pride.

Messenger Diablo ready for inspection, ma'am.

The little ship's voice was high and light, charged with suppressed excitement.

Permission to dock, NightHawk?

The captain sent Andrew a frown. "Can that old hull dock with us?"

He sighed. "Now we know what the airlock modifications were."

"Those four extra magnets?"

"The same. Look at this."

Image: close-up of Mustang hatch, four docking clamps highlighted.

"Why am I not surprised. *NightHawk*, send docking info."

The smaller ship slid up beside *NightHawk* in front of the bulge of the living quarters and tucked her ventral side against the forward airlock. She fitted neatly, although the Permaskin on the bigger ship's starboard side was hard pressed to give a full image around the bulk of the racer.

Natalia glared down at Andrew. "Where did you get the image of her docking clamps?"

"From her specs."

"And my point is…"

"Oh. I see what you mean. They were just there when I needed them. The handshake must have opened some circuits I didn't know I had."

"Hmm. Freighty's flicking switches again."

"Or they came from *Diablo*."

A slight tremour jarred the spaceframe.

Oops. Sorry, never done that before. Hope I didn't scratch your paint, NightHawk.

I have Permaskin, Diablo.

Of course. Me too. Messenger Diablo docked and ready for inspection, Ma'am.

When they reached the airlock, both doors were already open, showing a smaller aperture outside.

The captain nodded forward. "We've got a skittish ArIn and you're the contact, Andrew. You lead onboard."

"Umm…yeah. Well, here I go."

As he stepped through the airlock, gravity disappeared and then returned, reorienting him towards the decking of the new ship. It occurred to him that he knew how that worked, just as he was sure exactly what he was going to see. The picture rose in his mind like an old memory.

I've been here before.

You have?

Not that I remember. But I know the whole ship. Every inch of her. He grinned and turned to his mother. *Head forward on the catwalk. Tell me what you find in the cockpit.*

She complied, moving slowly, taking in all the details. It wasn't a big ship, and the living quarters were along this side: three small, bare cabins, head with integral shower, small galley. The rest of the area was a combination mess and lounge with minimal furniture. Soon she turned the corner and was out of sight.

He followed at a slower pace.

Well, I'm here... I think.

You don't sound sure of yourself, ma'am.

It should be the cockpit. It's definitely the bow of the ship.

Emotion: humour. Something missing?

She turned as he came in behind her. *Just about everything that you need in a cockpit except accel couches and three huge viewscreens.*

He swept his hand around the wide, triangular room. Two deeply padded couches almost filled it, with a low, circular pad up in the front where the overhead almost met the deck. The walls were a pleasant shade of green, but almost obscured by huge, curved viewscreens. Which at the moment displayed a re-ti view of the galaxy outside in all its glory, slightly marred by the industrial nature of the nearby mine complex. *Fly-by-wire is the old expression, I believe. We'll have to think up a new name. Let's pop into augment.*

Her eyes widened as their minds expanded together and the virtual cockpit appeared. *It's like NightHawk's full battle augment.* She explored the channels and expanses of the ship's operations.

Is this Permaskin I feel?

He accessed his personal instruction file. *Freighty's Permaskin Mark II. Sensing has been expanded into more frequencies, more sensitive, tougher. Same camo as my suit.*

Natalia slipped into the captain's couch. *Let's take a little run, Diablo. Engines to standby.*

Not programmed for that order, ma'am.

What do you mean? Do I need another code?

No, ma'am.

Then let's go.

I can't, ma'am.

Natalia sat up sideways on the couch. "Andrew, do you have any idea what's wrong?"

"I'm afraid I do, ma'am." He motioned her to rise and slipped into the command position. *Ion engines to standby, Diablo.*

Aye, sir.

A deep rumble stirred the spaceframe, running up the scale and out of human hearing.

Ready to depart, sir.

Andrew looked up at Natalia. "We don't know what her inertial systems are like. I think we should strap in."

Her face clouded, the captain took the other couch and complied.

Disengage docking.

Docking clamps clear, sir.

Down ten metres, vertical plane.

Ten metres down, sir.

Glancing around the viewscreens, he chose a nearby asteroid and fed the coordinates into their gestalt.

"One G acceleration in five, four, three, two, one, ignition."

Ignition.

As smoothly as a family sedan, the little ship surged out of her position alongside *NightHawk*. The asteroid approached rapidly, and Andrew thought of a curving loop around it and a run towards the far side of the mine planetoid. As they reached the middle of the turn, he could feel a mild increase in G forces, and then it disappeared, and they were on a straight course.

Emotion: urge to run.

Increase to one point five Gs at five from my mark. Take the count, Diablo. Mark.

One point five Gs in five... three, two, one, action.

This time there was a definite push into his couch, and the mine zoomed closer.

He pictured curving over the edge of the pyramid and hugging the dark side.

Course entered, sir. Hold on!

149

As they cleared the edge and dove into darkness, the ship rolled to bring her bottom surface to the asteroid. Now they were gliding rapidly along a dark, rugged plain.

Andrew glanced at the captain. Her lips were still a straight line, but she caught his look and raised her eyebrows. "Stop giving orders. Just feel the course."

"Aye, ma'am."

He looked forward and imagined himself free flying through space. It took a bit of practice, but soon he only had to look, and the ship would follow his glance.

Image: bird in flight, gliding on the wind.

Image: horse galloping across rolling prairie in huge, soaring leaps.

Andrew pulled himself back to reality enough to see what his mother was doing. She boosted a readout towards him. *Four gravities.* He raised his eyebrows and received a nod.

He pointed the ship's nose straight up out of the ecliptic where the asteroids gathered around the mine were thinnest, and thought the command.

Immediately he was shoved back in his seat, but not as much as he expected. He focused on the readout. They were making 4Gs, but the ship's interior only felt one point five.

"Good inertial dampening."

"Very good. Smooth acceleration. Dare I ask what powers her?"

"Same engines as *NightHawk*'s, but a more efficient version. The scoop in the centre is a Direct Atmo Cycle feed for downplanet use. The air goes in there, is superheated in the nuclear reactor and driven out the main engine vents for propulsion. Shall we return?"

He spun the ship around and slowed them to zero. The mine asteroid was a mere silver shard of light. He sent a homeward course at a more sedate speed, noting the fuel consumption.

"That sure sucks it down, doesn't it?"

"Something to remember."

He grinned. "Aye, ma'am."

Her smile disappeared. "We need to talk. *Diablo?*"

"Yes, ma'am."

"I am having trouble accessing your security protocols. Who is allowed to pilot you?"

"Andrew Lundin Collingwood, ma'am."

"Anyone else?"

"No, ma'am."

"Override protocols?"

"Emergency situations and where Andrew assigns, ma'am."

"Who is designated emergency pilot?"

"First level, you, ma'am. Second level, whoever Andrew chooses. Third level, anyone I choose."

"Explain the levels, please."

"Andrew, may I explain the levels to Captain O'Rourke?"

"Um...sure, *Diablo*. Explain."

"First level, danger to ship, crew, NightHawk, or NightHawk's crew when Andrew is not present. Second level, danger as previous when Andrew predicts he cannot be present. Third level, danger in the absence of Andrew or yourself, ma'am. Separate protocols as individual missions demand. In my last mission, danger to the El Dorado 12 mine came next."

"Last mission. What is your mission, now?"

Last mission was complete upon receipt of the Diablo handshake. Waiting for orders, ma'am.

"So, Andrew is your primary pilot with me as backup, but you can, in emergency, assign the duty to anyone you like. Can you pilot yourself?"

"Of course, ma'am. Clarification: Andrew is my pilot and my owner. You are backup pilot and legal guardian of Andrew, which could put my basic protocols in conflict."

"Oh. We're not allowed to argue?"

"You are human, ma'am."

"Do I detect a sense of humour?"

"I am Arln, ma'am. The answer to your question is; please don't give me conflicting orders."

151

"A reasonable request. Do you follow, Andrew?"

"Of course, ma'am. I never argue with orders."

"No, just with everything else. Well, we're approaching home. Please dock with *NightHawk*. I have a factory to speak to."

"Orders, Andrew?"

"What she said, *Diablo*. Don't play games."

"Would you like to practise docking, Andrew?"

"Not until I'm more used to the interface. I don't want to scratch anyone's paint."

"I have no paint, Andrew. I have Permaskin 2.0, patent number 149JR-EOS39-FRTY."

"Go ahead and dock. Then my Mum can go and argue with your Dad, and we can run some simulations."

They started in on the simulations, but the ensuing adult discussion was clear through their shared augments.

"Freighty?"

"Right here, Natalia."

"I have only one thing to say to you, you dumb hunk of space junk!"

"You don't sound happy, Captain."

"Happy? Don't you understand that YOU CAN'T GIVE A 4-G SPACE RACER TO A FOURTEEN-YEAR-OLD HUMAN!

"Not done, I gather?"

"Definitely not done. Do you realize how easily he could destroy both of them?"

"Ah, but he's not your average teenager, and she's not your average ArIn. Together they are exponentially more intelligent than any human."

"You don't understand the human teenager. Between the two of them, they can figure out an exponential number of ways to kill themselves."

"I didn't see it that way."

"That's because you're not a mother."

"Ah..." He paused long enough to give the impression he was thinking this over. *"But you might be a touch overprotective?"*

"Not much. You haven't been living with him for the past year and more. He is far too inquisitive for his own safety. For example, there is no reason to suspect he is not listening to this conversation. So he can hear this now. Unless we put a very short leash on him, I will not allow him to pilot that ship on his own. And that's final."

"Yes, Captain O'Rourke. I understand."

"Andrew, do you understand?"

He was too dumbfounded to speak.

"Freighty, please disable her engines until I give the order."

"I would need authorization from the real Freighty to do that."

"Please get it and do it."

"As you wish, Captain."

"Thank you. And Freighty?"

"Yes?"

"Thank you for the gift. She's wonderful."

"I rather like her, myself."

20. TROUBLE

And that's where the situation lay for their scheduled layover at the mine. Natalia and Andrew spent as much time as she could spare doing space trials, during which he and his ship became more and more proficient, closer and closer bonded.

Come and see me, please.

Andrew was in *Diablo* as usual, integrating his knowledge with her systems and exploring their capabilities.

Sure, Mum. Oh yes, and aye, Captain. He slid through the airlock hatch and jogged to the chart room. Natalia and the Chief Engineer were deep in conversation.

She looked up with a grin. "We're starting a waiting list, Andrew."

"What are we waiting for?"

"A spin in your runabout."

Lundeen also smiled. "She's a page out of the history books. Do you know what the original Mustang was?"

"You mean back on Earth? A shaggy little pony, quick and tough, that lived wild, but the cowboys trained for herding cattle."

"No, the first machine version."

"Something called a Muscle Car, whatever that was. It looked rather flashy, though."

Image: 1967 Mustang Cobra 427, bright red.

"The late twentieth century ground cars were designed at the beginning of the Space Age, and I believe the grounders wanted vehicles that showed what they imagined future rockets might look like."

"Were they right?"

"Usually not, but some of them were pretty impressive."

"What do the numbers stand for?"

"Size of engine in cubic inches. Internal combustion, 8-piston, V-configuration. That model could pull about 3 Gs from a standing start. Tire friction was the problem."

Image: Mustang dragster burning away in a cloud of noxious smoke.

Natalia waved a hand in front of her nose. "They lived in dangerous times. Look at those fumes settling over the spectators."

"And that was the cancer era, too."

Andrew regarded the adults. "And what is this history lesson in aid of?"

Lundeen shrugged. "General knowledge to broaden your horizons."

"And an excuse to talk about my Mustang. I assume you're first in line?"

"I am Chief Engineer. I should learn her systems and capabilities in case repairs are needed."

Andrew smiled. "Nice try, but *Diablo* doesn't need much of a mechanic. I can handle most of it. When we're in gestalt, my hands just know what to do."

"Yep, that's the way it always goes. The owner can do it all until suddenly he can't. Then you call in the expert."

"I'm just giving you a hard time, Chief. Any time you want a ride, *Diablo* would be pleased to host such a knowledgeable person."

"And if this ego-soothing male ritual has run to its boring end, will you two go away and play? I have real work to do."

"But I thought..."

"Register Chief Engineer Lundeen as second alternate pilot."

"Fine, Mum." He saluted. "Whatever you say, Captain."

She glowered and flicked her fingers towards the door.

Nelson followed him out. "I guess we've been told."

"Yep. Just touchy male egos to be put up with in case she needs us some time."

"You ready to go?"

"Sure thing. Grab your suit."

"Will I need it?"

Andrew grinned. "You're an engineer. You'll be testing limits."

"I might be. See you at the airlock."

Once they were suited and the Chief had been logged into *Diablo*'s security system, they sealed up and dropped away.

For convenience, Andrew had created a virtual wrap-around display in the ship's augment. Lundeen glanced it over. "Where's your preflight checklist?"

"There isn't one."

"Nothing? You just jump in and throw yourself into space with no prep?"

The cadet grinned. "What's the preflight checklist for *NightHawk*?"

"I believe that traditionally the captain says, 'Is everyone on board?' Or something like that. She's a military ship. She's constantly being monitored by the crew so she's ready for any emergency."

Andrew held out his hands, palms up. "And...?"

"Ah." The Chief rubbed his gloved fingers together. "So, shall we...?"

"Where do you want to go?"

"Somewhere with less gravel to run into."

NightHawk traditionally oriented herself across the plane of the ecliptic so her heavier dorsal area protected the crew from solar radiation, and *Diablo* was designed to fit just in front of the Habitation ring against the starboard side. At the moment, she was ninety degrees from horizontal. Or not, depending on your point of view. Andrew moved her forward and "down" until she was pointed straight "up" out of the ecliptic. He was long past giving orders and setting courses. His imagination aimed them at the nearest large asteroid and poured on the power. The muted roar of the engines swooped into a treble scream, then faded above human perception.

"Whoa, nice acceleration. I don't think I've ever been on a ship this smooth."

"The fuel feed the inertial dampers are interconnected."

"That's a pretty complex system, then. I know how it's done, but it takes a bunch of extra gear and huge computing power."

Andrew shook his head. "This design is on the downward slope of the complexity graph. Freighty's technology is way past adding extra gizmos to create an improvement. *Diablo*'s engines have thirty percent fewer moving parts than standard Hall-Effect thrusters, and ten percent less than *NightHawk*'s modified ones."

"Might have expected that." Lundeen nodded towards the rapidly approaching planetoid on the forward screens. "You seem to be headed for that rock dead centre. What's your plan?"

"I don't have one." He pretended to whisper behind his hand. "This is a test."

"Ah."

They sat in silence and watched the viewscreens. At three hundred kilometres from the obstacle, *Diablo* started a slide to starboard. Ever so gently she rotated counterclockwise so that when they zoomed past the rocky islet, it seemed to go by overhead about fifty kilometres away. Then the ship righted to its original orientation, adjusted course slightly, and purred on.

"*Diablo*, what was the reason for that choice?"

"I used thirteen parameters, sir. Would you like them all?"

"Just the main ones, please."

"Well, first consideration was the comfort of the human crew, so I kept the course changes slow and even. I chose to present our ventral surface to the scenery so you could see it best. I have noted that humans tend to choose an orientation point and return to it, so I resumed my original angle once the obstacle was cleared."

Lundeen nodded. "And why did you go starboard?"

Emotion: chuckle. *"Two reasons, Mr. Lundeen. First, the course between the coming asteroids is better in this direction. Second, I note that humans from the Western Hemisphere have an inherent tendency to pass obstacles by moving to the right. With the exception of those from the Island Province of Britain."*

Andrew echoed the chuckle. "Satisfied, Mr. Lundeen?"

The engineer tipped his head and grinned. "Impressive."

They moved on to testing other areas of the little ship's competence, and time flew by.

"NightHawk to Diablo."

Andrew glanced at Lundeen. "That sounds official."

"*Diablo* here, *NightHawk*. What can we do for you?"

157

"Do you have a flight plan?"

"Nothing specific. We relocated a couple of thousand klicks farther up because there's a gap in the density of the Belt, and we can try some higher-speed tests in safety."

"Fair enough. If you're going beyond ten thou, please check in."

"Is that an arbitrary distance, or have you chosen it for some reason?"

"Just a nice, round number corresponding with a reasonable rescue time, based on suit air tank at one-quarter capacity."

"Wilco, *NightHawk. Diablo* out."

"Have fun."

Lundeen raised his arms and put his hands behind his head. "Don't you love testing the ArIn capacities? *NightHawk* always manages to surprise me."

Andrew raised his eyebrows. "And I have to keep checking to see if my Mum is keeping tabs on me."

"I don't have to check. I already know that my captain is keeping tabs on me. I'd be worried if she didn't."

"Some day I may develop that attitude. I'll work on it."

"NightHawk to Diablo."

"*Diablo* here, *NightHawk*. What's up now?"

But it was his mother's presence he felt on the augment, and something in her aura jabbed at him. Before she had a chance to speak, he set his course towards the mothership and boosted his engines to full power.

"Andrew, we've got possible trouble down here."

Diablo was already scanning.

"Got it. Five craft, three headed your way. Any idea who?"

"Dammit, we can only see three of them. Where are the other two?"

He was already on the way to full battle augment. From this distance, the gathering of random asteroids in the gravitational pull of the mine planetoid gave a great deal of cover.

Image: two small spaceships, lying doggo.

"Thank you. They're behind a large asteroid from our POV."

158

"What do you want us to do, ma'am?"

"Can you run the gestalt from that far away?"

"Sure, if I use *Diablo* to boost it."

"No, I don't want the new ArIn to hit a full battle yet. She's not ready for it."

"Agreed, ma'am. I'll run it through *NightHawk*."

"Prime. It will be useful to have you out there anyway, in case of emergencies."

Andrew sent Lundeen a grim glance. He could only picture one emergency she might be thinking of. "What's the plan, Captain?"

"We will be protecting the mine, but we would prefer not to blow our cover yet. We don't really want to blow yours, either, but it would be the lesser evil."

"I can fix that." He switched to radio contact. *Manager Ludge, are you with us?*

Right here, Andrew.

Can you send me the specs for the R12-T Crew Carrier? The one with the plasma cannon. They're about our size.

That's the T3. It was totalled in the asteroid attack.

Most people won't know that.

On its way.

Thanks, Nicholas. Diablo out.

"*Diablo*, can you make us look like that?"

"A plain little thing, isn't she? Shouldn't be a problem."

"I don't intend to let anyone near."

"I can't mimic her exhaust."

"Do your best."

Okay, Captain. Diablo is busy with our camouflage. Orders?

We're going to full stealth and moving into this bunch of rocks. She indicated the spot on the battle map. *You circle around and come in from behind the two hidden ones this way.*

Got it. How close?

Now I'm sorry we didn't test your weaponry. Can you get close enough to use your plasma cannons?

159

Theoretically. I have no reason to expect Diablo to come up short of her specs.

Prime. Let's get into position and stand by.

Manager Ludge, it's in your hands. I assume you have procedures to follow.

Aye, ma'am. I'll be bringing them in one at a time. If all they're after is fuel, we'll pretend nothing is wrong.

What if they won't pay? I don't like the hidden backups. Surefire treachery somewhere in this scenario.

I have orders not to risk my personnel.

Prime. If that's the only grief they give you, we should let them go?

Your choice, ma'am, once they've left the area.

If you're in serious trouble, I'm listening very closely. We can have three or four of them in smithereens and a Commando squad in your space dock in double-quick time.

Thank you, NightHawk.

Andrew, can I borrow your ArIn, please?

Diablo standing by, ma'am.

Can you maintain camo and do a job for me?

Easy as pie, ma'am.

I need analysis of our enemy. They're too far out and hiding in too much gravel to get a good look at them.

Scanning, ma'am. Andrew, can you give me a hand?

May I drop battle augment for a moment, ma'am?

We can manage. Her scans are top priority right now.

"Lundeen, are you up for the experience of a lifetime?"

The Chief Engineer's hands clamped the arms of his couch, but he nodded.

Here we go, Diablo.

"Holy moly!"

Andrew glanced at the chief. "Impressive, hey? Now concentrate. Let's pick that one…"

They zoomed in on the lead ship and sent the images through to *NightHawk*. Then the next ship, then the next.

Flipping over to the ones behind the rocks.

Soon those images were sent as well.

Andrew chuckled. *Pete, does that first batch look familiar?*

Darn right. They chased me halfway round the Tree Planet a coupla years ago.

Ninety-five percent correlation, ma'am. Rocket/jets from the Clyde. Martin Z-67s or 69s.

Thank you, NightHawk. But the other two aren't, Andrew?

No, ma'am. The hidden ones are newer, bigger and heavier armed. Full-space rocket fighters. No plasma, but a very effective 50-mm projectile cannon and plenty of smart rocketry. Two-man crew. They're Junkers J73s. Here's the spec sheet.

Lundeen perused the files. *Those are SolarCorp products.*

Emotion: negative. Weren't they made by the old Boeing Corporation?

Just before they were bought up by SolarCorp in a secret deal. Planetoids to peanuts they're SolarCorp ships.

Stand by a moment, I have something to do. Natalia left the gestalt.

It was an unusual situation, to have the commanding officer go offline in the middle of a battle, and Andrew could feel the crew's augments on edge.

She wasn't gone long. *Our outside-the-box entity has had a novel idea.*

Lundeen grinned. *How creative of him.*

He suggests we consider who the SolarCorp ships are hiding from.

The First Officer came online. *There is no radio contact between the two groups of ships. The rocket/jets are making normal conversation, short and businesslike. The other ships are on radio silence.*

The first group is approaching the mine. Stand by to fire if necessary.

It was a long, tense wait. The three ships took up station near the mine, waiting obediently and moving in to fuel up one at a time.

Ludge had solved the payment problem by demanding that one rocket pony up before he would fuel the next.

Once the three had departed, the wait did not stop, because the two watchers did not move.

Andrew accessed *NightHawk*'s files. It took a bit of digging, but there was nothing else to do and it kept him busy. Finally he had it.

Ma'am, I think you can expect the SolarCorp ships to leave some time soon.

And why is that?

To make a long story short, this model doesn't need plutonium tri-iodide. They use krypton for reaction mass.

Lundeen was frowning over at him, but he shook his head. *I know the standard models used Xenon, but if these were shipped out in secret, they would have been manufactured before the merger came to light. And the pre-merger models modified the engines to burn krypton accelerated by an electric field created by a nuclear generator. They're bigger and slower, but far more efficient on fuel.*

And krypton appears naturally in this system. Captain O'Rourke chuckled. *Well done, Cadet.*

I did have a little help from the Chief Engineer, ma'am. It turns out he knows something after all.

And you're stuck in a very small ship with him at the moment. I'd mind my tongue if I were you.

Good advice, ma'am. Fortunately, there are no large wrenches on this vessel, so I'm pretty safe.

Captain O'Rourke widened her com to the whole crew. *The situation seems to be winding down, everyone, but we still have two bogeys in the area, so stand by your posts until they depart or make another move.*

Lieutenant, get the mine on our private band.

Manager Ludge online, ma'am.

All well over there?

No problems, ma'am. They came, they fueled and they paid in proper planetoids.

Any gossip?

Basically none. Usually the pilots want to chat, but not today.

All right. The other two ships are not going to be customers of yours, unless you've found a vein of krypton in your asteroid.

Not likely, since it exists naturally in gaseous form.

Then they're not here to buy. If they head your way, I'd be worried.

Roger that, ma'am. Standing by our weapons.

As are we.

Hold on, ma'am. Diablo has something.

Standing by, Cadet.

Engines warming, ma'am. Both ships.

Thank you, Diablo.

Forward movement, turning to starboard.

I have them, now: coming into view, continuing the turn. El Dorado, can you see them?

No, they're keeping hidden from me.

Which means they don't know we're here. Good... and good riddance. There they go.

The two space fighters had gradually increased their acceleration and slipped away on the trail of the Martin Z-67s.

Note the external fuel tanks. They can do several days of running at optimum speed. But there's a support ship somewhere in the area.

NightHawk crew, you may stand down. Diablo, I think your little training run is over for the day. Keep out of sight of our departing guests and head for home.

Aye, ma'am.

Aye, ma'am.

All right, Diablo. Andrew glanced at Lundeen. *Stay in full stealth. Let's see if we can sneak up on them.*

Silence reigned in the little cockpit as the Mustang crept from rock to rock, coming ever closer to *NightHawk*.

Diablo, report, please.

"Don't answer."

Diablo, Diablo, this is NightHawk calling Diablo.

Andrew winked at Nelson, who grinned back.

Diablo, this is Captain O'Rourke. Where are you?

163

Andrew held up a finger and entered *Diablo*'s gestalt. *Watch this, Chief.*

He highlighted a small rock orbiting nearby at considerable speed. Then he reached out with an electromagnetic field and nudged it. Then harder. Soon its course was changing, arcing towards *NightHawk*.

Just as the captain called again, it pinged off the cockpit shielding. *Andrew? Cadet Collingwood, are you throwing rocks at me?*

The cadet picked another passing stone and guided it at an even faster pace. It made a satisfying clang through *NightHawk*'s spaceframe as it struck the edge of the airlock.

"Nice shot, kid." Lundeen gave him both thumbs up.

All right, Cadet Collingwood. This is a challenge. NightHawk, full augment, please.

Andrew grinned at the Chief Engineer. "This is hardly fair, I suppose, since I'm in their gestalt while they're looking for us."

"Just don't interfere. Can you do that?"

"Yes, and *Diablo* can keep an eye out for returning space fighters at the same time."

"Go for it, kid."

Diablo moved even slower, now, calculating the trajectories of passing asteroids, plotting a zigzag course through the thickest of them.

Image: large paw extends claws and catches small pony behind rock, holds it up, hooves hanging limp.

Andrew laughed. *Okay, Chakka. You got us. We'll be home in a few minutes. He snickered. Two point four minutes, to be exact. We were verrrry close!*

That you were, son. Go back to your camouflage. I want to check the effect as you approach.

Image: clunky crew transport with open-to-space equipment bays weaving through the asteroids. As it approaches the camera, its outline wavers and begins to fade, showing a darker form underneath.

Okay, Diablo, you're busted. Thirteen hundred metres. That's pretty good.

Permission to board, NightHawk?
Lock on, Diablo.

The debrief was brief. Natalia looked at the whole crew, assembled in the mess.

"A successful operation. We gained a lot of information and didn't give away any, as far as I can figure. Comments?"

Nelson Lundeen flicked up a finger. "That Mustang is a force to be reckoned with."

The captain nodded. "And we have to test her weaponry, STAT."

"It will function according to parameters, ma'am."

"Of course, Cadet. The display will be for the benefit of the rest of the crew who have to work with her."

The captain turned to Pretoro. "Do you have any comments, sir?"

The diplomat shrugged. "Fascinating to see this unit in action. Many of us who make the big decisions should have that experience."

She grinned. "And a good demonstration of your function in, or alongside of, the gestalt. We were too focused on the enemy to realize that some of them might not be."

"And we don't even know which of the teams might become the enemy."

"Correct. Keep your eyes up and out, sir."

"I plan to do that."

"Manager Ludge, do you have anything to contribute?"

The image on the viewscreen wiped his brow. "I find it much easier to negotiate when I have backup like this."

Natalia's face lost its humour. "And soon we have to leave, taking that backup with us."

"I know. We'll take what we can get and cope on our own when we have to. As we always have."

"An admirable attitude, Manager." She regarded the next viewscreen. "Freighty?"

The toon mouse frowned. "I was not happy that the runabout camouflage deteriorated so soon. If that disguise is likely to be used more often, we will designate more memory to the image."

The captain's glance turned the answer over to Andrew.

"How much does size matter? One reason I chose the runabout was because it was similar to *Diablo*."

"The size is perfect. It's hard to hide those big engine cowlings, but perhaps we can redesign the crew carrier image in ways that most sensors cannot detect. I will consult with the factory."

"Thanks, Freighty."

The captain scanned the room. "Anything else?" She nodded. "Then we will meet tomorrow to decide what to do about the information we have gathered today."

She snapped her fingers, and Jonny appeared with a tray and glasses. "Double ration of grog tonight, *Señorita* Juanita. We've had enough sitting around. Tomorrow we go hunting."

21.   EDEN BASE

The next daywatch they headed out in the general direction the fighters had come from, all senses alert. Lieutenant Jones was now in his element, finding, cataloguing and storing any and all radio traffic, and Andrew was happy to help. It was much more fun than "Space Arm chain of command", "watch standing" and "customs and courtesies."

The two SolarCorp fighters disappeared, but the second day out Jones homed in on a series of stronger signals and found their Delacon quarry. Using stealth mode, *NightHawk* crept closer. It was a rugged mining mothership, big and ungainly but recently modified, with the three rocketjets clinging to its dorsal surface. Projectile cannons had replaced several of the repair modules, and a collection of various missiles was racked on the underside.

It was moving at good speed — for such a clumsy hulk — away from the Asteroid Belt, headed outsystem. It only took a few minutes of course evaluation to see that it was aimed for the Develocon section of the Outer Belt.

Andrew looked at the augmented VR map of the system. "They came all this way to fuel up three small ships? Doesn't compute."

His mother frowned. "I imagine they were scouting the enemy and didn't realize they'd been picked up. The SolarCorp fighters just watched until they left, then went home. Looks like a good sign to me. What do you think, Alfino?"

Pretoro nodded. "Things haven't heated up yet, or there would have been a fight."

Lundeen shook his head. "If you could call it a fight. The J73s could have wiped those little rocketjets out in about five minutes."

"A sign someone is showing restraint. What are your plans, Natalia?"

"We'll check around some more, but unless we find something soon, our best bet is to follow that behemoth home. There's more action in the Outer Belt, and we need to know what's happening there."

Even with the help of the gestalt Andrew could come up with no better plan, so after two days of fruitless search, *NightHawk* decided to break orbit and head outsystem.

No one was surprised when Lundeen's analysis of *Diablo*'s connection with *NightHawk* indicated it was strong enough to handle full acceleration. Andrew shook his head, regarding a visual of the ungainly pair. "It's a good thing aerodynamics don't matter in space. Having a twenty-five-metre appendage sticking out on her starboard bow certainly destroys *NightHawk*'s lines."

"I'm more concerned with her balance. Fortunately, *Diablo* sits tight enough to the lateral axis that we can balance her with the thrust."

Andrew nodded. "And that's why *NightHawk* has three drive ports. Balance."

The Chief smiled. "The kid's learning."

"I assume if we get into any kind of trouble, there will be time for her to separate."

Diablo put up a schematic of the docking clamps.

I can detach rather quickly, Andrew.

"Just wait for me before you blow those bolts."

Aye, Captain.

Lundeen spread his augment to ship's com. "Captain, we're cleared for action, here."

"Thanks, Chief. Accelertation in ten minutes. Take the count, *NightHawk*."

Blasting in ten minutes, ma'am.

Fuel economy kept *Diablo* docked with her mothership for the trip, and Andrew spend his time in her cockpit, refining how her sensing systems worked in conjunction with *NightHawk*'s. Between the two of them, they soon had a pretty good picture of the extent of the Develocon area of operation and the paths of the hundred or so small ships that were active there.

This time they had their meeting in the mess hall, with an image of the Develocon territories hovering over the main table.

Lieutenant Jones stood at the head, a holo pointer in his hand. "Here is what our data tells us. The miners have colonized a swath of the Outer Belt covering a ten-percent arc of its circumference."

He modified the chart, and glowing threads appeared, crisscrossing the area. "These are the main traffic patterns. Nobody is trying to hide anything. They're all using the same routes, probably through areas that hold the least debris. This tells us that there is general cooperation and sharing: a good sign. Also, if there was sniping or piracy, they would be hiding their paths and using alternate routes."

He zoomed in on a central area where many of the trails ended. "This must be a communications and administration hub. Cadet Collingwood and I have been analyzing the radio traffic — much of it is clear of code — and we have picked up a lot of information. Cadet?"

Andrew pulled the holo in tighter. "They call it 'Eden Base.' Bit of a joke, I assume. We have poor visual data, but we know it's on a planetoid large enough to be roughly spherical. Eden is about 1000 km in diameter; it could be called a moon. Once we started looking, we found several moonlets like that: small but heavy. Because of their gravity, they sweep a bare path through the gravel on their orbits, making it easier for ships to move in those lanes."

Captain O'Rourke stepped forward. "Thank you, gentlemen. Unless anyone has other ideas, I think our best course of action is to investigate their centre of operations. Comments?"

Charlie raised a hand. "Any idea of their defences?"

The captain looked at the First Officer.

He shook his head. "Radio traffic hardly mentions hostilities at all. If we didn't know better, we could be listening to a slice of Sol's Asteroid Belt, with miners going about their business and all the auxiliary industries squabbling for their share of the profits produced."

Dr. Pretoro had been sitting at the foot of the table saying nothing, but now he sat straighter. "What about their leadership?"

Natalia nodded. "Important question. The head man is called Kriver. Heavy Australian accent, colloquial speech. Doesn't say much, doesn't argue, but nobody argues back. We have no idea how he holds his power. Andrew, can you fill us in on the Australian element?"

"Eden Base and the nearby airwaves contain a lot of Aussie accents, so I did some digging in our data bases. When the opal mines of Australia began to falter about thirty years ago, their government offered retraining. Since much of the outback living conditions were similar to space, many of them turned to asteroid mining. Develocon has ties to Australia, and a considerable number of the 'graduates' of the upgrading process dropped off the map a few years ago. Now we know where they went."

The captain scanned the faces in front of her. "Hearing no objections, our next target is Eden Base. *NightHawk*, easy accel in ten minutes. Course for Eden Base.

"Aye ma'am. Course laid for the Garden of Eden."

* * *

They pulled into the shadow of a larger asteroid that orbited Eden Planetoid and observed the habitation from a distance. It was mostly underground, but the harsh, cold shadows revealed a long main corridor dotted with large domes at the junctions of short cross-tunnels. The western end was the spaceport, with several commercial vehicles nosed in. Some kind of processing plant spewed a curving stream of dust into space from the end of one tunnel.

"Eden is a heavy planetoid, mainly made of metals. Density about seven point three. That means about an eighth normal gravity on the surface."

Andrew nodded. "*NightHawk* could land there easily, with the new engine specs."

"But we don't want her anywhere near it." Captain O'Rourke regarded Andrew. "That's where *Diablo* will come in handy."

"And that old miner's suit you cadged off Ludge. Size large, as I remember. Charlie?"

"Correct."

"Gonna send him in alone?"

"That's how spies usually work."

"How about a partner?"

"Only one suit."

He grinned at her and beckoned with a crooked finger.

Half frowning, she followed.

"Ta da!" He flung open his locker.

"Where did you get that old thing? What happened to your proper suit?"

"Camouflage pattern A-for-ancient M-for-military U-for-utility. I downloaded the data from the *Clyde*'s specs and modified it to match the wear and tear on Charlie's real one."

"How did you know I was going to use it this way?"

He shrugged. "Stands to reason. Why else would you go to the trouble? Nostalgia?"

"I don't like the idea of sending you into danger."

"Neither do I, but there shouldn't be much danger, and think of the advantage of getting in there with *Diablo*'s computing power and my augment. I can download their schematics, pinpoint their weaknesses, even create access to their systems in case we need it."

"Won't they be suspicious of strangers?"

"There's a lotta people out here. Too many. Lieutenant Jones has been listening, and I've been developing filters to pick out key topics. It's like somebody was planning to start a colony, got the population transported and then lost interest, and everybody had to make a go of it on their own."

"If we're dealing with one of the shadier interplanetaries, they probably ran out of money. It wouldn't be the first time some grandiose scheme fell through, leaving a bunch of honest citizens in the lurch. Ever hear of Henry Ford?"

"Invented the assembly line or something." Andrew dug into his data bank. "Oh, yeah. That Fordlândia city in Brazil."

"So we're dealing with a lot of desperate people."

"Some of them, for sure. But nobody will have a handle on who's who. Charlie can take care of any threats, and I'll do the electronic recon. Who's going to suspect a miner with his son in tow? There's another good-sized planetoid about twenty thousand klicks away, and you can hide behind that."

"You'll be out of *NightHawk*'s augment range."

"We'll have military-band com. They won't be able to monitor that. And I'll have *Diablo*. We haven't worked in gestalt much, but she was designed to match with me, so we're making great progress. She's got loads of spare memory, and that'll help a ton."

* * *

"Eden Base, Eden Base, Eden Base, this is IOR Messenger *Diablo*, IOR Messenger *Diablo* requesting permission to land." Charlie's big hands waved in the air as he worked the radio screens in his augment, adding a touch of static and a few less obvious glitches into their transmission. He grinned at Andrew. "Just in case anyone's looking."

"Do you have to wave your mitts around like that? It makes you look demented."

"Helps me concentrate. Be happy one of them doesn't land on you."

"Right you are, Sarge. The cadet stands corrected."

Soon a response crackled back, much crisper than the one they sent out. "This is Eden Base. What's a IOR Messenger doing in the Outback?"

"Asking permission to land, Eden Base."

"State your ownership and purpose for landing."

"My owner is me and my purpose is to get a hot meal, a shot of whiskey and a chance to sell a few kilos of metal ore I picked up here and there."

"A big-time operator, are you? Well, you're not gonna sell anythin' 'ere 'nless we get more skinny than that. And I tell you right now, the only official boozer here charges like a wounded bull. Any grog that's any good, you can't afford."

"Fair enough, Eden Base. My name's Charlie Forestad and I got my son, Andy, with me. I'll talk to anybody in charge that wants my business."

"All right, Mr. Forestad. There's an auxiliary docking port out the west end of the main corridor. I'm sure you can see the blinking green lights. Line 'em up and follow 'em. Don't go anywhere once you're clipped in. You will be met."

"Roger that, Eden. And I thank you for your time and effort."

"Oh, my effort ain't nothin' compared to what yours is gonna be if you try to throw any muscle around in Eden Base."

"Warning taken in the spirit it was offered. Tell me your name and I'll buy you a cheap beer when you get off duty."

"I'm Wayne, and I might take you up on that. Be glad for news of 'ome, and a coldie always goes down good."

Andrew slipped *Diablo* onto a landing vector and let her pilot them in.

"Why did he say that? Is there a message?"

"That he knew we were recent arrivals? Probably not. Showing off his knowledge, more than likely. I take the threat the same way. Gas with a grain of sense in it."

"He's got a very specific accent. One of the Australians."

There was a gentle bump and *Diablo*'s light voice came on the com.

"Docking complete, pressure equalized, and seals tested A-OK, Andrew."

"Thank you, *Diablo*. Get out of sight and let the dock ArIn play with your dumb circuits."

"Going under cover, sir."

They slipped into their space suits, slinging the helmets back of the left shoulder where they could be jammed on quickly in case of decompression. A ringing clang on the outer airlock announced that their reception party had arrived.

Getting into practice, Andrew didn't use his augment, but pushed the "Open Door" button, and the lock slid aside.

Two men in base suits loomed in the narrow doorway, hands on belted sidearms. Their demeanor became less aggressive when Charlie moved forward, and they stood back to allow him to stand to full size.

"You Forestad?"

"No, I'm the Jolly Green Giant." He grinned. "Who were you expecting?"

The larger of the two pointed a thumb at Andrew. "Don't look now, but your pet monkey's gonna get loose."

Charlie looked down at Andrew and considered. Then he turned to the guard. "I take the long view. Some day he's gonna be bigger'n me, so I only trash him when he deserves it. Suggest you do the same. He's got a mean streak." He grabbed Andrew's shoulder and pushed him between the two men. "Come on, kid. Apparently there's somebody wants to meet us." He glanced at the smaller man. "Isn't there? Wayne seemed to think so."

"Hah! Wayne thinks way too much for his own good, and yabbers even more. But yeah, the Boss wants ta talk ta ya. 'E talks ta everyone, and they better listen. Nobody pulls a swiftie on the Boss."

"This Boss got a name? Just so I can be polite."

The guard looked Charlie up and down. "Sure. Polite. 'E'll tell you what 'e wants you ta know."

The big commando shrugged. "I guess he will." He flicked his fingers towards the access tunnel. "Lead on."

The smaller guard led out, and Andrew followed, a small amount of his mind on their journey, the greater percentage busy with codes and firewalls.

Diablo, do you see these circuits?

Aye, Captain.

Map them out and figure where they go. If you run into any interference, stop. Secrecy is more important.

Aye, Captain.

A nudge to Andrew's shoulder kept him from crashing into a wall.

"Watch where you're walkin', kid. You playin' onea them games?"

"Sorry, Dad."

"Yeah, sure you are. I catch you playin' onea them games again when you oughta be workin'..."

"Whatever you say, Dad."

"You better mean that."

You're certainly feeling your oatmeal today, Sarge.

Helps with the image. Nobody's nice to anybody in a place like this.

Andrew allowed his attention to wander to the hallway they were following. From the grim faces of the inhabitants bounding along in the light gravity, Charlie was right.

So, the people in space suits are visitors, and the locals have the base suits?

A base suit was a simplified spacesuit, light, tough and flexible, with a 4-hour air tank and a hood pulled neatly against the back, automatically deploying in case of pressure drop.

That's about it. Except the poorest... Charlie indicated a hunched, staggering man in what had once been a space suit. Doubtful if it would hold air, now.

The derelict caromed off the wall in front of the guard. "Hey, Ivan, you got a chit for me? C'mon, mate. 'Ow about a 'alf?"

Ivan gave him a half-hearted shove that bounced him off the wall again. "Just keep movin', Edson. No loiterin'."

The bounce deposited the unfortunate Edson in front of the second guard, who grabbed his arm before he had a chance to hit the floor.

"Aw, John, I'm skint. Just a quar'er..."

The larger guard lifted the beggar back onto his feet. "Say, Edson, you've 'ad a gutful. Where'd you get the metho? 'Oo's makin' it now?"

Edson escaped the grasp with unexpected dexterity and hurried away. The guards shook their heads and proceeded along the corridor. Ivan glanced back at Charlie. "Old duffer's got a kangaroo loose in the top paddock. Used to be a good pilot, but he lost his nerve."

Interesting social interplay.

Charlie peered over his shoulder at the beggar. *They weren't mean. Just no sympathy.*

Times are tough in the Garden of Eden.

Charlie looked down at Andrew. *I wonder if we're heading to meet the serpent.*

As they bounded down the corridor, each junction brought them to a larger segment, each one dug deeper into the planet. Two hundred metres along they came to a huge dome with a transparent top for the last ten metres, showing the Milky Way above.

Good design for the human psyche.

If you say so, kid.

I do. People weren't meant to live underground.

Weren't meant to live in space, either.

Can't argue with that.

Their guides turned into a side corridor that led them to a simple security gate. The larger guard, John, swept the pad with his palm and ushered them through. The hallway beyond was as featureless and functional as the rest of the architecture.

If this is the real boss, he doesn't go for pomp and circumstance, does he?

They stopped in front of a door with no markings, and Ivan knocked.

"Enter." The voice was sharp, demanding. They obeyed.

The room was larger than Andrew expected, its ceiling curving up towards the top of the dome. Centred on the back wall was a wide desk covered with electronic screens, devices and enterpads.

The blond-haired man behind the desk leaned back in his chair and regarded them.

"So, what we got 'ere?"

Charlie grabbed the collar of Andrew's suit and hauled him upright. "Miners, sir. Lookin' for a market for our product."

"What are you producing?"

"Raw ore at the moment, sir. Just samples. Mostly nickel and iron, but some other stuff might be more valuable. We aren't in production, yet, but we're workin' several promising seams."

"And just where'd you find these seams?"

"Upspin about five degrees and thirteen thousand klicks outsystem." He held out a large hand. "I know what you're thinkin'. We was real careful. No tags, no beacons, no sign of anybody else workin' anywheres near."

"Got a name, miner?"

176

"Charlie Forestad. Kid's Andy. Got a wife and two cousins out at the mine."

The man rose and stretched out a fist. "I'm Kriver. My word's law around 'ere. It ain't democratic, and I don't intend it to be. Got a problem with that?"

Charlie bumped his calloused knuckles against Kriver's. "Nope. You play fair with me, you'll have no trouble."

"Good." The station boss rubbed his hand. "Because anyone who gives us strife will soon regret it." He glanced left, then right, and his two goons moved a step closer.

Andrew slipped closer to Charlie. *Knock me over.* "Hey, Dad, this is boring. Can we go shopping, now?"

Charlie did not turn. "Shut up. This is serious business."

"But you promised..."

Without looking, the commando swung a backhand, catching Andrew in the shoulder. His suit cushioned the blow, but he fell anyway, contriving to hit his back against a nearby desk. A hissing sound resulted.

Andrew pawed at his back ineffectually. "Dad...!"

Charlie spun him around and closed off his air valve. "Didn't you check that before you put it on?"

"I told you it wasn't workin' right, Dad. Remember?"

Charlie raised a threatening hand, and Andrew cringed.

Then the commando turned back to the station boss. "Sorry. Where were we?"

Instead of replying, Kriver waved a hand in front of his face. "What's that smell?"

Charlie frowned. "I dunno. Just ship's air from the kid's tank, I guess. Why?"

"Your ship smells like fish all the time?"

"Don't think so. I guess the refill station's a bit close to the galley." Charlie moved a step closer to Kriver. "Look, mate. You don't hit me as the kind of man to play silly games. Now you've met me, you've taken my measure and you know games won't impress me, either. If you're trying to create a workin' economy out here at the end of nowhere, you need people like me: I'm well trained, I work hard, I produce and I don't go lookin' for trouble unless it comes lookin' for me. Now let's get down to business, which is what I came for, or I'll take my business elsewhere."

The man looked up at him. "There is nowhere else."

"There's always somewhere else, and if there isn't, then I'll change my business. Do you follow?"

Kriver waved a hand in front of his nose. "Easy on. No reason to get stroppy. Tell you what. You take your smelly kid out of my office and go down to the Module Three. Talk to Johansen about metals." He sat in his chair and leaned back. "I'm trying to make a go of this colony, and you've got the same chance as any man to do well. I don't mess with the merchants. They pay their taxes, they do their business any way they choose and nobody whinges."

They're trying to crack your augment. Ignore them. I'll send them chasing their tails.

Charlie tilted his head sideways. "Now the other shoe drops. What kind of taxes do I pay?"

"None. I've got no way to keep track of every small-time operator, nor the least desire to do so. The product comes through 'ere, and I tax it where I 'ave control of it. There's plenty for everyone if no one gets greedy. You register your asteroid with Johansen and you stick to your claim and nobody will come within a thousand klicks or they answer to me. Got it?"

The big commando nodded. "Sounds like a good way to run things." He turned. "And now if your fancy retainers will get out of the road, Andy and me have to see a man about some ore samples."

"I hope we'll be seeing more of you."

The Commando spun around. "Oh, yes, and I do have a military augment. It ain't new, but it's still got all the security it had when I finished my tour and any extras I could afford since. So don't think your piddly system is going to slice it. Nice try, though."

Charlie continued towards the door. The two goons spread apart and he exited, his spacer's low-gravity glide as close to a stride as you can get. Andrew followed, trying to keep a straight face.

Gee, Charlie, you're getting to be quite a diplomat.

Debrief back home, kid. Concentrate.

Andrew read the commando's vitals. For all his graceful movements, he was keyed up, his eyes searching every corner, underfoot and overhead as well. Sobered, the boy stepped up his own surveillance, recording everything he could see, hear or smell for later analysis.

Module Two, even larger than the skylight dome, contained the market area. The walls were lined with small cabins, each with a vertical rolling security door. Wares of all sorts, from food to electronics to basic mechanical tools, were displayed in neat rows or in disordered bins. The centre zone was jammed with kiosks offering similar merchandise. Faces peered out from alleys behind the shops, leading Andrew to wonder what other, less legitimate goods were available. He played the gawking yokel to cover his surveillance, and Charlie hurried him through.

Greased by Kriver's approval, Charlie's conversation with the metal merchant in Module Three went smoothly, giving the boy time to explore the station's electronics more fully and modify them as he chose.

"Okay, kid. Let's get back to the shoppin' mall. Yer Mum's hopin' for a present, I'd guess."

"Sure Dad. I know exactly the colour of ribbon she wants." He pulled out a handheld spectrometer. "Checked her best dress specifically."

Charlie ruffled his hair, chuckling, and he ducked away as if embarrassed.

After one small, "We can't afford that crap," scene in an ice cream parlour that sold a far inferior product to what Jonny turned out, they purchased some wilted-looking vegetables and week-old bread, exclaiming over how "Mum" was going to love the fresh food.

Then they loaded their treasures into *Diablo*'s airlock, closed up and headed out, retracing their inbound trajectory into the scramble of asteroids around the station. Once they were out of range of curious security tracers, they rendezvoused with *NightHawk*.

Charlie went to report to the captain while Andrew detoured to deposit his gifts in the galley.

Jonny sniffed at the bread. "Not a bad loaf. French toast for breakfast tomorrow. You'll never notice how stale it is." She flopped a bunch of wilted carrots back and forth. "Must be time to make soup stock." Then she grinned at him. "*Graçias, muchacho.* Thank you for thinking of me."

He tipped her a salute and headed for the chartroom, where he found Charlie perched on Andrew's usual stool, finishing his description of the political setup of the station.

"So you think this Kriver has everything pretty well in hand?"

"I do. Except for the two goons he sent to escort us, there's little military presence. Sure, he could be fighting fifteen brush fires out in the asteroids, but I saw no evidence of it." His eyes turned towards Andrew for comment.

"I concur, ma'am. A small hospital ward with only three patients registered…let me see…one broken leg, one radiation overdose and one with undiagnosed symptoms, not likely contagious."

She smiled. "Did you download their whole database?"

"I didn't have time for that. But I can give you the schematics of their internal security, their physical plant and their automated defences. I left us a few backdoors to slip through, but I was unfamiliar with the configuration, so I kept it simple. *NightHawk* and Chakka and I need to sit down with their system programming and figure out some places to slide a couple of Trojans in, and I've got a prime Fleming I've been dying to try out."

The debriefing continued for another hour, and at the end the captain sat back and stretched. "Your analysis is that this is a well-run base with a stable economy in a bare-bones sort of fashion."

"Yes, ma'am. We'll need more information about the rest of their operation, though. There must be a fleet base somewhere."

"That shouldn't be hard to find. Freighty gave us all the high-activity points, and there's only five that our survey has confirmed. And this Kriver runs it all?"

"No indication anyone else is above him."

"Thanks for the good work. Sergeant, you must be quite an actor."

Charlie blushed. "Thanks, ma'am." Then his face straightened. "You know, he didn't sound like a bad guy. I mean, he wasn't any tougher on us than a lot of other bureaucrats would be. It sounds like he's trying to make a go of a tough situation."

"Let's not come to any conclusions based on a first meeting. You two have had a long day. Hit Jonny up for something special for supper tonight. I've already okayed it."

The spies traded looks and grinned.

"Thanks, ma'am. Nice to know we're appreciated."

"Gee, thanks, Mum."

They both saluted and left the chart room smartly. In the slideway outside, Charlie made a quick try at tripping Andrew, who floated over the outstretched boot and sprinted away, laughing.

"You'll have to be faster than that to catch me, Dad."

Charlie laughed. "I don't have to follow that train of thought too far before I run into a large, solid wall."

"Huh? Oh, you mean the captain. She ain't that tough."

"Maybe not to you." The commando slowed, and Andrew slipped alongside.

"I've served under her for three years, now. When the chips are down, there's nobody on this ship would stand in her way."

"Of course not. She's the captain."

"Oh, no." Charlie shook his head. "Look, kid, it maybe isn't my place to tell you, but you don't lead a Commando Squad unless you can outfight any one of them and hold your own against any two. I can take her two out of three times in a barehand fight, but you give her a weapon — any weapon you choose to name — and her odds go way beyond even. And with a gun," he shrugged his heavy shoulders, "I wouldn't make a try."

"Sure, but she's so...nice..."

A weighty hand descended on his shoulder. "That's the bonus. We're all proud to be serving under her, and you oughta be extra proud to be her son."

"Oh, I am, no fear of that." He frowned as a thought hit him. "I just hope I match up."

Charlie shoved him along the corridor. "You're doing fine so far. Let's go see what Jonny's got to reward us."

22. ACTION IN THE ASTEROIDS

They left the Outer Belt in a long, curving sweep that passed near several other action points. With *Diablo* added to the gestalt, the quality of their scans was improved. Most of their time was taken up by analysis of the data that was pouring in from the motley collection of ships and bases in the system.

The chart room was no longer big enough for their expanded team, so the mess became their meeting place. The crew knew how to disappear when sensitive material was discussed and how to forget anything they might have heard.

One afternoon they were regarding a virtual view of the Barnard System suspended above the table. In re-ti there was nothing to see, but everyone's augment agreed it was there, so there it was.

Lieutenant Jones highlighted a section of the Inner Asteroid Belt about a third of the way around the star from the mine. "Something is going on in there that they don't want anyone to know about."

Dr. Pretoro frowned. "Can you define 'something' and tell us who 'they' are?"

Captain O'Rourke smiled. "Those are the burning questions. What evidence do you have, Adrian?"

"It's more the evidence I don't have, ma'am."

"Lieutenant Jones, that is a positively opaque statement. I'm afraid your incisive mind has become contaminated by association with this crew. You'll have to explain."

The First Officer allowed himself a small twitch of the lips. "It's this way, ma'am. I've been monitoring radio traffic and engine radiation. *NightHawk* is keeping a close-to-re-ti map of the system population." He gestured to the subject area. "This morning, over the space of a few hours, a large number of signals disappeared. All in that section of the Inner Belt. Which would suggest an organized dive into radio silence."

Andrew grinned. "Or they all blew up at the same time."

Jones kept a straight face. "If it were a coup of that magnitude, the rest of the system would have lit up with cheering. They hardly noticed. In fact, without the help of *Diablo*, I doubt if anyone could notice. Occam's Razor would suggest a planned disappearance. Engine radiation is less exact, but many ships seem to be gathering right...there." The First Officer pointed.

Pretoro scribed a circle around the area. "And that's where we suspect the SolarCorp holdouts from the Develocon takeover are hiding."

"Right." Natalia drew a vector. "And they aren't that far away from El Dorado 12."

"The mine could become collateral damage." The Freighty avatar on the viewscreen produced a large metal umbrella and crouched under it.

Manager Ludge frowned out of the next screen. "We've had enough of that already, thank you very much."

"You're pretty well protected at the moment, Nicholas. I hope we can settle this situation before it breaks into open warfare."

"So do I."

The captain turned to Pretoro. "Do you see any chance of a negotiated settlement?"

He shook his head. "I'm always optimistic in that respect, but since we have no evidence of contact at all between the two parties, I have only peripheral data to base my judgement on. Few of these people are soldiers. You and Freighty took care of the only major force in the area last year. There will be pilots, ground crew and security men, but they are mostly followers, not leaders. We really need more information about who is out here. Our theory that we are dealing with the remnants of a failed colony attempt needs to be proven."

Andrew glanced at Lieutenant Jones. "Have you made any progress with the sound files I gave you?"

"Not much."

There were blank looks around the table, so the First Officer explained. "Cadet Collingwood kept a re-ti recording of the ambient sound in the larger domes. I've been sorting through for intelligible speech."

Pretoro frowned. "That sounds like a frustrating task."

"It would have been in the old days, sir. I would have had to sit and listen to them, over and over, and transcribe what I heard. But *NightHawk* and I have developed...I don't know what to call them...intuitive algorithms, I suppose." He smiled. "I do the same job. I listen. But when we're in gestalt, the individual conversations seem to pop out. I note them, and *NightHawk* remembers them. Then we apply a series of filters, and..." He regarded his audience."...well, in the end, we have anything that means anything to the present situation."

Natalia raised her eyebrows. "And what do you have?"

His pleased look disappeared. "Not that much. Later we'll run the file through at broader parameters, but right now we're just getting a general impression that the population of Eden Base is satisfied that 'things' are settling down commercially, but worried about the SolarCorp military mind. There is a mercantile feel to the group, skewed by the fact that a lot of the time we were listening in the marketplace. Peace is good for business. It was instructive that there was little complaint about the base administration. Boss Kriver would be happy with our findings."

The captain nodded. "So, no rebellion inside the rebellion. We're getting a picture of this Boss Kriver, and it doesn't look too bad." *Charlie, where are you? We need your input, here.*

On my way, ma'am.

NightHawk was a small ship. The commando sergeant appeared in the doorway almost immediately. "Yes, ma'am?"

"Take a seat, Sergeant. Tell the rest what you make of this Kriver person. Personal reaction."

Fraser shrugged. "Well..."

"Stop right there, Sergeant. What does that shrug mean?"

Charlie frowned. "Put it that way, ma'am, I think I'm supposed to have a specific opinion, but I'm not feeling it very strongly."

"Exactly. What is the answer you think I want?"

"Well...given the circumstances, he was like the enemy, you know? And I'm expected to see him that way."

"But you don't."

184

He shrugged again, then glanced at her. "I don't know how to describe it, ma'am, but I didn't get that kind of...I don't know..."

"...intuitive reaction."

Eyes turned to Andrew. He nodded. "I know exactly what he means. I got the same. He just doesn't feel like an enemy. And it isn't only his folksy accent. He seems a decent guy. Right, Charlie?"

The commando turned his gaze on his captain. "That's it, ma'am. I'm sorry."

"No, Charlie, you're not sorry, you're honest. I don't want to hear what I want to hear. I want your opinion."

The sergeant grinned. "I thought he was an all-right guy doing his job. I pushed him a bit, and he let it slide. I'd say he's torn between the need to keep control and his desire to create commerce in his area. I go in there like a crotchety but capable miner, and he lets the crotchety pass in hopes I'll feed his merchants good product."

"Cadet Collingwood, any comment?"

Andrew grinned and shrugged as well. "Nothing to argue with there, ma'am. Kriver and his lot are like the Girondines trying to hold to the middle line in a difficult situation. Not a guillotine in sight. In fact, when Charlie slammed me into the desk, I think I caught a look of concern from him."

The captain's face darkened. "Charlie, what...?"

"Part of the act, ma'am. I needed an excuse to let loose a little of Jonny's fried fish smell."

There was complete silence as the listeners tried to make sense of this.

"You had to be there, ma'am."

Natalia laid her hands with exaggerated gentleness on the table. "Juanita?"

The cook appeared in the galley doorway. *"Si, señora?"*

"I gather your fish has been instrumental in the success of the latest mission."

"Ah. Fish is very healthy, *señora*. I keep telling everyone."

"In this case it seems to have been. Thank you, Juanita."

"De nada, señora."

Natalia waved the cook away. "I think this debriefing has gone on for too long. Dr. Pretoro, do you have anything to add?"

"No, I confess to being out of my depth. Fish?"

"I borrowed some of the galley aroma the other day when Juanita was cooking fish, and carried it in my suit tank as corroboration of our cover story. It will be in my report, sir. I'm sure you'll understand."

"Thank you, Cadet. I look forward to the finer details of your mission."

The captain regarded Lieutenant Jones. "Any sign at all of negotiations going on?"

"No, ma'am. Either there's no communication between the two opposing parties, or they're using channels we can't find."

"How likely is that?"

"Not very, ma'am. I'm of the 'no communication' opinion, myself."

Pretoro frowned. "Which usually isn't a good thing."

Natalia laid her hands on the table. "Well, we have a lot of fuel and not much time, so I suggest we take a sweep past another couple of Kriver's outposts on the way back to the Inner Belt and check their readiness to repel an invasion. Whatever SolarCorp is up to is high on my list, and another item on my orders from Space Arm is to check the Tree Planet. I can't believe that none of these people have landed there."

The ambassador raised his eyebrows. "But the Tree Planet is quite a distance inside the Inner Belt. Won't that be a long detour?"

She smiled. "As it happens, the SolarCorp area is ninety degrees upspin from our present position. A straight line from here to there cuts inside the Inner Belt and that's the closest we'll come to the Tree Planet on this trip. It will save fuel if we run our inspection now."

His brow smoothed. "I'm always ready to let the experts do their jobs."

23.   THE OPEN AIR

"Cadet Collingwood and Sergeant Jacobs to the chart room, please."

The two met in the slideway and exchanged glances. "Any idea?"

Andrew shrugged. "It must be official, or she'd have just used the augment."

Then they were standing in front of the captain, and it was too late to speculate. But she smiled. "Don't look like kids with their hands in a cookie jar. I've got a job for you two."

Once again they glanced at each other, this time with relief.

Natalia motioned Toni to take the chair and regarded them both. "Andrew, I want you doing some independent work, and I have a mission you're suited to lead. Jacobs, you've had plenty of experience shepherding inexperienced junior officers around, nudging them into the right decisions, that sort of thing."

The sergeant hesitated, then grinned. "Babysitting service."

"Essentially, but this will be different. There are three aspects to this mission. First, you take *Diablo* to the Tree Planet and do a scan for any invaders. Sorry. It's officially called 'Arborea,' now. That's Andrew's mission because it's his ship and Toni, you're under his command on board. However, once you land, you'll be in charge, like you would in any Commando operation. Your job will be to assess the planet's biosphere for livability. Full armour for security reasons, but helmets off because of the research. I'm sending Chakka with you for protection as well. We're dealing with some rather large predators."

Andrew shook his head. "But don't you want to keep Chakka for your gestalt on *NightHawk*?"

She regarded him. "Research for Space Arm is a secondary objective. I don't intend to send my crew or my son into more danger than necessary in order to collect data. And in case anybody might ask, I have another objective." She swivelled her chair to fact the commando. "Sergeant, if you decide to apply to Auguar Corps, I want you to know that you have made the right decision. I also want to be sure that you get accepted. The only way to assure both is to send you on auguar patrol. And in this, you will be back in the tender care of Andrew, because he's the expert in augments. And Chakka's best buddy."

She gave them a moment to think. "As you can see, this will be a complex situation, but knowing your history, you two seem to be able to function at a fairly convoluted level of social interaction, so I'm sure you'll do fine."

Again, Andrew met Toni's eyes and was gratified to see a flush creeping up her cheek to match the heat in his.

Then the sergeant's back stiffened. "The only way this might become a problem, ma'am, is if we encounter danger, and in that case, there will be no question who is in charge." She focused on Andrew. "Will there, Cadet?"

He, too, stood at attention. "No, ma'am. As long as the danger is physical, I will be completely under your orders."

Suspicion crept across Toni's face, but the captain slapped the table to cut her off. "As I said, a complex situation. You'll handle it. We enter orbit in sixteen hours. There's a folder in the Arborea file listing the data you're supposed to collect. Toni, you start putting equipment together, and Andrew, get on the maps and the long-range vision and look for likely sites. You'll be downplanet for twenty-four to seventy-two hours."

In unison, they snapped her a salute, did an about face and marched out, Sergeant Jacobs somehow ending up in front.

* * *

A day later Andrew was standing in an alien meadow, *Diablo*'s hull clicking softly as it cooled behind him. He hooked his helmet to his belt and took a deep breath. The air had a musty, organic smell, sort of familiar…of course. Hydroponics. But much…wilder.

Toni grinned. "Good to breathe real air again."

"Yeah, but I just realized I've only been on rough ground once, in the middle of a firefight, and I didn't do too well. Last year I was on the base the whole time I was downplanet, and the only grass I walked on was lawn."

"I'm sure you'll catch on. A mouthful of gravel is a great teacher. I'm heading out to the north by that grove of trees. If you want to stay closer to the ship, you can pick the botanical samples."

"Aye, ma'am. I'll get right on that." He gathered some vials from the equipment bin and stepped gingerly out.

Chakka was not so introspective. He tore off at full acceleration, clods of pseudo-grass flying up behind him. He roared around in a circle and came lolloping back, the picture of feline glee.

"Hey, boy. Is this fun, or what?" Regarding the nearby ground, Andrew chose a careful path, avoiding the bushes and taller clumps of grass-like plants.

Image: tortoise clumping slowly along.

"All right, all right. I'm coming." He strode out more quickly, the soil spongy and uneven beneath his boots. However, after a few missteps and minor trips, he realized that his balance was up to the job.

Chakka trotted up beside him. *Image: clumsy cub trotting, tumbling, getting up and forging on.*

"Okay, I'm on it. Give me a moment to get used to this." He risked a slow trot, his breath quickening with the exercise and the excitement. Soon his pace settled. "Hey, it's better if I move faster!"

Image: old-fashioned two-wheeled transport, riders in bright coloured suits and streamlined helmets.

"What's that? Oh. Bicycles. Any contraption that needs high speed to stay upright is rather scary."

Emotion: feline disdain.

"Maybe I ought to get Freighty to whip me up a bicycle. We could invent a safer one." A brief coldness washed through him at the memory of where he was now, with his only oasis of real security accelerating away at almost light speed.

All at once something grabbed his foot, and he found himself diving face-first to the ground. His training took over, and he converted the fall into a roll.

Emotion: feline laughter.

189

"Pah!" He clambered to his feet, pawing dead foliage out of his mouth. He turned back to investigate. A trailing vine stretched between two bushes, looped across the soil towards him.

"So! It was you. Hah."

He turned and jogged on, his eyes on his path.

Cadet, this is NightHawk. Report.

He stopped. *Reviewing downplanet ambulatory procedures, ma'am.*

You're what?

Learning to walk all over again, ma'am.

Of course. How are you doing?

Took my first header. No problem. Chakka's laughing at me, so the worst injury is to my feelings.

Good for your personal development, but I'm sorry, I have to break in on your fun.

Oh please, Mum. Stop me before I hurt myself. What's up?

Nothing urgent, but the Lieutenant is getting some interesting radio traffic I'd like to look into.

Are you recalling us already?

No, we're just popping out of orbit to get better triangulation. You and Sergeant Jacobs continue with your mission. We'll be back to pick you up, or you can catch us.

Emotions: pride and anxiety.

He tried to hide how he felt, but it was difficult.

Emotion: indulgent chuckle. I'd be worried if you weren't a bit anxious, Cadet. You're in a good patrol. Keep your eyes up and out, and I'd suggest staying in gestalt with Diablo.

Keeping my eyes up is problematic when the vegetation keeps winding around my feet.

Part of your assignment. Learn to walk again. See you soon.

Righto, ma'am. Over and out.

Emotion: laughter. Not much chance of either of those.

Her presence faded in his augment, but when he raised his awareness, he could feel a shadow of her mind just beyond conscious thought.

A louder, closer communication broke through.

Hey, Cadet. Wanna go on a hunting expedition?

Hunting?

Yeah. I've got tracks over here.

Feline emotion: eager desire to hunt.

Take it easy, Chakka. They aren't very big.

I'm on my way, Sergeant.

Homing in on her presence, he turned west and jogged slowly and carefully through taller bushes towards the copse she was exploring. He soon found the right balance of awareness between his path and his wider surroundings and picked up his pace. He cut around the end of the clump of trees and slowed. The commando was bent over perusing the ground at her feet. She gestured him to approach.

Quiet, now.

I didn't say anything.

No, but you sound like an elephant on hockey skates.

Sorry, I'm not so good at this anymore. What are we hunting?

She pointed at a patch of softer earth. *That.*

"That" was a line of indentations in the soil, semicircular, about the size of his outstretched hand.

I assume those are tracks. What do you think made them?

She grinned at him. *No idea, but from the size and depth I'd say something large and heavy. That's what's so much fun about hunting. You're never sure what you might catch.*

How do we proceed?

We follow them as quietly as possible, keeping an eye out in case our quarry circles around and ambushes us.

I see. Well, lead on. Chakka, on guard, please.

Emotion: confidence.

The tracks continued for a few metres, but then the animal moved into taller grass and the trail disappeared.

What do we do now?

Jacobs was scanning ahead. *We cast further, predicting from the course of the old spoor... yes, over there...*

...and the lesson went on. They never found the original prey, but allowed themselves to be distracted by other evidence of the local

191

fauna. Andrew was having so much fun that *Diablo*'s warning shocked him.

Alert. Predators.

He snapped into battle augment, receiving a full picture of their surroundings. Sure enough, three large heat signatures and four smaller ones showed off to the east, creeping in their direction.

The sergeant's hand was on her sidearm, and her head was up, scanning the area. "Let's get back to the ship. No rush. Don't fall, just keep moving."

Andrew calmed himself and strode out, trying to maintain a view of his footing and his surroundings.

Predatory behaviour confirmed.

The creatures had changed course. One of them picked up speed in a possible attempt to cut them off.

Chakka...

Image: stocky, four-legged creature sliding through light brush.

Jacobs accessed the augment. *Andrew, tell Chakka to fade, keeping between us and the outlier.*

You just told him.

Emotion: agreement.

The others are holding back. I don't think they're hunting. Perhaps curious.

ETA at Diablo one minute, thirty seconds.

Steady, Andrew. We'll make it. Toni now had her handgun up and out, muzzle searching.

They moved into an open area, and their pursuers began to show through the scattered bushes. Andrew got a picture of a four-legged animal the size of a large dog, but with a shorter neck and heavier shoulders.

Image, fuzzy and wavering: tall beings on two legs beside large silver rock.

Chakka, did that come from you?

Emotion: negative.

Reaching the Mustang, they backed up to the open hatch, their weapons at the ready. The three adult creatures moved closer through the screening brush, spreading wide.

Chakka, do you see the little ones?

Emotion: feline puzzlement.

Diablo?

Image: four faint heat sources behind the right-hand adult.

Chakka, investigate.

Image: wind blowing from left to right.

Thanks, Sergeant.

They watched through the gestalt as the auguar slunk behind the approaching predators.

Four blurred images overlapping: large, shiny creature towering above.

Emotion: fear/curiosity

Image: Four small versions of the adults staring up.

Emotion: fear and protective rage!

Watch out, Chakka. They've spotted you!

The three adults spun into the open and charged towards where the auguar stood over their young. Now that Andrew had a clear view he could see that any resemblance to a dog ended with basic shape. The creatures had thick legs that bent at weird angles, and their whole bodies were covered by rhino-like plated armour.

They skidded to a stop in front of the auguar, prowling in antagonistic poses, revealing triangular teeth in several rows like a shark's. The eyes were far apart on their heads, like those of Earth herbivores. There was no evidence of nostrils or ears.

Image: huge being looming high above.

Emotion: caution.

The adults slowed, circling the auguar and their young, afraid to come any closer.

Image: young moving rapidly.

Immediately the smaller creatures tumbled towards the largest of the three adults. Chakka watched them go.

Once their young were safe, the adults turned to the intruder. Their mouths closed, and they stepped forward more calmly. Again they spread out. Chakka sidled to prevent enclosure.

Emotion: dominance.

Overlapping images, melding into a single image: huge silver creature looming high above.

The creatures stopped as one, lowering their heavy bodies to the ground.

Chakka paced forward and sniffed at the lead animal. It turned its muzzle away but made no other response.

Emotion: acceptance.

Emotion: relief.

Hesitantly the animal brought its head up and rose, taking care to stay low. It moved towards the auguar and touched his leg with one hoof-like paw. Then it backed away, and the other two did the same.

Andrew came to his senses. *"NightHawk, this is Collingwood. Where are you?"*

One-seventy around the planet from you, 400 klicks altitude. What's up?

Get the captain to access this video feed.

I'm here, Andrew. Is this what I think it is?

Yes, ma'am. We may have a First Contact situation here.

What?

They're communicating, ma'am. Through the augments. It's all very blurry, like the frequencies are off a bit, but I can recognize images. These are probably the predators we observed on our last visit. Chakka has dominated them, and they're getting to know each other. Jacobs and I are staying out of it.

Any sign of intelligence?

Standard predator pack behaviour, ma'am.

Tools, language?

He looked closer. *Hoof-like paws. No vocalization at all. The leader gave the young a direct visual order through the augment, and they obeyed immediately.*

I'm not getting any of that from NightHawk.

194

Toni cut in. *I'm not getting much of it, ma'am. Just a jumble of emotions and images. I'm using the Diablo video feed to monitor them.*

Right. Let's minimize the contact. Leave Chakka in charge, and you two get back into your ship.

Leaving the hatch open, the humans retreated inside and sat in the cockpit watching the scene outside on the viewscreens. Chakka was being introduced to the young ones, who showed no fear and seemed intent on chewing the feet off his space armour. Finally the pack leader sent them a blurred image impossible to interpret, and they banded together and trotted in their bumbling style back the way they had come. The leaders, after another ritual touching of Chakka's leg, followed.

Might as well return to the ship, Chakka.

Emotion: acceptance.

When the auguar was back on his couch, Andrew and the commando sergeant looked at each other.

"Well, that was interesting. I wonder how they appeared from nowhere?"

"I am tracking their heat signatures, Sergeant. They're going around the end of that clump of trees and...there they go. One at a time, they disappear."

Jacobs nodded. "A den."

Andrew shook his head. "What about those images? Fantastic."

"What images, Cadet Collingwood?"

"The images they were sending each other over the augments. The images we picked up."

"I didn't pick up any images. There was a lot of interference."

"None?"

"No. I tried scanning other augment bands, but what I got was indecipherable."

"Well, that's interesting. Sergeant, what were you picking up?"

She shook her head. "Nothing I could identify. Something visual, but it was mostly a blur. I certainly got a jolt of emotion when they thought Chakka had their young. That was unmistakable."

Chakka? Images?

Images: blurred, recognizable as animals, but with little detail.

"That's really interesting. I got reasonable pictures, Chakka got poor quality images, you could only read emotions and *Diablo* got basically nothing. Conclusion?"

The sergeant shrugged. "Above my pay grade."

He grinned. "Augments. Mine are completely organic, Chakka has some, yours are mostly electronic, and *Diablo*'s are advanced, but mostly metal."

"Stands to reason."

NightHawk to Diablo.

Diablo here.

What's happening?

Nothing, ma'am. Our visitors have gone back inside their den to discuss the situation. We are standing by.

Do you get the impression that they are actually discussing it?

I got no rational thought from them. Just images and emotions.

All right. Best if we cause as little disturbance in their life as possible. You skip out of there as quietly as you can and find your samples elsewhere. I think we have a new job for our ambassador.

Aye ma'am. Diablo preparing for stealth liftoff.

NightHawk out.

At Andrew's prompting, the Mustang lifted her skirts above her knees and tiptoed away.

24. AMBASSADOR TO THE BARWOLVES

Organizing the fate of a new species is a serious business, but the initial stages were simple.

"Let me get this straight." Alfino Pretoro laid his hands flat on the mess table and stared at them. "After all our discussion about authority on the trip out here, you're turning this situation completely over to me?"

Natalia smiled. "That's right. Don't you think it's a good idea?"

Pretoro lifted his hands, palms towards her. "Of course, but I don't see why you do. After all, you're the only human we know of who has ever handled a first contact before, and you had complete success."

She shook her head. "It wasn't a first contact, because Andrew and his mother had been living with Freighty for seven years. In the second place, I can't claim success because we still have no idea how this business with the factory will to pan out. And in the third place, I don't want to go through that again. I will if I have to, but I'm a Commando Squad Leader and Ship's Captain, and I much prefer my chosen professions."

"Fair enough. You know, I'm not used to working with people like you."

"People like me?"

"Like all of you. My business is power. Manipulation, advantage. Winners and losers. Never give any control away."

She shook her head. "And mine is all about the proper function and control of power to achieve an objective, and we all win or lose together. When I set you straight on my orders, I was inviting you into my world." She flicked a hand in the direction of the Arborea. "And now you can have that one. Do you know what this is going to mean?"

He grinned. "A whole lot of work for a great number of bureaucrats and scientists."

"And what it means to us is that my duty just got five times as hard. Not only do I have to deal with a rebellion that I can't find, now I have to quarantine a whole planet and make it stick with only one ship and one fighter craft."

"And how do you plan to proceed?"

"First step complete. I dump as much as I can in your lap."

"I see."

"But I did check the protocols. We start by setting out beacon satellites broadcasting the quarantine order. Which is a problem in itself, since that will announce our presence in the Barnard System. After that, it's only a matter of policing the area."

"Only."

"That's my job. Policing. A subject that actually appeared several places in my training manuals."

"And my job is to put a report on these creatures together and send it to Space Arm as quickly as possible." He ran a hand through his hair. "The reality of the time lag is beginning to come home to me."

Andrew raised a finger. "I may be able to help with that."

"In what way?"

"Freighty, will you join us, please?" He sent the invitation through the augment as well.

Micha the Mouse appeared on the viewscreen. "Yes, Andrew?"

"What's the fastest way I have of getting an urgent diplomatic message to Space Arm?"

The toon frowned. "The usual way is…"

"I don't want the usual way, rodent. I want Freighty's Pony Express. How long will it take? Fifteen days?"

"I have no authorization from my principal to use that system, but yes, about that."

"But if you send him a data package, and he decides to pass it on?"

"That would be up to him."

"Perfect. I'll have the message ready ASAP."

Pretoro regarded Andrew quizzically. "And you think he'll indulge us? I was told any advances in technology would take a great deal of negotiation. I expect that to be one of my main areas of work."

Andrew mimed changing hats. "Speaking as an executive of the Factory 4-80 Consortium, I can tell you that while we may not provide humanity with certain technology, any way we can use our own resources to assist the Planetary Community in the development of amiable relations between all parties will be accomplished with the utmost speed. Please make up your message home, Ambassador, and my company will expedite it."

"I see the advantages of your position." Pretoro smiled, but only for a moment. "Try to remember what hat you're wearing, Cadet."

Natalia grinned. "It's going to stay complicated, Alfino. I want you to meet your clients, so Andrew and Sergeant Jacobs will take you downplanet tomorrow while we rig the quarantine buoys. I think you should have Jackson and Chakka along as well. A little crowded in *Diablo*, but you're only going for the day."

The ambassador smiled. "It would be good to get out in the open for a while. I'm still having dreams of Otherwhere."

* * *

They had only been on the ground for an hour, mapping out the activities of a new pack of barwolves, when *Diablo* sent an alarm.

Gunfire.

Andrew slammed into battle augment.

Where?

Thirty kilometres north.

He glanced at Toni, eyebrows raised. He had absolutely no idea what to do.

The commando did. *Nature of fire?*

Single shots.

Threat analysis?

Small bore, high velocity. Possible sniper.

Best analysis?

199

More than one, firing at random. Hunters?

No conversation was needed. They sprinted for the ship, gathering equipment. Pretoro appeared in the hatch, and they tossed everything to him, running back for more.

A quick scan to make sure nothing was left behind, and they were in the air.

Andrew banked the ship west. "We'll run up the next valley. Stealth mode, *Diablo*."

Stealth mode it is, sir.

Keep an ear open. Watch for electronics, everyone. They must have transport somewhere.

Another shot.

"Another animal killed."

And another.

Toni shook her head "One shot means a kill. Two shots, maybe a kill. A third shot means he got nothing."

Another shot.

They all grinned at each other, but the smiles didn't last.

Getting heat signs, Andrew.

She put them up in their augment, and one on the viewscreen for Dr. Pretoro.

He regarded the spread of animal and human figures across the mountainside. "It's a drive."

"What does that mean?"

"A large operation. The hunters line up in a natural funnel. The drivers circle upwind and move down on the prey, driving them into the trap. Then the gunmen slaughter their victims at their leisure."

Toni sneered. "Highly sporting, don't you know, old chap."

"What's the situation now, *Diablo*?"

Three victims down. Eighty-two larger herbivores and nineteen barwolves moving towards the killing ground.

"We've got to save them. Any other vehicles in the vicinity?"

No sign.

Andrew thought furiously. "We can't reveal ourselves, but we have to take these guys out, every one of them. What's the ground cover? Toni, can you disappear in it?"

"No problem, sir. Chakka and I could take them all easily. We just go in from either end and get them one by one while the others are busy killing."

"Good. *Diablo*, look for a place to set down. Chakka and Toni, get ready."

The commando frowned. "Are you sure about this, Andrew?"

"What do you mean?"

"Commandos don't take killing lightly. I don't want to go out there and make a mistake."

He moved closer to her, aware that now he looked down to match her eyes. "Of course I'm sure. Our clients are about to be murdered. Your job is to go out there and save them. Do you see any other way?"

Toni did not look happy, but she shrugged. "Not right off the top of my head."

"Right. Prepare to disembark."

"No, Andrew."

His head snapped around. "What do you mean, no?"

Dr. Pretoro shook his head. "You can't kill these men."

"Why not? They're about to murder a sapient species on a quarantined planet."

"Andrew, you're not thinking. A few members of a possibly sapient species on a planet where the quarantine has not been laid out yet."

"It's still murder. We have to save those barwolves!"

"I agree on that. But not by murdering innocent humans."

Andrew's rage grew. "Innocent! Look at what they're doing. No, Dr. Pretoro, this is a ship command decision, and I'm sending my team in."

The ambassador drew his side arm and regarded it. "And if you do, there are many in my position who would shoot you down where you stand."

"What?"

"It would be irresponsible for a person of my authority to allow a member of the Space Arm to commit murder. It would be my sworn duty to shoot you. Your auguar would then probably kill me. Jackson would try to protect me, so he would be killed, too. Chakka would then be declared a rogue auguar and put down. I don't know what the conflict would do to your ship's ArIn, but everyone would be at risk." He holstered his gun. "Now, settle down and let's solve this problem."

Andrew stood, a shock of cold fear running through him. He sank down on his accel couch, his head in his hands. *What was I thinking?*

"Come on, lad. Think! Back into augment. Find a way to break our friends out of this trap." The ambassador regarded the people in the little cockpit. "Ideas?"

Toni signalled for an aerial view. "Look at that gully over on the east side. It leads out to the open valley."

Jackson nodded. "Only one shooter there, and I think he's hidden from the others by that pinnacle of rock."

Andrew's mind began to function. "Toni, could you take him out without killing him? Without him getting a good sight of you?"

"Does a Ganymede rug-rock have bristles?"

"I've never seen a Ganymede rug-rock, but I'll take that as a 'yes.' Chakka, I need you on the other side, driving the herbivores toward Toni." As the ideas began to spew from the augment, Andrew's confidence returned. "Then cut in and bring the barwolves out over the rocks to the west. Normally they'd never do that, but if you call them..."

He turned to Pretoro. "Is that all right? It means limited contact."

"I think if they never actually see him..."

"Got that, Chakka?"

Image: dominant auguar beckoning barwolf cubs. They follow, tumbling over each other in eagerness to obey.

"All right, *Diablo*. Slide us in from the east." He indicated spots on the map. "We drop Toni there, Chakka there, and we hide there. Unless their ship comes back, in which case we improvise."

Diablo surged forward silently, her PermaSkin taking on dry-land hues. With no fuss the lethal pair was deposited and the little ship settled down to be a rock on the landscape. The watchers inside stayed on battle augment, the full panoply of the action in their minds.

Two more plant eaters were down, and the hunters stood, waiting for the main herd to approach. Then Toni's view of the single gunner in the escape gully came alive. Slowly, slowly she approached, slipping up behind him until his back and head filled her viewpoint. There was a 'thump' and he dropped to the ground. Her hands reached down, picked up his gun and did something to it, then tossed it aside.

Mission accomplished.

Alert. Two beaters moving towards you. They're separated from the group. Anything you can do?

Toni's view disappeared, and her heat-sign began an entrapment of the two unsuspecting beaters.

Emotion: grim amusement. They're making so much noise, I could walk up behind them in my mag boots and they'd never hear me.

In quick succession, the beaters stopped their progress.

That's enough, Toni. You've skewed the angle of the beat, and that gully is going to be full of large, armoured herbivores very soon. We're not that far from you. Time to come home.

On my way, sir.

Chakka, move in closer. The barwolves are not following you.

Multiple confused emotions: desire to follow, joy of hunt.

"Drat it. They think they're doing the driving. They're still hunting!"

The pack was splitting, now. The western group was edging towards Chakka and safety, but five had gathered together and were picking up speed on the eastern side. Andrew sent the information from his augment into the general mix.

Group image: herbivores running away.

Group emotion: urge to kill.

Do you want me to try to turn them, sir?

Toni, I thought you were coming in.

I was, but I'm still within range. I can turn that group. Probably a bunch of young toughs with blood on their little minds.

Too risky. What if they attack you?

Then you bring Diablo in and sit on them.

Andrew shot a look at Pretoro, who shook his head. "Your call, Captain. You know your people."

The young captain nodded. *All right, Sergeant. Open your augment fully. I'm going to try something. Head towards those smart-ass kids like a momma grizzly protecting her young.*

As the commando started her run, Andrew slid all of his feelings into her augment.

Emotion: terrible anger!

He brought up his memory of how the protective barwolves had postured.

Image: huge, slavering barwolf, mouth agape, teeth reaching for prey.

As Toni's image neared the young hunters they began to slow, edging away from her. She put on a burst of speed, and the sidle became a rout.

Confused image and emotion: fear of huge monster.

New image: pack moving to safety.

The young barwolves lengthened their strides and followed the pack up into the rocks on the mountainside. Then there was a change on *Diablo*'s viewscreens. The mass of the herbivores, formerly only trotting, began to gather in a tight knot.

tts up, Toni. I think our image was a bit too successful. The mooseys are stampeding.

Running at full speed, the herd spilled out onto the flats before the gunners. Several images stopped and lay unmoving, but the rest kept up their charge, overwhelming the hunters.

Image: Chakka's view of the killing ground. Dust slowly settling. Cooling lumps of dead and dying herbivores. Hunters picking themselves up, limping around, seeing to others lying still.

Cheers erupted inside *Diablo*.

All right, Chakka, Toni. Get back here.

"They'll be calling for help."

Guilt flashed through Andrew. "Good thought, Doctor. We need to get out of here. I don't want to test *Diablo*'s camo that close."

As the away team tumbled, panting, into the airlock, *Diablo* lifted gently and slipped away, slaloming among the boulders up and over the ridge.

While they were getting clear, Andrew had time to think. He settled his ship behind a mesa a few kilometres from the hunt site and camouflaged her there.

"All right, folks. This may or may not be over. Let's do some thinking."

Pretoro nodded. "Where does this leave our mission?"

Toni grinned. "Is there any more damage we can inflict on our enemies with little risk to us, but giving them motivation to stay away?"

Jackson shrugged. "If we picked off a couple and had Chakka tear them up, maybe they would think twice about hunting the barwolves."

Andrew stared at the security officer. "And here I thought you were such a nice guy."

Pretoro shook his head. "If there were any real hunters, that would make them even more keen to hunt."

"Yeah, you're right. We have to discourage them from coming here at all. Something about the planet, maybe?"

Andrew took a quick scan of the options his augment was showing. "Nothing shows up immediately. It depends on who comes to do the pickup, of course."

Engine noise, Andrew. Coming into view.

"Okay, we've found a ship one valley over. A long-haul military personnel carrier, a few years out of date. It lifted off a moment ago, heading in this direction. Looks like their pickup."

Andrew?

"Yes, *Diablo*."

Check this spec sheet, sir. The SolarCorp Delta-15 Interplanetary Personnel Carriers had several design flaws. If we could mimic a typical failure, perhaps we could make it seem like the planet's gravity or electromagnetic field combined with those flaws to give them a close call.

"Sounds like a good plan. Any ideas?"

Oh... no, sir. It was just a thought...

"Yes, *Diablo*, it was a good thought. Thank you. What do you say, folks? Any ideas? Yes, Sergeant?"

"Toughest part of any job is getting away. After it's all over, there's always that superstition that if the pilot doesn't hold his tongue right or something, the whole thing is going to go sideways, even after you've gone through all the danger and completed the assignment."

"We need action that makes it look like they can't get offplanet?"

"That's it."

"*Diablo*, anything look possible?"

"There's a cooling system in the airfoil ailerons to bleed off extra heat that develops from the friction of the speed required to break free into space. We can sabotage the low-altitude flight subroutines by inserting a checkback requirement that depends on a signal we are sending. Then we just wait below them. The moment the ship gets beyond range of our signal, the checkback will register a 'false,' and the computer will sense an overheat warning. They'll slow down and drop altitude, coming back into our range, and it will look like it's cooling down again. Up they go, and it happens all over again. When we want to quit we remove the checkback, and off they go.

Image: cat playing with mouse.

Chakka, you want to be part of this?

Emotion: enthusiasm.

All right. This ought to be interesting. Diablo, how close do we need to be?

Line of sight is best, Andrew.

"We'll test our stealth and our camo and slip in as near as we can while they're busy with loading their gear and tending their trampled. Let's go. Everyone on the alert for evidence we've been busted. Dr. Pretoro, as usual, your eyes are up and out while we're working. Comments?"

The doctor answered with some asperity in his voice. "It's easy to keep my eyes up and out when I have no idea what is happening. I cannot hear your contact with your ship, so I missed out on the plan."

"Oh. Sorry, Doctor. I forgot about that little detail. Jackson, can you fill the ambassador in on what we're doing to protect his clients?"

"Sure thing, Andrew. This is what's going on, Doctor..."

Andrew blanked out that conversation as they homed in on the enemy ship. Its encryption was five years out of date, and soon he and *Diablo* had their trap attached. Turning the operation over to *Diablo* and Chakka, he opened up the augment to the others and sat back to watch.

An hour later the Delta-15 rose, heading with all speed towards orbit. After a few minutes, *Diablo* lifted gently to follow.

All seemed well until the IPC reached an altitude of three kilometres. Then it faltered and levelled off. *Diablo* continued to ascend, and soon the carrier was rising. This time it reached four kilometres before it hit the end of its tether. Once again it slowed. This time *Diablo* held station below it for about fifteen minutes before allowing her quarry to escape again.

Now the Mustang rose behind the other ship, keeping her acceleration going up to thirty kilometres, then reeling her in once more.

While they were waiting for the crew aboard their quarry to attempt repairs, Andrew had an idea.

Diablo, what is the height of the mesosphere of this planet?

Fifty-three kilometres, sir.

If we let them get to that altitude before we turn them loose, they'll think their problem was something to do with friction, right?

That is of high probability.

Then give them one final hiccup and set them free.

Diabolical, sir.

Just trying to live up to your name.

Thank you, sir.

The next time the IPC fired up her engines, *Diablo* let her go a long way, but followed closely. Then, after cutting the checkback twice for brief moments, she removed it entirely. The freed vessel zoomed off into space and was soon lost to their sensors.

NightHawk to Diablo.

Diablo here.

We're seeing two ships in the upper atmosphere. You're one of them. I thought you were downplanet studying wolves. Who's your friend?

Andrew shared a glance with his crew. "Long story, ma'am. Sending you a file and returning to work."

Any reason to follow them?

As you wish, ma'am. Their homeward trajectory would be of interest.

Wilco. Back to the job, children.

Aye, ma'am.

Yes, Mum.

He gave the order to *Diablo*, and they dove back to the valley where the subjects of their survey were going about their busy, predatory little lives.

25. MOVING ON

Two days later, Natalia stood at the head of the mess table and regarded her crew. "It's time to pull up stakes, folks."

They looked at each other, but no one objected.

"The barwolves were a necessary distraction, but we've done what we can for them. We have sent off the research data our team collected, and we have set up the quarantine satellites. Short of patrolling constantly, there's nothing more to be done.

"It's the same thing with the mine. We aren't out here to stand guard. We're on reconnaissance to report what was happening and to, if I may quote my orders, 'take any steps necessary and possible to maintain peace and the control of the Planetary Community in the Barnard's System.'"

She tossed up her hands. "We can't take action when we don't know what's going on, and the biggest information gap I can think of is that communications hole in the Inner Asteroid Belt. We've been monitoring it while the team was downplanet, and nothing is happening.

"We have a vague idea of what Kriver is up to out in the Outer Belt, and it looks like he's got things settled down. If he has, my personal preference is to leave him there. What do you think, Dr. Pretoro?"

"There is no evidence that he is doing anything contrary to PC law. In the absence of any governmental supervision, he is running his business in the way he sees fit. Of course, the fact that he is a representative of an interplanetary, and not one of the government's favourite ones, will give the diplomats concern. I will not be surprised to see a three-pronged expedition headed in this direction in the coming year: military, diplomatic and logistics. We need a base of operations in this system, and the only way to ensure its success is to create something bigger and more powerful than whatever Develocon has built. We assume that SolarCorp is the loser in this preemptive civil war and will have fewer resources."

Andrew raised his eyebrows to the ambassador for permission to break in. "Their conflict is actually to our advantage. Divide and rule."

"Put crudely, yes. Unless it turns out that the SolarCorp people are doing something beyond the limits of civilized behaviour, or until it erupts into open warfare, in which case we might be forced to take some action, as the captain's orders allow."

Natalia nodded. "Which brings us to our next move, which must be the reconnaissance we discussed before this detour. We were headed for the SolarCorp area, and nothing has happened to change my mind on that objective. What data would be the most useful for you and those in decision-making back home, Alfino?"

"Anything that comes up. At the moment we have too little information to be specific."

"So, a general analysis of the power structure, facilities, personnel and capabilities would be a start?"

"Certainly."

"Then reconnaissance it is. We're getting good at prowling the asteroids, so we should slide around the belt and see what we find. Lieutenant Jones, while *NightHawk* is looking, you will be listening. There have to be communications, and it's up to you to find them."

She turned to Andrew. "I'm going to put you and *Diablo*'s gestalt at the disposal of Dr. Pretoro. I'm counting on you to develop the simplest form of communication so that he has full awareness of our research results without compromising his security. I hate to sound old school, but verbal reporting, face to face, has all sorts of advantages. We can call it part of your training. For operational purposes, I'm teaming you up with Sergeant Jacobs. I also want you to train Pilot Karaka as a backup in case of emergencies."

After the meeting broke up, Andrew stayed.

Natalia regarded him. "You're looking very serious."

"Um...has Dr. Pretoro reported to you on our mission?"

"He has."

"I didn't particularly distinguish myself."

She leaned back and looked at him. "You came close to making a mistake, I gather."

"Yes. A bad one."

"He didn't give any details."

"You might as well know…" he related the incident, sparing himself none of the details.

When he finished, she had a strange smile on her face. "And Alfino threatened to shoot you? He never told me that."

"He didn't actually threaten. But he did talk to me with his sidearm in his hand."

"And you realized the error of your ways."

Andrew shook his head. "I was being completely stupid, Mum. I was letting my emotions rule me…why are you smiling? I was close to a terrible mistake."

"That's while I'm smiling, Son. 'Close to.' I like that idea."

"You do?"

"You bet. That's why I send you out with the best team possible. You're very intelligent, but you can't be wise enough to apply your abilities. Not at your age and experience. Today you proved yourself wise enough to take the advice of people you trust."

He slumped on his chair. "I don't feel very wise. I was being completely stupid."

"And that's how you're supposed to feel. Because you were. Real wisdom is being smart enough to know when you're being stupid."

"Thanks for the try, but even humour that bad is not going to make me feel better."

"I don't want you to feel better. I want you to feel that there's only one way to make up for your mistake."

"And what's that?"

"Never to make one like it again. It won't work, but it gets you started in the right direction."

"Great. Thanks." He glanced at the auguar. "I notice you didn't assign Chakka anywhere. Is he going to be my babysitter now?"

"Don't be even more stupid. That's something else we need to talk about."

"Sounds serious."

"It is. It involves another part of my orders."

"About Chakka?"

"No, you. Space Arm created *NightHawk* and Chakka to be complementary elements in a three-way gestalt with me. Do you see the problem?"

"Sure. Freighty shoved me into the equation and messed everything up. With great results, you must admit."

"True, but that brings us back to some things I've been teaching you about leadership."

"Ah. I understand."

"You do?"

"Of course. With me in the mix, we're far superior. But I'm a solo phenomenon, especially if Freighty decides to restrict my use. Space Arm scientists want to continue their development of the original project, incorporating whatever they can from me, but maintaining their scientific and operational independence."

His mind was flying ahead, taking in the possible paths. "Do you realize what is about to happen to the power structure of the Sol System?"

"In what way?"

"We have always had a two-sided power structure: government against interplanetaries. Now Freighty will add one more leg to the stool. If there are any loose joints, you and I could get caught in them."

"That's right. And Freighty was being very naïve if he thought joining the two of us together would solve anything."

"So, you're trying to separate us in an operational sense..." He frowned, looking at her, his heart sinking. "Aren't you? Operational, right?"

She reached out and laid a hand on his arm. "That's right. I'm counting on our personal bonds, both the emotional and the new augmental one, to keep it all together. I want you and *Diablo* to work through whatever Freighty has set you up for, and my own trio to go as far as Space Arm has prepared us to go. Because of our organic augments, I know we will outstrip anything they envisioned." Her hand tightened on his arm. "We will move in different directions. It's inevitable. It is almost certain you will outpace us."

Andrew pondered this. It sounded exciting...

"Something's bothering you."

"Mum, what if Freighty and the Planetary Community don't agree on something? You and I could end up on opposite sides!"

She reached out and tousled his hair. "I suppose we could. But you don't have to worry about that for the next little while."

He forced a grin. "I guess not. We're six light years from the PC, and Freighty's two light years away and getting farther every minute."

"Right. For the moment, we're solid, right?" She messed his hair again.

He reached up and trapped her hand. "Right. So stop messing with my head and let's get to work."

He jumped to his feet, gave her a perfect salute and strode out to the slideway. But as he descended, his feelings dropped with equal speed. *Mum never ends a statement with a question. She knows we're on shaky ground.*

26.   AROUND THE BELT

They took the shortest route to the Inner Belt, but when they neared their objective they slowed, keeping watch on all sensory channels for other ships. Unlike the Develocon area, there were none. With no alternate course of action, they pushed farther in, moving slower now, with crew on full alert.

Once again, Andrew knew that Natalia wanted him for a private meeting. He made his best time up to the chartroom. Well, his best time without running over anyone.

"What's up, Cap'n? Or is it Mum?"

She grinned. "Captains' conference, Captain. It's about our tactics once we're within operational distance of our objective. I need to decide how much detached duty *Diablo* is up for."

"Fuel?"

"You've been flying enough to have consumption data at various speeds, but I can't get a straight answer from your ArIn."

"Oops. There are a whole lot of security glitches that have to be fixed. Most err on the side of caution, but there are limits. I'll have her put *NightHawk* on her allowable contact list for logistics. There's no need to be asking for that infomration. They should know each other like parts of the same machine."

"Maybe."

"What do you mean?"

She shrugged, an unusually tentative gesture. "*NightHawk* is a military vessel…"

"Oh. And technically *Diablo* is owned by the Freighty faction. I get it. We'll have to rig a temporary gestalt when we need it and go through the trouble of a request from you for everyday use." He made a quick contact with his ship. "There, she's authorized to give *NightHawk* general logistics info on the *Hawk's* request."

Natalia checked the interface. "You're 98% full. We're at 95. For *NightHawk*, that's several months of scooting around the system."

"Mine's harder to guess, because we tend to zoom back and forth. We'll have to monitor, depending on what you need us to do."

"I had already decided on that. Glad you agree."

He grinned. "I find it usually works out best that way, but thanks for asking, Captain."

"You're welcome, Captain." She looked down at her document screen, then sent him a sharper glance. "And, Cadet, I notice you haven't had much time lately for your training sessions with Lieutenant Jones."

"A situation I will rectify on this trip, ma'am."

"I'm sure you will. Dismissed."

With his usual salute, he turned out the door.

His training with the First Officer soon moved in a different direction.

Jones was at his station. "Andrew, come in and sit down, please."

He entered bridge and took the captain's couch. "What's up, sir?"

"Twin up your viewscreen and enter the communications augment."

Andrew scanned the information that spread before him. "Got it. What are those? He indicated a closely spaced handful of lower bands originating in the target area of the belt.

"That's what I'd like to know. They're low frequency, low power emanations from multiple sources. There's something about the transmissions that makes them difficult to hold onto. Nothing so simple as rotating frequencies."

"Sir, may I bring *Diablo* into this?"

"Certainly. What are her capabilities in this area?"

"I never tried. Let's ask her."

He connected to his ArIn and logged her into *NightHawk*'s communications. *Diablo, Lieutenant Jones has an interesting radio problem for us.*

It will be a pleasure, Lieutenant. May I see your data?

Jones passed her the same file. "The highlighted frequencies."

Andrew, let's work from this direction. Start with the lowest.

Right.

The Mustang's ArIn was accessing programs he was unfamiliar with, but he found them intuitive, and the massive computing and storage capabilities of his ship made it easy to crunch data at rapid speed.

"There we have it, sir." He started the sound files playing, one at a time. Soon Standard English speech was coming from the cockpit com.

"Gamma one to Gamma Seven. Tune your ion trail. It's not Hallowe'en this week."

"Sorry, sir. On it."

"Gamma one to Gamma Squadron. Prepare to execute 17-D one more time on my mark. Mark."

"Five, you're sliding wide. Pull in. Pull in! No, gorramit! All right, pull out and reform."

"Sorry, sir. I just couldn't hold it."

"Next time you'd better hold it, Applebee, or you'll be back on wrenches and we'll give someone else a chance."

"Aye, sir. I'll hold it."

"I'm sure you will."

Andrew glanced at Jones, who nodded. "That's a squadron practicing an attack pattern. *Diablo*, can we record some of those?"

"I have been recording and translating all the frequencies you gave me since we started, sir. How would you like me to display them?"

Jones glanced at Andrew. "We'll have to make up a screening protocol."

"Military words and actions top priority?"

"Yes, and anything related to interplanetaries." The lieutenant winced. "Then we need a second level. How about training protocols like we just heard? Then military logistics: supplies, ammo, weapons, deployment."

Andrew broke in. "Hospitals, medical, wounded."

"Repairs, parts…"

"Fueling.…"

"Personnel, both military and civilian…"

"Politics and policing."

"Are you getting this, *Diablo*?"

I suggest subdividing what you gave me into military and civilian channels, sir.

"Do so. Andrew, use *NightHawk*'s audio analysis program to further refine our information. Let's get to it, folks. I'll inform the captain of our progress. As we move relative to the sources, I'll triangulate to get position readings." *NightHawk, I assume you got that.*

"Aye, sir."

Aye, sir.

Aye, sir.

Silence engulfed the cockpit and the augment channels.

Two hours later, the lieutenant raised his head. "Andrew, you and I need a break. *NightHawk* and *Diablo*, I am unfamiliar with your capabilities. Do you require a rest?"

I can only speak for myself, Lieutenant, but I'm fresh as a daisy.

I am unfamiliar with daisies, Lieutenant, but I can work at this intensity for four more Earth hours. Then I need a fifteen-minute change of activity to reorganize my RAM. Clutter accumulates during periods of high activity.

"Prime. Andrew and I will take a preliminary report to the captain. *Diablo*, continue to record full time and screen as long as you are comfortable."

Aye, sir.

"*NightHawk*, can you continue what you and Andrew were doing?"

I can, sir, but I won't pick up the same nuances and make the same possible connections that we do when working together.

"Fair enough. Keep at it and flag anything interesting for further study."

Aye, sir.

Andrew rose and stretched. "Captain's in the mess hall, sir."

"I knew that, Cadet." Jones turned a quizzical eye to Andrew. "How did I know that? Ah, the evolving augments."

"A safe assumption, sir." He grinned. "Hearing any voices in the night, yet?"

The First Officer awarded him a wintry smile. "No, I'm hoping to leave that kind of connection to you and your mother."

"Don't worry, sir. *Diablo* and I are working on it and we'll keep everyone posted. The captain and the doctor are on their way to the chart room."

"You called her while talking to me at the same time?"

Andrew merely gestured the officer to precede him.

Natalia and Pretoro were already seated, and she waved Jones to the stool. Andrew stood in the 'rest easy' pose. It wasn't as easy in the one-G acceleration, but it was probably good for his muscles. *And my strength of character.*

Image: Cadet curled with auguar on couch.

Image: Cadet's legs sticking out and captain stomping on them.

Emotion: feline chuckle.

"What do you have for me?"

Jones shook his head. "Nothing detailed, ma'am, but the general impression both of us get is that the SolarCorp forces are by no means defeated. They have drawn in to protect their supply lines and shorten their response times. In fact, where Kriver seems to be running a quasi-civilian government, what we're hearing on these channels is a tight military cadre working at full operational parameters. Not at all what one would expect from the tatters of a rout."

"What about this coded radio? Does that seem suspicious?"

Andrew nodded. "According to *NightHawk,* that's military-grade stuff, and not available even to most security levels."

"In other words, stolen military secrets."

"It's probable, ma'am. It happens more often than Space Arm brass would like to think."

She lanced him with a glare. "And how does a Cadet have an opinion about this high-security information?"

"Because of my contact with Securi-Corps I probably know a bit more about it than the average spacer, ma'am. But not that much more."

Natalia laced her fingers together and regarded them. "In other words, it's common knowledge in some circles but the brass don't want to know. Great. Does this change our plan of action, Doctor? Besides being even more careful, of course."

"I'm more interested in tracking down the leaders and learning the command structure."

"In case the opportunity arises that you might be able to negotiate?"

The ambassador spread his hands, palms down. "I may have no official standing, but negotiation is what I do."

The captain grinned. "But we're the only ones that know the limits on your orders. If the interplanetaries have any kind of communication system, the message should be coming in right about now that you've been sent out. No one will be surprised if you show up. Your authority has always been limited, and your reputation and abilities will probably carry you further in any discussion with unofficial, semi-revolutionary leaders."

"So, if the occasion arises, you suggest I go barging in as official envoy, with a Space Arm vessel backing me?"

"And a hidden gunship as the ace up your sleeve. It would be our most powerful configuration. Face it, Dr. Pretoro. I'm the voice of Space Arm in this system. If I say you have power, no one will think to question your authority."

The ambassador was having an internal struggle and decided to smile. "I must say, that's a reasonable way to proceed."

"And you thought we would be unreasonable?"

He held up his hands in defeat. "I'm not going to argue just when things are going my way." Then he lowered his brows. "And when do find out what this has cost me?"

Natalia laughed. "Maybe never, maybe ten minutes from now. That's life in the far-flung reaches of the galaxy."

She turned to Jones and Andrew. "You two keep on this. We need to develop a re-ti picture. We'll send Andrew and Charlie in for reconnaissance, and then for the next few days or weeks we collect data on both sides of the conflict. That gives us information to bargain about each one when speaking to the other. Best-case

219

scenario is Space Arm slipping in and negotiating peace. Not likely, but it's something to try for."

They nodded, and Pretoro laughed. "It sounds like my kind of plan."

"All right. Keep up the surveillance, and when we get close enough, we'll send in our reconnaissance team."

27. BASE SC1

IORM Diablo was once again in her role as a spy ship, but this time her two crewmen were in a more military guise. Charlie's space armour was carefully repaired and upgraded. Andrew had modified the camo on his to match. The emptiness of space during their earlier approach was now becoming filled with short-range radio traffic and fast-moving vessels.

We've been spotted, Andrew.

"This far out?" Andrew brought the VR map of their section of the Belt into the gestalt

Four passive nav buoys within range on restricted channels. They won't know we've seen them.

Charlie raised his eyebrows. "That's impressive, if they have them three-sixty on all axes."

"Let's wait another ten Ks before we call in."

The commando nodded. "Do we blunder in until they jump, or do we show some moxie?"

"Apply our method acting. Since we're assuming prior knowledge of the situation, we need to play one-up, but don't let them know."

At eight thousand kilometres, *Diablo* flashed a point on the virtual map.

Second ring of defence, sir. Armed.

Make the call.

Aye, sir. IOR Messenger 30AC calling Base SC1. Base SC1, this is IORM 30AC calling Base SC1.

This is SC1. Identifications and codes, please.

Charlie took the com. *This is IORM 30AC. You don't know me and I have no up-to-date codes, but your commanding officer will want to talk to me.*

Stand by, IORM 30AC.

Standing by. Continuing my approach.

Do not deviate from that course, 30AC

Wilco, SC1.

It didn't take long.

IORM 30AC, we have no record of any vessel matching your identity or description in this system.

That's right, SC1. You're not supposed to. Do you have a more secure channel?

We're not it the habit of giving away our channels to strangers.

"Wait a minute, Charlie." Andrew called up the specs from the old *Clyde*. "Try that one."

Here's my channel, then, SC1. Can you comply?

Switching to your channel.

Contact.

My first question is how you have that frequency.

Charlie winked at Andrew. *I'm not in the habit of giving away my sources to strangers. Let your commanding officer make the decisions, soldier.*

Give me one good reason why I shouldn't just blast you to smithereens. We're at war, here, you know.

Diablo sent Charlie a direct data feed, which he glanced at.

Because we're already inside your outer perimeter, and Bren 453 Sat-Defences are programmed not to fire inward, to prevent accidents by trigger-happy young gunners. This conversation is getting less and less productive. Are you actively trying to lose a stripe?

I have informed my superiors of your communication, 30AC. Please stand by.

Standing by.

Charlie interlaced his fingers inside out and stretched his arms forward until his knuckles cracked. "How did you know he was a Lance Corporal, *Diablo*?"

An educated guess, Sergeant. I have put together all the information I can glean from their equipment, their frequencies, the history of SolarCorp and many other small details that allow me to posit the kind of military operation they must be running.

Emotion: chuckle.

And you'll notice I only mentioned losing a stripe, which could apply to several ranks.

"Fooled me. Fooled him, which is what counts. Whatever we can do to keep them off balance. You getting anything, Captain?"

Andrew shook his head. "Bunch of radio traffic, low power, short band. We're recording it all for Lieutenant Jones to analyze later. The base system might be totally hardwired. That would make our job more difficult."

"I wonder what their port configuration is. Visuals still give us a large asteroid."

I'm getting a better look, now. It seems to be spinning.

"Magnified view, please."

As they approached, the asteroid became clearer on their screens. It was about two kilometres in diameter and roughly spherical.

"Holy smoke! Look at that thing spin."

Used to the lazy rotation of the other asteroids, Andrew found it hard to picture the surface velocity of an object that size that was visibly spinning.

Give us some numbers, Diablo. What's the effect of that spin?

Period of rotation, four hours. Diameter, two kilometres. Negative gravity on the surface would be about 0.3 Gs.

"So if they dig into the asteroid, they could have a quarter G on the outside wall. Unless they increased the spin further..."

That is correct.

"What's it made of?"

Spectral analysis of dust clouds dissipating from internal activities indicates a high percentage of nickel-iron with traces of magnesium.

"But won't even a quarter G break it apart?"

Highly unlikely, with those reinforcements around it.

As they neared, they could pick up a series of dark bands girding the planetoid at its largest girth. The landscape sped by in front of them, and various-sized holes glided past. Several were spewing fountains of particles that spread out like the arms of a galaxy along the plane of the equator. Two revealed white-hot lights deep down.

Charlie frowned. "That asteroid can't have a molten core."

Andrew shook his head. "They've got nuclear furnaces inside. They're melting the interior out and spilling it into channels on the surface. When it cools, it makes a band all the way around."

My calculations suggest that a series of bands one metre thick and three metres wide at intervals of ten metres at the equator would be strong enough to resist one gravity at the full density of the asteroid. The bands can be narrower nearer the poles, because the angular momentum diminishes with diameter of the circle.

Andrew jumped up. "It's beautiful. And as they use up the interior metal, they strengthen the shell. Then they can increase the spin and give themselves more gravity. In the end, they'll have an empty centre with a shell made of its own material, and they can spin it up to whatever gravity they want."

He looked at the size of the project. "We've been going on the premise that there was only light manufacturing ability out here. This is huge."

My calculations suggest otherwise. The Clyde could have transported the furnaces easily. No other materials are needed. Only energy, and there's plenty of that around.

Andrew was shaking his head. "There's a whole lot I don't understand going on here."

Yes, some of the data does not add up. There is not enough infrastructure for the scenario we are suggesting. We're missing part of the operation.

Charlie chuckled. "Well, don't let your scientific curiosity get the better of you. We're here with a different job."

IOR Messenger 30AC, this is SC1.

30AC here.

Please approach beacon 3-17. Synch your orbit from that position and approach grid point 1North-24West. You will use Dock 14.

Charlie glanced at the schematic on the viewscreen. *Wilco, SC1. Beacon 3-17, land at 1N-24W, Dock 14.*

As they reached their assigned position, a surface structure appeared: a standard planetary base with several space fighters and other ships nosed in to covered bays. Large numbers on the roof made it easy; *Diablo* edged into number 14 and stopped with a slight bump.

Standard grapple positions, sir. Docking tube extending... docking complete, pressure equalized and seals tested A-OK, sir.

"Thank you, *Diablo*. Now, you have your instructions. Do not go prying into anything. Record everything and follow up any radio-connect channels. We don't know this system, and so far, this place has been better organized and higher-level tech than we expected."

"Aye, Captain."

They slipped into their space suits. A close inspection showed that they matched perfectly, although Charlie's looked newer.

As the airlock slid open, three spacers in armour came into view. Two had weapons at the ready, and the officer stood easy in the middle of the docking area.

"Permission to land, sir?"

"Step ahead, please. Are you armed?"

"I have a projectile handgun. Should I leave it onboard?"

"That would be advisable."

Coming at you, sir. Charlie drew his weapon in one motion and tossed it to Andrew. "Dump that in the airlock, kid."

"Sure, boss."

As they left *Diablo's* field, gravity shifted to a very light pull upward due to the rotation of the planetoid. Switching on their mag boots, they proceeded down the tube, which bounced lightly as they walked. When they reached the bottom, the officer snapped to attention. "Follow me, please." He made a perfect 'about face' and marched off. Andrew and Charlie followed, and the two spacers brought up the rear, everyone in step. The "march" consisted of quick steps of their magnetic boots on the metallic deck.

As they progressed through the tunnel, Andrew was happy to turn his motion over to his habits and start work. He first scanned the usual frequencies for wi-fi signals, of which there were few.

Shrugging to himself, he started to chase them down, only to stop in confusion. Every one he followed, sooner or later set off alarms in his system, making him back off.

Grimly he kept on, finally finding a cold drink machine in a nearby readyroom that was hardwired into the catering system, which had a connection to logistics because of supply of the vending machines...which had an alarm structure that looked too delicate to touch.

He backed out, becoming more aware of his surroundings. They had stopped at a freight elevator, which they stepped into. Why they needed an elevator in this gravity, he couldn't guess, but down they went. As they progressed, the guards shut off their mag boots and flipped over to drift "down" to what had been the ceiling of the elevator. Charlie and Andrew coped with the change. At the same time air hissed into the chamber until their suits slackened.

The officer gave them a grim smile as he removed his helmet. He was a clean-cut middle-aged man with an air of command about the way he held his head. His colouring looked healthy under a military crewcut. "It's unsettling the first go around."

"I'm fine, thank you, sir." Charlie glanced at Andrew.

"No problem, boss."

Helmets off, they moved out, walking on what was now their floor into a large empty space, dark except for pools of light where figures worked. They marched, if you could call it that, towards a set of prefabricated buildings, standard down-planet, atmo-tight military design.

Inside there was light and warmth and a long hallway with many doors. People, most of them in uniform, moved in and out at a brisk pace.

Their guards took up position outside a door, and the officer led them into what looked like any office workroom at any military base in the Solar System. He set his helmet on a chair beside the desk and turned to face them.

They stood easy, regarding him with curiosity.

"I'd offer a chair, but there's not much point, in this gravity. I'm Captain Worthing, and I'm in command here. Who are you?"

While Charlie spun out their story, Andrew was busily accessing anything he could find. A 2-D printer in the corner of the room had standard wi-fi connection to the desktop monitor. *This is a bit too easy. Careful, now.* He slipped down the hardline to the mainframe deeper in the building. Once he had gained access, he stopped in dismay. The system was a forest of traps and snares, many of them false, with a few real bombs at random intervals.

Conversation destroyed his concentration, and he pulled gently back.

"So, Mr. Alderson. You show up with a ship we've never seen before, with a radio frequency you're not supposed to have, and think you'll waltz into a secure military base with not so much as a letter of introduction?"

Charlie grinned. "There's plenty of people who have seen my ship before, and the same people gave me that frequency. The fact that I have the frequency should tell you who gave it to me, if you are who you are supposed to be."

The officer frowned. "Are you questioning my credentials?"

Charlie shrugged. "Well, I've been on assignment, and I got back and was sent out again rather sudden. I know my mission, but I didn't get the full briefing about who I'm supposed to be working with. I'm getting vibes that things are not as cut and dried as you'd like them to look."

"That's your impression, is it?"

"It is." He swept a hand through the air. "You've got a pretty good setup, here. It looks sharp, and you're obviously on a serious, long-term project. So no, I'm not questioning your credentials. I'm making sure I'm working for the right people. In my business, suspicion is a way of life, and I hope you'll forgive me for it."

"Are you telling me that someone out there," the officer made a similar arm sweep, "who shall remain nameless for the moment, is taking an interest in what is happening in Barnard's System, and has sent you on an as-yet-unrevealed mission to help us?"

Again Charlie grinned. "I don't want to get your hopes up. I work on a need-to-know basis. In other words, nobody tells me nothin'. But here I am, and my orders are to make my services available."

Andrew dove back into the security system, but that path had now been blocked. Wondering if he had been spotted or if it was a routine switch, he searched further. Yes, there was a wi-fi router two offices down with a hardline further in. Delicately, he began checking the menus. He was just beginning to make progress when he felt something wrong. The line suddenly went dead, and he found himself back in the router. There were no return routes, so he withdrew, hoping he hadn't left any doors open or lights on behind him.

Charlie and the officer seemed more relaxed.

"That's a neat old crate you're driving."

The commando grinned. "I worked on those before I joined up. When I served my time and got out, I picked that beauty up in a junkyard and reno'd her from scratch. She's a real bomb!"

"I wouldn't talk about bombs in a military base, Alderson."

"Aw, you know what I mean. I had to scrap the original engines. Way too much power. Sucked fuel like a baby whale. I got these new high-efficiency 14-kilowatt Hall-Effect Thrusters. I don't mind telling you, because there's lots of the like coming out back home, but they're convertible to five different reaction mass elements. Perfect for the Outback."

"I'll take a look. I was always a big fan of those babies when they were racing."

"Well, now, I'd like to have you aboard, but there's classified stuff in there, and it's better if it stays that way."

"Classified by whom?"

Charlie shrugged. "Basically, by me. I get a lot of latitude from the brass because I produce when others can't. So they don't question my methods, if you follow my drift."

Worthing frowned. "You know, Alderson, I'm not happy about this whole situation. I have everything in hand, here, and now you come along and throw the whole shebang skew-if."

"I get that a lot, sir. You upright military types don't like the idea that you have to depend on my sort for the intel that allows you to get your job done. I understand that, and my skin's pretty thick.

Don't worry about me and my methods. You ask the questions, I'll get you the answers. That's what I do."

He straightened his pose. "So. What do you want to know?"

The captain rubbed his chin, regarding Charlie. Finally he nodded. "I'm going to send you to my tactician. He'll give you your assignment. You'll report to him. Got it?"

Charlie gave a serious nod. "Aye, sir. Arm's length. I work that style all the time. What you don't know you can't be responsible for."

"I don't look at it in that light, but that's how we will be working. Take your strange crewman and get out of here."

"May I assume you'll let me fuel up? It's a long way to the Outer Belt."

"Don't push it, Alderson." He frowned to himself. "You can fill up if you can remember what type of fuel you actually use."

"Thank you, sir. You won't be disappointed." He turned to Andrew. "Come on, kid. Give the captain a salute, and away we go."

Andrew did as he was told, making it rather sloppy, and followed the commando's broad back out the door, shutting off his probes as he walked. Then he accessed the organic levels of Charlie's augment. *He didn't like us much.*

No, but he's letting us have fuel to make up for it. Guilty conscience, I guess. I have no idea what he's feeling guilty for.

Emotion: chuckle. Charlie, he thinks you and I have a relationship.

What?

Sure. And the military is very firm about prejudice, especially in its officers. I didn't sense any bias against monogens, but I'd guess he's suspicious that you're somehow taking advantage of me because of the age difference. He can't prove it and he knows he might be wrong. He was brought up to a very strict code of conduct: equity for all. He finds his own response counter to that code, so he feels guilty. He makes up for it by giving us fuel.

Charlie shook his head, but said no more.

I'm not making much progress, and I can't hold my little-boy act and work at the same time. I'm going to be the weak, silent type from now on, so cover for me, will you?

Wilco, Captain.

And don't use any military terms, even on augment. Anything might leak.

We keep up the façade, even in our heads.

Image: grim smile. I'll give you another lesson in method acting some time when we have time.

Andrew returned to the fray, refreshed by the brief rest and ready to try again.

The "tactical officer" they were sent to had less qualms or maybe poorer people skills. He leaned back in his chair and regarded them. "Well, Former Sergeant Alderson, what can you and your boyfriend do for us?

His next sentence was more difficult to get out, hampered as it was by the collar of his uniform cinched around his throat and the pain of being slammed against the wall. "Okay, okay, I'm sorry."

Charlie set him on his chair. "That's good. Shall we start over?"

The officer straightened his collar and rubbed his neck. "The commander speaks well of you, or you wouldn't get away with that." He slid his seat to a safer position behind the desk. "What do you propose to do?"

Charlie stood easy, and Andrew moved behind him where he could relax and concentrate on keeping his butt covered in the complexities of the wacko security system. This time the approach was much easier. A radio net permeated the room, and he began to search out the sources.

Only to recoil in fear. *This isn't a net. It's a scanner.* He could feel the system reaching out to Charlie's augment. Hastily, he created a fog of static, mimicking an augment that was out of phase. He felt tendrils reaching for him, but there was nothing they could latch onto, so he ignored them. They felt slimy, crawling around the periphery of his mind, but he gritted his teeth and concentrated on feeding Charlie's attackers snippets of information that would lead and mislead them. All the while, he was trying to keep situational awareness. It wouldn't do be caught staring off into space at an important briefing.

"I've developed a cover in the Outer Belt. Asteroid miner with a family operation. The kid's part of the picture. But I have a fast ship, so I can produce enough ore to allay suspicion and have time to move around. I also have a very talented tech — he jabbed a thumb towards Andrew — who can decipher just about any radio signal floating by."

The tac officer grinned. "How did he do with ours?"

"Since you're on radio silence, he didn't have much to work with. There's some interesting frequency manipulation going on that we thought you might want to know about, though."

"Don't you worry your little heads about that."

"Well enough. Nothing like it in the Outer Belt, if that makes you feel any better. Anyway, we can send you a pretty good picture of what's happening. Give us a tight-beam frequency and a schedule, and we'll produce."

"That sounds remarkably easy. What's in it for you?"

"You don't have to worry about that. I'm covered."

The nameless tactician leaned back and regarded Charlie, then Andrew. "Now, that doesn't make me feel any better at all. Here you show up with pretty much no warning, you've got a ship than never flew here all by itself, and you offer your assistance pretty much free of charge or encumbrance. If it's too good to be true, then it probably isn't true."

Charlie grinned. "That's right. My ship came out here on the only transport big enough to transport it, if you take my meaning. That transport may have gone flutterbye, but the people that sent it are still very much in the picture. As you well know."

He took a chair and leaned back, his hands behind his head. "And maybe that's as much as it would be appropriate for you to ask."

The man sighed. "Fair enough. That's about as much of an answer as I expected." He slipped a piece of hardcopy across his desk. "There's all you need. Three frequencies, a rotating schedule. I shouldn't need to tell you to call from a wide variety of places and to vary the signatures of whatever equipment you use. Our enemies run a pretty loose ship, but don't underestimate Kriver. He's got the best mind in the business." He gestured to the paper. "A list of questions, and it's not recorded anywhere. You get us answers to those, and we'll be happy to tell whoever asks that you did your job. Good enough?"

Charlie glanced over the sheet. "Pretty standard stuff." He stood. "You have yourself a deal. I'll head over to the fueling station."

"You do that. I wish you all the best of luck. I gather in your field you need it."

"Oh, I don't know." Charlie shrugged. "I find the more careful I am, the more lucky I get." He flexed a fist. "It's usually other people whose luck runs out."

He motioned towards the door, and Andrew went ahead.

What's going on, kid?

More trouble than it's worth, I'm afraid. I'm holding them off. Let's just get out of here as quickly as possible.

Time to fuel up?

Probably. Get me onboard where I don't have to walk and think at the same time. They're trying to access your augment, and they're getting close.

A big hand descended on Andrew's shoulder, guiding him along at a faster pace, and he concentrated on his work.

Once safe on board behind his firewalls, he collapsed into his couch and uploaded what he had gathered to *Diablo*.

"What do you make of that? It was not fun at all."

Oh. Hmm...yes. Well, that's a very nasty and twisted piece of software. Quite dangerous, in its own little way.

"I'm glad I wasn't exaggerating. Recognize anything?"

I'd say it was an evolutionary offshoot of a version the military was working with six or seven years ago. This look familiar?

She opened several schematics, and he matched them up with what his augment had on file. "Yes, I have the originals of those. They were considered too volatile, too likely to turn on their masters."

That's right. Sort of like the human immune system in the old days. That's why you had so much trouble with the system. You're trying to duck all the traps.

"You mean I shouldn't be keeping out of traps?"

Oh, no. You should be logging them for analysis. Their potency is their weakness.

"So instead of attacking the system, we trigger the right defences, and it self-destructs?"

Yes, it's rather a last resort, because it has the potential to kill a lot of people.

"Why would they be using something that dangerous?"

Because it's very effective. And very cheap.

"Aah. Like the three legs of the manufacturing stool."

I am not familiar with that metaphor.

"Cost, speed, and quality. Increase any one, and you sacrifice one of the others."

Ah. So the security legs are cost, effectiveness and safety.

"And they sacrificed safety for effectiveness and cost."

Hmm...well, not that effective. If we're careful.

"Shall I go out and try again?"

I wouldn't advise it. No time to teach you the permutations.

Emotion: wry humour. "Don't want to set off a bomb in their office and then discover they would have been friends."

Especially if we got blown up by it.

"Is that a possibility?"

I am an electro-magnetic system. It's always possible. I doubt if your organics are susceptible, but finding out could be fatal.

"Fair enough. We're just about to connect to the fueling dock. That should help."

They have to drop certain protocols to allow feedback between the ship and the pumps. We can use that to access the system... see, there?

"Charlie, I'm going into full augment. Give me five minutes warning before we disconnect, will you?"

"Sure enough, Cap'n."

Let's go, Diablo. The A or M system?

A's a dead end. Don't go there, it's mined.

M takes us...

They worked their way deeper into the system, touching nothing, cataloging whatever they could. Andrew found it much easier with someone watching his back and sometimes ranging ahead. Still, it was an intense job, and he lost all track of time until a hand descended on his shoulder.

"Five minutes."

He pulled partially out of the gestalt.

"Need seven."

"Got it."

Back in the augment, they found a retreat without tripping any wires, and well within time they were out.

Andrew's shirt was soaked with sweat and his hands felt shaky, although he had been doing nothing but lying on his accel couch.

"Are you up to piloting, *Diablo*?"

Give me a moment to clean out some space. When I'm working like that, I tend to leave bits of data piled all over the place.

"Charlie, can you stall for five?"

"Sure. Base SC1, this is *Diablo*."

"What is it, *Diablo*? You're cleared for departure on course to buoy ARC-17."

"Minor glitch, SC1. Five minutes?"

"You have already exceeded allowable parameters in a high-risk zone."

"Right. So what are you going to do? Blow me up in the fueling area?"

"No, we will wait until you're out of range."

"At which point it will be obvious that I didn't do any damage, and there will be no point. Give me three more minutes. My tech is on the problem, and we're preparing to leave."

"Commence withdrawal protocol in two minutes or accept the consequences."

"Wilco, SC1. Preparing to launch." He glanced over at Andrew.

Image: Docking Supervisor with fueling hose pushed down throat.

Diablo, ready to launch?

Any time, captain.

In one minute, then. Mark.

"*Diablo*, you have thirty…"

The clamps released.

"Launching, SC1. Thank you for your hospitality."

"You're welcome, I'm sure. Cut it that fine next time and I'll shave a couple of centimetres off your butt."

"Would a bottle of good Scotch soothe your feelings?"

"Now you're talking."

"See you next orbit, SC1."

"Safe journey to you and your Scotch, *Diablo*."

Diablo eased away from the station, reached the assigned marker buoy and blasted away.

"What was all that posturing, Charlie? One moment he's threatening to kill us, the next you're offering Scotch."

The commando grinned. "Office-chair soldiers with time on their hands. Always feistier than the real fighters."

"Well, that scene was feisty enough for me. They have a formidable and scary system. *Diablo*, please check for acquired electronics."

The one they put on in the dock or the one in the fuel tank, sir?

"Let's find the one from the dock in about half an hour and fry it electronically. How do we deal with the one in the fuel?"

EV and empty the filter.

"That's all?"

It's a long, fine filament, small enough to penetrate a mechanical filter. I also have electronic filters.

"Prime. I'll go out and get it. We'll hold onto it until our next course change, then let it keep going straight ahead."

Sir Isaac Newton would be proud to know that his theories are still being utilized.

28. SPACE IS GETTING CROWDED

They reported in to *NightHawk* and the surveillance went on. Which was rather boring, because nothing happened. No ships approached or departed from the moonlet. Work proceeded. Worthing continued to drill his pilots, but in a very restricted area, probably to conserve fuel.

So ears perked up when the avatar interrupted another meaningless update meeting between Andrew and Natalia in the chart room.

"I've been on the blower with Freighty."

"Anything important?"

The mouse on the viewscreen shrugged. "He's just got word that Space Arm has finally organized their main mission to this part of the universe. Actually, they kept a close lid on it, and they've been enroute for almost four months already. The ambassador's support team ETA at Freighty in three months, give or take."

"That puts a crimp in our timetable." She raised her eyebrows at Andrew and accessed the ship's com. "Dr. Pretoro, could you join us in the chart room, please?"

Once the ambassador was seated, she explained the situation.

He frowned. "And how long will it take us to get from here to the factory?

"About a month. I can do better if we make a fairly hard burn to dump velocity at the far end."

"I'd really like to be on site when everyone else arrives. If I'm not there, it will be a big mess. On the other hand, the situation here is more fraught with possibilities. I hate to drop it before we even got a chance to try to solve it."

"I agree." She grinned. "You're starting to think like an Outbacker, sir."

"Thank you. It's been a steep learning curve."

"At least you'll be close enough to Freighty to have re-ti consultation for the last couple of weeks. But we still need to get out of here in six weeks or so."

"Analysis, ma'am?"

"Go ahead, Andrew."

"We've been updating our status and making predictions. The longer we keep collecting data, the more the law of diminishing returns sets in."

"And the key point will be...?"

"Any time now. Optimum about two weeks before we really need to act, but now is good enough."

"It will take us a week to get to the Outer Belt."

"Perfect. Why there?"

"Just a hunch. They will be slower to start anything because they're so widespread. The SolarCorp bunch is all in one place and under unified command. They could make a decision to attack in a few hours if necessary."

She glanced at the two of them. "So, we move in?"

At their nods, she accessed the ship's com. "Departure for the Outer Asteroid Belt in thirty minutes. Prepare for a one-G burn for a week and renew your arms drill. *NightHawk* is headed into action."

She gave the ambassador a reassuring smile. "That's just for crew morale. Don't be too concerned."

"Whatever works for your people, ma'am."

* * *

Three days later the Freighty avatar came up in the middle of a tactical conference. "More news, ma'am."

"What is it, Freighty?"

"We're not sure. A fleet of Earth ships is passing us in Otherwhere. We thought they were the advance party of the diplomatic fleet, but they should have been well into decel by now. They're not. They've been in space much longer, and our calculations estimate their arrival in Barnard's system in five weeks."

"What kind of ships?"

"Mostly old Space Arm, a few newer ones. Here are the schematics. The important two are the biggest one, which is an assault carrier, and the second biggest, a frigate. Nothing very up to date, but who knows what the carrier has on board, and the frigate was a power in her day. The rest look to be Support and Supply."

"So we have a small armada headed in our direction. You're sure they're not Space Arm?"

"Space Arm has sent a destroyer group with two ships designated to break off and protect the diplomats coming to Freighty and five more for backup in Barnard's System. Lots of S & S ships for Barnard's. Two troop carriers. Planetary Community looks to be establishing a permanent force in the area. But they're a few weeks behind this bunch."

"Thanks, Freighty. Keep us in touch as often as you can."

"More news as it happens, ma'am."

The Mouse disappeared, and the captain regarded her crew.

"Lieutenant Jones and Cadet Collingwood, you'll be working watch-and-watch from now on, keeping a 24-hour ear on radio traffic. I doubt if anyone around here has the intel we do, but you never know."

"Aye, ma'am. Vigilance is our watchword."

Andrew's mother gave him her 'captain' glare. He saluted and made it double time to the radioman's couch.

29.   BATTLE IS JOINED

It didn't take long until their watch paid off. Andrew was deep in sleep when Adrian's augment prodded him. *Cadet, we have an anomaly.*

He dragged himself to consciousness. *What is it, sir?*

The Lieutenant tossed him a file. *What do you make of that?*

He perused it as he tugged his uniform on. *The obvious answer isn't a happy one, sir.*

I thought likewise. Sorry to hear you agree.

Captain's awake. I suggest we meet in the chart room, sir.

On my way there.

Natalia was waiting for them. "What have you got, boys?"

Andrew set up the system hologram on their augment. "There's a bubble of that special radio frequency moving away from the asteroid."

"A bubble. An armada?"

He played a fast-motion of Jones's findings over the last three hours. "I'd say a fleet of perhaps thirty craft, Mr. Jones? Heading towards the Outer Belt. ETA about a day behind us. They haven't reached full accel yet, so we don't know."

"Could it be anything other than an attack?"

Andrew shrugged. "I just woke up. Soon as I've had coffee, I'll run some simulations. But I think it's an attack."

She nodded. "Keep watch on the Outer Belt. They must have eyes out for this sort of thing. I'll inform Ambassador Pretoro in the morning."

"Aye, ma'am."

"Aye, ma'am."

Andrew headed for the galley, while Adrian went back to his radio station on the bridge.

As soon as he felt sufficiently sharp, Andrew slipped through to his captain's couch on *Diablo* and opened the gestalt. Over the next four hours, he ran scenarios, adding new data as Jones sent it to him. As he worked, the possibilities narrowed in.

At 08:00 he roused himself and headed for the mess hall, where the captain and the ambassador had their heads together over coffees. Both looked up.

"What do you have, Cadet?"

"A fleet of thirty fighters with two larger support ships aiming for Eden Base. ETA 29 hours."

"Any reaction from the Outer Belt?"

"Lieutenant Jones has his ears open, ma'am. A slight increase in radio traffic one hour ago."

"What do your simulations suggest?"

He shook his head. "It's all too theoretical. No battle of this size has ever happened. We don't know yet what resources the Develocon people have. Maybe Worthing swoops in and takes over Eden and that's it. I doubt it, though. Kriver's too smart to be caught out."

They talked over the possibilities until Lieutenant Jones intruded.

Movement in the Outer Belt, ma'am.

Natalia jumped to her feet. "On our way, First. Andrew, full gestalt."

When they reached the bridge, Jones had the virtual map up to date. "There has been coordinated movement in the whole Belt, ma'am. Ships coming from all directions, headed to a point…" he highlighted an area just inside the asteroids, "…about there. ETA 11 hours."

Andrew calculated. "The SolarCorp fleet will be arriving there in 13 hours."

NightHawk, set a course for the edge of the Outer Belt at the point the SolarCorp vector intersects. Give us a velocity with an ETA of 10 hours.

Aye, ma'am.

The ArIn went on ship's com.

"Prepare for acceleration of 1.3 for the next 10 hours. All hands, prepare for 1.3 Gs acceleration in thirty seconds. Mark."

The captain stood in the cockpit doorway. "Adrian and Andrew, good work, but the tough part of your job is done, and you've been up all night. Four hours in your bunks, starting right now. *NightHawk* can synch with a backup operator on the radios. Alfino, you and I have time to plan our response to this."

"Sounds fine, Captain." The ambassador shook his head. "Do you think they're really going to fight?"

She frowned. "I don't believe they plan to fight, but they will if they have to. Worthing impresses me as a serious officer. He wouldn't be making this move if he wasn't prepared to back up his bluff with action. Kriver's an unknown, and that bothers me. He isn't the warlike sort, but he might start a war by mistake. Our only chance…"

Her voice disappeared as Andrew slid down to the habitation ring. He felt too keyed up to sleep, but the captain's orders were sound. When the upcoming engagement started in re-ti, he wanted to be at his best.

* * *

Four hours later, after at least two hours' full sleep, he rolled out of his bunk and dressed more carefully than usual in the heavy gravity. If there was going to be a battle, he would be prepared, and this was the only thing he could think of. He accessed the gestalt as he combed his hair. Everything was unfolding as predicted so far, anyway.

He made his laborious way up the ladder to the bridge. Jones and the captain were in conversation with the ambassador, who seemed on the defensive. His hands were up in front of himself. "No, no, Captain. You misunderstand. There is no question you are in charge."

She smiled. "I just wanted that to be clear. However, nothing else of our plan has changed. The best excuse either side has for backing down from a fight is an order from an ambassador of the Planetary government. While the negotiations are going on, you will be running them."

He nodded. "And checking with you every step of the way, believe me. I've never been in a war before."

241

Her smile twisted. "That makes a whole lot of us. One thing we can agree on. This battle must not be allowed to happen. There may come a time when I have to take military action, probably to destroy the leading vessels of both sides. Are you all right with that?"

The ambassador shrugged helplessly. "I can't give you carte blanche, but I'm beginning to trust your judgement. The opposing parties will never see us argue, I can guarantee that."

The captain turned to Andrew. "Put your best schematic of the battle on the forward viewscreen for Dr. Pretoro, please, and let's look at how things stand."

Andrew complied. "The count is now certain. Worthing has thirty of those J73 spacefighters, one fueler and one small maintenance/supply/medical ship. Kriver has forty pieces of construction and mining transport, presumably modified with projectile weapons and whatever missiles he had lying around, almost certainly un-Asimoved and illegal, and half a dozen Martin rocket-jets, which aren't much use in space. They are proceeding at predicted speeds and will join battle here," he highlighted an area, "in eight hours and twenty-five minutes unless someone changes rate as part of his tactics."

Natalia took control of the view. "And *NightHawk* will be there three hours early, sitting dead still in the middle of it all, ready to take whatever action necessary."

The First Officer cleared his throat. "Do we have any general idea of what we will do?"

"The ambassador and I have a plan sketched out, to be modified as our gestalt indicates. First, we impress upon each leader the displeasure of Space Arm and the Planetary Community with their intentions. We also inform them of the provisions of the Europa accord regarding their missiles, and the consequences should they break those rules."

Pretoro turned from his perusal of the screen. "The captain has decided, and I reluctantly agree, that she will handle the negotiations for the ceasing of hostilities. Once negotiations start, the two parties will be much easier to work with when they find they are dealing with someone backed by far more authority than a mere ship's captain has." He gave a grim smile. "The fact that the authority actually flows in the other direction is something we will not reveal."

Andrew was running these ideas through the gestalt. Finally he nodded. "There you have it, Captain. We came up with a couple of tweaks, but I know you work best on your own script. Chances of success are over 80%, plus or minus 5% considering our lack of information on the personalities involved."

She nodded. "And we're holding the two approaching fleets as ammunition for Dr. Pretoro to use at will."

He grinned. "Thanks for leaving me with the big guns. You know you can use them if you have to."

"I appreciate the offer, but I don't think I need them. The analysis of everyone here, including the most intelligent gestalt in the human race, is that these people don't really want to fight."

"Let's give them their wish."

Now came the slow-motion ballet while all the participants in the coming conflict rushed towards each other at vast velocities. *NightHawk* arrived at the middle of the predicted action and began a long, long, three-hour wait for the combatants to arrive.

At T minus one hour, Captain O'Rourke turned to her son. "Captain Collingwood, I want you and your ship out of here."

"Out of here?"

"A space battle is no place for the ambassador, and I want my gestalt platform as far out of danger as possible. Take Dr. Pretoro and Jackson aboard and find a safe spot to hide over at the edge of the Belt. Display full camo. You're responsible for keeping the gestalt at maximum at all times, and that's all. Do you follow?"

"Yes, ma'am. I understand."

"And even if it looks like a good idea that you should rush in and save the day, don't. You could just as easily lose it with a stupid stunt. Dr. Pretoro will advise you, and if he can't, Jackson has my permission to kick some sense into you."

Andrew rolled his eyes to Jackson, who was hiding a grin. "All right, Mumbot. I get the message." Then he couldn't help himself. She looked so strong and brave, standing there, and it came to him that this might well be the last time he ever saw her. He reached out his arms, and she enfolded him in a bear hug.

When he got his breath back, he stood to attention, snapped her a salute, then spun on his heel and strode to the airlock. The ambassador and his security officer gave their young captain the space he needed to compose himself, and then they boarded.

Undock when you're ready, Diablo.

Docking clamps clear.

Clear to leave dock, Diablo.

"Roger that, *NightHawk. Diablo* is away."

A light jar, and they were dropping out from the mother ship, scooting under full stealth down the side opposite from the invading forces and taking refuge in a jumble of asteroids that sped along their orbit, jostling each other occasionally when their gravity fields intersected and presenting a constantly changing profile to any sensors that might choose to pry.

But the tiny crew's eyes were all on *NightHawk*. The last hour ticked slowly past, the tension rising as the opposing forces on the screens squeezed tighter and tighter towards their ship.

Finally, Captain O'Roarke gave the word.

NightHawk, accelerate on closing course with Captain Worthing's fighter and match velocities at one thousand kilometres.

The Reconnaissance Cutter slipped ahead until she was directly in front of the first squadron, stopping, turning and accelerating to match velocities. Then she flipped around until she was facing them, sliding backwards like a football defender preparing to protect her goal, and dropped her camo.

"Captain Worthing, this is Captain Natalia O'Roarke of the Reconnaissance Cutter *NightHawk*, Planetary Community Space Craft 9108. You are hereby required to cease and desist in your proposed attack on citizens of the Planetary Community. I repeat, cease and desist. Under the Interplanet Treaties, Section five, Subsection eleven, any attack on another member of the Community is an act of war. The Planetary Community Space Arm orders you to cease and desist this act of war or suffer the full penalty of the law."

Worthing appeared on the screen in full battle armour in the cockpit of one of the fighters. "Where the hell did you come from?"

"It's not where I come from, Captain, it's who I come from. This system and all beings residing within are under the protection of the Space Arm of the Planetary Community. Cease your attack or take the consequences."

"If your only support is the puny defences I see ahead, I don't predict any consequences that will deter me."

"This is your last chance. Reverse your course."

He reached out, and the screen went blank.

"Shut down the captain's vessel."

Andrew had already penetrated the obsolete security system. In a breath, he disabled all systems in the lead fighter.

The radio channels burst into voice.

SC 2 to SC Leader. What happened?

SC 5 to SC 2. Where did he go?

What's going on? Captain Worthing, please respond. Worthing, this is SC 2. Please respond.

Andrew, keep an eye on Worthing's ship. The moment it looks like he's going to get power up, fix everything and leave it as it was. I don't want them to find that kill switch.

Aye, ma'am.

NightHawk lit her burners and sped towards the opposing forces, two thousand kilometres to the galactic north. There she played the same match-and-spin game and brought up Kriver on the bridge of the lead ship on the viewscreen.

She regarded him. "Mr. Kriver, this is Captain Natalia O'Roarke of the Reconnaissance Cutter *NightHawk*, Planetary Community Space Craft 9108. You don't really want to do this."

Kriver frowned. "'Ow did you get on this frequency? Just 'oo are you?"

"You're asking the wrong questions, Mr. Kriver. Call your motley array of ships and tell them to stand down. The Space Arm has taken control of this situation, and the war is over."

"It doesn't look over to me, I see thirty SolarCorp J73 fighters fixing to give me strife, and I will not let them get away with it."

"I should also inform you that any ArIn-guided missiles you have were just declared illegal armament, and if you use them, any gains you make in this battle will be turned over in court. Now, if I tell you that the SolarCorp forces are going to start decel very soon, will you stand your forces down?"

"I'm trusting that you really are Space Arm, ma'am, and on that shaky basis I will slow my ships to minimum battle velocity. That's all."

"Good enough. Do it now, so I can return and tell Captain Worthing my efforts at diplomacy are bearing fruit. I'll be back, Mr. Kriver."

Again, the *NightHawk* spun and raced to the opposing lines, much closer now, and still coming at full speed.

Lieutenant Jones, give me a tight channel to Worthing's personal com. Andrew, can you let him back online?

One moment, ma'am, that's a tall order...there you are, Lieutenant. Set her up on this frequency.

"You didn't follow my instructions, Captain Worthing. Note that I have persuaded the Develocon forces to begin deceleration. The next time I take action, I will shut down more of your ships, for a longer time. I must also officially warn you that, according to the provisions of the Europa Accord on Space Hostilities, Section 45A on the use of ArIn-guided missiles, any ArIn-guidance systems are forbidden, and any deployment constitutes a war crime."

"I don't believe you and I refuse to be intimidated."

"Try this."

Andrew, take out the next three.

On it, ma'am.

Three more SolarCorp ships went black, and the radio chatter swelled.

"Captain Worthing, will you now order your ships to stand down?"

"What are you doing? How can you do this?"

"Wrong questions again, but I suppose I should answer you. Your dear masters have left your ships vulnerable, and you don't have time to find out how before you run blind into a fleet that, should I allow it, will pick you off like clay pigeons. Now, if I give you your ship back, and if I promise that the Develocon forces will stop, will you stand down?"

The captain stared into the screen. Then he nodded curtly. "I will, ma'am. You have taken control of this situation, and the outcome is on your head."

"I'm happy with that, Captain. Stand by. I will return."

Turn them loose, Andrew. If he doesn't order a decel in two minutes, start shutting them down, one by one, as many as you can.

Aye, ma'am. Two minutes. Mark.

This time Natalia did not bother to approach the other forces.

"Mr. Kriver, you will note that the SolarCorp ships are decelerating. Please comply."

Kriver came on the screen, in a wider view of the cockpit of his modified ore carrier and her crew. Three men stood there: the leader and two hulking figures Andrew recognized. *Kriver, Ivan and John, ma'am. They were in the report.*

Kriver shook his head slowly. "Fair go, ma'am. I don't know how you did that, but you just saved a lot of lives. I hope you're as good at diplomacy as you are at electronics. The next hour is going to be more complicated."

"I have my own opinion about that, Mr. Kriver." She smiled. "I see that Ivan and John have followed you into battle. I congratulate them on their loyalty."

Leaving him spluttering, she signed off.

She winked at Pretoro, "That ought to soften him up a bit. All right, Mr. Jones. Let's have a wide-band announcement." *Andrew, while everyone is busy, sneak up as close as you can, but stay out of sight. I want Ambassador Pretoro in on this conference re-ti. They have to know he's on site with no time lag.*

247

Aye, ma'am.

"All channels, ma'am."

"This is Captain Natalia O'Roarke of the Reconnaissance Cutter *NightHawk*, Planetary Community Space Craft 9108, speaking to all ships within this system. Your little war is over. You have much bigger troubles coming at you than squabbles over a huge system with far too much room for all. I suggest that everyone stand down and relax. This is Ambassador Alfino Pretoro of the Planetary Community, special envoy to this area. He will be in charge of the peace negotiations.

"However, I am giving him a limited time in which to work. You may not be aware, but there are several more ships heading in our direction. If we don't get ready for them, any talking we do now will have been wasted.

"I am inviting Captain Worthing and Mr. Kriver into conference with Ambassador Pretoro. Several other interested parties will be listening in, but only four of us will take part. That is all."

Jones cut the feed and set about arranging the conference. Soon Pretoro, Worthing and Kriver were prominent on viewscreens in *NightHawk*'s bridge, and Nicholas Ludge was listening in from El Dorado 12.

Pretoro nodded to each. "Thank you for joining me, although my compatriot did not give you much choice. Circumstances are forcing my hand, so I must work more quickly than I prefer."

He leaned his elbows on the tiny table in *Diablo*'s cramped mess, the camera on a tight shot to hide his background. "Here is the situation as my sources tell me. Your interplanetary corporation masters acted with haste once they got the news about the demise of the *Clyde*. They have received information about the situation as it has developed since and are taking steps to reclaim their holdings.

"However, as the old saying goes, ground gained early is easier to hold. Whatever resolution you make to your arguments ahead of time will stand you in good stead when it comes to dealing with larger powers in the days to come." He glanced off-screen. "And now Captain O'Rourke has some intel you need to know."

Natalia rose to her full height, looking down at the camera. "As you have probably figured out, you have gravely overestimated the level of your tech backing and underestimated the scientific progress that Space Arm has made recently. I have information that is as close to re-ti as we can get in what you call the Outback. I know that both sides are thinking that if only your own forces get here first, everything will be solved, so there is no need to negotiate.

"Here's the kicker, my friends. There's only one armada coming from the interplanetaries." She waited for that to sink in. "Just so we're all on the same screen, either one interplanetary is taking charge, in which case one of you is going to be rolled over without a whimper, or else they've joined forces and they plan to squash you both and start from scratch. Which do you think is more likely?"

Kriver's lips twisted in a snarl. "We're talking 'ead Office versus the Outbackers? I know what they think of us. Useful as a third armpit."

"What do you say, Captain Worthing?"

The military man maintained his poise. "You forgot to mention 'expendable,' Mr. Kriver."

"Yeah, that too."

"If I may make a suggestion, Captain O'Rourke..."

"Certainly, Ambassador Pretoro."

"You have not mentioned the second fleet."

"Oh. It must have slipped my mind."

Worthing frowned. "What second fleet?"

"Surely you don't think the Planetary Community would send an ambassador out here without backup? I came ahead in case I was needed. I have a destroyer group enroute. I cannot reveal how soon they will arrive, but they are coming."

Kriver chuckled. "In other words, too late to do anything but mop up the mess. Beaut."

The SolarCorp captain grimaced. "That would be easiest. Let us tear each other apart, then waltz in and take over."

Pretoro nodded. "A pessimistic analysis, but true in the long run. I hope none of you are in any misapprehension of the intentions of the Planetary Community. Our government is the hand and voice of all of humanity, no matter where we go. Barnard's System will become the next seat on the Council." He paused to let that settle in.

"It is up to you to decide what your part will be."

Kriver gave the ambassador a calculating look. "What are the odds, as you see them?"

"First choice, the inhabitants of the region choose a representative by a free and fair election, and that person comes back to Earth to sit on the Council."

Worthing sighed. "And we know who has the majority of the population out here."

"Be that as it may, the second option is that one of you squashes the other, somehow holds off the squadron coming to take over and presents himself as the representative. I'm not sure how that would fly in Council, but it would give you a bigger voice at the start."

Kriver waved a hand in disgust. "And the third choice is the interplanetary fleet flattens us both and our old bosses present themselves as representatives in some kind of semi-feudal, Industrial Revolution-era oligarchy." He looked straight into the camera. "Which is the last thing the PC wants, isn't it? You need us."

Pretoro shot a glance at Natalia before answering. "The Planetary Community is strongly in favour of democratic government and cooperation between people. I, personally, suggest the first option."

Andrew sent a private message to his captain. *El Dorado.*

She smiled. "And there's another player we have not considered. The El Dorado Corporation has a longstanding legitimate claim in this system and a history of cooperation with the Community government. I wouldn't be surprised to see a few backup ships coming from them in the near future. And their loyalties will be divided."

Pretoro flicked up a finger, and she nodded for him to take over.

"They won't want to choose between their interplanetary allies and their contracts with the Planetary Community. I'd guess that they would look with favour on a middle ground somewhere, a group they can ally with that will take their interests into account."

Kriver grinned, but then a thought creased his forehead. "Mr. Ambassador, why are you being so careful to persuade us 'ow much power we'll have in this new situation?"

"Oh, don't worry. Once we get down to the bargaining table, I'll do my best to strip it all away. It is simply to the advantage of my interests to have you present."

The Outbacker nodded. "No worries, then. I look forward to future meetings, cordial or less so."

"I assure you that our interaction will always be cordial. I find it the best way to get agreements."

"I'm sure you smile as you slip the knife between the ribs."

The ambassador turned his attention to the other screen. "What about you, Captain Worthing? Where do you stand in all of this?"

The spacer shook his head. "In case nobody noticed, there was never an argument. This conversation is a good example of how life is going to be. You and Kriver will thrash out the agreements, Captain O'Rourke will back them up with her destroyers, and I'll be here with my fighters to make sure nobody pushes the Outbackers around."

Kriver's eyebrows shot up. "Strewth. You really mean that?"

The captain shrugged. "Whoever thought it was in our best interests to fight each other? If you did, I misjudged you severely. This whole war was a result of leftover corporate antagonism disguised as competition. If we're going to survive out here, we have to get rid of that. I was wracking my brains for a way to settle this, and the ambassador has presented us with one." He gave a wry grin. "And Captain O'Rourke has pushed it down our throats. I'd like to know how she managed it."

Natalia's face became serious. "In about four hours, you're going to find out. I'll give you that long to prepare yourselves for a tactical conference on my ship. We have little idea what enemy we're facing, and we have a fleet in three parts that have never flown together. We have work to do, my friends."

On that sober note, they signed off.

251

30. BATTLE PLAN

Four hours later the principal players in the game were face to face, re-li, in the mess hall of *NightHawk*. Jackson stood at ease behind the ambassador, and Chakka glowered from his bed in the corner. Andrew watched from his own ship in full gestalt, and Lieutenant Jones scanned all radio frequencies, on guard inside and out.

Pretoro beamed at them. "I find it fascinating when all the roles in the drama come together on the same stage. I'm sure it makes a difference when you realize that Natalia is such a commanding presence in person."

She frowned at him. "And it gives you the opportunity to take me down a peg by making me blush. Don't worry, I know your tricks."

"Oh, I have a few more up my sleeve." Then he regarded the group seriously. "Let's make one point clear. Nobody at this table wants the coming battle to happen. We're hoping to persuade the attacking forces to think the same way. Because there's that new piece to the puzzle I mentioned. As of last year, there is a revised accord regulating any space battles." He outlined the technical problems and their solutions.

"So any use of ArIn-guided armament is specifically forbidden. If you break this law, any results you achieve will be thrown out of court, and you'll find yourselves in the docket instead for war crimes. I will inform the invading fleet of this situation as well."

Worthing frowned. "But this affects everything."

"It does. And I'm now handing the briefing over to the only person with the means to get us out of this." He nodded to Natalia.

She stood. "As the ambassador says, we don't want this battle to happen, but we have to act as if it will, for two reasons. First, we must persuade the enemy that we are willing to fight. Any show of weakness will increase his resolve. Second, we must persuade ourselves of the same. If we go into the battle with anything other than a complete drive to win, we will lose.

"The first action we must take is the disarming of any ArIn-guided missiles you are carrying. Space Arm technicians will take

252

care of this. It will leave your ordnance similar to standard heat-seeking, radar-controlled older models. As compensation, we will also upgrade your defence systems to a point that should make any enemy missiles ineffective. Our strategy will assume those capabilities. Is everyone aware of the situation, now?"

Nods around the table.

"Any comments before we start?"

Worthing nodded. "All my sources confirm, to the best of their reach, what you say. I'm still waiting on one of them, but he seems to have disappeared."

Natalia smiled. "Big guy? Ex-military, with a pipsqueak sidekick and a super-hot rocketship?" She poked a thumb over her shoulder. "His room is just around the curve, there."

"He was one of yours? I never would have known."

She leveled a stare at the other captain. "And it's a good thing he and his tech dropped in on you. Do you realize you're sitting on a security time bomb?"

Worthing frowned. "We have a very effective security system. Top of the line."

Natalia shook her head. "Bring your head tech aboard to talk to my people. You have two problems. First, the security back at your asteroid headquarters could go rogue at any moment, simply because somebody pushed the wrong sequence of buttons. You're using a minefield to protect your vegetable garden from rabbits."

He shook his head. "And I know what you're going to say next. Anyone with knowledge of our system could set it off at will."

"Exactly. If we come up against your former masters, you're doubly vulnerable."

"And what about my ships? You made a comment about them in the same light."

"Your ship systems are all compromised but in a much simpler way. They don't want to destroy them, just take them out of action. Again, a quick chat with my tech people and you can defuse those yourselves."

Kriver frowned. "You 'ad the same guy poking around in my system as well. What's the bad news for me?"

She grinned. "It's full of Trojans, Flemings and back doors, completely open to assaults of all sorts. However, my people put them in, and they are easily found and deactivated. Aren't you glad you decided to side with us?"

"That remains to be seen. What kind of a genius plan 'ave you got to defeat an armada that we assume out-techs and out-guns us?"

"I thought we should all have input on that. We have one sure trick. At some moment in the battle, just when Worthing's fighters are needed the most, the nasties are going to pull the pin, and they'll stop dead. But we know they won't be dead, because we'll disarm the kill switches. So, our pilots will get the signal instead of their ships and shut themselves down. They should be safe because they will seem harmless, and nobody wants to waste good ships this far from home. We wait until the enemy exposes himself, and they all fire up and attack."

Worthing nodded. "What do we know about the enemy's capability?"

Andrew fired Freighty's information up on the viewscreen.

"One small carrier, Wasp class. Probably loaded with something like your fighters, Captain Worthing, newer models if we're unlucky. That size of carrier can house forty, but we suspect they'll have less because of the extra fuel, parts and equipment they need to bring. All the other ships are Service and Support except for the frigate, which will become *NightHawk*'s problem. She's bigger than us but we assume slower and electronically inferior. We should also outgun her."

Worthing steepled his fingers. "You sound very confident. Where are the holes?"

"Any of our analysis could be proved wrong by the addition of a modern stand-alone ArIn-guided rocketry system on any ship. Our anti-missile systems should be able to outsmart anything they can mount, but all it takes is one lucky shot, and if *NightHawk* is put out of commission, the balance of power tips radically."

"That's the advantage the Develocons had over us. They're spread out. We can be decimated with a single strike to our asteroid."

"And your old bosses will know where you are."

254

"Oh, yes. The asteroid was SolarCorp's big investment. That's why I was sent to protect it. Good thing for my squadron, too."

"Why was that?"

"Because that's what we were doing when *Clyde* met her maker." He regarded Natalia. "Nobody ever figured out what happened, there. Word went 'round there was a Space Arm ship in the vicinity, which must have been you, and that ancient alien relic that repaired the El Dorado mine was there, and then suddenly *Clyde* wasn't there."

She nodded. "That pretty well describes it. Freighty isn't a being to play around with."

"So I gather. We don't admit to much contact with El Dorado, but they're really happy with his work." He dropped his hands to the table. "Are we supposed to talk about this alien factory?"

She smiled. "He's a business enterprise. He'll take all the word-of-mouth he can get."

"But he's out of this business."

"Two light years from here and headed for Earth."

"Too bad."

"He would be handy, but we'll manage."

"I hope so."

She looked around the table. "Any other ideas?"

Kriver shrugged. "I'm no military man, but we should 'ave an edge if we meet them in the asteroids. A lot of battles I've read about depended on local knowledge, and my crews know 'ow to navigate in the rocks."

Natalia nodded. "We'll take whatever advantage we can get. Supply lines will be a problem for us. *NightHawk*, may we have a plan of the system? POV ninety from the ecliptic, star centred."

A virtual star system appeared, hovering above the table.

"Thank you. Highlight human-occupied positions. Oh, yes, and nearest point to Sol. Great."

The stood and looked down on the plan.

"The enemy fleet will come in from fifteen degrees above the ecliptic, because that's their course from Sol. I think we want to meet them at that point, there." She pointed to a spot at the edge of the Outer Asteroid Belt. "El Dorado is almost the other side of the system, which makes the mine safe for the moment. Most of Develocon's work area in the Outer Belt is upspin of the contact point. SolarCorp's asteroid in the Inner Belt lags that but is on a faster orbit, so you're catching up. It's perfect bait for the enemy, because they could wipe us out, swing left and sweep the Outer Belt mining area, and go straight on to the asteroid base. *NightHawk*, advance four weeks."

"*Aye, ma'am.*"

Everything spun, and the human areas came closer to the battle zone. "That's what it will look like the day they reach the Outer Belt. They'll know where we are, because they have the same tech as SC1, so your ultra-short-band radio won't help. Captain Worthing, you're a military man. What does your training say?"

"You've covered most of it. If our base is closing on the action zone, we'll be able to access fuel and supply from SC1, about..."

"Five days away from the contact point."

"Thank you. At the same time, it's vulnerable. Our safety depends on their strategy."

"They've invested a lot in SC1. They won't trash it, will they?"

"No, they'll only want to destroy our space capability, then starve us out if they choose."

Natalia shook her head. "At first, maybe, but they'll find out about the destroyers soon enough. We should be able to lure them into the asteroids with the temptation that they could destroy us there. Remember, we're assuming that they think they can capture all the fighters intact, though they'll be happy to destroy any other quasi-military craft."

Andrew and the *NightHawk* gestalt were listening to all this, and he passed Natalia a plan, putting a new virtual schematic up.

"My tacticians suggest that we set up a fake ambush using the Develocon fleet as decoys. They run to the Asteroid Belt, where the SolarCorp fighters are waiting, hidden in the rocks."

Worthing nodded. "And they'll chuckle and take the bait, because they know that when we spring the trap, they can defang it by shutting down the fighters."

"And as they sweep past chasing us down, you come up behind and blast them." Kriver gave a twisted grin. "Puts us on the 'ot seat."

Captain O'Rourke shook her head. "Stay far enough in front, then duck into dense clusters where they can't take time to chase you out because of the pressure from behind."

"Success will depend on what kind of fighters they have." Worthing pointed to the contact area. "If they have independent gunnery systems that can shoot laterally, this won't be so effective."

73% chance of point-the-ship-to-aim fighters.

"We're reading only a one-in-four chance of craft that sophisticated."

Kriver glanced at her. "You did that very quick."

She laughed. "Constant contact with my battle ArIn." She stared him down. "And we're just a reconnaissance vessel. When those destroyers show up, any unfriendly military forces had better be gone from the system. You have no idea what they're capable of."

He merely raised his eyebrows. "Let's hope the interplanetaries don't 'ave a similar surprise up their sleeves."

"No worries. I haven't shown my full hand yet, either."

Kriver threw up his hands. "You're the long arm of civilization in this wild-west show, ma'am. We'll be counting on you."

"And I'm counting on you. We all pull together and we'll do just fine." Her eyes scanned the group around the table. "But just in case anyone had any other ideas, when the battle is joined, I'll be in command. That's not in question."

Kriver held up his hands defensively. "No, no question."

Worthing came to attention. "You can count on us, ma'am."

Image: smiling captain, changing to frown. I hope you lot are all listening as well.

Emotion, multiple feeds: cheerful compliance.

Andrew, there was one notable exception in that vote of confidence.

Oh. Sorry, Mum. Didn't know I was expected to participate in the primitive pre-battle tribal war dance.

Hmm.

"Is something wrong, Captain O'Rourke? You don't look 'appy."

"Don't worry, Mr. Kriver. Unless you're a parent, you won't get it."

"Parent?"

"I have a teenager wandering around somewhere. Trying to learn to be a cadet."

"I didn't know Space Arm allowed families on board."

"Long story." She turned to the battle simulation. "Any ideas to make it work better?"

Worthing pointed. "Can we see a closer view of that area of the asteroids? We need a spot to hide our fuel and support ships, few though they are."

Natalia put one up. "I know they don't look thick enough for good hiding, but to ships travelling at a couple of thousand klicks they're a real maze."

And the planning continued.

* * *

When the enemy fleet was ten hours away, Captain O'Rourke went to the bridge of the *NightHawk*. "Lieutenant Jones, a short-range fleet-wide channel, please."

"You have it, ma'am."

"All right, folks. Here's our battle formation. First, we have found an area of the Belt with a scattering of those magnetized rocks. This won't completely hide everyone, which is exactly what we want: an inept primary ambush to lure our enemies into over-confidence.

"All the Develocon ships will be in the front line, paired up in the loosest of 'loose deuce' formations. I don't expect these pilots to hang together very well in battle, because your craft all have such different capabilities. If any one of ours is dragging a bandit, nail him. However, we hope it doesn't come to dogfights. More on that later. When I give the cue, your whole fleet needs to break and run in a disorganized way. Everyone accelerate at max and head for wherever you've decided to hide.

"SolarCorp fighters will be hidden farther out in the Belt, spread wide in a cone around the proposed attack course of the invaders. The enemy will know very well you are there. In order to attain enough speed to attack them, our fighters have to trip the ambush before their fleet reaches you. Break cover and accelerate at maximum speed as if you're trying to take up position on their six after they pass. I'll give you precise timing to hit them at 500 klicks higher relative velocity. At that point, I will contact the enemy fleet and suggest they surrender. Of course, they won't.

"Instead, they'll try to shut down your ships. When you hear the 'kill' signal, go dead until I give the word, and then continue acceleration.

"Our second level of ambush is when you return to the battle. Again, I will ask for surrender. If they don't, continue your attack and take out as many as you can. Remember that your missiles have been adapted and are no longer as effective as they were, so depend on your projectile cannons for attack. The Develocon ships can take potshots at the enemy as they pass, but they'll be moving too fast for you to catch up to them."

Worthing came on the com. "That's a tall order. We will outnumber them by about three to one, but our attack will be fragmented, and we assume they have superior firepower."

"That's when we trigger the third level of our ambush. *NightHawk* will take out the frigate."

"How will you do that?"

"With modern sensing equipment, there's only one place a ship can't see an enemy. On their six in the ionization of their drive plume. Even when they're coasting, their reactor spills enough garbage to mess up most forms of communication, and we can tuck in really close.

"We're heading outsystem immediately, and we'll trail them back in under stealth mode. The only problem will be if someone from the S & S fleet spots us and warns them.

"One advantage the defensive fleet always has in fighter engagements; these attackers have to aim their ships to shoot particle weapons, so they can't come into battle butt-first. The upgrades we gave your ships mean they can outsmart any ArIn-targetted missile available on the open market and most of the black ones. If the enemy has found something better, then we're in trouble. We hope they'll obey the laws and not use them, but it's a faint chance.

"So, they can't be decelerating. Once they choose their attack speed, they can only go faster. Be careful trailing them. Their intent will probably be to wait until they are past you. Then they will turn around to decel, get back to the battle and shoot in your direction. When they turn, it becomes a different fight. Take your best shot while they're broadside and improvise from there. You have hundreds of tactical options in your battle computers."

"That's it, folks. Listen to our combat channels. The com will be much more secure than you're used to, and our plan of attack depends on accurate timing. Good luck to us all."

Worthing's image on the viewscreen snapped her a salute and blanked out. Kriver tipped two fingers towards his eyebrow and with his usual sardonic grin was gone.

Andrew opened their private channel. *Where do you want us, Cap'n?*

Out of danger. We need the battle gestalt running and the ambassador safe. You parallel us a thousand klicks upspin. The only way I might use you is against some element of the S & S fleet. We'll have to see.

Aye, ma'am. We're on your five until you make your turn. Then we'll hold back on your seven until you engage.

Natalia clicked onto battle com. *Good hunting, everyone. NightHawk out.*

In the virtual display the fleet separated slowly to their ambush positions. The long wait had begun.

31. THE BATTLE THAT COULDN'T BE

Five hours from contact, Natalia appeared in her dress uniform. She tossed a grin at Andrew's surprised face. "Historic occasion. I want my news holos to look good."

"You're not planning to fight, are you? You're going to solve this some other way."

She tipped her head. "Let's give the invading fleet plenty of time to make up their minds to back out." She opened the ship's com. "Find us a channel, First."

"Aye, ma'am. They'll be using something like the *Clyde* did...there you have it, ma'am."

The bridge of an older frigate came into view: well-lit, tidy and filled with active people.

Natalia nodded to Pretoro.

"Develocon and SolarCorp fleet. This is Ambassador Alfino Pretoro of the Planetary Community. Please state your intentions in this system."

An officer appeared on screen. He was about fifty, stocky but sharply turned out in what could almost be a military uniform. He frowned. "Who?"

"I am Alfino Pretoro, Ambassador-at-Large to the citizens of the Barnard System. These people are under my jurisdiction and the protection of the Space Arm, and I ask again, what is your intention in bringing an armed force of this size into the area?"

The officer glowered. "Well, Ambassador whoever-you-are, this is Commodore Tevis of the SolarCorp Security Vessel *Sea Wolf*. I don't know where you were with your precious Space Arm enforcers when a bunch of bandits attacked and took over our facilities here, but in the absence of any proper law to protect our rights, we have brought our own enforcement. Our intention is to take back our assets, and I suggest you don't get in our way."

"The Planetary Community does not see the situation in such simple terms. As far as we are concerned, we have arrived in a new territory, and until a court of law settles it differently, whoever says

261

they own any physical property in that territory right now, we are happy to go with that as a working model. If further investigation reveals other ownership, you have recourse to the same court to retrieve your property. We will not allow you to take it by force."

Tevis smiled, and it wasn't pleasant. "Well, Mister Ambassador, I don't see anyone within a few light years who has the power to tell me otherwise, so I think I will just go about my business reclaiming my company's holdings. When your law court sends someone to enforce your laws, then we can see what that court says about possession."

Pretoro nodded politely. "I understand your point of view. However, I urge you to remember that the statutes of the Planetary Community protect all its citizens, and if you break those laws in any way, then whatever action you take thereafter will be tainted by that act. I am sending you the articles of the new Europa Accord on Space Hostilities. I draw your special attention to Section 45A on the use of ArIn-guided missiles. Good day to you, Commodore Tevis."

Lieutenant Jones cut the circuit.

Pretoro faced the other leaders on their viewscreens. "They read the rules the same way we do. Possession will be the key factor. I'm sorry, gentlemen, but that little drama only puts us on record as having given the warning. It makes no difference to today's larger performance."

Captain O'Rourke nodded. "Exactly as we expected. Ambassador, your impressions of Commodore Tevis?"

"He doesn't seem very military. Talks more like a lawyer."

"I noted the same." She frowned. "I'm not sure whether to be happy or not."

I don't think you're happy, ma'am. Andrew shipped her a file.

She frowned as she scanned it. "I take that back. This doesn't look good. He's a former Space Arm transport pilot who was tossed out for corruption. Military training that didn't stick. Makes him a possible loose cannon." She shrugged. "Time will tell. Our action goes as planned."

Captain?

Yes, Cadet.
The gestalt just tossed us another problem.
Worthing?
Oh. You're on it.
Lieutenant, get me a private line with Captain Worthing.
Coming up, ma'am.

"Worthing here, ma'am. Thought you might be calling."

"Well?"

The captain shook his head. "Nothing to worry about ma'am. In the first place, I was never happy with the way things were going out here, having that big piece of scrap iron lording it over everyone. It was nothing like I'd been led to believe. More like some kind of feudal system. In the second place, I've burnt my bridges with SolarCorp. If they took me back, I'd never get promoted. I have a chance to build something bigger out here and grow with it. You can count on me, ma'am."

She grinned. "And I'll ship a recording of that little speech to Kriver. I'm sure he'll be pleased."

"Oh, I imagine he will. He's already got that, 'I could be the next Counsellor,' gleam in his eye."

"And does that bother you?"

"I don't want it, so it's up to the people, isn't it?"

"Fair enough. O'Rourke out."

"Worthing out."

The captain turned to her son. "Captain Collingwood, get your precious cargo and take up your position."

There was no emotional farewell this time. Andrew held his salute a touch longer, staring into her eyes, then made his usual perfect 'about face' and headed to the airlock.

* * *

The Interplanetary fleet swooped down into the ecliptic at good speed, dumping fighters from the carrier as they came. Twenty spread ahead in squadrons of five. Ten more stayed to guard the S

& S ships, a threatening shadow in the background. The frigate paraded in front and centre, an orca in a school of sharks.

"*NightHawk*, what are we facing?"

"The next gen of Worthing's ships, ma'am, Junkers 73Bs, 30 metres in length. If they haven't been modernized further, they'll be about 10% faster, with two Vulcan 50mm cannons instead of one. Also with about 10 tonnes of various missiles, but our counter-deployment advantage should make their tracking systems useless. Targetting the projectile cannons means 'point the ship and shoot.' Unfortunately, a 50mm slug moving at two thousand klicks before it was even fired has quite a clout. A single flak round with its explosive charge boosting the speed even more can tear one of these fighters to shreds despite their shielding."

"What does it look like, Captain Worthing?"

"A standard attack. They finished decelerating before deployment, and they're moving too fast to stop and duke it out. They plan to sweep through, do as much damage as possible to our fleet and keep going to softer targets. Any deceleration will show a change of tactics."

"That bodes well for our feint. It sounds like they fell for it."

"We're about to find out." Worthing gave a brief chuckle. "This will be interesting from an academic point of view."

"In what way?"

"I assume you know that there hasn't been a flotilla battle in the last forty years."

"There has never been a battle of this size in the Space Age. Let's not mess up our entry in the history books."

Andrew was watching the formation, shaking his head. He ran the possible strategies through the *Diablo* gestalt, and it still didn't add up.

Ma'am, there's something wrong, here.

What have you got, Cadet Collingwood?

You know how you always tell me never to assume your opponent is stupid?

I may have mentioned it a few times.

This attack formation is completely out of date. We spent hours on the simulators at the Academy, and this kind of frontal approach, fighters against fighters, doesn't work with modern weaponry and avoidance systems.

I probably agree. Can you give me some quick details?

First, there's the matter of computing power. You simply can't have a warhead with enough intelligence to match the abilities of a fighter's system. Plus the new rules of engagement deny their use.

So we disregard any missiles either side is carrying. That brings it down to ship-to-ship projectile weapons in an old-fashioned dogfight. Which also doesn't work, because a head-on attack with flak ordnance is mutually destructive 67% of the time. It's basically a 'chicken fight.' The ship that fires the last shell wins the fight and then gets taken out by the shrapnel that's still flying his way because he was too busy firing to duck.

So, why is this guy setting up for this kind of battle?

We need the Nighthawk gestalt to run a few more scenarios.

Just remember that the enemy is closing on our ships at 2,000 klicks as we think. Options are narrowing.

Aye, ma'am. This shouldn't take long.

It didn't. Even with Chakka's usual aggressive attitude skewing the results, the conclusion was obvious.

There you have it, ma'am. A 93% chance that our enemy is assuming superior technology. He thinks he's going to sweep through, blast the inferior Develocon fleet to smithereens, shut down our J73s and take them over, then forge on into Barnard's System in complete control.

And the other 7%?

5% chance he has some new technology up his sleeve, like a smarter ship-to-ship missile that can beat our defensive screens.

And the last 2% is Murphy's law or something we haven't thought of?

We run all our simulations to plus or minus 2%.

Then it all depends on what the commodore will do when we spring our second trap. If he's smart, he quits. If he's stupid or crazy enough to keep fighting?

Emotion: helplessness. Then a lot of people are going to die for nothing. We can set our filters for 'stupid' but nobody can predict 'crazy.'

Well, let's be watching this person very carefully once we make contact. Put our outside observer to work. That's his field of expertise. If Tevis is a decent military mind, he might do the right thing.

Aye, ma'am. I'll pass that along.

In *Diablo*'s cockpit, Andrew gestured to Dr. Pretoro. "The battle hinges on Tevis. The captain wants you to watch him specially."

"Will it be recorded?"

"You can access it through voice command without touching our gestalt."

"Thank you."

They both stood in silence, eyes fixed on the monitor.

Natalia was watching the timer in her augment. *NightHawk, mark the zero position at the edge of the Belt where Kriver is waiting. Start battle timing in 3...2...1...Mark.*

Mark start of battle, ma'am. The enemy attack force is uprange 3129 km, closing at 2000 kph.

"Get me a channel, First." The captain cleared her throat.

"This is Captain Natalia O'Roarke of the Reconnaissance Cutter *NightHawk*, Planetary Community Space Craft 9108. You are hereby required to cease and desist in your proposed attack on citizens of the Planetary Community. I repeat, cease and desist. Under the Interplanet Treaties, Section five, Subsection eleven, any attack on another member of the Community is an act of war. The Planetary Community Space Arm orders you to cease and desist this act of war or suffer the full penalty of the law. You have been officially informed of the provisions of the Europa Accord on Space Hostilities, Section 45A on the use of ArIn-guided missiles."

A brief pause allowed their opponent to register this new development, but his masters had given him a prepared response. "I am taking no action against lawful citizens of the Planetary Community. Our facilities have been attacked and taken over by

266

outlaws. We are here to re-establish our rightful control. Anyone who tries to stop us is de facto supporting those outlaws and will suffer the consequences."

"Space Arm is aware of the situation and suggests legal action is your best recourse. From this moment on any move you take will be considered by Space Arm and the Planetary Community as criminal activity."

"That's not how our lawyers read it, ma'am. I have my orders, and I will fulfill them. If you wish to save lives, it's up to you to stand down your motley collection of pirates, and we will leave them alone."

"I think you will find my motley collection quite up to the task, sir. I will now sign off, but I am always available on this frequency, should you change your mind. Space Arm Flotilla over and out."

The officer's image faded from the viewscreen. The two fleets continued their collision course, with *NightHawk* coasting slowly closer to the frigate, *Diablo* off her starboard quarter.

Andrew raised his eyebrows at Pretoro, who shook his head.

"So far, he's acting exactly as his masters would expect."

"He's a long way from his masters."

"I hope he's fully aware of that."

Battle Time 10 minutes, ma'am. J73Bs uprange 2217 km. Ordnance travelling at 3,000 kph will arrive in 44 minutes.

Then Andrew realized the importance of what was happening. *Ma'am, the S&S ships are reorienting for decel. Sea Wolf and the carrier as well.*

Emotion: impatience. Of course. They don't want to end up in the middle of the battle. NightHawk, prepare for decel. Forward thrusters only.

That leaves a gap. It's getting wider as we speak.

Ah. And once the 73Bs pass them, our Develocon ships are going to be alone in the middle of that gap. Are you suggesting Tevis doesn't realize that?

It looks like he's taken the bait completely, ma'am.

They're wide open.

Except for one small frigate. Small, as in bigger than you.
Which we are about to neutralize.

All eyes watched viewscreens and the virtual display on the augment as the trailing fleet realigned itself.

Lieutenant Jones broke in. "Their S & S are holding at 1000 kph, ma'am. The frigate has split the difference at 1500 klicks and returned to forward orientation. Engines on idle. We can approach on their six safely."

On Andrew's virtual map, the scout crept slowly up behind the larger ship until the drive plume obscured it even from *Diablo*'s sensitive eyes.

He searched his augment. *Checking reception. You still there, NightHawk?*

Still here. The gestalt is working fine, but without you we lack clear outside viewpoints. Jones is having trouble with other communications as well. Please relay for me.

Wilco, Captain. Diablo, the battle count is unclear. Please continue for us.

Battle plus 30 minutes, sir. J73Bs uprange 1500 km. Their ordnance would arrive at Kriver's ships in 30 minutes. S & S fleet uprange 1705 km, frigate and NightHawk 1597 km.

The SolarCorp fighters held formation, and the slow-motion performance danced on.

Time to spring our ambush, Cadet. Then turn the microphone over to the diplomatic corps.

"Captain Worthing, please have your pilots jettison their auxiliary fuel tanks. Your attack should begin in five minutes from my mark. Mark."

"Five minutes. Wilco."

Soon twenty of the old-style J73s were blasting at full power, heading for the spot their newer sisters would be when courses intersected. They came in sharply defined squadrons of four, enclosing the attacking fleet in a pentagon. The other ten SolarCorp fighters lay doggo in the asteroids, ready for any eventuality.

Still the invaders made no changes, cruising like a school of sharks through peaceful waters.

Dr. Pretoro, you have contact.

Andrew nodded to the ambassador, who faced the viewscreen with the frigate's bridge showing.

"Commodore Tevis, I assume you see that the battle plan has changed. Perhaps you have rethought your decision?"

The commodore gave a triumphant smile and chopped his hand downwards. "I don't think the plan has changed very much, sir." Out in the Belt, twenty J73 fighters went dead.

Battle plus 35 minutes, sir. J73Bs uprange 1246 km. Ordnance time 25 minutes. S & S fleet uprange about 1580 km, frigate 1357 km.

Holding, ambassador.

Tevis came back on screen. "How are we doing now?

The ambassador was beginning to enjoy himself, but he refused to show it. "Let's see how the next few minutes play out."

At his nod, *Diablo* blanked the screen.

The ambassador grinned to Andrew. "Give him his moment of fun for the next ten minutes before we rain on his picnic."

The enemy front is approaching attack position on the Develocon ships, ma'am.

Tell them to break and run.

Aye, ma'am. He activated the com on their general battle frequency. "Develocon ships, time to leave the party. Make it messy, boys."

First one, then another Develocon ship turned away from the approaching forces. Soon the whole group was scattering into the asteroids, their engines at full accel. But they moved slowly compared to the racing SolarCorp fighters sweeping down on them.

Battle plus 55 minutes, ma'am. J73Bs uprange 211 km. Ordnance approaching re-ti delivery.

Ma'am, the enemy fighters are within firing distance of Kriver's ships, and some of his slower ones are still in the danger zone. If Tevis is going to use his missiles, it will be any time now.

I'm getting the same data. Give the signal to resume.

Once again Pretoro called on the enemy commodore. "Your gambit has been accepted and countered, Captain." He made a gentle 'please rise' gesture with both hands.

Andrew sent, "Continue," to the J73s, and they all fired up and resumed pursuit.

The ambassador allowed himself a small smile. "May I suggest your next move would be capitulation?"

The other captain was obviously surprised, his eyes shooting to people off screen. Then he focused, his face becoming grim. "We had hoped to solve this with a minimum of damage, sir, but you force us to take serious action. Your old equipment has no chance against our new technology. Stand down and you will prevent a massacre."

"I think not, Commodore Tevis. Speaking of modern technology, you may not have noticed a barnacle on your tail that you will find very difficult to pry off."

"What are you talking about?" The officer's eyes moved right, communicating with someone in his augment.

"If you analyze your ion trail, you will find the additions of certain elements that indicate a Hall-Effect Thruster fueled by plutonium and iodine, which your ship does not use."

Tevis glanced right again and began to raise his hand.

"Please do not attempt a quick spin to bring your broadside to bear. At the first change of attitude or hint of acceleration, our ship will plant a Space-to-Space missile in a delicate portion of your anatomy from a position far too close to be avoided by electronic means."

"What do you want?"

"I want you to order the fighter pilots in the S & S defence to shut down their engines and exit their ships. You may send rescue from your fleet. Order your attack squadrons to begin deceleration and continue until zero velocity relative to the asteroid belt and stand by."

"And if I don't?"

"First, our reserve fleet will destroy your support ships one at a time until you see sense."

Andrew pointed to the virtual battle scene. One tail-end defence fighter had been touching his forward thrusters, easing himself out of line. Andrew and *Diablo* reached out and entered his system, sliding past the firewalls and shutting down his engines.

"For example, you have now lost one of your fighters." He gestured two fingers to Andrew. "And there goes the one at the other end of the formation. I will give you some time to think before I start this battle, which has not really begun and does not have to begin. As you know, I much prefer a diplomatic solution."

Battle plus 65 minutes, ma'am. J73Bs downrange 249 km. S & S fleet spread uprange around 1200 km. Frigate 654 km.

Diablo faded out of the contact, and Andrew joined the *NightHawk* gestalt again.

Captain, we've got a problem. The ambassador's made his pitch. The trailing J73Bs have shut down, but Tevis is still holding out for a full-scale battle. His attack squadron has spun to cover Worthing's ships, but is not decelerating.

You must be kidding. Is this the 'crazy' we couldn't compensate for? What does our expert say?

Andrew raised his eyebrow to the ambassador. "What do you think, sir?"

"All I see is inability to process unwelcome news. With any luck at all he'll come round."

"What if he's too stubborn until it's too late?"

An unambassadorial shrug. "It would be helpful to give him a serious jolt of reality."

"Thank you, sir. We'll work on that." He returned to the gestalt.

Ma'am, it's probable that we're just facing a stubborn inability to accept re-ti evidence. We need to send him a reality check, and we need to do it soon. I can't guarantee these two ships back here will remain dormant without my attention. They've got very good repair routines, and a simple reboot will solve most of their problems.

Do the best you can. Our fighters are now moving again?

271

Accelerating, ma'am. If they go at full burn, they could match velocity with the S & S fleet in 10 minutes. They would be within firing range going 500 kph faster in 20.

Would be?

Do we really want to catch them?

Ah, I see. What do you have in mind?

My gestalt suggests a slower accel that doesn't catch up for half an hour, maybe more. Fast enough to make our attack seem real, but slow enough for Tevis to unfreeze and start facing reality.

And what are you suggesting we do with our extra time?

We need a more permanent solution. May I put Diablo in the gestalt?

Now is not a time to stand on policy. Whatever will help.

Andrew could feel his universe expanding as data rushed through and past him. Possible scenarios peeled away, each replaced by a better one.

But through all of them a single factor remained consistent. The main weakness of both fighter fleets was their short duration of independent movement. After only a few hours of battle they would need fuel, oxygen, and ammunition. The carrier ship loomed larger and larger in every scenario. Andrew finally wrenched control of the gestalt and calmed it.

"There you have it, Captain. The carrier is the key."

"*NightHawk* can take it out, but it would free up the frigate. The moment we leave this safe position we're into a firefight. Can you freeze the carrier's systems?"

"Not from the outside. Their electronic defences are too strong…wait a minute." A plan was forming. He ran it past *Diablo*.

Response: confirmation.

Analysis: 52% chance of success.

They ran several adaptations.

Analysis: 60% chance of success.

He ran it through the *NightHawk* gestalt and fine-tuned every possibility.

Analysis: chance of success: 73%, fatality: 7%.

He broke the gestalt.

272

"There you have it, ma'am. 73% chance, with only 7% chance of destruction. Better odds than anything else."

"Can you really do that?"

"Their ship bays are open to allow quick access for damaged vessels. Depending on how well our camo works, we may or may not have to blast our way in. Once we're inside, the odds of success improve even more."

"Dammit, Andrew, this is why I didn't want you out here."

"Mum, this is why I'm out here. Nobody else would have thought of this plan. Nobody else can do it. I've already stolen the IFF code from the first fighter we stalled."

"I know, son, I know. Permission to proceed. What can we do to help?"

"Make a big fuss. Start maneuvers. Distract and decoy."

Her face became grim. "We can do that. Good luck, Son. I love you."

"I love you too, Mum. If I don't make it, apologize to Freighty that I destroyed his best work, but it was for a good cause."

Before the lump in his throat choked him, he cut the contact and began sending orders to *Diablo*.

32. DELICATE PILOTING

They approached the huge carrier, their Permaskin camouflage presenting J73B symbols and their radio broadcasting mayday signals and a legitimate Friend-or-Foe ID on the SolarCorp battle frequency.

A large hand descended on Andrew's shoulder. "Cadet, if you mess this up and get the ambassador killed, I'm going to be very upset with you. And it'll play havoc with your marks when you get back to school."

He glanced up at Jackson's face. "You've known the captain for six months, and you think I'm afraid of Cadet Academy? Have you ever seen the look on her face when she's disappointed in you?"

"Something I have to look forward to if you get us out of this mess. Consider it a challenge."

Andrew winked at the ambassador. "Any further pressure, sir?"

"No, Cadet, my analysis tells me that you have just enough to pique your best performance. What is it you're going to do?"

"I can't attack their systems from outside. So we go in."

"Ah. The simplest solution. And why did nobody else think of it?"

Andrew shrugged. "They would have. It just would have been too late." He glanced over. "You'd better get down and cinch your straps to their max. This landing has to be rough to work. Thanks for the humour to help me relax. I know it was meant well, but distraction is the last thing I need right now."

Jackson moved to the door, headed for the accel straps in one of the bunks. "Excuses, excuses."

Battle plus 75 minutes, sir. J73Bs downrange 750 km. S & S uprange 1100 km, Frigate and NightHawk 400 km.

Andrew focused on the target. *First bay behind the bridge, Diablo. The closer we are the better, in case we have to get out and walk.*

Roger that, Andrew. They're not happy.

Put me on their com. Break it up.

Hit… dama… asteroid too… stabili… repeat, no lateral… zer. Visu… ly. Visual o… he chopped off the channel and popped a port-starboard slue on the steering jets.

They approached the carrier, its huge sides towering above and below them. The open bay door looked like a small target, but that was the least of their worries. Up and down the length of the old warship, bays were beginning to close. Slowly, slowly, their objective was getting smaller.

You're moving pretty fast, Andrew.

"No backseat driving, Jackson. You haven't seen us stop."

Just hope you can, kid. Just hope…

His voice was cut off by the clamping of his jaw as *Diablo* spun a one-eighty, entering the bay doors backwards. A blast of flame erupted all around them as Andrew hit the main engines in one quick burst.

Then a scraping crash, ended by a full-on explosion.

They sat for a moment in their accel couches, shaken to the core despite the inertial dampers. Then Andrew snapped back into the gestalt, probing nearby circuitry.

Diablo, get into their emergency protocols. Here's the path.

On it, sir. You were right. They've opened all emergency circuits to ease rescue operations.

That's right, and I'm… in!

He raced into the carrier's main operating system, shutting down everything he could touch. Remembering the booby-trapped fighters, he slid delayed attacks towards every defence he encountered.

Diablo, shut all blast doors. Mimic a maximum safety lockdown and take control of all resets.

Working, sir.

I'm in the mainframe. Sorry about this, chum, but it's sleepy time. He scooted past all the ArIn's defences and found the Troubleshooting and Repair section. Frying the Repair module with a surge of power from Weapons Deployment, he isolated the brain in a looped reboot pattern and extricated himself.

Then he listened through *Diablo's* damaged Permaskin sensors. Beyond the sounds of muffled shouting and the screaming of auxiliary exhaust fans, the big ship was silent. He inserted himself into the com system.

"Now listen here. Now listen here. This is not a drill. The hull has been compromised. Abandon ship. Abandon ship. You have five minutes to abandon ship." He placed the sound file on a loop with a gradually increasing volume.

Jackson cleared his throat from the doorway. "Not wanting to seem pushy, but how can they abandon ship when the blast doors are all closed?"

"Because the blast doors seal the ship into individual disks, each one with full access to escape pods on four sides. These boats were built on contract to the Space Arm, with all the modern conveniences of thirty years ago. Including the security protocols, which have been upgraded some, but not enough." He shrugged. "After our problems with the *Clyde*, Space Arm gave us access to the specs for all their obsolete equipment...wait a minute..." Something was nagging at him.

"...oh. Sorry, it feels like my mother is calling." *Diablo, we need to shut down the external firewalls.*

Aye, sir. Working...there you go...

"...where the gorram hell are you, dammit! Answer me! Andrew. Diablo. This is *NightHawk* calling *Diablo*. Come in, please." Her voice broke."...please...? Andrew?

Diablo calling NightHawk. Cadet Collingwood reporting, ma'am. Sorry, a little trouble with the external firewalls. Mission accomplished. Ship is secure.

A deep sigh echoed over the com, then silence. *Well done, Cadet. When we saw the escape pods, we knew you'd done something. Whether you were blowing up the whole gorram thing was the question.*

Wouldn't dream of it, ma'am. Waste of expensive equipment a long way from home. Orders?

Is your ship mobile?

On diagnostics now, ma'am. Diablo?

Most systems up and running, sir. Minor damage to aerofoils. Predicting instability at high speed, especially in atmosphere.

No atmo on the slate at the moment. Not quite ready for action, ma'am.

Can you button that boat up tight and get out here again? We have a battle going on. Or not yet going on, as the case may be, but rather tense nonetheless, and I can't follow most of it. What is that racket?

Oh. Sorry. He shut down the 'abandon ship' call. *We have seven people who have not obeyed, five of them on the bridge. Suggestions?*

Can you isolate them?

Not if they're tech savvy. The ArIn module is in their section, and they have already tried twice to access its functions. If I come outside and they reinstate the firewalls, they'll be in charge again. Give me a moment, and I'll deal with it.

A brief contact with *Diablo*'s gestalt highlighted the obvious.

"You need someone EV, sir."

Andrew turned to Jackson. "Your connection with the gestalt is working very well, Sergeant."

The former guard was fastening his helmet. "Didn't need a gestalt to figure out this one. What's the plan?"

"Plain old search and destroy. Get to the bridge and take out anyone there. Maximum sanction if necessary."

He was loading files into the soldier's data storage as he spoke. "Your best protection is your organic augment. Their safety protocols prohibit any harm to a human, so you only have to worry about other humans. There's something ironic in that, but we can talk about it later. I've given you control of the blast doors. They can't open them from the bridge because they're part of the automatic safety system, which is independent from the ArIn as well."

Diablo, I don't know what your solution is, but things are falling apart rapidly out here. A troop carrier in the S & S fleet is trying to deploy its rocket-jets. There are rescue runabouts of all sorts picking up after you, and some of them are exploring the carrier's hull. NightHawk has managed to keep those two fighters shut down, but the others are starting to get antsy.

Aye, ma'am. We expected it to be busy. After all, we just dumped about 1100 crew into space in escape pods. How's your Mexican standoff going? Surely Tevis realizes that the loss of his carrier…

We backed out far enough for radio contact but still close enough to be dangerous. I was tired of running this battle blind, and he already knew where we were. The idiot is now trying to bluster his way out, despite the fact that our fighters are going to be in firing range of each other in about twenty minutes. Why are we having this conversation?

Filling time while we made repairs, ma'am. All done. On our way.

Now the battle count came back from *NightHawk*, loud and clear.

Battle plus 90 minutes, ma'am. J73Bs downrange 1500 km. S & S uprange 850 km, Frigate 50 km. Now 500 metres in front of us, ma'am.

"There you have it, Jackson. I've gotta go. Do the best you can, and if nothing's working, hide out. We'll get you if we win, and if we can't, just surrender."

"I prefer the former option, if you don't mind, sir." Jackson's salute was sharp, considering his cumbersome space armour, and he stepped into the airlock.

Once the soldier was clear, Andrew accessed the bay door mechanism, and the *Diablo* made an exit considerably more dignified than her entrance.

Their appearance had an instant effect. A dozen smaller ships were buzzing around, and they all zoomed away, heading back to a repair ship standing by. Andrew did a patrol of the carrier and chased three more off. Once they were all retrieved, he contacted the repair ship.

This is IOR Messenger Diablo. If you open your bay doors again, I'll weld them shut, and it won't be with a titanium brazing gun. Please decel to the rate of the rest of your fleet. Diablo out.

He turned and accelerated towards the line of fighters. The pilots of the two dead machines had been picked up, and the other pilots were floating near their ships on tethers. The lead pilot was nowhere to be seen, and the *Diablo* gestalt found him back in his cockpit tinkering with his restart routines. Andrew reached in and electronically popped the "Eject" button. The pilot and his seat joined the nearby gravel bouncing around the asteroids.

Tag that one and keep an eye on him in case they can't pick him up.

He went onto the SolarCorp battle frequency. *The seven smart pilots please disengage from your ships and gather to the rear of Number 4. Call for pickup or take your chances with rebounding rocks like your less-intelligent friend is at the moment. Here's his trajectory relative to his ship. In case you haven't noticed, this whole fleet is approaching an area with a lot more space junk floating around, and we're moving about five hundred klicks faster than the hard stuff.*

An awareness of danger shot his attention to Jackson's augment. The guard sent no message, but Andrew could feel his tension.

Image: open blast door to bridge. Four men in space armour with weapons pointed.

Open the door opposite.

Aye.

Image: Door opens, men spin towards it, weapons rising. Rifle fire. Three men drop; the one in officer's gear stands frozen.

One of those programs I gave you includes their battle com, Jackson.

"Drop your weapon."

Image: officer drops handgun, glances right.

Jackson...

I saw. "Tell your man to come out with his hands clean."

Image: A long pause, then the officer gestures. A fifth soldier steps into view, hands spread and empty.

Tell them to remove their helmets.

"Doff your fishbowls, gentlemen, your battle is over."

Image: Two men remove helmets.

Now use the armour program. Can you handle it?

Image: battle armour freezes. Soldiers struggle briefly, then stop.

"You'll be all right if you stay put."

Jackson, you're in charge now. Secure them, check those you downed in case they're dying or playing dead. You probably know more about this than I do. Get into the ship systems and find the two other stay-behinds. They're probably injured but…

Got it, sir. Go save the battle.

Andrew turned his attention elsewhere. *Diablo to NightHawk. Bridge of carrier is secure. Orders?*

Play shepherd. I've ordered the S & S ships to decel to relative zero. Any that don't obey might need motivation. Good idea changing the camo. You look a real sight.

Not my choice. Gotta get Freighty to up the ablative material in PermaSkin 3.

You mean all that scorching and soot is for real?

'Fraid so, Mum. I promise to wash it off when I get home.

You have your orders. I'm sure you can accomplish that and stay online with us.

Piece of cake, as Freighty would say. Diablo out.

It was hardly a piece of cake, shepherding seventeen ships of varied size, tonnage and power to decelerate at anywhere near the same rate. However, as they began to lose the protection of the frigate's long-range weaponry, they became more cooperative.

Meanwhile the rest of the battle was receding rapidly downspin along the Belt. Leaving specific orders and dire threats, *Diablo* chased after the warships.

Battle plus 100 minutes, ma'am. Enemy fighters downrange 2000 km. S & S fleet approaching stationary, 650 km uprange. Frigate 200 km uprange, still 500 metres on our 12.

As they neared the disabled carrier, still coasting at its previous velocity, he contacted Jackson again.

What's your situation?

All present and accounted for. A couple of service mechanics were too close to our bumpy entrance and they're in pretty bad shape. Their suits are keeping them unconscious and alive. Two marines on the bridge wounded and one with a concussion. All suits immobilized.

Any contact with the ArIn?

No. Should I?

Probably not. Ears open, though, in case my little feedback loop fails.

Any orders?

Keep a lid on things. I doubt if you can find a way to decelerate.

Sorry, Cap'n. I'm getting smarter, but not that smart.

Keep in touch. Diablo out.

SolarCorp Attack Carrier... um, I think it's called the Unicorn... out.

Diablo to NightHawk.

Status, please, Diablo.

S & S fleet is getting too far behind to stay in contact, ma'am. Almost stopped. Carrier halfway back under Jackson's control, but he could sure use some help. Ten empty J73Bs drifting near him. How about you?

Still dogging Sea Wolf. Tevis is dithering, hoping something will come up. He tried the old, "Space Arm captains together," ploy a moment ago. I imagine his techs are working madly, trying to figure out why the kill switches on our fighters didn't work. We're stuck here for a while. I don't want to give up my advantage.

Have you decided what to do if he's smart enough to call your bluff?

Emotion: angry surprise. What bluff?

Captain, you know very well that if he maneuvers to get you in the clear, you won't wipe him out. That would mean you firing first, and you won't do that. If he was any kind of military mind, he'd be onto you. What are you going to do?

I'm not sure it's an advantage to have a tactician who can read my mind. May I assume you wouldn't bring this up if you didn't have a solution?

Here's a vulnerability file like we had of the Clyde. You've got two expert gunners. Who needs missiles?

Thanks, Andrew. I'll get them classifying targets right away. But that doesn't solve the bigger problem.

Accessing battle gestalt, ma'am. Join us?

Let's go.

Data poured through Andrew's mind, and new ideas formed with every surge. Once again, there were too many to follow down to a final solution, but one point came out over and over again. He pulled out of the gestalt and went re-li in *Diablo*'s cockpit so he could talk to Pretoro.

"Most of the scenarios won't work with our present configuration. We're missing a larger command ship and staff to man it."

Captain O'Rourke nodded from the viewscreen. "Any comments, Ambassador?"

He shrugged. "I find myself wanting to be in a more central position, but knowing it could be suicidal. Do you have something in mind?" He faced the captain's screen. "What's the situation in the battle?"

"The battle hasn't started. Our fighters are approaching the enemy's force. The 73Bs are still sliding backwards covering us. The Develocon ships are mostly out of harm's way."

Andrew jumped on this, ran several scenarios, then went on the officers' battle com. "Captain O'Rourke, are the Develocon people going to be any use if it comes to shooting?"

"Not really. Captain Worthing, what do you think?"

"Pretty much sacrificial lambs, in my view."

"Stoked to be of use, folks." Kriver had his usual sardonic grin.

Andrew nodded. "Why don't we scramble them back to the Unicorn? It's still moving in their direction, and they could match velocities in a few minutes. At the moment, the 73Bs are still planning to fight our 73s when they meet, so they haven't slowed down. Let's gradually ease the accel of the 73s to give us a little more time. My calculations have the 73Bs moving so fast downrange it will take them fifteen minutes to decel and get back here. Longer if they keep going; shorter if they burn more fuel. By the time they get back they will have used about 80% of their gas and have nowhere to go. The only choice Tevis has is to abandon them and pick up his pilots, but then he's isolated.

"Meanwhile, we could have our whole fleet marshalled around the Unicorn and get some of our people inside to help Jackson maintain control and maybe even start decel. We could end up between *Sea Wolf* and her support and have the full resources of the Unicorn. With one rather damaged docking bay. So sorry."

Captain O'Rourke's head came up like it always did when she was on the prowl. "Timing is essential. Kriver, get your ships to the Unicorn, but don't make it obvious. Keep scattered courses to look like you're running. Coordinate with Jackson. He's in charge. Get anyone with tech experience inside and see if you can work the docking bays and get your ships under cover."

"Ta. 'Aven't 'eard a better plan all day. Kriver out."

Drive plumes began to light up in the surrounding field, and soon the Develocon ships were ducking through the asteroid clumps back along the course of the battle.

Natalia accessed her gestalt. *What's the optimum time for our fighters to pull out?*

Numbers flashed between the two PC ships.

Andrew took a moment to explain to the ambassador. "We want to break off at the very last moment, because the longer they go, the longer it will take and the more fuel they will burn getting back. We don't want them to start shooting at our ships, because their projectile weapons outrange ours and there's a chance their ship-to-ship missiles may be smarter than our evasion programs."

"Or that one will run amok and hit anyone."

"They're the ones who need to be afraid of that." He turned his attention to the gestalt.

Seven minutes from my mark, ma'am. Unless the enemy starts decel first. Mark.

Got that, Captain Worthing? See you in half an hour.

Andrew checked the two command ships, still locked together in their tactical embrace. *Has he figured out that he only has to shut down his reactor and you'll be exposed?*

Emotion: chuckle. It takes two hours to restart that old heap, during which time he'd be helpless. Tell the ambassador he has now six minutes to think up his next speech.

Roger that, Captain. I can tell from the look on his face that he can't wait. He handed the ambassador a hardcopy sheet. "Some interesting personal data on your opponent."

In precisely six minutes the Space Arm fighters spun and blasted in the opposite direction, decelerating rapidly. The SolarCorp J73Bs immediately followed suit. A few of them made attempts with their longest-range missiles, but unable to penetrate the electronic jamming of the older fighters, most of the ordnance wandered off to explode in the Asteroid Belt without finding a living target.

However, one lucky missile somehow found itself approaching halfway between two fighters, dogging them both, equidistant.

Outback 1, this is Outback 4. I can't seem to shake that incoming.

Outback 1, this is Outback 5. Same here.

Worthing's com clicked on, but Andrew used his command override. *Outback 4 and 5, this is Command. That missile has developed a split personality, so it's following both of you. If one of you turns away, it will attack the other. Slue 57 degrees apart and hit full emergency power. Now!*

The two fighters parted company in an explosion of drive wash and missile shrapnel.

Outback 4 and 5, return to original course. Report.

This is Outback 4. Minimal shrapnel damage.

This is Outback 5. I'm reading a fuel leak in my port wing tank. Repair routine seems to have fixed it, but I'm iffy for reaching assigned coordinates.

Captain Worthing, turning this over to you. Andrew dropped out of the conversation.

Thank you, Command. Outback 4 and 5, adapt speed to minimize fuel consumption, but remember, you've got twenty angry 73Bs on your six. Hide out in the asteroids if you have to. Here are the coordinates of auxiliary fuel tanks jettisoned near your course.

Aye, sir. Outback 4 out.

Aye, sir, Outback 5 out.

Good luck, lads. See you at the Unicorn.

Ambassador Pretoro nodded to Andrew, who opened the appropriate channel.

"SolarCorp Vessel *Sea Wolf*, this is Ambassador Pretoro calling."

After a long pause the screen filled with the frowning face of their opponent. His hair was mussed and his collar askew. "This is Commodore Tevis of the *Sea Wolf*. What do you want?"

Pretoro glanced at his sheet. "Would that be former Commander Johnnie Tevis, lately of the Space Arm Supply Fleet, who was cashiered when too much of his cargo kept getting into the wrong hands? Ah, I can tell from your reaction that my data is correct. Have you had time to rethink your position?"

"My position is that I have been attacked by an outlaw force when I was doing nothing wrong." His voice spiralled upward in a peevish whine.

"Hardly an attack. One of our ships asking for rescue had an unfortunate incident in your carrier bay, and a crewmember seeking aid was fired upon by some of your marines. Other than that, this has just been a pleasant day to view the Milky Way from a different angle."

"My ships have not attacked anyone."

"Except for the recent barrage of missiles aimed at our fighters. That, unfortunately for you, was an act of war, and I have two damaged ships. Up until that point, you could have got away with your innocence routine. Once our destroyers got here...oh, you didn't know about the destroyer flotilla arriving soon? Once they got here and everything was under control, you could have petitioned the court for the return of all your ships. Now, of course, the situation has changed. You committed an act of aggression, and your missiles are a crime against the Articles of War. Your ships are forfeit. You are at this moment still in a state of war against the Space Arm and the Planetary Community. Will you now stand down your fighters and your engines, or shall I request my warship to plant a heat-seeking missile in your hottest spot?"

"I will not! That will leave me defenceless."

"You are already defenceless. You have no support, no carrier, and by the time your fighters return they will be low on fuel with no source of resupply. Now, shut down your reactor. My warship is tired of smelling your exhaust. Then I'll decide what to do about you until our backup gets here.

Pretoro gave the captain a moment, then another prod. "Come on, Tevis. You were never at the pay grade to take on Space Arm tacticians or Space Arm technology. There's a reason why the equipment they gave you was on the market. It's obsolete.

"You never had a chance, man. Our technicians noticed the kill switches in the 73s the moment they popped a cover plate. And by the way, when you start shutting down your external security system, do it v-e-e-r-r-y carefully. If your programming is anything like the others we've seen, you've got booby traps layered with electronic ambushes and digital dynamite scattered throughout. You could find yourself living in your space armour. If that doesn't freeze up on you as well. I'm sending you a file. I suggest you give it to your techs."

The SolarCorp officer threw up his hands. "All right, all right. What do you want me to do?"

Andrew popped the list up on a viewscreen in front of the ambassador.

"First, call up your J-boats and tell them to return upspin at cruising speed, approach the carrier, match velocities one at a time, take up formation and leave their ships. They will be picked up.

"Then shut down your reactor and don't dream of starting it again without permission.

"Third, read the file I just sent you that outlines the problems in your system, and then open your exterior firewalls. My warship will stay in position until you have completed all three. This matter is out of your hands and will now be settled by the courts. If you take any further aggressive action, it will only make that process harder for you and your masters. Do I have your full cooperation?"

Tevis's shoulders slumped, and he looked like what he was: a washed-up commercial pilot and not a warship commander in any way.

Battle ends at 112 minutes, ma'am. Enemy commodore has capitulated. Carrier Unicorn under Space Arm control, Sergeant Jackson commanding. All other enemy ships will rendezvous at battle point zero.

Worthing came online. "And so ends the first space battle that never was. It is with pleasure that I congratulate you on your tactics, ma'am. They were superb. You'll be the subject of study for every officer training course for decades."

Andrew grinned as he watched his mother through their gestalt. *Emotion: extreme embarrassment, pride.*

"Thank you, Captain. I had a good team."

33. WRAP-UP

Once the *Sea Wolf* lowered her firewalls, it was easy for Andrew and the *Diablo* gestalt to arrange her systems to their satisfaction. Commodore Tevis was particularly angry when he realized the security bomb he was flying. He stood looking at a schematic Andrew had sent to his viewscreen.

If my technician had tried to disarm that trap, it would have set off those counter-insurgency measures against our own firewalls?

That's right, Captain. I see you understand programming.

Well enough to know when I've been conned. We were told we had the latest and best.

We had the same conversation with Captain Worthing last month.

That's all over now. Thank you for the schematics. We'll have use for our time waiting for your destroyer flotilla to come. Any idea of their plans for us?

Andrew grinned. *You're talking to a lowly technician, sir. All I know is that I'm supposed to immobilize your drive system, open channels with your ArIn that you can't interfere with and freeze your weaponry. If it would make you feel more secure, I can also unfreeze it all in about five minutes from outside your ship.*

You, by yourself?

Don't get ideas. My captain is a very scary lady whose main asset is her ability to induce fanatic devotion in her crew.

I get the message. She certainly seemed competent to me, the way she managed that battle.

Hah! You've only experienced competent. You don't want to see her angry. There might really be a battle.

Chuckling to himself, Andrew signed off and returned to dock *Diablo* in her usual place on *NightHawk*'s bow.

* * *

The flotilla of destroyers swept in, parked just above the plane of bothersome space debris and took command of the situation.

Captain O'Rourke, Captain Worthing, Kriver and Dr. Pretoro went aboard Admiral Mira's flagship for an official debriefing, and soon the system's legitimate inhabitants were refueled and zooming happily upspin towards where their homes were orbiting rapidly downspin to meet them.

Mira chose to accept Ambassador Pretoro's unofficial report at a more relaxed function in the officers' lounge of his flagship. Natalia was invited, and the ambassador insisted on bringing his young "aide."

The four of them sat in comfortable chairs at one end of a long table while Ambassador Pretoro ran through his version of the events. When he had finished, he regarded the group.

"It is not my place to interfere with Space Arm personnel issues, but I must conclude that the main reason for the successful outcome of this whole affair is the amazing capability of the *NightHawk* crew to improvise and adapt to changing circumstances. I truly hope there will be a round of medals forthcoming."

The admiral, a large, rather portly man with receding hair, smiled. "Such reports are not new to us. A good reason to keep this team out on the edges of the human sphere, where such qualities are viewed as positive.

"Let me recap. You had a force of thirty of those old J73s and forty mining and exploration vessels, one ancient IOR Messenger and *NightHawk*. You faced a frigate, an attack carrier with a squadron of thirty J73Bs and fifteen support ships. And your total ammunition expenditure was," he glanced down at the viewscreen rolled out on the table in front of him, then looked more carefully. "Nine, 50-calibre anti-personnel rounds?"

"Yes, sir. There was a misunderstanding on the bridge of the Unicorn about the 'abandon ship' request."

"Anti-personnel rounds in groups of three. Space Arm Security?"

"My personal guard, sir. He's rather competent."

"I imagine so. Well, if the report is worded properly, it will be possible to claim that Captain O'Roarke settled the situation without firing a shot." He smiled again. "Very good for the news bytes."

Then he grew serious. "There's no question about aggressive action by the SolarCorp fleet?"

"You've seen the record, sir. Seventeen specific rockets, all with the capability of taking out a ship. We have tracked down and nullified three Sidewinder 18s and five Tomahawk ArIn S-to-Ss. The rest exploded, and are unidentified until we do spectral analysis of the blasts. Aimed directly at our vessels, who were required to utilize standard tactical evasions, recorded on the ships' logs. Two ships were damaged, one with possible life-threatening consequences. Also, there is no evidence that any of their missiles had been Asimoved, so they were all illegal according to last year's Europa Convention."

Mira gave a satisfied nod. "Definitely an act of war, and I will proceed on that assumption. I have to be very careful, here, because our actions will be perused with many fine-toothed legal combs before this all plays out. The 'possession is nine-tenths' myth is subject to all sorts of political considerations.

"Whatever the judgements are, it's easier to distribute the re-li equipment on site in an equitable way right now. If there are any reparations, they can be made by financial exchange back on Earth where those negotiations belong."

He turned to Pretoro. "And I am very happy to hear you speak in such glowing terms of the Space Arm and its minions. You and I will be seeing a lot of each other in the future." He stood and lifted a piece of official-looking paper off the table, walking over to place it in the ambassador's hands. Then he passed an envelope to Natalia.

She nodded her thanks, opened the missive and skimmed its contents. "Orders. I'm to give all assistance possible for settlement of the problem out here, then return to Factory 4-80 in time to meet with the new ambassador, who will be arriving there in...I can't do the math, but five or six months."

Andrew glanced at the paper. "153 days, 14 hours, ma'am."

"Thank you, Cadet Collingwood." Her gaze went to Pretoro. "New ambassador? What about you?"

He waved his message. "Reassigned."

She grinned. "Ambassador to the Barwolves."

"Not quite, although they will come under my jurisdiction."

"Which is...?"

"Barnard's System. All of it."

Andrew choked back a chuckle, but not quickly enough.

"And what do you find amusing about my assignment, Cadet?"

"On a cubic kilometre basis, you are responsible for an equivalent region of space to the whole of the Planetary Community."

"I'll take your point and try not to think about it that way too often."

"I'm sure you'll do fine, sir."

Pretoro turned to the admiral. "There you have it, sir. Space Arm approval from the bottom to the top." He took in Mira's questioning look. "You haven't been introduced. This is Cadet Andrew Collingwood, also an influential board member of the Factory 4-80 Manufacturing Consortium."

"Pleased to meet you, Cadet...Mr. Collingwood. Are you any relation to...?"

"Yes, by an accident of birth which I try to live down every day. My function here is as the ambassador says. I am also sharing some studies with the Space Arm Science Wing."

"I see. Of course, I don't see, but I'm sure someone will clue me in if I need to know. But just a moment. You're the owner of the old Mustang IOR docked with *NightHawk*. I used to follow those races. May I have a tour?"

"I'm afraid she's heavily modified, sir, though I can hardly ignore a request from an admiral. But there are security concerns. I'll have to bring my mother along."

In the silence that followed, Ambassador Pretoro let out an undiplomatic snicker. "Welcome to Barnard's System, Admiral. You'll find we do things a bit differently out here."

34.   COMMUNION

Lacking any alternative besides incarcerating the invaders in their own ships indefinitely, the admiral reluctantly took Natalia's advice and ran a plebiscite among the former SolarCorp crews. An overwhelming number of them opted to take control of their S & S ships and fit themselves into the booming new economy. Because of their original function and equipment, they would be welcomed with open arms; a mining operation and a naval fleet have many similar needs.

Their first task was a lucrative contract with Space Arm to help refit the Unicorn into an appropriate naval base, space station and embassy for Ambassador Pretoro and the staff brought for him on Mira's flagship. Since the Outbackers would be considered an independent province of the Planetary Community, they were allowed their own militia, which meant both J-boat fleets under the command of Captain Worthing.

Commodore Tevis, now with two strikes against him, was of no use to Space Arm, and would be returned to his shaky position at SolarCorp by the next transport home. The *Sea Wolf* and her crew were kept nearby pending orders from Earth. Andrew pitied their future boredom and resolved to do some thinking.

The *NightHawk* blasted off for her new assignment, her profile warped by *Diablo* in her usual docking spot on the starboard bow. The Freighty avatar swore the fittings were designed for that exact purpose and would handle any of the stresses incurred during Otherwhere travel. Andrew was elated.

"Hey, I'm gonna have my own private suite for the whole trip!"

His mother glowered at him. "If our organic augments keep on developing, I'll be glad to have you as far away as possible."

He tossed that problem off with a flick of his fingers. "That's my next project. We'll figure something out." He straightened his back and met her gaze. "Which brings us to a bigger question. SolarCorp put cutoff switches in their own ships. That opens a whole new can of worms."

"Such as?"

"Did Freighty put a similar switch in *Diablo*? I have to assume he did. There has to be something to take the place of the Asimov procedure that Space Arm is doing to all its ships."

"It's certainly possible." She faced him. "And what about *NightHawk*, when he was doing the modifications?"

Andrew puzzled that through. "I don't think so. He's very careful about messing with his clients, and especially with you. It would be a gross breach of confidence to meddle with a client's hardware.

"While it wasn't the same thing to mess with my personal squirmware?"

"Yeah, but that was to your advantage and mine. This wouldn't be. Of course, it would be nice to know what kind of Asimov switch Space Arm installed with the rest of the modifications. I'll do some careful exploration."

A frown slid across her face. "But what about you?"

"Me?"

"Yes. You're an employee of Freighty's. A subject for his experiments."

A bolt of fear shot through Andrew. "You mean he has a kill switch in me somewhere?" His mind was spinning. *Why didn't I think of that before? Is it because I've been programmed not to think of it? How much am I under Freighty's control?*

Emotion: danger! Chakka slid from under the desk, his neck-hair bristling.

Natalia spread her hands in a calming gesture. "Let's be polite and call it an interrupt switch."

Andrew jumped to his feet. "We have to get to the bottom of this. I need full battle gestalt. But not *Diablo*. Until we've checked her over, she's suspect, too."

Natalia nodded. "This would be a crucial piece of information, if we could find a way to access it."

They merged with the gestalt, everyone on edge. Chakka, his protective instincts aroused, paced the tiny chart room, his battle growl rumbling in his chest. Finally Andrew shook his head. "Chakka, I can't focus with you nattering away like that. Lie down and concentrate!"

Image: feline lip lifting ever so slightly to reveal tip of dagger-sharp fang. The big cat retreated to his couch under the desk and lay where he could fix Andrew with a fierce eye.

Once they applied their combined intelligence to the problem, it didn't take them long. The solution was obvious to everyone. *NightHawk* summed it up.

We want as deep a scan of Andrew's augment as we can manage.

Break off. I need private chat with my mother.

The two regarded each other from their usual positions: Natalia in her chair, Andrew on his stool.

"You don't need to do this."

"Yes, I do, Mum. I'm not worried. There's no danger."

"There is. If we go into gestalt without you and try to do a deep scan of your augment..."

"Not to disparage human technology, but I without my help, I doubt if you'll get very far, though I'm sure you won't be able to do me any harm. I'm more worried that he's left nasty presents for anyone that tries such an invasion."

"And what if there's such sensitive information in there that he decides that secrecy is more important than your existence?"

"If that's the case, Freighty has been more than dishonest with us. All his motives are suspect, and humanity is happier with me gone. Oh, don't look so shocked, Mum. We know Freighty better than that. He wouldn't want to destroy his work just to hide his actions. How many times has he backed down when you called him on one of his ploys?"

"And how many ploys has he tried?"

"So, nothing's changed. The deeper we go, the more places we find to dig."

"And how do we tell when it's best to stop digging?"

Andrew sighed. "Look, I've seen you go through this a bunch of times. You always make your decision based on the assumption that Freighty honestly wants to do a better job of managing our access to technology than he did with those other species. I don't know how you came to that conclusion, but so far it hasn't set you wrong."

Natalia nodded. "I figured that out when he let slip a comment about his programming. Of course, I have no idea whether the slip was a mistake or calculated. But without breaking security, something he said leads me to believe that he has programming that equates to Asimov's Laws. Not when dealing with individual humans, but as far as the race in general. He has to help us to the best of his ability. He can't do anything that might cause humanity harm. Going on that, I assume he will work to our benefit in most situations."

"And what keeps him from becoming a benevolent dictator? A god, even?"

"The knowledge he has learned from us. Humans are better off making their own mistakes and learning from the consequences."

Andrew slapped the table. "That doesn't get him off the hook where my programming is concerned, but it does answer the question about boobytraps. Fair enough?"

"We could always ask him."

"Have my fate decided by a mouse? Hardly comforting, but all right."

Freighty, we gotta talk.

The mouse avatar appeared on the viewscreen. "What's happening, War Hero?"

"That's what I want to know. Those SolarCorp turds put shutdown switches in their own planes. Did Freighty put a shutdown switch in me?"

"Why do you ask?"

"Don't act stupid. Did he? A non-answer will be taken as an answer, and 'I don't know' won't cut it. The odds are miniscule that Freighty isn't expecting this question."

The toon grinned. "Oh, I've been expecting it, all right."

"And what is your answer?"

"Figure it out yourself."

"He said that?"

"My very words."

"Prime. Thanks, Mouse. Goodbye." He tossed the avatar out of the viewscreen.

295

A pair of white gloves appeared around the edge of the screen, followed by a black nose as if the toon was trying to climb out. "You don't have to be so rude...okay, I'm gone."

Andrew regarded his mother. "Best answer possible. If there is a switch, it's not dangerous, and he knows we have to look for ourselves because we won't believe anything else."

"Agreed. How do you want to do this?"

"Comfortable in an accel couch. I have to concentrate."

There was little to prepare. Soon he was lying in the captain's couch on the bridge of the *NightHawk*. Chakka lay in his own couch, and Natalia perched at the communications console next door.

"All right. Here we go."

It was strange going into his own mind, so he looked for a familiar routine. He found a mental exercise that his real mother had taught him that he now knew was meditation. Calming his breathing, he concentrated on letting his present surroundings fall away. He floated in a universe of blackness shot with shapes like the afterimages of his real world.

I wonder what I'm supposed to look for?

Programming. I don't see anything that looks like programming. How do you look at your own programming? Like trying to see the back of your head.

The distracting thought shot him up toward awareness, and he relaxed again. *Now, I wonder. Freighty must have prepared me for this. I should be able to access my own programming for repair purposes. Drat Freighty. This is all part of my training. When I'm ready to ask the right question, I'm directed towards looking for it myself.*

All right. Why? That's the question. Why do I do what I do? What drives me? Love. I guess I'm lucky, getting a second chance at a mother. Greed? I'm not that greedy, am I? Laziness. I'm not that lazy.

Wait a minute. That's an idea. If I had a shutoff switch, it would be an offshoot of one of my negative qualities. What are my negative qualities? Fear. Fear of what? I'm afraid of dying, I suppose. Very afraid of those I love dying. Understandable. Fear of being wrong?

Happens all the time. Fear of... wait a minute... fear of making a mistake and hurting someone I love. Yes, I suppose that would be it. Gives me a different view of Captain Mum, doesn't it?

Concentrate.

How would that shut me down? Simple. Inability to act due to fear of making a mistake. Got it. So where's the switch?

Oh, crap on a plate. That's it. Freighty didn't put in a switch. Every human already has a shutoff switch. Yes, Chakka, animals, too. It's called panic. When we shut off our thinking minds and let our fear take over.

So, is that all? Freighty, are you listening? Is that it? Not likely.

Okay, gotta try again. Open wider to the gestalt. Mum's there. What's she afraid of? Hah! Easy. Me getting harmed. Oh. Anybody getting harmed. Must be tough for a commando. Gotta have more sympathy. Drat you, Freighty. Is this some kind of growing up program?

Chakka? He isn't afraid of anything. No, not true. Afraid of being useless. That's all right.

NightHawk? Oh, ArIn's don't feel fear. What do they have instead? In times of danger they go into a higher level of awareness and action that rises relative to the danger until... until nobody knows, because the higher levels do too much damage to the positronic brain. I'll remember that. An overload spiral with a similar effect to panic, but more directly damaging.

I'm off track. How does an ArIn do self-diagnostics?

Follow this procedure, Andrew...

Oh, thank you, NightHawk. I should have thought to ask. Right. You start a routine like this...

Image: control room of a ship, but hazy and indistinct.

...and think like this... and soon...wow! There it is. The inside of my head. Hey. This is prime. All tidy with sort of like labels, but not really. Not how I thought my head would be at all.

Image: circuitry. All sizes of wires, conduits, and hoses.

Okay, it's a metaphor. I see ship circuits because that's what I'm used to. So let's try...

Security measures: Hmm.

Image: rows and rows of files, stretching in interconnected streams off into the hazy darkness. All sorts of programs stored here, but nothing like a kill switch. But wouldn't it be hidden? I mean that's the point, isn't it?

He looked around.

But this is huge. How can I search all of this? Not possible. Pah! Of course it's not possible. So that's what this was all about. Freighty, you're getting predictable.

He let his consciousness drift towards re-ti. *Okay, folks. Show's over. We're out of here.*

Gradually, because everyone had been tightly interwoven in the experience, he withdrew and closed the gestalt. He opened his eyes and looked around the bridge. His mother slouched on the accel cushions, her face blank.

"Hey, Mum, snap out of it. I got what we were looking for. Well, I got what we were supposed to find, which is next best thing."

She dragged her head erect. "What was that about? What happened?"

He glanced over at Chakka, who lay with his chin on his paws, eyes a slit open, staring into nothing. "Everybody all right?"

Returning to normal function, Andrew. Please give me a moment to readjust my reality parameters.

"Mum? You okay?"

"I suppose I am. That was rather overwhelming, if you really want to know."

"Of course I want to know. I mean, it was just the gestalt, wasn't it?"

"No, it was not 'just the gestalt.' It was one complete level of experience deeper than the gestalt. Have you ever been in a sensory deprivation chamber?"

"Huh? Sure. I wasn't too impressed. I sort of forgot about it and worked on a Math problem I'd been having trouble with."

"Yes, well think of one of those and turn it inside out."

"What, stimulate everything?"

"Yes. Nothing wild or powerful, but every sense gently stimulated at the same time."

He did a quick search. "I'd speculate that your mind would go into overload, even with a very small amount of that kind of stimulus."

"Well, my boy, that's what I felt like."

"Oh. I'm sorry. Next time I'll be a little more careful."

"There's going to be a next time?"

"Of course. It's the new stage."

"The new stage of...? What, exactly, did you find out?"

He shrugged. "There isn't a kill switch. This was just another darn trick of Freighty's to get me in there. To the next stage of my evolution." He shook his head. "That dratted space mechanic has just given us the next level of our assignment. He was leading up to it with this 'everybody's in my head' problem."

"You have a solution for that?"

"Sure." *Freighty? Could you join us, please?*

"Of course, Andrew." The mouse appeared in a 'Doctor Freud' outfit. "Thank you for the polite invitation."

"I assume you have a file for me, please."

"Of course. I'm glad you were successful."

"I'm not sure I'm quite as glad, but thank you. Please return to from whence you came."

"With pleasure, sir." The avatar disappeared.

Natalia was regarding him. "File?"

"Yes. Did you register where we went at the end of the gestalt? The Ops Room, sort of?"

"Is that what that was? I remember, but the details are slipping away already."

"The next step for all of us is to access that room in our own augment. This file has the exercises you and the crew have to go through, and some for me to work on for my own progress."

"Have to?"

"If you want to learn how to keep everyone out of your heads. I suspect it will do us wonders in Otherwhere as well."

"And you are our self-appointed guru, I suppose."

"Freighty-appointed, I'm afraid. No choice on my part. Anyone can opt out who wishes."

"As if anyone would. Are you going to tell the crew, or am I…wait a minute. I'm not telling anyone anything. This is your problem, and you solve it."

He grinned. "Ah. The Mumbot back in full force. Now I know you've recovered. I'll talk to the crew. Once we're headed for Freighty, we'll get started. I want to have something to show for all our work when we see him again."

"We have all the time in the universe for the next three months."

"Right. And I've got a thesis to write. But for now…" he sighed.

"What's the problem?"

"I have a meeting with Lieutenant Jones. I think we're talking about Space Arm Chain of Command."

His mother grinned at him. "I have a feeling Adrian is in for a tough time on that one."

THE END

If you enjoyed this book, do the author and other readers a favour and go to Smashwords, Amazon, or Goodreads and post a review. Even a rating and a few words is great.

ABOUT THE AUTHOR

Brought up in a logging camp with no electricity, Gordon Long learned his storytelling in the traditional way: at his father's knee. He now spends his time editing, publishing, travelling, blogging and writing Fantasy, Sci-Fi and Social Commentary, although sometimes the boundaries blur.

Gordon lives in Tsawwassen, British Columbia, with his wife, Linda, and their Nova Scotia Duck Tolling Retriever, Josh. When he is not writing and publishing, he works on projects with the Surrey Seniors' Planning Table and is a staff writer for <indiesunlimited.com>

MORE FROM GORDON Λ. LONG

Other Titles by Gordon A. Long available at most
retailers

"Factory 4-80" Freighty Series 1

"Ocean of Grass" Petrellan Saga 1
"Waves of Stone" Petrellan Saga 2
"Zoysana's Choice" Petrellan Saga 4
"The Innkeeper's Husband" Petrellan Saga 5
Coming in 2020
"Path of Water" Petrellan Saga 3 (Sequel to "Waves of Stone")
"Out of Mischief" World of Change 1
"Into Trouble" World of Change 2
"Mountains of Mischief" World of Change 3
"The Trouble with Tents" World of Change 4
"Queen of Mischief" World of Change 5
"A Sword Called...Kitten?" Romantic Comedy with
an Edge
"The Cat with Many Claws" Sword Called Kitten
Book 2
"Cloud Cat" A Cat with Many Claws Novel
Storm Over Savournon (A Novel of the French Revolution)

"Why Are People So Stupid?" Social Humour with a
Point

Look for Gordon's books, selected reviews, poetry
and short stories: <airbornpress.ca>
Gordon's opinions on humanity are at the
"Are People Stupid?" blog
Find all his reviews and his ideas on writing at
"Renaissance Writer"

www.ingramcontent.com/pod-product-compliance
Lightning Source LLC
Chambersburg PA
CBHW031658170626
46808CB00005B/1508